KNUCKLEBALL

The Uncertainties of (a) Life

To Susan —
A great friend and
IU alumna !

Enjoy ! **Ken Beckley**

Ken Beckley

author·HOUSE®

AuthorHouse™
1663 Liberty Drive
Bloomington, IN 47403
www.authorhouse.com
Phone: 1-800-839-8640

Certain characters in this work are historical figures, and certain historical developments and events portrayed did take place. The development and setting of the Evansville College campus is factual. Every effort has been made to describe the handling of all health / medical situations involving the fictional characters in ways that actual professionals could have managed them. However, this is a work of fiction. Except for historical figures, all the other characters, names, and events as well as places, incidents, organizations, and dialogue in this novel are either the products of the author's imagination or are used fictitiously.

Published by AuthorHouse 3/13/2012

ISBN: 978-1-4678-7421-2 (sc)
ISBN: 978-1-4678-7420-5 (hc)
ISBN: 978-1-4678-7419-9 (e)

Library of Congress Control Number: 2011962046

Scripture quotations are taken from *The Living Bible* copyright © 1971. Used by permission of Tyndale House Publishers, Inc., Carol Stream, Illinois 60188. All rights reserved.

Any people depicted in stock imagery provided by Thinkstock are models, and such images are being used for illustrative purposes only. Certain stock imagery © Thinkstock.

This book is printed on acid-free paper.

ACKNOWLEDGMENTS

I am indebted to the Rev. Dr. Kent Millard for encouraging me to follow my passion to write, to authors James Alexander Thom and Scott Russell Sanders for their invaluable advice, and to my wife, Audrey, for her encouragement and support.

Others who contributed or led me to significant information also have my gratitude. They include the following:

Greg Beckley	Ed Kahle
Nola Beckley, my mother	Brandt Ludlow, MD
Larry Beckley	George Lukemeyer, MD
Roger Beckley	Tom Mayer, MD
Beth Ann Bohnert	Tony Mobley
Matt Bojrab, DDS, MS	Randall Pemberton
Richard Conroy	Art Rettig, MD
John Durkott	Max Schumacher
Judy Edwards	Tracy Smith
Carl Erskine	Brad Sutton, OD
Judy Fiddick	Gene Tempel
Stan Fox	Libby Troeger
Bob Gildea	University of Evansville
Bob Hammel	David Williams
Tom Healy	Jim Williams

Aja Mason & the Warrick County Coal Miners Museum
Boonville Warrick County Public Library
Evansville Vanderburgh Public Library
Indianapolis Marion County Public Library

I am thankful to my proofreaders, Jo Anne Mayer and Beva Rikkers, and to the editors and custom illustrators at AuthorHouse.

CHAPTER 1

Standing on the pitcher's mound on a hot, humid Sunday afternoon in August 1955, I couldn't have imagined what would happen to me over the next thirty-five years.

Focusing intently on the catcher's mitt, I bit the inside of my right cheek to keep from grinning when I saw my favorite sign, three fingers pointing toward the dusty clay ground. *Knuckleball.* Digging the tips of the middle three fingers of my right hand into the hide of the baseball, I went into my windup and threw, the ball traveling with no rotation whatsoever and dipping suddenly just as it reached home plate. The batter stood frozen, the bat never even leaving his shoulder.

"Strike three!" shouted the umpire. "Game's over."

With that, I, Davie Miller, had tossed my third no-hitter of the season, a summer in which I painfully learned *life* can be like a knuckleball—unpredictable, and sometimes the bottom drops out.

■ ▨ ▬

I had an incredible life. I just wish some of it hadn't happened.

Fifteen years prior to that August afternoon, I was born David Harold Johnson—Harold being my father's name—in the front bedroom of my parents' small, one-story, white, wood-frame, charcoal-shingled home on a gray, rainy June afternoon in Barclay, a town in far southwest Indiana. My mother said I was withered-skinned and thin but from all appearances healthy when I was delivered only fifteen minutes after her sister, Sarah Mae Hutchison, summoned our family physician, Dr. John Clark. Mom said when he slapped my butt, my face turned beet red and I let loose

1

with enough noise to convince him my lungs were strong and clear. Aunt Sarah Mae was visiting from Illinois when the labor pains first appeared and then suddenly intensified and was bedside to hold my mother's hand and keep the perspiration that developed on her forehead from being a nuisance. But this wasn't Mom's first delivery experience, and although one should never presume there could be no problems, she told me giving birth to her third child wasn't something she feared. The delivery was painless, thanks to an injection from Dr. Clark. I arrived a week earlier than expected. In fact, my dad was at his job at Crescent Creek Coal Mine and caught off guard when a pit boss delivered the happy news, which Aunt Sarah Mae had passed to him when she called the mine's office.

My sister, Peggy Sue, was born in 1937. A brother, Charles, had died only eleven days after delivery in 1936. In those days, the medical term *sudden infant death syndrome* (SIDS) was unknown; Charles just died, and the doctor could give no explanation as to why. It was a horrible time for my parents. Certainly, life's knuckleballs can impact anyone at anytime.

The area where I grew up had a huge impact on how I developed as a person. As I look back on it, I believe the land; the simplicity of life in a rural, small-town area; and what I refer to as "good ole down-to-earth people" gave me wonderful experiences and helped shape my views and philosophies as I grew to adulthood. As a result, I never considered myself pretentious; I always tried to display humility and never took anything for granted. Hard work was the way of life for the people who lived in and around Barclay, and so that was all I ever knew for myself. My best friend, Billy, and my next best friend, Bobby, grew up with the same experiences, but their lives turned out far different from mine.

When I was born in 1940, our town had a population of 1,200; it was by far not the largest in the area but not one of the smallest either. It had only two traffic lights; both had been installed three years earlier, one at the intersection where two state highways crossed on the north edge of town and the other at Main and Second Streets, the heart of the downtown. Religion was important, as evidenced by the fact that there were nearly as many churches (nine) as commercial establishments combined. The two grocery stores, a hardware store, a pool hall, two banks, three gasoline stations (Gulf, Sinclair with the green dinosaur on its tall sign on Main Street, and Texaco), two taverns, and two restaurants were all locally owned. Religion would play a key role in my life, as it did for my parents and grandparents. Education would, too. There were two elementary schools and a high school. There's not much to say about my elementary school experiences, but high school was something else.

As with any small town, Barclay had its characters—people just outside the norm, people who make life extra interesting. Charlene Helbert was one of them, and I learned about her background from my mother when I was older. A small, red-brick building on Main Street housed the telephone exchange, a switchboard filled with small holes into which black-covered cables were plugged to connect one caller to another. Mom said everyone knew the spinster Charlene, the primary switchboard operator, listened in on conversations, because what two people thought were secrets soon became public knowledge. Charlene was said to be the instigator of more gossip than any other twelve persons put together. "Charlene, you've got to stop eavesdropping," the small phone company's married president, Homer Cawley, was rumored to have admonished her, almost pleading because of all the complaints he'd received. But Charlene paid no attention to him. Further rumor was she had the upper hand, because he was making late-night visits to her boudoir.

Then there was "Shorty" Hill, a never-married, thirty-eight-year-old, mostly unemployed, town character who lived alone in a run-down, spooky house near the town cemetery and who had the uncanny ability to remove the metal caps on glass soft drink bottles with his teeth. I always suspected Shorty, who got his nickname because of his physical stature—five-three at the most—had "little man syndrome" and dealt with it by getting attention for his bizarre antics. He reveled in drawing a crowd outside a restaurant or tavern by announcing he was going to pop the top off a soda bottle with his teeth. Placing the neck of the bottle inside his mouth and gripping the cap between the upper and lower molars, he somehow removed it as he pulled up on the bottom of the container. The crowd would grimace, gasp, and clap, delighting Shorty and making him feel like a "big man." He'd smile from ear to ear, his yellowed, heavily decayed teeth repulsively displaying their ugliness for all to see.

Despite the characters, residents took pride in the town and how it looked. No one owned what was considered a big, expensive home; lawns were generally well-kept; the abundant trees were regularly trimmed; and seldom was trash seen lying around.

"'There's just no future for me in farming, Mary June,'" my mother quoted Dad as saying to her when they were dating in the first half of the 1930s. The hours on a farm were long—work started before sunup and lasted to after sundown—and too much of a family's potential for income depended on the weather. I wish he hadn't, but my father made the decision to apply for a job in the riskier coal-mining business—risky from a personal safety standpoint.

Dad had been born and raised on his father's farm, which was located about two miles north of Barclay. The homestead consisted of eighty acres on the day of his birth in 1913, but ever the opportunist, his father purchased more land as it became available, so that by the time Dad left the farm, went to work in the mines, and married Mary June Hutchison, it had grown to 250 acres.

Grain prices plunged in the early 1930s as the Great Depression enveloped America. But my Johnson grandparents and their sons, John and Harold, grew most of the vegetables they needed and were fortunate to have hogs and chickens for meat. I'm told that their having less money was not an extreme hardship. My miserly great-grandfather Christian, an immigrant from Wales, had originally owned the farm and left Grandpa Johnson the property and more than five thousand dollars in savings at Barclay National Bank when he died. What a gift! Using his own savings and some of his inheritance, my grandfather purchased land from nearby farmers who couldn't cope with the Depression's hardships and needed to raise cash just to feed their families. Our family was fortunate it hadn't invested in the stock market and thus wasn't financially devastated by the market's crash in October 1929.

"Your father went to work at Crescent Creek Coal Mine in July 1935, only six weeks before we were married," my mother told me years later. "He was *so* excited to work at the same mine as his best friend, Henry Thompson." Dad and "Hank," as he was known, graduated together from Barclay High School in 1931. Although my father was tall, Hank was considered a giant of a man at nearly six feet six and was stoutly built with muscular arms. He had a ruddy complexion, blue eyes, and wavy blond hair. He'd always lived in Barclay. His father was a miner, and there was no doubt where Hank would be headed immediately after high school graduation.

In the mid-1930s, Indiana was one of the nation's largest coal producers—most of the state's black fossil fuel coming from southwestern Indiana strip mines. Several privately owned mines were located within a twenty-mile radius of Barclay. Two others were part of publicly owned conglomerates. Dad worked for one of the latter, Lakeland Corporation. Owner of Crescent Creek, Lakeland had an immense interest in bituminous coal because it provided coke necessary for steel production at the company's huge foundry along Lake Michigan at the northwest corner of Indiana. The coal industry, like nearly every employer in America, had been hit hard by the Depression, but signs of recovery were beginning to show by the summer of 1935, a fortuitous situation, considering my father wanted desperately to leave farming.

▬ ▬ ▬

Unfortunately, too many children don't take time to talk with their parents about the past. For whatever reason, they let the years slip away, and then it's too late. I'm glad I did on several occasions in 1974 when I was at a low point in my life and wanted to know more about my family and how Mother dealt with tough times of her own. She was quite willing to share the past. As she got older, she seemed to think about it a great deal more, which is a pretty typical part of the aging process, I suppose.

"Our wedding day was the first 'happiest day of my life,'" Mother related to me when we sat in her living room on a rainy Sunday afternoon in May of '74. "It was September 10, 1935. Seems like yesterday." She and Dad were married at Ebenezer Lutheran Church, less than a mile from the farm where he grew up. My grandparents had been married there in 1909 and Dad's brother, John, too. They were a religious family, never missing church services on Sunday morning and praying as a group at every meal and individually when they went to bed at night. They read the Bible at the supper table, and the two boys were raised to fear God but trust in his goodness and support.

Ebenezer was the white, wood-frame, hilltop church home to most of the farm families of the surrounding area and was lovingly cared for by them. It had a cross atop the tall steeple that rose above the front double doors and was surrounded by tall oaks, with a few maples in the lawn between the church and parsonage. Six concrete steps with black-painted iron handrails at each side led from the lawn to the front doors. "I fell in love with it the first time your father and I attended not long after we began dating," she said. They'd been introduced by her close cousin, Jane Frapwell, shortly after my mother graduated from high school in neighboring Southern Illinois.

Jane had urged her to come to Barclay, knowing Mom wanted to get away from her overbearing mother. That's my description of my grandmother Hutchison based on what all I'd heard about the way she acted in those days, although I never found her particularly warm myself. I once overheard Grandpa Johnson remarking to Uncle John, "She wears the pants in the family." I knew whom he was talking about. Perhaps it was her mother's domineering manner that caused Mom to need someone who was kind and caring. At least she admitted to me she quickly fell for that good-looking young farmer Harold Johnson after first meeting him.

Mom was born and raised in a small Illinois town, the daughter of a preacher at New Carlisle Church of Christ. She was two years younger than my father and confided to me that despite being a pastor who should be a model in forgiving, her father was so angry he and her mother didn't attend the wedding. "I pleaded with him to be there, even to participate in the ritual, but his strong feelings about me being too young, his belief of a better life if I'd attend Southern Illinois Normal College and graduate with a teacher's degree, and the fact I dared get married in 'a Lutheran Church of all places,' were too much for him to handle." The dispirited tone of her voice suggested her parents' absence caused her pain she'd carried all these years, almost forty of them. I couldn't help but feel so very sorry for her. I think hearing her words made me even more determined not to be hypocritical in regard to my expressions of religious beliefs.

Mom related that Sarah Mae, her only sibling, three years her senior, unmarried, shorter, and heavier, was her maid of honor. "Poor Sarah Mae, she always had a weight problem." Cousin Jane also stood with her before the altar. Uncle John was the best man, and Hank Thompson joined them. The family invited neighbors, friends, and relatives, and fifty-seven attended.

Many times prior to the inclement 1974 Sunday afternoon with my mother, I'd seen a black-and-white photo—a formal pose—taken after the wedding, and she was striking in a white dress. Dad wore a tie and dark, plain suit. He stood about a half foot taller than she. She was blond, trim, and nice-looking, with not a wrinkle in her face. They flashed smiles that spread from ear to ear. I can remember how strong and handsome my dad was. Mom described him as six-two and about 215 pounds when they got married. He had coal-black hair and dark eyes. I'll never forget his hands, which dwarfed mine; his palms etched by a maze of lines from years of hard work, and his fingers seemingly triple the size of mine when I was four years old.

"My, we didn't have much money when we got married," Mom related. "I'd worked as a teller at Barclay National since the summer of 1933, extremely lucky to get the job. Only a few months earlier, President Franklin Roosevelt closed all the nation's banks because people had lost faith in the banking system. Needed confidence was restored when Congress passed emergency reforms. Meantime, our only competitor here, Hopewell County Bank, nearly collapsed as so many of its customers lost their jobs and withdrew what little savings they had, just to survive. Thousands of small banks around the country closed.

"You might not be able to relate to this," she said, looking at my face for some reaction, "but initially, I earned twenty cents an hour, progressing to only twenty-four cents by the time I was married. Harold's wage as a welder was $5.47 ½ a day for eight hours of work. Sort of funny, isn't it, that someone would earn a half cent?" She waited for a reply. I smiled and raised my eyebrows to reflect amazement. "All the miners' wages were set by company contract with the United Mine Workers of America for each type of job, such as welders, electricians, drillers, pumpers, and shovel operators. All the workers were protected by the UMW."

Mom and Dad had $1,113 in savings at Barclay National when they married. And they had a brown 1931 Ford coupe they drove twenty-five miles to a one-night honeymoon in Moonlight Motel near the Ohio River on the southern outskirts of Evansville.

As I sat on the sofa, my mother in a light oak rocking chair near one of the living room's two large windows, I thought she had aged a great deal; perhaps it was good she'd quit working for a living five months earlier. Her once perfectly smooth facial skin had given way to numerous lines, and her eyes were more sunken than in the past, but she still radiated a pleasantness and a positive attitude exhibited by few despite the major heartaches she'd suffered. If her qualities were the result of a life of following her faith, then she was a testament to the rewards of willful servitude to the supreme being.

She wore a simple blue, shirtwaist dress with a tie belt of the identical cotton material and gestured often with her slender, smooth-skinned hands as she spoke, especially to make points of emphasis important to her. Occasionally, she glanced out the rain-streaked windows.

Mother's eyes lit up as she talked about most of the past, no doubt thrilled that I had any interest at all in it. Unfortunately, not all of it had been pleasant and I was about to get details.

"We set up housekeeping in a small wood-framed, two-bedroom white house with an outhouse at the rear on Seventh Street here in town. It was five blocks from Barclay National, so I could walk to work on Main Street each day. Rent for the house owned by Chester Brummett, my bank's president, was fifteen dollars a month, which was about average since we only had two other rooms, a kitchen with a small, white metal table and a living room with a coal-fired potbelly stove that was the only heat during the winter months. As a mine employee, Harold could purchase coal for less than the general public." She chuckled. "The fireplace in the living room wasn't used, because too much heat from the room escaped up the chimney, and firewood was too expensive anyway." She paused, looked down and then back up at me sheepishly, and said, "I have to admit, the one thing I struggled with was getting accustomed to using the outhouse as the toilet. The house where I'd lived with my cousin for two years had a bathroom that consisted of a sink and toilet. Yes, I know, that was almost unheard of, but Jane had one. Now, the outhouse your father and I had was only ten steps from the back door, but going there in winter snow or howling, frigid wind and sitting over the hole in the cold wooden bench of a seat was something I quickly learned to dread when winter arrived in early December."

"What was it like working at the bank?"

"Well, I was a teller, one of six employees. We were open from nine to three, Monday through Friday. People around town sarcastically called our schedule 'banker's hours.' But we were also open three and a half hours Saturday morning, something no other banks in the area did. Mr. Brummett reasoned that the Depression had everyone on edge regarding their money's safety, so the thought of having easy access to it six days a week was soothing to our customers.

"Harold's day at the mine began at six thirty, so he'd arise at five fifteen, eat breakfast, pack food in a small metal lunchbox, and leave the house by six, all while I slept. The welding shop where he worked was located in a metal-framed building near the coal-processing tipple eight miles from our house."

— — —

"Only four weeks after our wedding, I began experiencing nausea in the hours before going to work," Mother revealed. "It was difficult, but at the bank I did my best to hide how awful I felt. After a week of watching me suffer, your father convinced me to see Dr. Clark. Was I ever shocked when he told me I was pregnant!" Again, she chuckled. "That had been the farthest thing from my mind. Harold and I'd talked about one day having a family but certainly not this soon. We wanted to save enough to buy our own house and then have children. My visit to the doctor that Saturday afternoon in October certainly changed things."

I saw her eyes drift, a look of satisfaction on her face. "June 17, 1936, was the second 'happiest day of my life.' Your brother Charles Arnold Johnson was born in our bedroom. We chose Charles because it was your father's middle name and your grandfather Johnson's given name. How lucky we were that Mrs. Calhoun had offered to care for Charles while I worked at the bank each day. She was a godsend." How I remember Winifred Calhoun! What a dear lady—although there were times when she'd take a hairbrush and use the backside of it to tan my rear end when I didn't mind. Mrs. Calhoun was a neighbor when Charles was born. She was sixty years old, a widow, and needed something to do with her time. Her modest charge was fifty cents per day.

"My mother insisted on coming from Southern Illinois to assist while I recovered in bed for a week. She returned home as soon as I was up and about," Mom said. I can imagine that being left alone with her baby to nurse him without the stares and comments of my know-it-all grandma Edith Hutchison came none too soon.

"Harold could hardly wait to return home from the mine about four each afternoon, sit in a chair in the living room, and hold his sleeping son. I'll never forget watching him stare without saying a word for what seemed like hours, looking at the perfectly formed face, eyelids, and tiny nose and at the smallness of the hands that together didn't fill the palm of one of his. Charles had thick black hair, just like his father."

— — —

Mother's facial expression suddenly changed, and I knew what was coming, a life knuckleball. She ceased rocking. "Everything seemed so perfect in our lives, and I remember that on the evening of June 27, Harold and I laid in bed, wrapped in one another's embrace, and I whispered, 'How lucky we are.' Charles was asleep in his bassinet that rested in the cradle of wooden folding legs just past the foot of our bed. He nursed every three hours, but at one thirty, when the clock on the fireplace mantle dinged, for some reason waking me, I realized it had been four hours since Charles had nursed."

It was nearly four decades later, but tears welled in her eyes as she continued, talking in an almost trancelike state. "Sensing something was wrong, I slid from bed and rushed to the bassinet but couldn't hear or feel any breathing sound coming from Charles. I picked him up. His skin was cool, almost cold.

"I'm certain Harold never forgot my piercing screams. 'Charles isn't breathing! Charles isn't breathing!' I was frantic. Your father flew out of bed, took our son, pressed an ear to his mouth, then began to gently shake him. All I could do was continue to scream, 'Do something, Harold! Do something! *Why isn't our baby breathing?*'

"Harold had the sense to get to the phone on the wall in the kitchen and ring the switchboard operator. He was holding Charles and yelled into the phone, 'Call Dr. John Clark! This is an emergency!' I admit I was still incoherent and didn't hear what else your father said, but it wasn't long before our back door opened and Dr. Clark rushed in.

"We stood holding one another while the doctor used his stethoscope to listen for a heartbeat, gently forced open Charles's tiny mouth to see if anything was lodged in his mouth or throat, then used his stethoscope again. Nothing. I'm not sure what else Dr. Clark did. All I can remember ..." Her voice trailed off.

Then Mom looked at me, such a forlorn expression on her face. "Oh, Davie, I pray you never experience the loss of a child, never hear the words 'I'm sorry, your baby is dead.' I began pleading with Dr. Clark, actually probably screaming, 'Charles can't be dead! No, no. Oh, Dr. Clark, do something! There must be something else you can do!' I didn't even give him a chance to answer me. 'I fed him only a few hours ago. He was fine.' I begged for an answer, 'What could have happened?' I saw the hurt showing on his face as he shook his head. He hadn't a clue."

We both sat there, neither of us saying anything, and then our silence was interrupted when she, staring out a window, said as expressionlessly as anyone could, "I can remember almost everything that was said and done in those frantic moments as though it was yesterday. I've recalled it nearly every day of my life for almost forty years."

There's a small gray headstone in Barclay Community Cemetery with the inscription, "Infant Charles Arnold Johnson. Born June 17, 1936. Died June 28, 1936." With no visible signs of illness, it would never be known why my brother died.

The emotion in what my mother related had us both somewhat wrung out and in need of a break. She'd prepared iced tea earlier that day, so we walked to the kitchen to fill two glasses and then returned to the living room. Mother wanted to talk more. It was good we had a chance to be alone.

"The days that followed were filled with silence in our home," she began. "The mine office had told your father to take as many days as needed to be of support to me and cope with his own emotions. We spent a lot of time in prayer, asking God for understanding and strength, and we sought comfort from family, friends, and our pastor at Ebenezer. My mom and dad called from time to time to check on us and offer what emotional support they could give from a distance."

Mother's voice suddenly perked up a bit, but the impassive look on her face didn't change. "Did I ever shock your father when at the supper table a month after Charles died I told him I wanted to have another baby! You should have seen the look on his face. He was dumbfounded." No doubt it felt good to share this with me, because she displayed an ever-so-slight smile. "I told Harold, 'I've thought a lot about it, and I want that wonderful feeling that comes from holding a baby, knowing it's mine and yours; besides, we have the opportunity and responsibility to raise a child and prepare it for the world.' We hadn't planned the first pregnancy, but we could the next one. I told him that despite the horrible loss we'd just suffered, despite the Depression, despite the fact we didn't own a home yet, despite so many challenges that likely lay ahead, it's a wonderful world, and there was no need putting off having another child as soon as we could. In fact, I hoped we'd have at least two more." Mom paused and then in her witty way added, "Bet you're glad we made that decision." We both laughed.

But getting pregnant didn't come so easily this time; just as she said friends had told her over the years, even before she was married, when you want a baby, nothing happens as quickly as you had planned, and when you don't, an unwanted or unplanned pregnancy suddenly appears. In March 1937, nine months after Charles died, Dr. Clark informed Mother she was going to have another baby. She was already three months pregnant.

Peggy Sue was born on my parents' second wedding anniversary, September 10, the end of fifteen months of emotional ups and downs. This was a new beginning, and they were ready for it.

CHAPTER 2

Mother's description of the next two years was a period of happiness and growth. She and Dad were well thought of where they worked, and Peggy Sue had been a happy baby and then a joy as a child, the image of her mother, including the color of her blond, curly hair and the dimple in her right cheek. The only concern, and not anything that preyed on Mom's mind and Dad's, was news the first day of September 1939 that Germany had invaded Poland and thoughts were being expressed nationally that Adolph Hitler would not stop with the seizing of just one country. Poland was on the other side of the world—in fact, my parents weren't exactly certain where it was among that jumble of countries over there—and the United States wasn't involved, so they felt there was really nothing to worry about.

In November, Mom learned she was again pregnant. She and Dad hadn't wanted Peggy Sue to grow up as an "only child," and without ever talking about it, each hoped they would have a boy this time.

"We met that winter with Mr. Brummett, and he assured us the bank would loan us money, within reason, to purchase a house whenever we felt ready to do so. I know it doesn't sound like much in this day and age, but we had nearly $3,300 in savings and decided we wanted a three-bedroom house, so we reduced expenses wherever possible and slowly, steadily increased our savings. On June 5, 1940—my, was it an ugly day outside, windy and rainy—you arrived in the same front bedroom as your sister and brother. How lucky we were. We had another boy. You were so thin but a little longer than most babies, with long fingers, and a full head of black hair."

In July, just past my one-month birthday, I was baptized at a Sunday morning worship service at Ebenezer Lutheran. Mom was proud to tell me I wore a white dress—*a dress!*—my grandmother Dorothy Johnson had worn when she was baptized in 1891. Peggy Sue also wore it in her baptism in 1937.

■ ▒ ■

War was about to envelop the United States. No one, absolutely no one, thought it would happen.

"December 7, 1941, was much like any other Sunday, except it was chilly in Southern Indiana with the high temperature expected to be in the upper twenties," Mom told me. After attending church and eating noontime dinner, she and Dad had no particular plans for the afternoon other than to play on the living room floor with Peggy Sue and me. "I will never forget the Glenn Miller Orchestra's 'Chattanooga Choo Choo' was playing on the radio." Mother's specific recollection didn't surprise me. It would be the same if someone were to ask me what I was doing the moment the news broke that President Kennedy was murdered or that Neil Armstrong had stepped on the moon. Those are things you just don't forget.

But the tranquility of that moment in our house shortly after 1:30 p.m., as perhaps at any home in Winston-Salem, North Carolina; Iowa City, Iowa; Sheridan, Wyoming; or anywhere else in America, was broken by the sudden announcement that the Japanese had attacked Pearl Harbor in the Hawaiian islands, a territory of the United States that housed a huge American naval base. It appeared there was great loss of life, airplanes, and ships in the horrendous, devastating, unexpected bombardment.

Mother's voice was almost a whisper. "Your father and I, not fully comprehending what had happened in a place we didn't know existed, just sat there, not knowing what to say. We were aware of fighting among other countries over the past two years in Europe and had been hearing the Japanese were a threat to American cargo ships in the Pacific, but this? Not even the government—President Roosevelt or anyone else— expected this.

"You children. You precious children. You were oblivious to all the horror, the concern, the fear. Peggy Sue played with three rag dolls made from muslin feed sacks, and at eighteen months, the spitting image of your father, you were trying to stack small wooden blocks with colored numbers and letters of the alphabet carved into the sides.

"I remember exclaiming to Harold, actually whispering, 'Oh, my God, will they attack *us*?' Harold had no answer. His eyes, like mine, were glued to the small, ivory-colored Silvertone radio we'd purchased from Sears and placed on a shelf in the living room so you couldn't reach it." She smiled in saying those last five words.

"As the afternoon wore on, news reports continued to update what reporters in Washington, London, Manila, and elsewhere could find out. I admit I was frightened, certainly from a very personal standpoint." In September, Congress had passed the Selective Training and Service Act, the first US peacetime draft system in history. It required all men twenty-one to thirty years of age to register that fall. My dad was twenty-seven. After he registered at the Hopewell County Courthouse in Pemberton, eight miles south of Barclay, all he could do was hope and pray war would never involve the United States." But it would.

"December 8, President Roosevelt asked a joint session of Congress to approve a state of war with Japan, and the request was quickly okayed. Everyone I knew was now jittery. It's all we talked about at the bank.

"Three days later, Germany and Italy declared war on the United States. In response to a request from FDR, Congress passed a joint resolution declaring war on both of them.

"Your dad could be such a grouch, but I always understood why." Dad's hours increased each day at the mine as the demand for coal by Lakeland Corporation grew to enormous quantities for its northwestern Indiana steel mill. Steel plants throughout the nation shifted to all-out war production for building anything that contained steel and was used by the military. "Day after day, he came home physically dragging. What had been nine-hour days prior to the war became eleven and sometimes twelve. But he knew workers everywhere were sacrificing similarly, so he wouldn't complain. As it turned out, the Hopewell County draft board didn't call up any miners who had young children at home. But a few of Harold's Barclay area friends and acquaintances—married and single— were either drafted or volunteered." The latter included his brother John.

Uncle John's career had been in farming with my grandfather. I learned he wasn't built like my dad; he had the same dark hair and eyes but was about four inches shorter and twenty-five pounds lighter. But like Dad, he didn't have an ounce of fat on him. He was in perfect physical condition for what lay ahead. Two years older than Dad, he and his wife, Ann, and their eight-year-old daughter, Marcy Lynn, lived on the family property in a small house about a quarter of a mile down a gravel lane from Grandpa's. Losing Uncle John to the war effort would be a huge hardship for Grandpa, but he admired his son for feeling such an obligation to the nation.

As though I might have had any doubts, Mom made it clear that Dad really struggled with whether to enlist. She said he and his brother had long conversations about it, and while Uncle John felt a sense of duty to enlist, he was adamant he would never have any animosity toward Dad for not doing the same. Mom said Uncle John emphasized that his daughter was older than Peggy Sue and I, and if the worst should happen to him while in service, his parents were there to take care of Ann and Marcy Lynn.

"Your Grandpa and Grandma Johnson had us and John and his family for a Sunday-night supper at their house, and I remember how solemn it was. Very little was said, and no one did a good job of keeping tears from showing, because John was leaving for the Armored Service School at Fort Knox, Kentucky, the next day, April 13, to train as a tank soldier. Ann told me he wrote at the end of his seventeen weeks of training that he felt somewhat prepared for what lay ahead. She was scared to death."

I was fascinated; I wanted to learn about what had happened to the family during the war years, I could hardly wait for each of the subsequent sessions with Mom that spring of '74. Except for one thing very grave, I had little recollection of the early to mid-1940s.

"When your uncle left for overseas in 1942, Harold was working as a driller on an explosives team with his buddy Hank and earning $14.48 a day," Mother related. She'd gotten small notebooks out of a closet where she'd kept them all those years. Income and expenses were meticulously recorded in pencil. "Our family and savings had grown to the point a different house was necessary and financially possible. Peggy Sue was making it clear she didn't want you sleeping in the same room with her." Mother chuckled.

"We were excited when we found this house we're in now. It was the answer to our dreams for a larger home." Like our home on Seventh

Street, the green, wood-frame residence at Conley and Third wasn't a long walk to the bank for Mom, and she and Dad felt the asking price of $5,150 was reasonable. "Mr. Brummett loaned us $1,150, so on July 4—it was a Saturday—with assistance from a few friends, we moved here." Mother looked at me with a sparkle in her eyes. "Guess what was the most exciting thing of all about the house." Without giving me a chance to answer, she said, "It had an *indoor toilet!*" and she smacked her hands together. "Good-bye, outhouse." How she laughed, and I did too.

Our home at 309 S. Conley Street had a bedroom on the ground floor, just to the right of the front door and living room. The dining room lay between the living room and kitchen, which was tucked back to the right. The bathroom with toilet and lavatory was inside the back door, just off the kitchen. All the floors, except the kitchen, were dark hardwood. Tile, in a not especially attractive shade of yellow and shaped in square blocks, covered the kitchen floor. All the rooms, including the two upstairs ones, were wallpapered. There was a basement, a porch across the entire front with a large wooden swing hanging by steel chains just to the right of the front door, and a large backyard.

Peggy Sue and I had our own bedrooms upstairs, which were accessed by wooden stairs at the left back corner of the dining room. Since I was only two, Dad built and installed a handrail for those stairs within days of our moving in. There was no toilet upstairs, so a white enamelware container, a "pee pot," was placed there for nighttime needs.

The basement was accessed from just inside the rear door by the kitchen. A water heater sat in one corner, near a coal-fired furnace. Adjacent to the furnace was a small coal bin. A shower head hung above a drain cover near another corner. Wooden shelves attached to the cinder-block wall at one side of the basement had ample space for sacks of potatoes and onions and canned goods. Grandma Dorothy Johnson always canned sausages, garden-grown vegetables, and blackberries and raspberries picked from bushes in the bottoms near some of the farm fields, and she shared them with her sons and their families. Now there was room for Mother to accept even more of the quart Ball glass jars. The previous homeowner had had three clotheslines strung from one wall to another, and those would be used to dry clothes in the winter. Two steel poles in the shape of a "T" supported two galvanized clotheslines in the backyard.

A hand-dug cistern in the backyard held water for our many uses— toilet, shower, lavatory, cooking, and drinking. A system of pipes carried rainwater from the roof gutters through underground rock filter boxes and into the well. In extremely dry weather, Dad hired a commercial supplier to fill it with water from his tank truck. Also at the rear of the house was a plot approximately sixty feet wide by forty feet deep that the previous family had used as a vegetable garden, and we would, too.

■ ▒ ▬

"The next three years were difficult," she continued. "At various periods between early 1942 to late '45, the government issued ration booklets that limited the amount of gasoline and certain food items, such as sugar, coffee, and meats, that could be purchased. Thank God for Dorothy's canned goods and the garden in the backyard. We had only one vehicle, a black 1936 Ford pickup truck, that Harold drove to work each day, and we rarely went to Pemberton or Evansville, so gasoline rationing wasn't a hardship."

She raised her shoulders and chest slightly, her pride showing when she declared, "My colleagues and I even had roles in the effort, selling war bonds that helped the government finance the fighting. They could be purchased for as little as $18.75 and redeemed in ten years for $25. Mr. Brummett offered each of us five cents for each bond we sold. It wasn't much of a bonus, but his intent was genuine. I was making an additional dollar to two dollars a week and placed every penny of it in our family savings account."

Mother paused and sighed. "Poor Ann. She occasionally received letters from John, but he wasn't at liberty to describe what he was doing or where he was located. She believed he was in North Africa. When she read in *Life* magazine in May of '43 that twenty-three soldiers from the small city of Red Oak, Iowa, were missing in action in North Africa, her ever-present fear intensified. Ann wiled away the hours tending to a vegetable garden behind the small farmhouse. She dubbed hers a 'Victory Garden' in keeping with the national effort for families to raise their own vegetables to help deal with possible food shortages. She said the plantings gave her a feeling of having at least a minor role in the war effort. Ann confided in me that John ended every letter by telling her how much he loved her and Marcy Lynn and asked that she also give his love to his parents and to Harold and his family. She always did, and we were pleased to receive his regards, although it didn't stop us from worrying.

"Oh, Davie," Mother said, the saddest look suddenly covering her face. "Our lives—yours, mine, and your sister's—were about to be turned upside down."

Another knuckleball was on its way.

It was August 7, 1944.

Having talked about it with Mom more than once during the years since then, I'm well aware of what happened that day. Dad, Hank Thompson, and two other men had formed an explosives team of what were called shooters. They usually operated four hundred to six hundred feet from the men and machinery on the floor of the pits below, using explosives to break up dirt and thick layers of rock so the mammoth electric-powered Bucyrus Erie shovels with their massive buckets could expose the coal by scooping the tons of overburden and dumping it to one side of the pit. Dad's team used a drill to create holes approximately forty feet deep, and then they filled two-foot-long cloth bags with lampblack, dipped them in liquid oxygen, attached wires, and lowered the explosives into the holes. A steam whistle would warn all miners that a blast was about to occur, and then, after a suitable period of waiting, the other ends of the wires would be touched to a battery approximately two hundred feet away to set off the explosives.

It was a rainy, windy day with poor visibility. Dad and Hank were working as a two-man team, which was totally against company regulations but the others had called in sick that morning. For reasons he couldn't adequately explain later, Hank thought that after dropping explosives into the holes Dad gave the all-clear signal. Hank activated the warning whistle, and after waiting for what he thought was an appropriate amount of time, he set off the charge. He later explained it was a typical explosion—thunderous with dust, dirt, and rock rising high into the sky and then the earth giving way.

As the dust settled, he looked for Dad. Hank told investigators he panicked immediately as he thought, *Where the hell is he?* They were out in the open; Dad couldn't have just disappeared. Hank said that walking close to the edge of the highwall where the ground had broken away, he spotted a few pieces of flesh and a piece of boot and was instantly overwhelmed by a sickening feeling. *My God, was that Harold?* he thought.

It was said that Hank began waving his arms wildly back and forth and cupping his hands around his mouth, screaming at all the miners far below, "Stop! ... Stop! ... Stop! Jesus Christ, Harold is missing! Son of a bitching mother fuck, where is he?"

As men yelled to one another, machinery was halted. The investigative report says, "Mr. Thompson admitted he was frantic and his eyes dashed everywhere. He said he called out to the other miners, 'Look anywhere ... for anything! Harold's missing!'"

Fellow miners later said they'd feared the worst. And they found it when they reached the area of the blast—shredded pieces of clothing and a section of a miner's Bakelite hardhat with jagged edges. Why Dad hadn't gotten clear of the blast area after the warning was sounded would never be known.

▬ ▨ ▬

Mom related that she noticed the mud- and gob-smeared pickup truck park along the street, parallel to the sidewalk in front of the bank and watched two grim-faced miners get out. Rain was falling heavily in Barclay. For some reason, she glanced at the large clock on the wall above the front door. It was shortly after 2:00 p.m. "Mine superintendent Barney Oxley and Gene Hyatt, the pit boss, walked right past my teller's window without even looking at me or speaking to anyone, yet I didn't think anything of it except that Barney had always been so friendly toward me. They went straight to our president's office. Within minutes, Mr. Brummett appeared at the lobby and asked me to come with him." Her colleagues told her many days later how horrible they'd felt when they heard the unforgettable, agonized sounds—the screams of disbelief and denial and the wailing—that came from behind the closed office door. They said they stood looking at one another, sensing what no one ever wanted to learn. Death in the mines, although not common, was a fact of life, and it had come to one of their own families.

Mom stopped at this point, sitting there on her sofa, her head lowered. I dared not make a sound. She needed to be lost in her own thoughts until she felt like talking again. I couldn't imagine what her struggle on that day in '44 had been like. She had lost her husband eight years after the agony of the death of a son. As I look back on it, I really think that what she suffered and how she dealt with it somehow strengthened me in life. She'd been kept strong by the faith she always exhibited, and that certainly impacted my life and likely led me to deepen my own faith as well. Goodness knows, I had to rely on it a lot.

She cleared her throat and looked at me, her eyes moist. "As shaken as I was, I went home and mustered the courage to tell you and Peggy Sue that 'Daddy' wouldn't be coming home again. At seven years of age, your sister clearly understood what 'killed' meant and took the news particularly hard. She and Harold had had a close relationship, although I never believed he felt the attachment to her that he did to you. I don't know if that was because of an innate father-son thing or because he'd lost a son, which caused him to want to be closer to you. But you were only four and I knew you couldn't quite comprehend. Your sister wanted to see your father, but I wasn't about to describe why there was nothing to see."

I got up from the easy chair and went to the kitchen, leaving Mother to sit in silence for a few moments. The glasses of water were refreshing to each of us.

I sort of remember that what was called "visitation" was held in the living room of our home. Such a setting for viewings was common in those days. Some of it came back to me as Mom described it. "The first of two nights of visitation began two days after your father's death, starting at six that evening and lasting three hours. A black wreath hung on the front door where friends entered, paid their respects, and then exited through the kitchen. At the end wall of the living room, what little there was of your father's remains along with his extra set of work clothing, pair of boots, and hard hat were in a regular-sized closed casket. Our black-and-white eight-by-ten-inch wedding photo sat in its dark wood frame atop the casket. It was the best visual of who he had been."

I let Mother take her time. "I was comforted by my parents and sister, Cousin Jane, Dorothy and Charles, and Ann, although they were overwrought as you would expect.

"I was physically and emotionally spent after the second night of the calling and still had the funeral the next day. Ebenezer Lutheran's capacity of two hundred was nearly filled. We sang one of Harold's favorite hymns, the old standard 'Nearer My God to Thee,' but I thought everyone was fairly listless. Reverend Paul Schumacher used Old and New Testament scripture to assure us that Harold was with God and at peace, that he was being rewarded for the good life he had lived on earth. Honestly, and

I hate to admit it to you, Son, but I barely heard a word of it. My mind seemed to be elsewhere, thinking about how my children and I were going to cope.

"I did snap out of it and hear the minister's eulogy. He did a fine job of recounting your dad's life from farm to coal mine, his love for family, and his faith in God and Christ. The service ended with the upbeat 'I'll Fly Away,' but none of our family had much enthusiasm for the lyrics at that moment."

I vividly recall that at the town's cemetery, two workers had hand-dug a grave. I remember because as a little child I'd never seen one and was fascinated by such a hole in the ground. I learned later that what I saw in the hole was a concrete vault above which sat the gray metal casket supported underneath by straps. Our family sat in two rows of fourteen white wooden folding chairs under a small, dark-green canvas tent that warded off the late-morning sun. Peggy Sue was quite distraught and perhaps that took my mother's mind off her own grief, as she did her best to comfort my sister. I basically had no reaction to the proceedings. Following a brief scripture reading, we all watched as Reverend Schumacher sprinkled a handful of dirt over the casket and said something, which I later learned was "Ashes to ashes and dust to dust."

"My parents drove back to their home that afternoon, but I accepted Sarah Mae's offer to stay with us until Sunday," Mother recalled. "That night, lying in the quiet of my bedroom, I finally let my emotions go and sobbed uncontrollably until, exhausted, I fell asleep."

The army had relayed the news to Uncle John, now involved in Lieutenant General George S. Patton's Third Army's major offensive in France and offered him a brief furlough from the fighting but not enough to get back to Barclay. In letters to family members, he revealed that he took the news hard, as any brother would, and had no one to share his emotions with except a sympathetic army chaplain. He said he was somewhat hardened toward death because he was around so much of it, but to lose his dear brother and not be home with his grieving family was a difficulty he could hardly bear. He wrote a most soulful letter to my mother and one to his parents, expressing his deep feelings for my father and his emotional and prayerful support for Mother and Grandpa and Grandma Johnson. And he promised them he would be all right and would return home one day to work on the farm again.

Mother revealed that Hank Thompson didn't show up at the visitations, nor would he be seen at the funeral. Instead, he relayed through the mine superintendent that he wanted to meet privately with her, if she would see him. Without hesitation, she agreed. She didn't blame him any more than she would blame God and told him such when he came to our house in the early afternoon the day after the funeral.

"Unfortunately, Hank had turned to bourbon whiskey to drown the incredible guilt that had wracked his body, and though he appeared sober, his breath and gestures revealed otherwise. In fact, I was the one who did the consoling while he fumbled with words, rarely looking at me with those deeply reddened eyes. I did my best to assure him that I recognized his remorse.

"Can't you just picture that big, tall, physically strong man, slump-shouldered and his spirit completely broken as he sat next to me on this sofa? I looked directly at him and tried my best to speak with kindness. 'Hank, you mustn't carry any burden with you. I know Harold was your best friend and the two of you loved working together. No doubt you were an excellent team. What happened was an accident of mining. We can't look at it as anything more, or our insides will be eaten out and *our* lives will be lost, too,' I said.

"I placed a hand on his lying in his lap. 'Harold loved you, and I do, too. If it weren't for you, Harold wouldn't have gotten a job at the mine, and his and my life wouldn't have been as good as it was, because we wouldn't have had the money he earned and he would have been miserable working on the farm. You made it possible for him to have a special period of life and you must—you *must*—understand that I will always be appreciative to you and will continue to consider you a special friend.'

"I was certain Hank left our house that day feeling some relief, but I was also certain he still carried guilt."

Hank Thompson never recovered from the tragedy and his role in it, and eventually, he killed himself.

▬ ▬ ▬

It was so important to me, learning all that I did about my mother and those dark days in the mid-1940s. I knew if I ever had children, I'd want to share this with them, so they'd have an appreciation of their father's background and an understanding of the lives of their grandparents and great-grandparents.

Mom related that the day Dad was killed, Chester Brummett told her to take as much time away from her job as she wanted and needed. He even said he'd pay her regular hourly wage for as long as she was gone. She hadn't thought much about the reality of her financial situation because of all the activities of the week, but it slowly began to sink in during the weekend after the funeral. On Monday morning, when she awoke, she suddenly panicked. Reality had arrived.

But as she calmed her mind and began to reason with herself, she took a pencil from the small desk in her bedroom, got a notepad, and began to think.

Fortunately, she and Dad had been frugal. Also, fortunately, he had purchased, with cash, a used but newer black Ford pickup truck in 1943, so another vehicle was one expense she wouldn't have to worry about.

Crescent Creek didn't have a life insurance program for its employees but decided to pay all the funeral expenses and give Mom five hundred dollars because Dad and Hank should never have been allowed to work only as a two-man team the day of the accident. She said she gave no thought to suing the company. Lawsuits by an individual against a large company were unheard of in those days, especially in an area like Barclay. Mom was thankful for what she considered to be the mine's generosity.

She was starting life anew with a five-dollar monthly loan payment for the house and the regular costs of utilities and maintaining the residence. Then there was food and clothing for the family, gasoline for her small truck, and Mrs. Calhoun's weekly charge for taking care of Peggy Sue and me. On the income side, she had just over $1,250 in savings and was making an hourly wage of eighty-nine cents, which amounted to $32.04 for a thirty-six-hour week. After studying all the figures, she felt a bit of relief. Had she known what would happen when she returned to work at Barclay National on Wednesday, she wouldn't have had any concerns at all. She'd tell you God was looking after her.

▬ ▬ ▬

Thirty minutes before the bank closed for the day, the president called her to his office.

From everything Mother shared with me about him, I began to see

Chester Brummett as a tough-minded, successful businessman with a huge heart. He cared for his employees and customers and was a good family man. He participated in civic organizations as a way of trying to improve the community and served as a deacon in Grace Baptist Church. As a businessman, he always tried to do what was best for his stockholders, him being the majority owner with 12 percent of the shares. There were just over one hundred shareholders of the privately held bank and many of those had received their stock from departed relatives who were among the original owners of the bank when it was founded in 1858.

"I took a seat in front of his large dark oak desk," Mother told me. "Mr. Brummett leaned forward, elbows on his desk pad, hands folded together just under his chin, and he looked me squarely in the eyes. He was mostly bald, about average height for a man fifty-five years old, and slightly overweight; he had a kind voice most of the time and overall, a pleasant disposition. I had no idea why he wanted to talk with me, but I felt at ease.

"He said, 'Mary June, I'm so very glad you're back, and I hope you were ready to come back. As you know, I wanted you to take your time.'

"I responded, 'I do know that, Mr. Brummett, and I thank you for your kindness and concern. The children are fine. They'll miss their father more when the realization that he won't be home again sets in. Peggy Sue is certainly more aware than is David, but he, too, will begin to understand more as time goes by.'

"I remember tears developing in my eyes as I told him, 'I can't thank you enough, nor repay you with the proper words for all the goodness you have shown me. To offer to pay me as long as I needed to be away was an overwhelming comfort, and it just again demonstrated what I have known about you since shortly after I began working here eleven years ago.' I paused. 'Can you imagine that, I've been here eleven years!' Perhaps it was rude, but I didn't give him a chance to comment before I continued, 'But I didn't need to take more time. I know that although Harold was taken from me, God has a plan for me and my children, and I have the faith that our lives will be fine. Besides, I didn't need to spend more time with my thoughts alone in my house; I was ready to return here to be with my bank family.'

"Mr. Brummett nodded as though he understood, then paused, cleared his throat, and began to speak almost in what I would call a formal executive tone, which suddenly made me wonder whether he was about to deliver bad news. *Was I about to lose my job?*

"He was so dignified acting. I'd never seen him this way. Perhaps it was because I was paying such strict attention that I can remember his words almost verbatim. 'Mary June, my responsibility is to operate this bank in such a way that we'll make sound judgments in regard to the investments of our money; make wise loans that will get repaid over time; hire and retain good, decent, quality people who will treat our customers with great care; and have an organizational structure that allows us to be efficient.

"He cleared his throat again and continued, 'I firmly believe that once this war is over—and it *will* end—good times will return to America. I foresee peaceful times once again, a confidence in our nation that you and I have never seen before, along with prosperity. Yes, I believe there will be opportunities for growth, the like of which we could not have imagined ten years ago.' He paused as though preparing to announce something to me. 'As a result, this bank has to prepare itself for the future and growth that is going to come, not tomorrow, but as soon as the war is over. Mark my words. Growth will come.'

"How wise he is, I thought, *yet where's he going with all of this?*

"Then it came. 'Mary June, I want to make you a vice president of our bank.' I didn't move, didn't react. I was stunned. Nothing would come from my throat, as though the air inside it had been locked in.

"He saw the look on my face and continued, 'I'm going to do some reorganizing of our staff, to prepare us to be ready for the growth that will come. I'm placing you in charge of something I'm calling 'customer service' and in charge of getting new accounts and keeping those customers and our current ones pleased with us. Your personality and your work ethic make you perfect for these responsibilities.'

"I could feel euphoria developing in me, and finally, I said, 'Oh, Mr. Brummett, thank you, thank you. I'll never let you down.' I wanted to cry, and my eyes were probably moist, but I didn't dare show such emotion—probably unprofessional of a person who was going to become an officer.

"Fortunately, he quickly responded, 'I know you won't, Mary June. That's why I'm promoting you. I have complete confidence in you.'

"Then came the second surprise. 'Oh, I almost forgot. Your pay.

Instead of paying you an hourly wage, since you'll have more responsibility and I'll expect you to work a few more hours each week, you'll receive a salary. You'll be paid forty-five dollars per week.' Son, my head was now almost spinning, instantly realizing thirteen dollars more per week meant more possibilities for our family. Basically, what I remember saying was 'Thank you, Mr. Brummett. Thank you.' And I reached across the desk, and both of my hands shook his right one. It was a bit awkward, but it was a genuine gesture on my part.

"I was so pleased the staff took the news well when Mr. Brummett announced it to them just after the bank closed for the day. Everyone seemed so very happy for me.

"I felt like I'd sprouted wings and could leave the truck at the bank and fly home, but I stopped at Montgomery's General Store, bought a quart box of hand-scooped vanilla ice cream and six sugar cookies from a large glass display jar, and drove home.

"You may not remember this, but I announced loudly when I walked in the back door, 'Children, Mrs. Calhoun, we're going to have a party!' As you two came running to the kitchen, I said, 'It's time for some smiles around here.'" Mother giggled when she said, "Poor Mrs. Calhoun. When she walked into the room, she just stared at me, having seen a somber, still-grieving woman leave the house that morning and now return in an entirely different mood. She probably wondered if I'd lost my mind. When I told her the news, she gave me a hug that took my breath away. She seemed as happy as I. Then she gathered the two of you to her side and said, 'David and Peggy Sue, we're going to dance,' and with that, the three of you did a most uncoordinated jig of some kind. I thought my sides would burst from laughing so hard."

● ▧ ▬

By this time in my life—the latter part of 1944—my family had stopped referring to me as "David Harold," unless my mom was mad at me. I had simply become "David." Peggy Sue remained, well, Peggy Sue. There was something about a lot of little girls that seemed to require the use of both their first and middle names, especially if Sue was the middle one. There were many of them: Karen Sue, Bonnie Sue, Wendy Sue, Rebecca Sue, Dottie Sue. But in pronouncing my sister's name, it seemed people didn't place a millisecond of a pause between Peggy and Sue, almost as though her name was "Peggysue."

Records Mother kept showed both my sister and me to be of average height and weight for children of our ages. I remember Peggy Sue was very pretty. She always wore her hair long, and it was quite curly. I didn't like her hazel eyes because they could be almost sinister-looking when she got mad about something I'd done. As for me, my eyes were dark brown and my hair straight and black.

CHAPTER 3

I know, from reading history, that when spring arrived in 1945, so did events that would change the world forever. The White House announced that FDR had died April 12 while vacationing in Warm Springs, Georgia. He'd been ill for years, more than the public knew, and the American population was so caught off guard there was fear as to what his passing would mean for US leadership. Vice President Harry S. Truman, somewhat unknown although elected with Roosevelt, was sworn into office. At the same time, the war effort was going exceedingly well for the Allies in Europe. In rapid succession, tyrants fell. Italian dictator Benito Mussolini was captured trying to flee Italy to Switzerland and was executed by partisans in late April. Two days later, German dictator Adolph Hitler committed suicide in his fortified Berlin bunker as Allied forces closed in. In early May, all German forces surrendered to the Allies, and spontaneous celebrations erupted throughout much of the world. May 8 was declared Victory in Europe Day in the United States with formal celebrations being conducted in cities across the wildly happy and relieved nation. Staff Sgt. John Johnson would soon be on his way home.

In August—the fifteenth, to be exact—Japan surrendered only days after the United States dropped atomic bombs on Hiroshima and Nagasaki. The war was over. The United States could now be at peace with the world. It was time for the prosperity Chester Brummett had prophesied.

I remember very little of it, but Mother provided all the details. Saturday, October 6, Barclay held a "Welcome Home" celebration for its seven

29

men and one woman who served in World War II. Uncle John, who'd developed broad shoulders and gained fifteen pounds of muscle since he'd enlisted; five other men; and the lone female, Army Nurse Julia Scales, rode on a wagon pulled by a tractor. All wore military uniforms. The wagon sported a patriotic theme, with large American flags at each corner and dozens of small ones attached inside bunting of red, white, and blue around the sides of the bed. All but one, Bob Thompson—no relationship to Hank—stood and waved throughout the parade. Thompson was one of three of the men who had been wounded in combat, but his injuries were so severe he'd spent months in an army hospital in Italy before he was able to return home in late May. He sat in his metal folding chair.

The temperature was a pleasant 70 degrees, and the sun shone brightly as the 1:00 p.m. parade began, led by two high school bands—Barclay High and nearby Clarkson High, also in Hopewell County. The procession featured marching units of area veterans whether they had served in wars or not. Most were members of American Legion and Veterans of Foreign Wars posts, and all wore their previous military uniforms, although the combination of years and too much food and drink made some a little snug. Boy Scout and Girl Scout units, the part-time town manager, the state senator and the two state representatives from the area, and US Congressman Charles Powers, whose district included Barclay, also participated.

The parade started at Barclay High, proceeded along several neighborhood streets, and entered a blocked-off Main Street from the south. It seemed every building on Main was displaying the Stars and Stripes in one fashion or another. Cheering and appreciative children and adults, some with tears rolling down their faces, some outwardly crying, lined all the streets, most waving small American flags. The community swelled on this day with the addition of hundreds who drove from throughout Hopewell and surrounding counties to join the display of gratitude.

The appreciative throng stood, used chairs they'd brought with them, or simply sat on streetside lawns or curbs along the parade route. When the procession ended near the heart of the business district, just two blocks north of the signal light at Second Street, the forty-member bands joined as one in front of a platform that had been built in the middle of the street. Barclay High in its red and black wool uniforms and Clarkson High in their green and white faced the south toward all of the other parade participants who stood in the street, with the crowd many persons deep along the sidewalks. My entire family stood together, about thirty feet from where Uncle John would be sitting. Mother said I was pretty fidgety, and it was a challenge keeping me interested.

The seven honorees were ushered to the stage and sat in white, wooden folding chairs on the painted white platform that rose about four feet above the street. On the other side of the simple dark-brown wooden lectern, which had a plain front and a small American flag on top, sat the various government officials. One chair on the military side was purposely left empty.

As planned, to get the crowd's rapt attention, the two school bands began playing the National Anthem. Platform participants and audience alike stood with right hands, some clutching caps or hats, over their hearts and faced the nation's flag in a floor stand on the corner of the stage, to the crowd's left. The state flag stood at the other front corner. Performing together for the first time, the bands did so with gusto, the reeds of a saxophone or two squeaking from time to time and at least one cornet making a mess of the high note at "*rockets' red glare.*" But the good effort was there, and the crowd showed its appreciation and pride with rousing applause. In fact, the applause was sustained by the emotion of the song mingling with the feelings of just being there to celebrate the end of a horrific war and honor the town's brave representatives in it.

As master of ceremonies, Town Manager Edwin Rogers rose from his chair, and as he walked to the lectern, the enthusiastic crowd quieted. Speaking into a microphone attached to a steel floor stand next to the lectern, his words boomed on the portable public address system when he began, "Our honored and distinguished servicemen and woman—" but the crowd drowned him out with roaring applause, shouts, cheers, and chants of "Hip, hip, hooray! Hip, hip, hooray!" Except for Bob Thompson, the special military guests stood again, and they and Thompson waved, all but two flashing ear-to-ear smiles. Those two showed no facial expression, either because the war had drained them of emotion or they were somewhat embarrassed to be the center of attention. No doubt sensing the display of exhilaration might not end, Rogers spoke loudly, repeatedly saying, "Ladies and Gentlemen," so he could be heard on the electronic speakers hanging on metal stands along the sidewalks and waving his arms above his head, signifying a call for silence. Continuing with the introductions, Rogers got to the last one, paused, and remained silent for a moment more as he looked solemnly at the crowd.

Dropping the volume of his voice slightly, he said, "We are so extremely thankful for these brave people seated here, but our hearts are heavy because one of our sons from Barclay who went overseas to serve our country didn't get to come home to celebrate. The empty seat at the far end of the row of our honored guests is for Army Sergeant Donald Phillip Clark, who lost his life on D-Day, June 6, 1944, during the assault at Omaha Beach. Let us have a moment of silence in respect for the ultimate sacrifice of Donnie Clark and thank God for him and his service in the defense of freedom." There was rustling in the crowd as nearly all bowed their heads, followed by a chorus of "Amen" after Rogers ended the silence with "Amen."

Each of the politicians spoke, with Congressman Powers claiming he was "speaking on behalf of the president of the United States." If not exactly true, no one questioned that Powers's praise was what President Truman would have said had he been there.

Finally, the part of the program everyone had been waiting for arrived. Town Manager Rogers called the military guests to his side one at a time. Even Bob Thompson, seated closest to the lectern, now managed to stand and hold on to it. Rogers introduced them with their service rank and full name and told where they'd served and for how long but didn't refer to the medals or ribbons on their uniformed chests because some had more than others and this was no occasion to make anyone seem less special than anyone else. The exception was to call attention to the Purple Hearts worn by the three who had been wounded in combat.

Each of the honorees was presented with the gift of an American flag secured in a large square dark marble base that displayed a light gold metal plate engraved with the words, *"Presented to (name) by the proud citizens of Barclay for sacrifice and distinguished service in the defense of freedom. October 6, 1945."* A similarly worded gift was presented to the still-grieving mother of Donnie Clark (her ex-husband had left her and Barclay years earlier). Clark had been buried in Barclay Community Cemetery in 1944, his name hand-cut into a five-foot-tall limestone monument dedicated to Barclay residents who'd lost their lives in other wars as well—the Civil War and World War I. The three-foot-wide by nine-inch-thick monument displayed seven other names, all men, and stood just off the sidewalk in an alcove between Barclay National Bank and the Corner Café, which was at Fifth Street and Main. The monument had been erected by veterans' organizations after World War I.

Mom said she'd been told all those who were honored had been given an opportunity to speak but informed Rogers prior to the parade they would not. She opined it was a duty and an honor to serve, but none of them wanted to look like they were taking special credit for it. Besides, some had been in such awful combat and for so long they didn't think they would ever talk about it even with their families. Uncle John wouldn't, not with Ann or Marcy Lynn or even with Grandpa Charles whom he respected deeply. But Grandpa, with just as much respect for his son, told me he never asked.

Just after Rogers called for one last round of applause and thanked the crowd for coming, the bands began playing "God Bless America," followed that with "America the Beautiful," and ended with "My Country, 'Tis of Thee." While they played, many in the audience hurried to the stage to shake their heroes' hands, and some even sought out Virginia Clark, Donnie's mother, to express their feelings to her, too.

My guess is that for the people of Barclay and the surrounding rural area, the war finally came to a close that day.

CHAPTER 4

My mother found love again.

"Children, I've invited Matthew Miller to have supper with us this evening." I was seven and in the second grade, and Peggy Sue was ten and in the fifth when we heard those words after Mom got home from the bank one late afternoon in October of '47. She was certainly in a cheerful mood. "Mr. Miller's a friend of mine. You'll remember him from the ball game we attended this summer." Mom's announcement didn't mean much to me although except for relatives and the preacher, I didn't recall any man being in our house since shortly after Dad died. My sister had an odd look on her face, which I now know to have been one of skepticism. As if to convince us, Mom kept saying things like, "He's a very nice man" and "You'll like him," emphasizing *nice* and *like*.

Mom revealed to me in our 1974 conversations that she'd gone out with a couple of men since Dad had died, but not until 1947 and the occasions were primarily social events. She'd wondered if she would ever have special feelings for another man, and then she met Matt Miller, and she knew she could.

"I fell for Matt the first time I met him. My good friend Karen Smith and I went to an evening high school musical production near the end of the 1946–47 school year. Since all teachers were required to 'volunteer' at extracurricular activities, he was taking tickets at the entrance to the auditorium. My, was he handsome with those dark eyes and that thick, wavy black hair. His build reminded me of photos I'd seen of Charles Atlas; just perfectly shaped, it appeared.

"Apparently, my captivation with him showed, because Karen teased me about it when we took our seats and she flashed a devilish grin at me throughout the play. I must admit that when we talked with him at intermission—he made a point of seeking us out—I was overwhelmed by his charming personality and those dreamy eyes." Mother blushed.

"A month later and one week after the school year ended, I was busy with paperwork and didn't notice him until a teller came to my desk on one side of the bank lobby. 'Someone's here to see you,' she said. I looked up, and there he stood, no more than fifteen feet in front of me. I can still picture his smile and those perfectly aligned white teeth.

"Matt said, 'I've come to inquire about transferring my checking and savings accounts.'

"I learned later that he'd already decided he should begin doing business at our bank if it meant opportunities to drop by and see me. Making inquires of friends in town, he'd been able to learn a little about me, that I was a widow with a young son and slightly older daughter, and he knew where I worked, but the busyness of the closing weeks of the school year, and perhaps a tinge of shyness, had prevented him from contacting me previously.

"He said he'd moved back to Barclay two years earlier and opened checking and savings accounts at Hopewell County Bank because he'd been a customer there when he was younger. 'Friends urged me to be with your bank,' he said. Whether that was true or not, it didn't matter to me. He said he and a fellow teacher painted houses in the summer, and he played semi-pro baseball in a league on Sundays. In fact, he invited you children and me to the game that Sunday afternoon. It was your first time at a baseball game, Davie," she said with the obvious pride of having introduced me to the sport I would fall in love with. It would play a major role in my life.

"He gave me a brief history of himself. He was thirty-three, a year older than I, and taught physical education. A Barclay native, he'd earned his bachelor's degree in phys ed from Indiana University and while there tried out as a pitcher for the baseball team but wasn't selected. Although he looked fit as a fiddle, he'd had a chronic heart murmur that in 1942 prevented him from being accepted by the military. He said he begged the army to take him even for a desk job somewhere, but his request was denied.

"In the summers of his college years, he played semi-pro baseball, a mixture of amateurs like Matt and older men who'd had some professional experience, mostly in the minor leagues, but had given up on those dreams. He described himself to me as a decent pitcher, with a fastball, pretty good curve, and something unusual in those days, a knuckleball. During the school year, he kept his arm in shape as an assistant coach on the high school baseball team, throwing the ball in the normal course of teaching the players and pitching batting practice on occasion."

━ ▬ ▬

"I can remember it was unusually hot for a June afternoon—close to 90 degrees, if I recall correctly—when Matt picked us up at our house. He had a dark-green 1945 Ford sedan. I had some sugar cookies I'd made and a thermos filled with water. He'd advised me there was no water or food at the ball field.

"The first hiccup of the day was after church service at Ebenezer that morning. It wasn't anything major, although it could have been embarrassing. As the entire Johnson family was standing together outside, you told Grandpa Charles you were going to a baseball game that afternoon and you were excited. 'It's my first!' you proclaimed.

"Charles said, 'Oh, who are you going with, and where's the game?'

"Well, I about fell over. I had to think fast. I'm certain I blushed when I responded we were going to watch the Barclay Reds play at the high school diamond because I thought it was time to introduce you to baseball. It seemed enough of an answer to satisfy Charles, and nothing more was said about it."

The baseball field was the same one I would play on in high school years later, located behind the gymnasium at the rear of the school. Volunteers had erected a twenty-foot-high screen made of chicken-wire fencing attached on the playing field side to poles similar in size to telephone poles but not as tall, to serve as the backstop seventeen feet behind home plate. One unshaded, wooden, dark green bleacher of seven thirty-foot-long rows was set back along each base line. The infield was clay dirt, the top inch or so loosened by men using rakes prior to each game.

The outfield fence also had chicken wire attached to small poles about five-feet high. The ground in the outfield, never watered by anyone except Mother Nature, was a mixture of grasses and weeds that got mowed nearly every Saturday morning. If for some reason the grass didn't get cut that week, it wouldn't be mowed on Sunday. People were expected to attend worship service somewhere. Regardless, there was a tacit understanding in Barclay that no one worked or participated in any organized activities until after noon on Sundays.

"The second hiccup of the day was my not taking enough water to the game. I learned a big lesson. At first, you sat with me and watched the players, but it wasn't terribly long before you lost interest and began playing with little metal toy cars and trucks in the dirt behind the bleachers. Your sister sat beside me, entertaining herself with two Raggedy Ann and Andy dolls. I can remember being enthralled with how Matt looked in his uniform but knew he must have been dying in those wool pants and flannel shirt.

"As the game progressed, you and your sister went to a nearby playground and entertained yourselves on the swings, teeter-totter, and wooden merry-go-round. From time to time, I'd go there to offer cookies and make sure you drank water.

"As the ninth inning began, both of you came to the bleachers and said you wanted to go home; you were hot, tired, dirty, and thirsty. The thermos was empty. 'It won't be much longer; the game's almost over,' I said. 'Please sit here for me and let's cheer for our team. Okay?' That appeared enough to satisfy both of you for the moment, although neither of you was too happy about it.

"I remember that after the game Matt came over to us and said, 'Hey, what'd you think?'

"To which you replied, 'I wanna go home.' Your and Peggy Sue's hands and faces were smeared with dirt, and your clothing was covered, too. And that was your introduction to baseball." Mom smiled.

"I went with Matt to several Sunday-afternoon games that summer, some at Barclay, some in other towns, always relying on Mrs. Calhoun to take care of you two. We were together often on weekday evenings as well. It wasn't a secret to some in Barclay that we were seeing one another, but the Johnson in-laws were oblivious to it."

— — —

Mother seemed to love telling me about Matt. His life experiences had been much simpler than hers, although not without their challenges. After graduating from Indiana University, commonly called IU, in 1935, he got a job as a teacher at a high school in Huntington in Northeast Indiana. While there, he'd met a teacher his age who lived and taught in nearby Columbia City. But their two-year marriage wasn't one of much happiness, and fortunately, they had no children when they divorced in 1940. It was Matt's dream to return to Barclay, so through the years, he'd kept in touch with the school principal, his friend Reid Fichter. When the opening for a physical education teacher and assistant baseball coach was revealed to him privately by Fichter, Matt jumped at the opportunity and moved back to Barclay in the summer of 1945.

He was born Matthew Raymond Miller—he, too, had his father's first name for a middle name—in 1914 at home just outside the town's corporation limits and lived there until he went off to college, although he was home each summer. He was an only child. His father worked at Hedlund Corporation, an Evansville manufacturer of airplane parts, a job of national importance once the United States entered World War II, and his mother was a homemaker, which was typical of women in those days. Matt's summer jobs as a teenager and later a college student were almost exclusively on farms, working in the hayfields. After his enrollment at IU, his summertime income became vital in supplementing the money his parents paid to send him there. He loved baseball, a sport he'd learned as a child, played with passion as a teenager, and then continued to participate in as an adult. His dream of playing professional baseball ended with not being accepted on the team at the university. He was deeply hurt the coach felt his abilities weren't up to the level of those who played in the Big Ten Conference, but he didn't dwell on the decision for long, accepting in his heart that he just wasn't good enough.

CHAPTER 5

"Children, you remember Mr. Miller," I recall Mother saying as soon as Matt walked in from the front porch for that late October supper. "We went with him to the baseball game this summer." I had remembered him but only vaguely. I recalled a little bit about the game. It was the first time I'd ever seen the uniforms, and I thought it would be neat to wear one.

Mom had told us to be on our best behavior when he arrived. I wasn't shy like my sister, so I immediately announced, "I've got a baseball," ran from the living room, and bounded up the stairs. When I returned, Matt was sitting in the large easy chair, Peggy Sue—staring at the floor—was on the sofa, and Mom was in the kitchen. "Look, my baseball," I practically shouted as I rushed across the dining room. I was unaware it was a ball Matt had asked my mother to give to me after that game we'd attended. She'd been careful not to confide in us that she had been going to games and seeing him at other times as well. Anytime we'd asked her on evenings or Sunday afternoons where she was going, she'd respond, "With friends." That was enough to satisfy us.

I remember holding out the grass-stained ball, which overfilled my seven-year-old palm, and Matt telling me I was lucky because "lots of little boys don't have a baseball of their own."

"I like to throw the ball with Mommy." I could tell by his reaction it was news to him, my mother tossing the ball back and forth with me in the backyard. I didn't have a baseball glove, so Mom would toss it underhanded, often letting it hit the ground and bounce up just in front of me.

"Do you have a glove?" Matt inquired.

"I don't have one. I'm going to get one," I remember replying with youthful innocence, having no idea if or when I'd get one.

I had only spoken with Matt for a few minutes in my entire life and already had good feelings about him. He seemed very interested in Peggy Sue and me, asking lots of questions about us. I could tell he listened intently to everything we had to say. He touched on the subject of baseball and his role in it at the school but had sensitivity for my sister and the fact the game meant almost nothing to her. After all, baseball was a boy's sport. In later years, I would realize he was so well-liked as a teacher because he took an interest in every student he taught.

"Time for supper," Mother announced. My mom was quite a cook.

She told me in '74 there were certain things that always stood out in her mind. She could recall precisely the details of events that meant a lot to her in life. One was this meal, the first she ever prepared for Matt.

"We had pork chops, sweet potatoes, orange Jell-O, and homemade apple pie. I'll never forget Matt said it was 'delicious.' What a relief to hear that word because I'd been so nervous not only about preparing the food but whether you and your sister would behave at the table. Well, it was silly of me to be concerned about either one. The evening couldn't have been more perfect.

"I didn't want him to help, but he insisted on washing the dishes while I dried. Standing at the sink in the kitchen, I told him, 'You were wonderful with the children. I can tell they like you.'

"Without looking up, he replied, 'They're great kids, and they've been raised well by their mother. I'm impressed.' Those words meant everything to me. I remember lying in bed that evening and thinking perhaps there was a future for the four of us together."

What a lovely look Mother had on her face as she gazed out the living room window.

Then she looked at me, and her expression turned serious. "Well, what happened after church that Sunday was about as ... embarrassing ... actually, I don't know if that's the right word; I know I could have hidden under a rock. We were standing on the church lawn with Charles and Dorothy, and you blurted, 'A man came to our house for dinner.'

"My heart raced, my knees weakened, and I was suddenly flush with anxiety as your grandfather responded, 'Oh, and who was that?'

"Peggy Sue answered, 'Mr. Miller, a teacher at the high school.'

"Charles and Dorothy shot glances at one another, and I instantly interjected, 'Matt Miller, the phys ed teacher at Barclay High.' I wanted to say more but was so stunned I could hardly make a sound. It seemed like an eternity for me to gather my composure, and then I motioned toward a nearby tree and asked if we could talk over there.

"Thank goodness you children ran off to a swing set while we three adults found privacy under a tall, wide-spreading maple whose leaves had turned to shades of red and yellow, some of which were at our feet. Other parishioners greeted and talked with one another near the front steps, but none of them came over and interrupted us. What courage it took for me to tell your grandparents what they needed to hear. 'Please believe me,' I said, 'I didn't want you to find out this way. I have so much respect for you and love you so much. I had intended to talk with you after worship, but David …' I couldn't complete the sentence. Somehow, I found the inner strength I needed. 'Matt Miller and I met at the bank one day when he came to open accounts. I went to some baseball games with him this summer; he was a pitcher for the local semi-professional team on Sunday afternoons. I've also been with him on other occasions and invited him to our house for dinner Friday night.'

"I remember so distinctly that neither Charles nor Dorothy said anything. All I saw were two stoic faces, and I thought they were really mad, perhaps terribly hurt. I couldn't bear the sight and that led me to begin struggling not to cry, although I know tears began developing. 'I've been a widow now for over three years,' I said quietly. "I loved Harold with all my heart. We were meant to spend our entire lives together but were robbed of that.' The tears now rolled down my cheeks, but I forced myself to face the two of them and said, 'I never looked with interest at another man for all that time since Harold died, until this summer. Please don't think it wrong of me or disrespectful to Harold's memory to see another man.'

"Then Charles very calmly asked if it was a serious relationship. I responded that I didn't know, although that was hiding the truth. 'But we've enjoyed being with one another, and I thought it was time for the children to get to know him. I didn't want them to hear rumors, just like I didn't want you to find out the way you just did.' Then I told them I was so sorry and asked if they would forgive me. At that point, my emotions wouldn't let me say more, and the tears increased although I wasn't sobbing.

"I couldn't have asked for more than what came next. Charles and Dorothy looked at one another, and then he said—and I can remember how tender he was in the way he expressed himself as he placed an arm around my shoulders—'Mary June, Dorothy and I have talked many times about you and your future. We wondered how long it would be before you would begin seeing men. We're not offended. God would never want us to be so. He wants us to continue to be loving and supportive of you.' You could have pushed me over with a feather.

"Then he pulled away from me and stood looking me squarely in the eyes. He said, 'Yes, you and Harold *were* robbed of your life together, and he of his, but you shouldn't be robbed of life without another loving man. We understand that and want you to know you must live your life in a way that will be a blessing to it, a blessing to your children, and a blessing to yourself.'

"Dorothy wrapped her arms around me, hugged me, kissed me on a cheek, and said, 'God bless you, dear. We'll always be here for you and our grandchildren. We want nothing but the best for you, especially your happiness.' At that moment, you children came running up to us. Peggy Sue wanted to know why I was crying. Your grandmother told her they were tears of joy because I was telling them how happy I was.

"I remember as we were driving home, I couldn't have been more relieved, both at how Charles and Dorothy had taken the news and how they responded. Now, it was my parents' turn."

Mother told me her folks invited us to their home for Thanksgiving. When her mother called with the invitation, Mom courageously told her about the relationship with Matt and asked if he could come with us. "Although often overbearing, your grandma Hutchison had an under-standing heart, and after several questions about Matt, she said she'd be delighted to have him, too, and would inform my father. But I told her I wanted to tell Dad myself. I felt I owed it to him and didn't want that responsibility to fall on her.

"Dad used a room he'd converted into a study so he could work on sermons without leaving the parsonage, which was about a hundred feet from the church. Besides, he could see everyone who entered the church during the week, his way of keeping up on all who were giving their time in serving the Lord through New Carlisle Church of Christ." It was quite unusual to hear my mother mock her father the way she said, "giving their time in serving the Lord through New Carlisle Church of Christ." She loved him very much but didn't care for what she considered his self-righteous ways, as though there was only one church in the world, his, and his expectations were that every one of his flock would give every ounce of themselves in serving it.

Grandpa Warren Hutchison was twenty-four years older than Mom. I can remember even back then he was fast losing his hair on top. It was still light in color—one might call it blond—and it masked the gray that was rapidly creeping in. He was of average build for a man his age, his face round. No doubt his deep voice commanded attention from the pulpit, but he always softened it when speaking with Mom, even though his remarks could sometimes be biting. Grandpa was much different from his wife; in some ways, he was far more understanding than she, a necessary trait of a good minister. Mom always said he was compassionate but definitely resolute about the philosophies of his church and not open-minded about those of the various denominations of Baptists, the Methodists, or, God forbid, the Lutherans. For whatever reason, he didn't care for the Lutherans. Mom never knew why.

She said that when she broke the news about her relationship with another man and asked if Grandpa would mind if she brought Matt with her, quickly adding that her mother had no problem with it, he said he didn't either, although he asked a lot of questions about the teacher from Barclay. "Of course, he wanted to know right away if Matt attended church. I told him, 'Occasionally, at First Methodist, here in town.' To my dad, church attendance was all important." She laughed in recalling, "When he learned Matt had been a lifelong St. Louis Cardinals fan, his interest was piqued even more." Living in Southern Illinois, Grandpa was a diehard Cardinal. I can remember while growing up I knew never to try to talk with him about the strengths of the Brooklyn Dodgers, New York Giants, and others in the National League. Dodgers, Giants, the Lutheran church—it didn't matter—if he didn't like them, they were inferior.

These many years later, the relief on Mom's face told me a lot. No doubt the four-hour drive to New Carlisle had been nerve-racking. "Thanksgiving Day couldn't have gone better," she said. "You children were models of good manners at the dinner table. My folks and your aunt Sarah Mae were extremely cordial to Matt. And the meal was sumptuous."

CHAPTER 6

Christmas 1947 is the first one I remember something about, but, as with other subjects we discussed, much more came back to my mind when Mother described it. I think she enjoyed sharing those memories, because it was a period of so much joy for her.

"Matt met the Johnsons for the first time when we went to Christmas Eve service at Ebenezer, and they couldn't have been nicer to him. I think he felt a bit uncomfortable being there. After all, I was still Mary June Johnson and they were my in-laws. We sat with Charles, Dorothy, John, Ann, and Marcy Lynn."

This part I remember: the worship portion was brief, and we kids were anxiously awaiting something else. We thought it was nice Jesus was born, but Santa Claus was a lot more important. He brought gifts, and it seemed there were tons of them under the tall pine tree standing in the slot of a wood base on the floor in front and to the right of the altar. Just when it appeared we were about to burst from anticipation, Reverend Schumacher announced, smiling widely, "Children, we have a special guest with us tonight. Who might that be?"

With that, all of us yelled from the top of our lungs, "Santa Claus!"

On cue, Santa strode into the sanctuary from a doorway to the right of the tree. "Ho, ho, ho. Hello, boys and girls." We were so excited and jumped up from our pew seats, but I saw two or three little ones who were scared and started crying. Like them, I believed Santa was real. Even at ten, Peggy Sue sort of did, too, although some of the kids in her elementary school class had been saying he wasn't.

Gesturing widely with his arms, Santa said, "What's tomorrow, boys and girls?"

Almost as though we'd rehearsed the response, we screamed in unison, "Christmas!"

His next statement was one I couldn't quite comprehend. "Tonight, I'm going all over the world to take toys and goodies to children everywhere, but I wanted to stop here and see all of you." *How could he do that?* Even at seven and a half years of age, I knew the world had to be pretty big. But I didn't dwell on my skepticism. Santa asked us if we'd been good boys and girls during the year, and we all shouted we had, although I didn't think Peggy Sue always minded our mother the way she should have. Santa then started handing out presents. We raised our hands whenever our names were announced, and some of the mothers served as elves to bring the gifts to us in the pews.

I received a *Tommy Tittlemouse* nursery rhymes book! Were they kidding me? Someone of my age getting nursery rhymes? But I didn't say anything. Then Santa told us he had a busy night ahead. He asked that we be good and mind our parents throughout the year, waved good-bye, and left. As we all left the church, each child was given a small brown paper bag containing candy, peanuts, and an orange or apple, and Mom let us eat anything we wanted. After all, this was a special night.

My sister and I could hardly fall asleep, partly from eating too much from our goodie bags, but mostly from anticipating the excitement of the next morning. I think it was about 6:00 when she came to my room to wake me. We went down the stairs as quietly as possible, but some of them creaked and we were scared we'd wake Mom. We were excited Santa had eaten the cookies and drunk the milk left for him on a chair near the lighted cedar tree Grandpa Johnson had cut down on his farm.

"Well, let's see what Santa brought us," Mom said, surprising us as she came out of her nearby bedroom. We hadn't been so quiet after all. She had us run upstairs and get robes and socks on while she went to the basement and put more coal in the furnace.

When we returned, Mom was wearing a red-and-white Santa's cap and said she'd be Santa's helper and hand out the gifts. Peggy Sue had counted fifteen of them, but we were informed some were for other members of the family we'd see that day.

I remember getting some plastic toy trucks and a dark-green metal military fighter airplane. My sister got a Betsy Wetsy doll and a book from the mystery series about the fictional young amateur detective Nancy Drew. She loved reading, and Nancy Drew was her favorite character. Mother gave us a large package and said it was a joint gift. I loved my sister. Even though we were three years apart in age and she had her own set of friends, we got along well together. But sharing a gift was something we'd never been asked to do.

We tore the wrapping paper to bits. I'm certain I sat there with my mouth open when I saw the illustration on the top of the box. We both yelled, "A train! A train!" It was a black Lionel locomotive with a coal car, an oil tanker, two boxcars, a caboose, and an electric O-gauge track.

Mom found putting the straight and curved sections of metal track together not to be as difficult as she'd feared, and it didn't seem to take long before the train was running. It was a steam-type locomotive that produced its own smoke and had a built-in whistle. The caboose was lighted on the inside. It took Peggy Sue no time to learn how to control the speed with the transformer, but for me, that was another matter. I insisted on full power all the time, and as a result, the locomotive jumped the track more than once, which put the joint sharing of a gift in jeopardy. My sister would complain to our mother who would patiently ask me to use the proper speed, which I wouldn't or couldn't do, which would result in Peggy Sue complaining again.

Mom was saved by the clock. She suddenly realized time had gotten away from her; there was food to prepare for Christmas dinner with our Johnson family at the farm. She told us to unplug the train, go wash our faces, and put on the clothes she'd laid out the night before.

"I called Matt at his parents' to wish him a Merry Christmas," Mother recalled with fondness.

"Peggy Sue and Marcy Lynn were a big help to Dorothy, Ann, and me as we prepared the meal. Men just never helped get dinners ready. Women were left to do all of it from cooking to clearing the table and washing dishes afterward."

While the food was being prepared, I went with Grandpa and Uncle John to check the cooling unit in the milk house. I always loved going there, because the room was so cold. The two of them milked forty-three Holsteins every day at 5:00 a.m. and 5:00 p.m. The milking area in the barn had eight stalls, each fitted with an electric-powered machine. Prior to purchasing the devices, they'd milked by hand. Each cow's milk was taken to the cooling unit, poured into ten-gallon cans, and kept cold until "the milkman" from a commercial dairy operation that purchased it came every other day to pick it up.

As the women worked in the kitchen, mother said Grandma reminisced, "It's so wonderful having electricity. I know we take it for granted, and I remind myself from time to time how lucky Charles and I are to have it. As far back as I can remember, before electricity, we used coal oil lamps for our lights throughout the house. I grew up with an icebox, and that's all Charles and I had for years after we were married. A route man brought ice to our house two days a week. Water was drawn from the well out back, and I had to heat it on the stove." Looking at the cast-iron, wood-fired stove, she added, "Of course, I still use it, but at least we now have a water pump for the well out back and a water heater."

This Christmas dinner, like every Christmas meal I can remember, was similar to Thanksgiving's, except there was no ham. We had chicken and dumplings, cranberry sauce, gravy, mashed potatoes, green beans and corn that Grandma had canned late that summer, homemade yeast rolls, chocolate cake, and cherry pie.

After what seemed like hours to us kids, Grandpa announced, "Let's go see what's under the tree," eliciting Grandma's immediate rebuke that there'd be no gifts until the dishes had been washed.

For different reasons, each of us was excited as we drove home that afternoon. Mom had received a Kenmore chrome-finished electric roaster and three sizes of cast-iron skillets. I'd gotten an all-steel red scooter, although despite the fact there was no snow on the frozen ground, Grandpa's gravel-covered driveway disappointingly made it impossible to use. I was a little jealous Peggy Sue got two gifts, a compact Philco electric radio and a set of deluxe Kingston all-metal, solid-wheel, ball-bearing roller skates. I just knew that when she tightened the toe clamps onto her shoes, buckled the leather straps around her ankles, stood up, and tried to skate, she'd fall on her rear end. I was right, and did I ever laugh, bringing a "Stop that!" from my mother. Peggy Sue had gone out to Grandpa's concrete front porch and immediately plopped down. She was skinny as a rail, so there wasn't much physical cushion for her to fall on. I know her bottom hurt.

Another round of food and more gifts awaited us at home. My

Hutchison grandparents and Aunt Sarah Mae had driven over from Southern Illinois and were preparing the evening meal when we arrived at 5:00. They spent the night with us after another round of gift-exchanging. The next afternoon, a Friday, they left, so Grandpa could have a full day to prepare his sermon for Sunday morning. But yet another "Christmas" lay ahead that night.

"A baseball! A brand-new baseball! Now I've got two!" I remember crying out when I tore the wrapping paper from a small square box Matt gave me. Peggy Sue and I were glad he'd joined us at our home that evening. Her shyness around him had evaporated by then, and she'd said enough nice things about him to me that I knew she was as fond of him as I was.

Mom shared with me years later that Peggy Sue struggled for about a year in dealing with our father's death, so it probably took longer for her to warm up to Matt than it did for me. Basically, he was the first man that I remember being in my life except for Uncle John and my grandfathers.

That night, I also recall seeing the glow of the tree lights that made my mother's face shine with the big smile she displayed as she sat with us on the floor while we opened presents. She seemed quite happy, and I paused because I thought, *How pretty she is.*

Matt told me that when the weather got much warmer, he'd teach me how to throw and catch a ball. Suddenly, I was glum. "But I don't have a glove. I can't catch the ball without a glove. It hurts my hands when Mommy throws to me." He responded that maybe I'd get one someday. Then he acted surprised, looked at an unopened gift at my side, pointed, and said, "Why, I wonder what might be in *that* package."

I'd momentarily forgotten there was another to open. "A glove, a glove! My own glove! Oh, boy, I can play baseball now!" I exclaimed after I ripped the paper from the box and yanked out the tan Rawlings fielder's glove. It dwarfed my left hand when I slid my fingers and palm into it.

"It's a little big for you now," Matt stated. "But it's the smallest size made and your fingers will grow into it."

Mother recalled that I jumped up, blurted, "Let's play now!" and pulled the ball back as though I were going to throw it. Instinctively, she and Matt ducked and threw their arms in front of their heads, fearing I'd hurl it toward them.

She remembered Matt declaring, "No, no, not now!" almost laughing at my childish exuberance. "There're still gifts to open; it's dark outside, and I'm certain your mommy doesn't want us playing ball in the house."

"You said, 'Darn,' and slump-shouldered sat on the floor as our attention shifted to Peggy Sue, who'd been busily opening her presents and not saying anything only because there hadn't been an opportunity to do so."

"Thank you, Mr. Miller," Peggy Sue stated, holding a white brushed rayon robe and matching slippers to her chest.

"You are most welcome, Peggy Sue, but you must do me a favor and call me 'Matt.' I much prefer it. 'Mr. Miller' is too formal. I'm 'Mr. Miller' at school. Here, I'm just 'Matt.'"

Mother and Matt exchanged their first-ever Christmas presents which she described as a narrow, smart-looking Hamilton wristwatch with dark brown leather straps for him—"It's about *time* you got a new one," she said and shook her head as she recalled her pun—and a pair of black, sheepskin-lined gloves and black capeskin leather jacket for her. "I couldn't believe the *expense* of what all he got me!

"Later, as Matt and I sat in the living room—it was gratifying to hear you children having fun upstairs. Big band music was playing softly on the radio. He said, 'I have a feeling 1948 is going to be a special year.'

"I responded that I hoped he was right. It was a wonderful feeling at the moment that the country was not at war and I could see through customers' activities at the bank that people were doing well again. Just as Mr. Brummett had predicted three years earlier, prosperity was returning to much of the country. Our bank grew from the savings of workers who were making more money and from the demand for loans to people who wanted to build houses and purchase newer vehicles. My income had increased, and I felt more secure in providing for our family.

"Of course, I didn't know that a major change was just around the corner."

CHAPTER 7

"Davie, your life, Peggy Sue's, and mine changed in a very special way on New Year's Eve. Mrs. Calhoun had agreed to spend the entire night with you and your sister. Matt and I went to a party for about twenty at a friend's house. The evening was fun, and no one drank much beer or hard stuff. Of course, we all sang 'Auld Lang Syne' at midnight.

"Less than an hour later, Matt proposed to me at his house, and I was thrilled, to say the least. We were very much in love, and still are." She pointed to her ring finger. "He'd purchased the engagement ring and wedding band from Throgmartin Jewelers in Evansville. Paid $159.95. Of course, that was a lot of money for a teacher back then." As she held out her left hand toward me, Mother said the engagement ring was fourteen-carat gold. It had a centered diamond accompanied by two small diamonds on each side. The wedding band had six small diamonds.

"There were lots of immediate questions. Which church for the wedding was a major decision we'd have to make. The same one where I was a member and you children and I attended every Sunday? Or perhaps the Methodist church where Matt worshiped? He wasn't a member and didn't attend regularly, but still it was the church he knew well and he liked the preacher. There were other choices where we could begin attending and then get married: General Baptist, Free Will Baptist, Southern Baptist, and Missionary Baptist. Although we didn't know if they all did it, we knew some would baptize people fully clothed by submersion in ponds or creeks, and we didn't care for that. I'd never forgotten the sight of my friend Miriam Logan being baptized in a lacy white dress on a hot summer Sunday afternoon. As the minister and Miriam stood almost chest deep, he had her hold her nose tightly as he bent her head backward and seemingly under the water for at least a minute. Was Miriam being baptized or drowned? I wondered. The pastor declared Miriam was 'baptized in the blood of Jesus,' but all I could see was a beautiful dress covered with the muddy water of a pond.

"We also didn't like the Bible-pounding style of preachers who'd loudly declare 'the Kingdom of God and the Judgment Day are upon us, and you've got to be saved if you don't want to go to Hell' or that they relied on the Old Testament instead of the more modern concepts of the New Testament, which were easier for us to understand. Other choices in town were the Church of Christ, the Reformed Church, and Calvary. Oh, my, Calvary had an area reputation as 'holy rollers'—the preacher and congregation shouting, arm waving, and becoming ultra-emotional in their services. There were no Jewish people living in Barclay—still aren't—and the few Roman Catholics in town attended Holy Redeemer in Pemberton.

"Answers could wait. What couldn't was informing you, my parents, and Matt's.

"I was relieved you children took the news as well as could be expected. I knew both of you had grown fond of Matt, so I believed the thought of him becoming your new father would be acceptable to you. You two had lots of questions, such as where we were going to live, would you be going to your same school, and would your names still be Johnson. Interestingly, neither of you asked about a wedding. I guess it wasn't something of importance to you. Matt and I answered as best we could. We weren't positive where we'd live, but it was entirely possible it would be here at 309 S. Conley. Regardless, you would still be in your same school and with your same friends. In regard to your last name, that hadn't been discussed but would be."

I learned that answers to everyone's questions came over the following several weeks. The wedding would be a family-only ceremony in the parsonage of First Methodist Church on May 29, just after the end of the school year. Additionally, Mom thought it best that she start a new church home. There were too many memories at Ebenezer, and she and Matt being there might be uncomfortable for the Johnsons and others whom she'd known for a long time. Matt wanted to attend services on a more regular basis; he just needed someone to push him, and Mom would.

In fact, it was an expectation on her part that the family attend church every Sunday. All of us began attending First Methodist regularly in late January. We went to Sunday School classes and then attended worship service together.

Another major question was answered with the decision our current residence would continue to be our home. Matt's $3,500 salary combined with Mother's meant the pressure of her income taking care of all the expenses of a house and raising two children would be eased greatly, and they could also build up savings in the bank. She said Matt hadn't been the best saver in the world, so developing a plan for putting money into an account each payday would be important for their future.

■ ▬ ■

I vividly remember hounding Matt through the winter months about playing pitch and catch, but snow or low temperatures kept us confined to our makeshift diamond in the basement. He purchased a hard rubber ball, about the size of a baseball, and the two of us would roll or bounce it back and forth to one another because the ceiling was too low to permit tossing. "Okay, David, let's learn to hit the circle." Matt took red chalk and drew a circle about eighteen inches in diameter in the middle of the light-gray cement-block wall at one end of the basement, believing that even at seven years of age, not far from being eight, it was time for me to learn accuracy.

Many days when he was visiting, we'd play our basement version of pitch and catch and then turn our attention to the red circle where he taught me how to throw the ball. I would try my best each time to hit the middle of the circle—not just inside the circle, but the middle—on the big red dot he'd made. A white chalk line on the floor, only ten feet from the wall, Matt reasoned, was far enough for a young guy to throw from and be in the proper position to catch the ball as it bounced off the wall, then the concrete floor, sometimes at speeds or angles that were too difficult for me to handle; it was a good learning method nonetheless. Learning the "art" of pitching, he would say, would begin much later, maybe another three years later when my arm was more developed as my body grew. Matt taught me it wasn't how hard I threw the ball, but whether it hit approximately the center of the circle that was important. And he tried his best to explain that I shouldn't aim the ball but just release it naturally, a concept that was a little difficult for a youngster to grasp.

However, he was amazed at how quickly my accuracy developed. It seemed to come naturally to me. Of course, there were times the ball would slip from my hand and strike the wood studs of the uncovered ceiling. Good thing there wasn't a window at the top of the wall. Mom was a good sport, getting accustomed to the sound of the thuds under the flooring that were more frequent in the early weeks of "her boys" playing downstairs but becoming less so as time passed. She told me she was just happy I had a man in my life.

Mom's parents and sister, Matt's parents (Ray and Emma), Peggy Sue, and I were the only attendees when First Methodist pastor Earl McElroy performed the simple marriage ceremony on the last Saturday in May, just days from my eighth birthday. I think I was more interested in the fruit punch and cookies Mrs. McElroy had prepared, but I could tell Peggy Sue thought the wedding was special because Mom had asked her to hold a small bouquet of flowers and stand beside her during the ceremony. I did think it pretty cool—I'm not certain I used that word for a descriptive back then—we got a new white Bendix automatic washer out of the deal, a surprise gift from the Miller and Hutchison grandparents. Mom sure had been complaining about the washer in our basement that wasn't working very well. The new unit even had an attached clothes-ringer assembly so she could run clothes through it before hanging them to dry. The years of ringing out water by hand would now be a thing of the past. But the gift that was the biggest surprise came from my Johnson grandparents. Understandably, they'd not been invited to the wedding, but when Mom and Matt arrived home from the wedding, there on the front porch of our house, with a big red bow on it, stood a tall, dark-colored RCA radio. It would be our source of family entertainment for years to come.

▰ ▰ ▰

That summer, the best friend I ever had—but sadly for too short of a time—moved to a house three doors away on South Conley.

CHAPTER 8

Billy Thomas was the same age as I. I always thought it humorous his formal name was what amounted to three first names—William Dean Thomas—and I teased him about it. We were inseparable, like the closest of brothers. Billy was slightly thinner and a speck shorter, with brown eyes and curly, dark-brown hair that always appeared to be out of control. He hated combing his hair or having his mother comb it for him.

We'd go out to Grandpa Johnson's farm that first summer and watch men work in the hayfields. Threshing was a dying method of harvesting oats and wheat. It was a process only for the hardy, which most farmers were, but more-modern machinery was starting to be used on many farms to bale hay and straw and stack the bales in barn lofts. Neighbors helped neighbors when threshing time rolled around in July and August. The days were almost always hot and humid, sometimes with a lack of wind that made conditions almost unbearable. But there was no choice when crops were ready for harvesting. The process had to be undertaken when Mother Nature dictated, not man.

A few days prior to the day of threshing, oat and wheat stalks were cut in the fields and then placed in shocks to dry. Threshing was a major event. A dozen men or more showed up, all wearing overalls, long-sleeved flannel shirts, and straw hats. It seemed every one of them had a large, dark-red or dark-blue handkerchief with an imprinted border hanging partly out of a rear pocket of their overalls. Handkerchiefs were a staple, used throughout the day for wiping sweat and clearing dust from eyes and noses. Teams of horses pulled wagons to the fields where men threw the shocks onto the flat beds.

Grandpa Johnson let us serve as "water boys." He'd fill thick-glass gallon jugs, use corks as stoppers, and tie a jug on each side of the saddle horn, and then Billy and I'd ride Old Blue to the fields to give workers something to drink. Why the horse was named "Old Blue" when he was a chestnut color, we never knew and never asked. He was simply Old Blue. I sat in the saddle, Billy just behind me, on the bare back. "Now don't you tarry none in the fields," Grandpa would warn us. He knew men were often not productive "if they was a-runnin' low on water." The routine of riding out to the workers, leaving filled jugs, returning to the farmhouse with empty ones, filling them, and doing the process all over again was something we never tired of doing. And we were never afraid of Old Blue, because he just plodded along. The added entertainment was to see rabbits dart or black snakes slither when their hiding places were exposed as the shocks were picked up and pitched onto the wagons. I learned early on Billy wasn't afraid of anything, and he'd push himself off the horse and chase the snakes—he never caught one, of course. He was tougher than nails, certainly unlike me when I was around snakes.

In the barn lot, dust and chaff swirled about as the hired owner of the special equipment, with bandana over his nose and mouth, stood on wagons and used a pitchfork to throw the bundles of oat or wheat into the feeder of his Allis-Chalmers threshing machine. It was quite a contraption of belts, pulleys, and cylinders, all powered by a J. I. Case steam engine. The chugging noise of the equipment, black smoke from the coal that heated the steam engine's water, and chaff and dust produced the "awfulest" scene, we told our parents the first evening we worked. But the ugly-looking thresher did its job, separating grain heads and blowing the stems through a long snout into the barn loft. This process went on all day and then again the next.

Billy and I really looked forward to midday, but so did the men. Their stomachs told them it was time for nourishment, and their bodies said it was time for rest. Everyone gathered at the farmhouse where Grandma Johnson and six other women prepared a noontime meal that rivaled Thanksgiving and Christmas combined. Could those men ever eat! One after another removed his dust-covered and sweat-soaked shirt in the rear yard of the house; lathered his face, neck, and torso with one of the bars of homemade lye soap; cupped his hands; and while leaning over a water trough similar to one used for cattle in the fields, repeatedly scooped up water and dumped it over his head, shoulders, back, and front. Grandma had several large pieces of cotton feed sack material lying on the grass near the trough for the men to dry themselves. To be presentable to the women as they moved single file through the kitchen and piled plates high with meat, vegetables, and bread, the men always put their shirts back on, but as soon as they got outside and sat on the ground in the shade of the large, tall maple trees, shirts came off or at least were unbuttoned down the front and sleeves rolled to the tops of the biceps. An hour's rest and a full stomach from a meal that included pie and/or cake prepared a man for a long afternoon back in the sun.

The last year of threshing on the farm was 1949. The harvesting of oat and wheat became the job of a John Deere combine pulled by an Allis-Chalmers tractor, and straw and hay were baled by machines.

■　▬　▬

By the summer of 1950, in our circle of friends, everyone was referring to me as "Davie." Funny, it seemed everyone I knew had a name that ended in "y" or "ie": Billy, Denny, Jimmy, Suzie, Betty, Becky, Debbie, and so forth, although their mothers never referred to them by their nicknames. Mine certainly refused. I would be "David" to her until much later in life. Sometimes, Mom would become even more formal, especially if she got upset, like one very late afternoon in July when I was playing in Billy's backyard. From three houses away, I heard her call out loudly, not knowing exactly where I was, "David … time for supper!"

Billy said, "That's your mom. You'd better go."

I ignored her, and we kept playing. Minutes later, "David Harold … time for supper!"

"You better go. Your mom wants you home," Billy advised, now concerned.

I didn't even look up from pushing one of my toy cars around in the dirt and declared, "Naw, I don't worry 'til she yells 'David Harold Johnson,' then I know she's mad and I'd better get home."

During the two years since the May 1948 wedding, my new father and I often talked baseball and played together outdoors whenever we could. I'd developed a smooth throwing motion by the time I was ten. I'd grown to five-three and 107 pounds, according to Mother's records. I was a little taller than most of my friends. Matt had become "Dad" to me, and he was the first in our family to start calling me "Davie." I just loved this man in my life, and to this day, I don't think I ever back-talked him.

Billy and I also loved throwing and hitting baseballs when the ball diamond of our nearby elementary school wasn't in use. Buddies—we were all nine or ten years old at the time—would often join us and we'd choose up sides even if each team had only five players, or even four. I had a wooden Louisville Slugger bat, as did another classmate, Bobby Hatcher. We usually had four or five baseballs among us, so there was enough equipment to fill the hours until it was time for lunch or supper or until we got into such an argument about whether someone got tagged trying to run from one base to another that we'd quit, only to show up the next day and start all over as though nothing had happened.

There wasn't any organized baseball league to play in until a boy was either eleven or would turn eleven that year, which was unusual for a community the size of Barclay. Apparently, no adult wanted to take responsibility for organizing and overseeing a league for younger kids.

Because of Dad's keen interest in major league baseball, especially the Cardinals, and the National League, I picked up on comments he made while reading the *Evansville Courier's* box scores and write-ups of games played the previous day. He so loved Stan Musial, Red Schoendienst, Marty Marion, Enos Slaughter, and the other Cards that he'd developed a great dislike for the league's opponents, especially the the seemingly always outstanding Dodgers. Perhaps it was his verbal dislike, in part, that led me to the Dodgers. When I learned that first baseman Gil Hodges and star pitcher Carl Erskine were from Indiana—Hodges from Petersburg and Erskine from Anderson—and the shortstop with the funny name of Pee Wee Reese was from upriver Louisville, Kentucky, I really became interested in the team. What solidified it for me for life was something that happened on my tenth birthday, June 5, 1950. Dad took the family to Evansville to see *The Jackie Robinson Story*, a newly released movie about the first black man to play major league baseball.

I've read so much about this man I can recite it accurately from memory. Jack Roosevelt Robinson was born January 31, 1919, near Cairo, Georgia, in a region with a history of slavery, where Negroes—the descriptive term commonly used throughout America until the early '70s—were hated by white people. Lynchings had not been uncommon in that part of the nation even at the time he was born. His mother,

Mallie, was a sharecropper and raised him, his three brothers, and one sister mostly on her own since her husband was often absent from their home. In 1920, when Jackie was not quite one and a half years old, Mallie and the children moved to Pasadena, California, at the urging of a family member who lived in the Los Angeles area. The family was poor and even in California endured racism. But the mother instilled in her children a belief in the power and protection of God; she taught them to fear God, read the Bible, and lead good lives.

Jackie became an outstanding four-sport athlete—football, basketball, track and field, and baseball—at the University of California, Los Angeles. During World War II, he served in the army but not overseas. Enduring racism even in serving his country and dealing with a temper that got him into trouble from time to time, he was honorably discharged, setting the stage for something that would change major league baseball forever.

In 1945, God-fearing Branch Rickey, general manager of the Brooklyn Dodgers, ordered scouts to look for prospects who were playing in the Negro leagues, to find any who were capable of playing at the highest level of organized baseball. Robinson was highly recommended, and in August, he signed a contract with the Dodger organization, starting in 1946 with the club's minor league team in Montreal. It was a daring move, and Rickey firmly warned Robinson there would be more to playing professional baseball than hitting, running, and fielding. He would have to endure the worst racial taunts, threats, and opposing players' rough play. But if he were to succeed, he would have to turn the other cheek, hold his quick temper, and never fight back except by the way he played the game, to prove he belonged. On April 15, 1947, Jackie Robinson became the first black man to play major league baseball.

He soon learned that life on and off the diamond wouldn't be easy. There were hotels that refused to admit him and restaurants that would not serve him, even though he was with his teammates. Fans and players of opposing teams viciously shouted at him, calling him "nigger" and "black boy" among other insults. There were threats against him and his family. Some of his own teammates at first didn't want to be on the same team with him. But, as Mr. Rickey had demanded, he proved himself with his play on the field and showed he belonged. Robinson was an exciting, daring base runner, hopping up and down, back and forth, and feigning he was going to try to steal the next base. He was a hugely frustrating distraction for opposing pitchers. His forte would be something most uncommon in baseball: stealing home plate. In his first season, he led the National League in stolen bases and received the coveted designation of rookie of the year.

Two seasons later, Robinson led the league in hitting (a .342 average) and stolen bases and was given its highest honor: most valuable player.

The movie made a great impression on me as a child, especially the part where the mother gave her little boy his first baseball glove. I've never forgotten the surprised and happy look on young Jackie's face. It reminds me of how I felt when I got mine one Christmas. Even though I was ten when I saw the movie, I left the theater feeling pity for the hardships Jackie Robinson had dealt with and admiring him for being a fiery player on the field. He became not only a hero to me but also my idol, an interesting choice because no blacks lived in Barclay and I'd never been around any except to see them on sidewalks in Evansville when my family went shopping there. I'd heard the word *Nigger* used around Barclay but didn't know it to be a derogatory term, until I saw the movie.

"Four Giants for three Dodgers." Billy knew how to get under my skin by demanding an extra baseball trading card from me if Jackie Robinson was one of the ones I wanted. I hated him for it. Sometimes, I wanted to slug him. We started trading "bubblegum cards" in 1950, purchasing small packets that contained cards and thin, flat pieces of bubble gum at grocery stores. I had to earn my money by doing chores around the house. I was jealous that because Billy was an only child, his parents gave him about anything he wanted, especially money. He didn't have to help them do anything.

Initially, Bowman and Leaf were the most popular brands among my friends, but Topps soon gained the upper hand. Black-and-white action pictures of players on cards with imprinted autographs could also be purchased at the county fair by inserting a penny in a machine and cranking a handle. Photos of ballplayers and movie stars were inside the lids of Dixie Cup ice cream cups. Dad claimed my most prized possession was Bowman's Stan Musial rookie card of 1948, but I was far more interested in the Dodgers. I hated the New York Giants mostly because Billy liked them and bragged about them. We'd make even trades of our teams' players—Carl Erskine, Roy Campanella, and Duke Snider for Bobby

Thomson, Larry Jansen, and Sid Gordon, as an example. And when Billy issued his four-for-three demand when Robinson was involved, begrudgingly, I always gave in. When we exchanged cards, he'd just sit there with that stinking, lousy smile on his face. Dad would call those "a-possum-eating-shit" smiles. I never used that phrase around Mom.

Solidified as a Dodger supporter after seeing *The Jackie Robinson Story* in 1950, I could hardly wait each morning to read the *Courier* to find out how my team had fared the previous afternoon. On July 1, the Dodgers were in third place, a half game behind St. Louis and the Philadelphia Phillies, who were tied.

On September 1, Brooklyn had climbed to second place but was now six games behind Philly. The previous night, Indiana native Hodges hit four home runs off the Boston Braves' Warren Spahn, Norm Roy, Bob Hall, and Johnny Antonelli. Four homers in one game tied the major league record held by five others, including the legendary Lou Gehrig of the 1932 New York Yankees. Hodges also drove in nine of the Dodgers' nineteen runs. Fellow Hoosier Carl Erskine pitched his first complete game of the season, giving up eight hits and three runs.

▬ ▬ ▬

Exactly one month later, my parents were worrying about another war. The previous day, General Douglas MacArthur—supreme commander for the United Nations—called on North Korea to surrender and release all prisoners of war or "complete destruction of your armed forces and war-making potential is inevitable." But world affairs weren't on my radar screen—not by a long shot—my focus being on something I could understand: the pennant race. *My* Dodgers had slashed the staggering Phillies' seven-and-one-half-game lead on September 21 to one game with one to play, against one another on this day, October 1, and I went to school in complete confidence because I "just knew" Brooklyn would beat Philadelphia and go on to the World Series against the Dodgers' American League nemesis: the Yankees.

When I learned from a friend that the Phillies had won, four to one, in ten innings to capture the pennant, I was heartbroken. "At least look at it this way," Dad tried his best to encourage me, "the Giants finished third and the Cardinals fifth." His words helped, but then he couldn't refrain from teasing me that *his* Stan "the Man" Musial won the batting title and

Jackie Robinson finished second. When he saw I wasn't taking the issue well, he backed off.

"Mom and Dad, the Thomases have a new television." For months after delivering that news to my parents, I was in complete envy that Billy had a "1951 Model" Philco television with black-and-white picture tube that his parents had bought in September of '50. A small percentage of Barclay residents owned a television, a new source of entertainment and information. Its popularity would grow, but the price—Billy bragged to me his folks paid $249.95—was more than most people could afford or were willing to pay for an invention that might not have much of a future. The Thomases' television had a sixteen-inch diagonal picture tube inside a mahogany veneer cabinet that they set on a small but sturdy table at one end of their living room. Dials below the picture tube changed channels and raised and lowered the volume. The unit even had a built-in antenna system although being so many miles from the stations in Evansville and Louisville, the system was practically useless. As a result, the family purchased a large antenna and attached it atop a thirty-foot metal pole that was cemented in the ground next to their house.

Mr. Thomas and Billy were kind enough to invite Dad and me to watch some of the World Series that October.

▬ ▬ ▬

The summers of my eleventh and twelfth birthdays were nearly identical. I was now David Harold Miller, having been adopted by Dad early in 1951. It took some effort to get accustomed to the Miller name, especially for Peggy Sue's and my friends, who had known us as Johnson all of their lives.

In the summer of '51, Billy and I began playing baseball in a league for eleven- and twelve-year-old boys from Barclay and the rest of Hopewell County. Our team finished second to Pemberton.

Billy, Bobby, other buddies, and I loved the summers, because it gave us freedom in a largely rural area to explore the wilderness areas just outside of town. What wasn't farmland or spoil banks, also known as "stripper hills" left over from coal mining, were rolling fields of tall grasses, dotted with thistle and cocklebur bushes; wild yellow and bluish-purple flowers; small, lonely maple and sassafras trees that sprang up here and there from seeds birds had dropped; and meandering creeks that often abutted forests filled with tall oak and hickory trees, as well as maple, tulip, gum, sycamore, elm, and dogwood.

The forests, or "woods" as people around town referred to them, were carved with ravines that lay sixty to one hundred feet on a diagonal from ridgelines. We'd walk the ravines, play "cowboys and Indians" or "army," trying to hit one another with hickory nuts while dashing among the trees. In winter snow, we'd take sleds and create long, twisting trails through the trees from the ridges to the bottom. It was a dangerous activity since the sleds picked up quite a bit of speed as they traveled downhill.

"Billy, you okay?" Bobby screamed when he saw Billy fail to make a sharp turn and slam almost headfirst into a hickory. To me, at the time, it seemed he must have been going forty miles an hour; it was probably nothing like that, but it seemed really fast. We all ran through the snow to him. Billy just lay there, the glancing blow to the head having knocked him unconscious for a moment. "My right shoulder's killing me," he moaned as he began regaining consciousness. We knew he was hurt if he'd admit to an injury. Billy's arm was in a sling for two weeks, fortunately for nothing worse than a severely bruised muscle.

The stripper hills comprised many square miles around Barclay. Crescent Creek and two other coal companies had mined areas near the town in the 1920s and expanded their operations farther away in the decades since. When coal was mined, huge electric-powered shovels and draglines created deep open cuts in the earth as they removed the overburden and dumped it to one side, exposing seams of coal that would be dug out by steam-powered Marion coal loaders and processed back at the tipple. The earthen swath, typically ninety to one hundred feet wide, might be a mile or more long, depending on the length of the coal company's property or the veins of coal underneath. When the shovel reached the end of the area to be mined, after the coal was removed, it repeated the process by going in the opposite direction and dumping the dirt and rock into the open pit it had created. Thus, when an area of hundreds of acres, referred to as a "coalfield," had been completely mined, at least one open pit was left, as were the tall mounds of dirt, shale, sandstone, limestone and other types of rock beside it. Rain eventually filled the pits with water, creating fishing and other recreational opportunities.

Crescent Creek's ownership stocked pits with fish and covered their spoil banks with trees, all to provide recreation for residents and a natural habitat for animals, especially deer and wild turkey. Over the years, the company planted more than two and a half million white pine, scotch pine, tulip—the official state tree of Indiana—black walnut, locust, and varieties of oak trees. Parts of the spoils were too dense for us to walk in, and we had to be extremely careful maneuvering near the "highwalls," the walls of the pits that could range from thirty to eighty feet from the top to the water. One slip of the foot on loose dirt and rock and we'd plunge far below. Even if a person knew how to swim, the greatest danger in falling wouldn't necessarily be hitting the water but huge hidden boulders that lay just below the surface near the foot of some walls.

— — —

"Why do we have to stay for 'church' when the preacher is soooo boring?" Peggy Sue would inquire.

To which I'd add with my strongest frown and turned-up nose, "Yeah, it's boooorrrring," drawing out the word's pronunciation just to give weight to Peggy Sue's exclamation.

My sister and I could agree on one thing for certain: we were not in love with Sunday-morning worship services.

As would be natural for me throughout the remainder of my life, Sunday mornings were occupied by worship and Sunday School classes. I loved the teachers of the latter, especially Mrs. Walters, who taught the eleven- and twelve-year-olds. A kind, gentle, salt-and-pepper-haired woman of slight build, probably in her sixties, she showed a love for each child, encouraging us in her soft-spoken way to "be kind and respectful of everyone" and to follow the teachings of Jesus in that regard throughout our lives.

On the other hand, my sister and I thought of the fiftyish Reverend McElroy as "ancient" because of the dry delivery of his sermons, which he always read, rarely looking up at the congregation. He nearly bored Peggy Sue and me to tears. The songs the choir director selected didn't help matters. They seemed to us to take forever to be sung, such as "The Old Rugged Cross"—I swore they must have sung it "twenty times a year"—"Amazing Grace," and "The Church's One Foundation" (all *five* verses). The pianist had the unwelcomed ability to take a song like "I Love to Tell the Story" and turn the 4/4 meter into something like a funeral dirge, which made the piece agonizingly slow. When the congregation stood to sing one of the songs that seemed to us to drag on for an hour, Peggy Sue and I would look at one another and roll our eyes to show our total displeasure with the moment. As she seemed to need to do every Sunday, Mom would remind us that "the Sabbath" was an important day, and although we might not enjoy the worship services, we would look back one day and realize how important it was that we attended when we were young. In her eyes, it was part of foundation-building for our lives.

∎ ▦ ▬

The good news in late summer was Mom and Dad decided to purchase a television, an RCA Victor with a twenty-one-inch diagonal black-and-white screen. Family entertainment had always been the radio, which brought comedy shows, such as *Amos and Andy* and *Burns and Allen*; sports; news; music; cowboys like Hopalong Cassidy; Dad's favorite the *Grand Ole Opry* because of his love for country music; and my sister's and my favorites *The Green Hornet, Inner Sanctum,* and *The Shadow.* The hair-raising openings of the latter two set the stage for suspense that would have our eyes darting about the room, especially at the doorway, to see if something evil was about to pounce on us. Stormy, gray Sunday afternoons with occasional flashes of lightening that danced on the bedroom walls served to intensify the setting. We would lie on the floor of her room and hear the dissonant cord of an organ followed by the eerie sound of a creaking door slowly being opened and then the haunting voice of "Raymond, your host ..." who would tell us, "We have a very special guest of horror with us." Thus, *Inner Sanctum* put us on edge from the beginning.

But the same could be said for the detective mystery series *The Shadow,* each episode typically opening with slow, dark orchestral music followed by "Who knows what evil lurks in the hearts of men? The Shadow knows!" and then a long, sinister laugh. It was enough to keep both brother and sister in rapt attention throughout the program and make sleep more difficult that night.

Sunday evening meals were simple—typically hot, stewed tomatoes spooned over bread, fried cornmeal mush covered with syrup, or crackers and milk (saltine crackers crumbled by hand and dropped into a glass of warm milk, stirred, and then dipped out by spoon and eaten). Mom permitted us to eat in our rooms, and more than once, glasses of the crackers-and-milk concoction were knocked over at the words and creepy laughter that followed "The Shadow knows!"

While radio was "television of the mind," the real thing was something quite special. For the first time, our family saw what Lucille Ball, Red Skelton, Jack Benny, and others looked like in person. We were also entertained by the goofiness and humor of Groucho Marx's *You Bet Your Life* and enthralled by the solving of police cases in the *Gang Busters* series. The existence of a television in our own home was so exciting that in the beginning, we'd even watch the test pattern that preceded the start of programming each day.

▬ ▦ ▬

To me, the 1951 National League baseball season became a laugher. No doubt the Dodgers were going to the World Series. After winning the first game of a doubleheader on August 11, Brooklyn led the Giants by thirteen and a half games. The season was all over but for the shouting. Or so I thought.

Following one of the most famous collapses in history, the Dodgers and Giants were tied after the second game of a three-game playoff to determine the league champion. The season finale was October 3 at the Giants' home, the Polo Grounds. At school that day, my mind was on the outcome of the game, not my studies. When the bell sounded to end classes, I rushed outside and found Billy's mother listening on her car radio in the gravel parking lot. "Davie, it's the bottom of the ninth, and the Giants just scored a run. It's now four to two, Dodgers!" she exclaimed. "The Giants have two on and only one out. Bobby Thomson's at bat."

The Dodgers changed pitchers. Would it be Carl Erskine or Ralph Branca? The manager chose Branca to get the final two outs. The first pitch was a strike, and I smiled. But in only a moment, history wiped the expression from my face.

Thomson drove the next pitch into the left-field stands, and I was haunted the remainder of my life by Giants' announcer Russ Hodges screaming over and over, "The Giants win the pennant! The Giants win the pennant!"

"That's impossible! That's impossible! It can't have happened! It can't!" I cried, agonizingly twisting my body and turning my feet in the gravel beside the car. But it had. Tears welled in my eyes and then rolled down my cheeks.

I tried to hide them but couldn't, and that lousy Billy, who'd arrived at the car just before the pitch, took no mercy, quickly moving close to my face and sarcastically taunting, "The Giants win! The Dodgers lose! The Giants win; the Dodgers lose! Ha, ha, ha, ha, ha!" I was so distraught, so physically drained I couldn't talk back or muster the energy to give Billy an agitated shove. I took the abuse and, slump-shouldered, slowly began to walk home, refusing Mrs. Thomas's offer of a ride. The last thing I wanted was to be trapped in the backseat of a car with Billy.

I refused to eat dinner and stayed in my room, not studying, just lying on my bed and staring at the ceiling. I was such a diehard Dodger fan and had built my hopes so high that the team's fall from grace was more than I could handle emotionally. Finally, about a half hour before I was to be in bed for the night, I ambled downstairs and without any energy in my voice whatsoever asked my mother if I could have something to eat. Mom's intuition when supper ended more than an hour earlier had led her to set food aside. A plate for me was sitting in the refrigerator.

I dreaded the following day at school because I knew the taunts by my baseball-following buddies—and others who weren't close friends— would be unending. But it was Thursday and if I could endure two days, the weekend would save me.

As I look back on it, the effects of the Dodgers' historic fold actually turned out to be a good lesson. I learned the hard way that if one dishes it out, one has to learn to take it as well. My season-long teasing when the Dodgers were running away with the pennant had come back to ensnarl me. I would be less willing to taunt anyone about anything in the future.

CHAPTER 9

The next year, I had my first taste of the business world, a newspaper route in Barclay. I began delivering the *Grit*, a weekly newspaper that was published in Pennsylvania primarily for small, rural towns throughout America. It carried the subtitle "America's Greatest Family Newspaper." I picked up the route from a church acquaintance, sixteen-year-old Randall Troeger, who'd tired of the weekly grind of Saturday-morning delivery and collection. Each edition cost customers ten cents, with two pennies as my commission, the remainder sent to the *Grit*'s headquarters in Williamsport, Pennsylvania. There were sixty-two customers and if delivering the paper were the only responsibility, doing so would have taken less than an hour, but collecting the money was time-consuming. If a customer wasn't home when the *Grit* was delivered, I had to return later in the day or later in the week.

The route, which I kept until 1955, taught me many lessons—responsibility, the proper handling of funds, the importance of thanking customers for their business, and the nature of people, especially those who purposely avoided me on Saturday so they wouldn't have to pay. I soon learned that if customers didn't alert me they'd be away from home on a given Saturday and unable to pay that day, I had better not deliver their paper the following Saturday or until they paid their bill. Regardless of who was home or not, I knew I had to write a check for $4.96 to the newspaper each Sunday. Mother established a checking account for me, but in her name at her bank and worked closely with me to ensure that I kept accurate customer records and my own financial accounting.

As with every summer, Mom and Dad required my sister and me to help with the vegetable garden behind our house. Fresh vegetables alleviated the need to buy them at the grocery. The plot was approximately sixty feet by forty feet, and in late March or the earliest days of April, Dad hired a local man to turn the earth with his plow horse. Hiram Pugh did odd jobs for a living. He hitched *Bess* to a steel single-blade wooden-handled plow, and with a slap of the reins, a verbal "Giddy up," or a clucking sound Hiram made out of the side of his mouth, *Bess* would plod forward until he said, "Whoa!" or pulled a rein right or left to turn his partner and repeat the process over and over, loosening the soil so it would be ready for a harrow to cultivate the ground by breaking up the clods and producing a smoother surface.

I was fascinated by Hiram, an older, rough-handed, rugged-faced, gray-haired, never-married man who was slightly stooped and weathered by a hard life in the sun. He smoked cigarettes that he held between his yellowed, uneven teeth. He'd stop *Bess* and then withdraw a small sheet of thin cigarette paper from a pocket of the flannel shirt under his bib overalls, lay it over the first two fingers of his left hand, and use the thumb to create a crease into which he'd pour a small amount from a red can of Velvet pipe and cigarette tobacco he held in his right hand. Then he'd slowly lick an inside edge of the paper and with both hands, roll the paper so that its edges stuck together with the adhesive of the saliva. Withdrawing a small box of wood matches from the chest pocket of the overalls, he'd remove one and strike the head across one of the metal buttons that held the overalls' straps together just below the front of the shoulder. After lighting the cigarette, he'd command, "Giddy up," and *Bess* would start moving down the garden again. I watched in awe as Hiram handled plow, reins, and cigarette without skipping a beat.

Mom and Dad were disciples of *The Old Farmer's Almanac,* an agricultural bible of sorts used by farmers and others to know when to plant seeds. The *Almanac* was a proponent of planting "by the light of the moon," meaning planting in daylight when the moon at night was new to full. Thus, if the publication said April 14 to 24 was the best time to plant green beans, then that's when our family placed bean seeds in the ground and covered them. The same would be true for every vegetable we'd produce—corn, potatoes, peas, cucumbers, cabbage, radishes, lettuce, onions, carrots, peppers, and tomatoes. What my sister and I disliked most was the weekly, or more often if necessary, weeding of the rows, especially on hot, humid days. In fact, we just knew nature had a grudge against us, for the days we were to weed were the days that seemed to be the hottest.

Despite all the moaning, complaining, and hard work, nothing was better than fresh buttered and salted corn on the cob with sliced tomatoes, cooked green beans, mashed potatoes with butter or milk gravy, and fried chicken. And there was dessert, always dessert, an evening staple for our Miller household. Mom came home from work each day and prepared food in abundance. It was something women did, an expectation. Additionally, every summer, she canned several quarts of beans, a mixture of peas and carrots, and cucumbers, which were made into pickles. All those jars would be stocked on basement shelves to be used during the winter.

In baseball, I played well in my summer league, pitching more than the previous year but also playing shortstop. Our team finished third behind champion Clyde. Brooklyn won the National League pennant. I taunted no one. But the dreaded Yankees won the World Series four games to three. Thus, three out of the six years I'd been following the Dodgers, they'd lost in the World Series to the Yankees. Would they ever win?

My academic studies went well that fall. Especially enjoyable was English, my introduction to writing creatively. I had a penchant for expressing myself orally and in the written word, and "Miss" McCarthy—a title given all female teachers whether married or not—was a bear in demanding perfect spelling. She would downgrade a completed assignment by one letter for each misspelled word. It didn't take long for students who misspelled four to learn that an "F" was no laughing matter. I recognized years later that Miss McCarthy, though demanding and sometimes harsh in her criticisms, had a profound influence on my life. I loved the challenge and learned the appreciation for good writing. What I couldn't understand, with the emphasis on perfect English, was why the principal of the elementary school continually talked about the importance of the basic educational skills of "readin', ritin', and 'rithmatic." He even wrote them that way in printed materials given to parents and students. *Some way to set an example!*

CHAPTER 10

When school began in late summer 1953, I was thirteen and in the eighth grade. Peggy Sue was now a junior and almost sixteen.

She'd been a challenge for our mother for the past year. I later learned the sometimes testy relationship was nothing unusual for a mother and teenage daughter who was going through physical and emotional changes as she grew older. Peggy Sue, who was now about five inches shorter than I and very trim, began having menstrual periods when she was twelve, but I thought nothing of her mood swings since I had no idea periods existed. It wasn't something she shared. All I knew was she was "weird" sometimes. I was caught completely off guard, however, one morning in July when I opened the bathroom door.

That spring, Dad had had a local carpenter/plumber install a bathroom upstairs between our bedrooms, carving out space by reconfiguring the size of the bedrooms and closets and installing a tub, sink, and toilet. The only shower in the house remained in the basement. Since water was brought in by tank truck whenever the level in the cistern fell too low, Mom and Dad always instructed us to conserve. "If you get water out of the tap or from our glass water bottle in the refrigerator, you have to drink all of it; there mustn't be any waste. If you pee in the toilet, don't flush it until you smell an odor. We can't afford to flush every time."

My sister and I always maintained our individual privacy, whether in our bedrooms or the bathroom, but one early school morning, without thinking, I pushed open the slightly ajar bathroom door and was startled, as was Peggy Sue. There she stood, in front of the mirror behind the sink, nude, hands above her head as she brushed her long, wavy blond hair. Instinctively, she turned toward me and just as instinctively twisted away, her face looking back and frozen in fear, her mouth open, and her catlike eyes with a startled look of someone who had just gotten caught doing something she shouldn't have been doing. "Daaaavieeeee!" came with the full force of her lungs. "Get out of here! Get out of here!" With that, I turned and bolted, not even taking time to close the door. "Mother! Mother!" came the high-pitched voice from the head sticking out of the door as Peggy Sue was closing it. "Mother, Davie was peeking at me. And you'd better do something about it!" she demanded as she slammed the door shut.

"David Harold, what were you doing? You know better than that! Shame on you!" my mother yelled from below the stairs.

"It was an accident, Mom!" I yelled back in self-defense. "I didn't mean anything. I just forgot to knock. I didn't know she was in there." It was the truth. My explanation seemed to work, but I stood there, thinking about what I'd witnessed. The bumps on my sister's chest that I last saw about three years ago had now become breasts that were forming with small nipples. And hair. She had lots of blond hair in a triangular area below her navel. I'd only seen pubic hair in photographs that we boys secretly passed among ourselves and in cartoon pictures in "eight-pagers," little erotic comic books that could easily be stuffed inside a back pocket of blue jeans or hidden under a mattress. I'd discovered my own sexuality a summer ago, and there was a hint of dark fuzz in my pubic area, but seeing a girl nude, in the flesh, was life-altering even if it was my own sister. I would see fully clothed girls differently from now on—forever.

■ ▨ ▨

I'd describe my baseball performance that summer as "good" but nothing special and our team as "fair." *My* major league team cruised to the National League pennant, winning by thirteen games over the second-place Milwaukee Braves, who had moved from Boston following the previous season. Jackie Robinson and Carl Erskine had stellar years, and despite Erskine setting a World Series record of fourteen strikeouts in game 3, four off the rising star Mickey Mantle, the outcome was the same old, same old. "The Bronx Bombers" won in six games. For Dodger fans everywhere, the rallying cry of "Wait 'til next year" was all they had. In my mind, "next year" might as well be "next lifetime."

Certainly, a change in my baseball life the following spring would end up being a pivotal one in life itself.

CHAPTER 11

"Davie, it's time to learn the knuckleball."

In early spring 1954, Dad decided my fingers had grown to the point I could handle a baseball better than ever, so he would begin teaching me two pitches to supplement my fastball—a curve and a knuckleball. "I wouldn't let you try curves when you were younger because throwing them required an arm movement that could damage undeveloped muscles and ligaments." He explained that to the contrary, the knuckleball wasn't damaging, since to be effective, it shouldn't be thrown as hard as a fastball or curve. The initial key to being able to throw the "knuckler" was to have fingers long enough to grip and control it. It was a very difficult pitch to learn; therefore, few adults had ever tried to perfect it when they were younger and as a result had no experience to teach boys. Lucky for me, Dad was an exception.

He told me that when he moved back to Barclay in 1945 and joined the town's semi-pro team that summer, he'd been introduced to the knuckleball by Eddie Handley, a crafty old pitcher who threw "junk," a mixture of mostly slow pitches that could curve, drop, hop in the air, and seemingly do about any other contortion possible as they baffled batter after batter. "Why in the hell can't you hit that son of a bitch who's thirty years older than you assholes?" opposing managers would yell at their batters time after time when they returned to the bench after striking out, hitting weak pop flies or slow rollers. Handley was an agent for Clark Insurance Agency in Barclay—"*We Insure Your Life from Beginning to End.*" In 1945, at the unheard of ballplaying age of fifty-two, he was in his nineteenth year of Sunday-afternoon semi-pro ball. Before moving to

Barclay, he'd had an eight-year career in the minors and majors—mostly the minor leagues—with the Boston Braves organization.

Dad said Handley told him, "You need to learn a knuckler. You've got a good fastball but a pretty damned weak curve. The knuckler will make you a hell of a lot tougher to hit." Over several summers, Dad worked on perfecting the pitch as best he could, so he knew what it took to teach me.

We began practicing after the school day starting the first week of May. With utter enjoyment, I listened to everything Dad said about the art of throwing all three pitches—fastball, curveball, and knuckler. There'd be more to teach the following year, such as where to attempt to pitch the ball (low outside edge of the plate, high inside, and so forth) and how to change speeds on the fastball, turning it into more than one pitch (fast, medium, and slow). Dad didn't want to fill my head with too many facts at a time, so we worked only on one pitch each day. But he was extra careful not to let me attempt to throw too many pitches, especially curves. While a curveball could make a one-summer star out of a youngster who was throwing it against thirteen- or fourteen-year-olds, damage to an elbow and shoulder could take years to heal, if it ever did.

There wasn't one single grip for a knuckleball, but the theory was the same. When it was introduced into professional baseball in the early 1900s, pitchers used their knuckles when gripping and throwing it. As time went on, others found it easier and more effective to use the fingertips. Whether using the tips or knuckles of two fingers or three and whether digging the tips or nails into the seam or into the smooth cowhide covering, the pitcher would go into the same windup as for any other pitch and with the same motion release the ball toward the plate; except with the knuckleball, it was almost as if the pitcher pushed the ball out of his hand.

The difference between a knuckler and other pitches is that it was "dead," not motionless but without spin. What it would do on its flight path was unpredictable—to the batter, the catcher, and even the pitcher himself. The knuckler was a phenomenon. It could float toward the plate with no lateral or up-down motion whatsoever or move slightly right, left, up, or down, and sometimes dive at home plate, as though the bottom had fallen out. On a day when a pitcher "had it"—and not every day was the same—hitters were nearly helpless. On those days, pitching was pure joy.

"I just can't get the hang of it," I protested to Dad, trying to find an effective grip and release. I used two fingertips and then three, and I tried placing them in the seam and then the hide. By mid-June, I had found that for my finger length, three fingertips pressing against the so-called fat part of the ball—the large smooth area—proved the easiest way for me to have control, but the ball wasn't very "dead." What a struggle. Often the ball'd hit the dirt about halfway between the mound and home plate or sail high above Dad, who was acting as my catcher, or far left or right of the plate. It was as frustrating an experience as I'd ever faced, but I wasn't about to give up.

I'd try the knuckler in games that summer, initially without much success. "Dang," my teammate and catcher Billy would say, "you're gonna break my nuts if you keep throwin' that thing into the dirt. I've heard children come from them, so don't ruin 'em."

By the end of the season, I was commanding my three types of pitches pretty well, and we won seven of the ten games we played. I was in the outfield the other three games. Unfortunately, I couldn't hit worth a darn, so if I had any future in baseball, I knew it had to be as a pitcher. Bobby Hatcher was our best hitter, and Billy was about second or third best. In the league for thirteen and fourteen-year-olds, our team ended the season with the best record, but there weren't any playoffs, so we were named the champions. Each of us on the team got a small trophy, a gold-leafed player completing his batting swing, mounted to a small wood base that had a small engraved gold plate that read: *Champions—1954.* It was my first trophy, and I placed it on a lamp table next to my bed, so I could see it every night before turning off the light.

■ ▩ ◼

Of all my friends, Billy's language was the worst. He constantly mispronounced and used incorrect grammar. Southern Indiana residents were known for lazy or sloppy speech, perhaps because so many Southerners had settled above the Northern Kentucky border and influenced them. "Tires" were "tars"; "windows" were "windas"; "arthritis" was "artheritis"; a "realtor" was a "realator"; and "Illinois" was "Illi-noise." Interestingly, Billy's parents didn't speak that way, but he'd use "is" when the plural "are" was called for and "seen" for "saw" and so forth. "I seen him runnin' that a way," he'd say, or, "We's goin' git that in town." Asked what he thought about an apple my mother gave him one day, he replied,

"Them's good." Billy just didn't care. He was hard-nosed, hardheaded, and determined to do certain things his way, no matter what anyone said. It's a wonder he didn't fail English in school.

He and I loved fishing with our cane poles and red-and-white plastic bobbers that summer, although cleaning a stringer full afterward was no fun at all. "It's all part of the process," Dad would lecture. "It's one thing to catch fish, but unless you release them back into the pond, you have to clean them when you get home. Fishing isn't just fishing and eating; it's fishing, *cleaning*, and eating."

Billy was always the leader of our small gang of friends, leading the way to mischievousness, rarely anything worse. We delighted in tipping over outhouses at Halloween, always hoping someone would be inside, but that never happened. We got fresh cow manure and scooped it into brown paper bags, set them afire on concrete porches and knocked on the front door, then watched from behind bushes, overjoyed when the unsuspecting but alarmed resident stomped out the flames. Our success was measured by the quantity and quality of cuss words that spewed forth. When old man Rufus Preo stormed back into his house and returned to the porch to fire his twelve-gauge shotgun into the air, we decided we'd gone far enough.

Our dads taught us how to fire shotguns and a rifle that fall, choosing a safe area in the spoils for target practice. "First and foremost," Mr. Thomas warned, "you *cannot*," he emphasized the word by repeating it, "cannot be too careful with these guns. One mistake and you could shoot someone, and you sure as hell don't want to live with that on your conscience the rest of your lives."

So he and Dad showed us how to hold the guns, to keep the safety locks on while loading, and how to load them. "Always treat any gun as though it were loaded. Assume that it is," Dad warned. "Never, never, never point a gun toward anyone when you're holding it, and never, never, never assume it doesn't have a bullet or shell in it." He paused. "There've been numerous tragedies when people assumed they were holding an unloaded gun while showing it off to someone, pulled the trigger, and …" He didn't have to complete the sentence; we got the point.

Our fathers took us hunting a few times, sometimes as a foursome and sometimes as one dad and two neophytes. They never let us hunt by ourselves. Maybe next year, they said. But "next year" would never come.

CHAPTER 12

Peggy Sue graduated from high school in May 1955 and made the decision to enroll at Evansville College that fall to become a teacher. She said Dad's love of teaching had rubbed off on her, and she wanted to remain near home. The truth be known, she had a boyfriend, a classmate who would also enroll at the university. A year earlier, Larry Jones had given his gold BHS-initialed high school ring to her as a sign of their "undying love" for one another, and she'd wrapped several layers of white adhesive tape around the band so it would stay on the ring finger of her right hand. Occasionally, she'd place the ring on a thin gold necklace and wear it around her neck. "Going steady" with someone and displaying a visible sign of it was a big deal to Peggy Sue and others her age. I could have cared less.

By that summer between our freshman and sophomore years, both Billy and I had grown, but in different ways. He was about three inches shorter than I – about five-seven – but probably a good fifteen pounds heavier and stouter. I was as skinny as a rail despite eating everything placed in front of me at the dining room table and snacks in between meals. Billy and I loved life and were rarely apart.

▬ ▬ ▬

The nearest pits to Barclay were about a mile out of town, and a group of us friends had been riding bikes there since the previous year. My parents always warned me about the pits' dangers and urged extreme caution when going there. But they weren't ones to watch my every movement and felt I had to learn responsibility as I grew. Billy's folks had done the same, and generally, we were careful. It was rare we'd dive off any pit wall higher than thirty feet above the water. We always selected diving areas where the footing was good and the walls were relatively straight down, not jagged with large boulders projecting outward either above or below the surface. The areas also needed to have access for footpaths from the water back to the top. Occasionally, one of our group would daringly walk to a point to dive thirty to forty feet up from the surface, but that was the absolute limit and even that was scary to fourteen- and fifteen-year-olds. One particular pit was our favorite; we'd begun diving and swimming in it the previous summer. We became quite familiar with the underwater sides and knew where to dive to avoid hidden rocks below. The water's depth was believed to be about seventy feet. By the time we arrived in late spring '55, we were unaware of what had transpired since our last swim in September.

Elmer's Wrecker Service was a popular business in Barclay, Elmer Yoder being known as a good ole boy around town. I knew from hearing men talk that he built his reputation on service, that he'd help any motorist with a recalcitrant vehicle in any type of weather. His one and a half acres in a Westside residential area had become an eyesore, because it was filling with wrecked cars and trucks—grotesquely-twisted vehicle bodies, many void of parts Elmer had salvaged for resale or reuse.

Because he was running out of space, in December 1954, Elmer secretly pulled several vehicles to the pits and without permission from the coal mine that owned the area, pushed them over the walls and then watched as they sank in the water below. He chose those that had been on his property the longest and whose bodies were in various stages of rust. Included was a trailer that had belonged to Ed Morris's long-distance tractor-trailer operation in the nearby town of Calvin. The hinges of the two eight-and-half-by-twelve-foot steel doors on the rear of the trailer were slightly rusted, so the doors were stuck partially open when Elmer pushed the *Ed Morris Long Haul Service* trailer over the edge and heard a thunderous splash below.

▬ ▬ ▬

Just after noon on Saturday, June 4, the day before my fifteenth birthday, Billy, Bobby, Randy Fenton, Danny Bean, and I rode our bicycles to our favorite pit for the first swim of the summer. We'd had baseball practice that morning, preparing for the summer league's games that would start the next weekend. All but Danny were going to be sophomores in high school that fall. He was a year older. Several minutes later, Dickie Abel showed up on his bike. Dickie hated his name, Richard Nicholas Abel. Anyone named Richard or Peter was certain to be teased unmercifully by adolescent peers who'd say, "Let's see your dick, Dickie!" or "How's your peter, Peter?" then giggle as though no one else had ever thought of the embarrassing and always irritating reference. In Dickie's case, the teasing could get worse. "Dick Nick" became a despised nickname for awhile until he beat the shit out of a taunting Terry Krider, two inches taller and a year older. That got attention, word spread, and no one, absolutely no one, teased Dickie anymore.

As a group, we six friends couldn't have been happier. School was out for the academic year, and we'd have no cares in the world until classes began again the day after Labor Day. It was a bright, sun-swept day, and the mercury in the large rusting tin Double Cola thermometer on the front of Pearson's Grocery registered 75 as we rode by. The temperature of the water in the pit, however, was something else. Although cold water never really bothered us on a warm day, it was considerably colder than the outside air and even colder the deeper we got from the surface. All but Bobby had brought swimming suits. Typical for our absentminded friend, he'd forgotten his and said he'd make his way along the narrow, winding, rocky path to the water's edge where he'd strip and swim naked. "I'm not going to bust my balls jumpin' off this wall without any clothes on!" he exclaimed.

As usual, the ever-daring Billy was first to dive. All of us almost always jumped feetfirst, although Dickie and Danny had tried going headfirst from thirty feet last fall without a lot of success, experiencing painful belly whoppers or creating somewhat grotesque forms before slamming into the water on their backs. All of us were determined to learn to dive headfirst this summer and were making plans to haul a long board we would secure at one end by a number of large, heavy rocks so we could spring to the swimming hole below. In fact, Billy boldly announced he'd be the first to do a backflip from the board sometime this summer and said anyone else who didn't try it would be "a chicken." No one ever wanted to be tagged "a chicken."

"Splash," was the sound the water made as Billy's feet hit and his body went straight down in the depths below. Before his momentum eased of its own accord, we could see him suddenly begin flailing his arms and kicking his legs to stop the speed and shoot his body back to the surface. "Whoa!" he screamed. "Whoa, guys, there's something down here! I brushed it with my left arm on the way down. It scared the shit out of me." Kicking his legs and swimming awkwardly to get away from the area where he had just broken through the water, he yelled, "Don't dive over there. There's something under there." For Billy to appear frightened was a big deal. Nothing ever scared him—*nothing*.

"What is it?" we yelled almost in unison as we watched Billy tread water never taking his eyes off the area above the object below. "I don't know, but it's hard. I bet I'll have a huge scrape mark on my arm. Don't jump there." Pausing, he then exclaimed, "I'm going back over there!"

I yelled, "Wait for us!" and the four of us sprang from the cliff one at a time, shivering almost uncontrollably when we broke back up through the surface. By early June, the increasingly warm weather hadn't begun to reach very far into the deep pit, so "frigid" would be a good description of the water temperature. Yet, we were boys, and we didn't dwell on low temperatures as older folk did.

Billy led us to the general area where he'd entered the water and proclaimed he was going down to investigate. The rest of us treaded water, slowly adapting to the coldness, until he resurfaced. Some pits had murky water. This one was relatively clear, although from above darker in appearance because of the depth that started almost immediately from the edge of the wall. In recalling all of this numerous times later, I could imagine that with his head down, eyes open and holding his breath as tightly as he could, Billy kicked his feet, held his arms straight down in front of him, and cautiously moved toward the object below. As he slowly pulled his arms in backward motions, he maneuvered closer and saw an outline about fifteen feet below the surface. Quickly, he resurfaced. "It's a truck!" he yelled. "A truck of some sort." After catching his breath, he said, "I'm goin' down again." I followed him. The other three continued to hold their spots by treading, with Bobby now at the edge of the water but still clothed and staring wide-eyed at the area where Billy and I disappeared. Billy went deeper. I was close behind. He moved downward along the side of the object, which was resting at a steep angle to the surface and tilted toward the right, away from the underwater pit wall. I could make out the words "*Ed Morris Long Haul Service*" through the dim refracted sunlight on the upper side. Billy continued toward the front of the form and then shot to the surface again. I was close behind, heart pounding from the lack of oxygen and the mystery of what we had discovered.

"It's a semitrailer," he announced, barely able to get the words out. "Let's get to the edge. I gotta rest a minute." The five of us swam to the shoreline and sat on the narrow strip of hard-packed rocky soil below the high-wall with our feet on rock that barely protruded from the wall below the water.

"Maybe there's someone in the cab," I blurted.

"No, the cab's not there," Billy replied, still trying to catch his breath.

"There's nothing but the trailer. Odd I didn't see the rear end of it before I jumped. The front must be about twenty-five feet down; the rear about fifteen."

"Maybe the cab got separated," Danny suggested.

"Nah, I don't think so," Billy gasped. "But I could see the back tires. The doors are just barely open, and the front end is down at a steep angle resting against some rock. I don't know how the thing's hangin' there. Looks like it could slide off pretty easy."

"Let's all go look!" Danny exclaimed. And with that, all but Bobby pushed away from the wall and swam approximately eighty feet where we hovered over the higher end of the form everyone could now detect, thanks to Billy's description. One after another, we arced our bodies and moved headlong toward the forty-five-foot-long trailer that had been resting precariously in its watery grave since sometime after we swam there late last summer. After exploring as best we could with the amount of breath we could hold, we resurfaced.

"How'd it get there?" Dickie wondered breathlessly.

"Somebody musta pushed it over. It sure wasn't here last year," Danny replied.

"I wonder what's inside!" Billy exclaimed as all of us treaded water.

"Don't know, but I'm sure not gonna find out," I said to him.

"Well, I am," Billy declared.

As I was saying, "No, don't …" Billy was under the water again, determined to explore the inside of the trailer for contents.

Moments later, he resurfaced. Each of us had been kicking legs and pushing arms up and down to stay afloat. Billy gulped air. "I got one of the doors to open a little more." He quickly shared with us that the heavy, partially open upper steel door now had an angled gap of about four feet and allowed a small amount of sunlight to penetrate just inside.

As I saw him pull in more air and prepare to go under again, I pleaded, "Billy, please don't go down there. It could be dangerous. Please."

"Yeah, Billy, don't!" Bobby yelled from where he stood at the pit wall.

Without thinking twice, in an instant, Billy disappeared. And in another instant, we followed.

Billy carefully snaked his way through the trailer door opening. I'm guessing that in the dark water, he made his way to the floor and felt nothing attached to it and then moved higher and pushed his arms about to determine whether anything was floating and felt nothing there either. I could swear I saw a slight movement of the trailer itself while he was in there. Needing breath, Billy saw the sunshine-illuminated opening through the rear doors, kicked his legs, and pulled his arms in downward motions as he proceeded toward the surface once again, bumping hard into the partially open door with his left shoulder as he exited. I noticed the slight collision must have loosened the hinges because the door closed slightly. When he and I resurfaced, the others were already there, gasping for air.

"I haven't found anything yet," Billy announced. "It's dark in there, impossible to see anything, so I had to feel my way around."

"Billy, you're crazy. Let's just dive and swim and forget about that trailer," I pleaded.

"Just once more," Billy panted. "Just gotta satisfy my curiosity."

"Yeah, 'Curiosity killed the cat,' my granddad used to say," Randy retorted. But Billy being Billy took in as much air as his lungs would hold and went under again.

I'm recreating what I think happened. As he reentered the trailer's interior, Billy noticed the door was not as far open as it had been, but I'm guessing he thought little of it and began his underwater inquiry, going deeper, toward the front this time. Perhaps he felt something attached to a wall and tried yanking as hard as he could. When he did, he probably heard a creaking sound as the unstable trailer suddenly began to roll to its right, breaking loose from the rock shelf that had so delicately supported it. He would have instantly let go of the object as fear swept through him and began searching for the dim light of the open door, but the light was quickly fading as the trailer rolled slightly and started sinking toward the bottom. The water inside the trailer was now totally dark, and Billy was floundering, disoriented, as he tried to find the doors. His breath was rapidly diminishing, not helped by his panic. He realized he was trapped.

From above, the rest of us saw water movement on the surface and sensed something was happening below. We were all getting tired but without thinking about it and without anyone saying anything, instantly and frantically, we plunged back under, only to barely make out the image of the trailer slowly disappearing. It was a horrifying, sickening feeling, not knowing whether Billy was inside. Our heads and eyes darted left, right, up, and down as we swam downward. All we could make out was the trailer sinking toward the bottom. Feeling our lungs would explode, we resurfaced and frenetically looked to see if Billy had, too. I screamed at Bobby standing at the edge of the wall, "Have you seen Billy? My God, he's disappeared. Oh, God, where could he be? Oh, my God!"

With that, I was back under, followed by the others. Furiously, we kicked our legs and moved our arms upward as fast as the pressure of the water would permit and moved toward where the trailer had been, then further toward the bottom, but conditions were so dark we could see nothing. Each of us swam in different directions desperately trying to see anything, especially Billy. Again, we rose to the top.

All of us were now screaming hysterically and kicking our legs to stay afloat. "Bobby, go get help! Oh, my God! Oh, my God!" I cried out, overwrought with fear. With no regard for how much our lungs hurt, each gulped in more air and went under again, frantically looking for Billy, not knowing that even if we'd found the trailer, it was too late. Inside, his lifeless body floated against the roof as the trailer sat on the bottom. That's where he was found.

It seemed like hours, but in actuality, it was about thirty-five minutes before a Barclay Fire Department truck and a Hopewell County Sheriff's cruiser with flashing lights and sirens blaring made their way through the rugged fields to near the edge of the pit wall. Within five minutes, a county rescue unit towing a boat arrived. Bobby, who'd never undressed at the pit, had pedaled his bike as fast as he could and stopped at the first house he came to at the edge of town. Luckily, elderly widow Ruth King was home and quickly telephoned the fire department, reporting "a boy is missing" and describing the location of the pit where my friends and I were now huddled against the rocky wall, exhausted from our efforts, crying and screaming denials that Billy might have drowned.

The rescue crew found it extremely difficult to lower the boat down the pit wall. It was far more difficult an hour later for my friends and me to accept that Billy would never play with us again. His body was brought to the surface.

━ ▬ ━

Mom and Dad found it impossible to console me. I cried and yelled incoherently the remainder of that afternoon and evening, refusing any attention or to believe Billy was dead. I demanded to be left alone and stayed behind my closed bedroom door, sitting huddled in a corner on the floor and then in a fetal position on my bed, crying, sobbing as my body shook uncontrollably. I rolled onto my back and slammed my arms onto the bed, shouting, "No! No!" I had lost my birth father eleven years earlier but had little memory of him. Now the one thing that mattered most to me, more than my parents, more than my sister, more than my grandparents, was gone. And I felt my world was, too.

Sometime before daybreak, I fell asleep, physically and emotionally spent.

"Davie," I heard my mother say in a hushed voice, "it's Mom and Dad. May we come in?" I had awakened moments before the light knock on my closed door, shortly after 1:00 p.m.

"Davie, please let us talk with you," my dad pleaded, softly. "It's important that we talk."

In her calm, reassuring tone, Mother said, "We love you deeply, Davie, and want to talk with you. We hurt like you do, and it's important that we're all together." I could tell they were not walking away from the door. I wasn't in any mood to talk but finally, listlessly made my way from the bed and slowly turned the knob. The moment I opened the door, I was struck by the compassion I saw. I can't describe it, but the look in their eyes, the expression on their faces told me they cared deeply about me. What they saw in return was a sloop-shouldered, red-eyed, ashen-faced son whom they embraced with such tenderness the memory would never leave me. There was no crying; I was too exhausted, and it seemed no more tears were possible.

As we stood there for what seemed several minutes, their arms enfolding me, Mom spoke. "Sweetheart, we don't know exactly how you feel, but we want you to know we anguish, too. We loved Billy almost like a son, and we know he was like a brother to you." Gently nudging me, they guided me to the edge of the bed, and we all sat together.

"Why did God take Billy?" I asked so softly they could barely hear me, my head facing the floor.

Tenderly, Dad responded, "God didn't take Billy." His eyes locked on mine when I looked up, surprised at his answer. "God doesn't cause people to die. He's not that type of God." He paused to make certain I was comprehending. His voice was soft, but he was firm in his conviction. "God puts us on earth to do good things, to help people, and to make this a better world. Sometimes, horrible things happen. There are tragedies. People die far too young. But these things happen. God doesn't cause them to happen. My saying this doesn't make Billy's death any easier to accept, but we mustn't blame God. If you can do it, take time to pray to God to take care of Billy and to give you strength as you deal with his death."

I was staring unfocused at the floor and declared, without emotion, "I should have stopped Billy. We told him not to go back down there, but he wouldn't listen. We should have stopped him."

Still gentle, Dad asked, "How could you have, Davie? You were in very deep water. What could you have done to stop him? If you'd been able to grab an arm, he'd've just broken away from you and gone down anyway. There was nothing you could've done." Speaking as though Billy were still alive, Dad continued, "You know Billy, when he makes his mind up, he's going to do what he wants, regardless."

We sat there, no one saying anything, and then Mom, ever so careful not to sound demanding, said, "When you feel like it, come downstairs, and I'll fix you something to eat. You need something to give you strength, even if just a little food." It was my birthday and no one mentioned it. It was unimportant.

By this time, my sister had entered the room and walked quietly toward us, although I didn't know it at the moment. When Mom and Dad stood up to leave, I saw Peggy Sue's feet just in front of me, and I looked up. She took a step and a half forward and placed her arms around my shoulders, pulling my head to her stomach and holding me there. She and I had always been close, but this was the tenderest expression I can ever remember from her. I needed support, and she was also there to give it. She did not speak, but her embrace was an expression of a thousand words.

Later that afternoon, I summoned the courage to walk to Billy's house, knocked at the back door, and waited, not knowing what I would say. The door opened, and there stood Billy's drawn-faced, auburn-haired mother. "Mrs. Thomas" was all I could say before I began to cry while stepping into the opening and putting my arms around her waist, burying my face in her bosom.

Holding me tightly, she started crying, too. "Oh, Davie ..." she managed to say before her voice trailed off, and we just stood there sobbing.

Pulling back from her but with my arms still at her waist, I pleaded in anguish, "I tried to stop him, Mrs. Thomas. Please believe me. I told him not to go back down there. Oh ..." My voice broke before I could continue, and I hugged her even tighter.

I won't forget her words of assurance. "I know you did, and the other boys, too. Dave and I talked with the sheriff's deputy. We certainly don't blame you."

Deputy Greg Bland was the lead investigator on the case, the one who'd arrived at the scene the same time as the fire department. His written report hadn't been completed, but based on interviews with the five of us boys and the divers who recovered the body, he believed it was a situation of a boy being too adventurous despite the pleadings of his friends.

Later, the official report placed blame on Elmer Yoder for the trailer being in the water, but there was no law against the wrecker service owner pushing the unit into the pit so he wouldn't be charged. The fact Yoder entered private property with the intent of ridding himself of several worthless wrecked vehicles was a matter that would be between him and the coal company. Billy's parents wouldn't sue. They were not litigious people. Besides, even though the coal company turned its head in regard to swimmers, fishermen, and hikers, the six of us were on private property and knew there were risks swimming in the stripper pits.

Viewing for Billy took place on Monday and Tuesday nights at Flanagan Family Funeral Home; it was the only full-time funeral home in Barclay and only three blocks from Dave and Debbie Thomas's residence. The town wasn't large enough to support two funeral homes, but there was another, on the south side, that was owned by a company in Pemberton and operated only when the Flanagan family was overwhelmed with business.

Bobby, Randy, Dickie, Danny, and I sat together on the second row of white, wooden folding chairs that took up much of the space in the plain, rectangular room as Billy's parents greeted the line of consoling friends and others at the foot of their only child's open, gray-steel casket for three hours each evening. From where we sat both nights, we couldn't see Billy and just stared at the cloth-covered white interior of the open lid, occasionally standing to embrace a classmate or other friend. Otherwise, we didn't move or talk. We weren't about to leave our buddy. Our minutes alone with Billy's parents were difficult as none of us could adequately express ourselves. But we understood words weren't necessary. Our sunken eyes and sad faces expressed it all. Most important, we felt they didn't blame us. For them to have done so would have been a terrible burden to carry throughout our lives.

— — —

Mom, Dad, and Peggy Sue didn't say a lot to me after Wednesday's funeral, letting me absorb myself in thought, as I mostly stayed in my room, feeling pretty listless. Their support was not in question.

Late Wednesday afternoon, Dad knocked on the door frame and entered the open door to my room. I was lying on my back in bed, staring at the ceiling. "Here, I brought you something. Mom made this grilled cheese sandwich for you. This and some milk will be good for you." Dad set the food on the nightstand next to my bed and sat down beside me.

"It just isn't fair that Billy's gone," I stated without expression and without turning to face Dad. "It just isn't fair."

I remember my father placing his right hand on my chest and assuring me, "No, it isn't. Billy didn't deserve to die. This is difficult for everyone—for you, for us, for your friends, and especially for Billy's parents. But Billy would want one thing from all of us: that we continue to live our lives to their fullest and not consume ourselves with grief to the point we do nothing, or almost nothing. If you want to do something special for Billy, dedicate your life to being the best you can be in whatever you do."

I turned toward Dad. I longed for assurances. "Be the best person you can be; be the best ballplayer you can be; be the best student," Dad stated in a quiet, challenging tone. "The important thing is that you try. Not everything will turn out as you want, but if you always try your best, that's what will be important. Billy would want that from you." Without saying a word, I raised myself and hugged my father with all of my strength and then continued to hold him until I eased myself onto my back. I needed his challenge. I needed something to break out of the deep funk I was in. Looking into Dad's eyes, I smiled ever so faintly. He kissed me on the forehead and then left me to spend time in thought. He was correct. I needed to dedicate myself in everything I tried to do. Billy *would* want that from me. He certainly wouldn't want me moping around the rest of my life. I could just hear him, "Hey, Miller, get off your butt and do somethin' with your life!"

■ ▦ ■

Thursday morning, as my parents and sister were sitting at the breakfast table, I surprised them by coming down the stairs, with baseball glove and ball in hand. "Dad, can we play pitch and catch when you get home from painting this afternoon? I gotta get ready for the season." The five of us who were with Billy in the pit were given permission not to play in the summer's first game that Saturday. None of us was yet in the mood to play.

That Thursday afternoon, I was as focused as I'd ever been, not saying much, just concentrating on the target of Dad's catcher's mitt. The pitches were sharp, the fastballs lively, the curves still barely curving, and the knuckleballs showing more deadness than they had before. We would work together until team practice sessions the next week.

On Saturday, June 18, I pitched my first game of the season, against Hardy, a team also from Hopewell County. All I could think about was Billy and that I was dedicating this game to him. I was angry because he wasn't there to be my catcher, and I took it out on the opposition. I don't want to brag, but I must say I was about as sharp as a pitcher could be. We won eight to nothing, and the team mobbed me at the mound when the last batter struck out. It was my thirteenth strikeout. I'd given up only two hits; neither base runner advanced past first base.

My first no-hitter ever came the following Saturday, against nearby Clarkson. I knew my knuckleball was already being talked about in Barclay and among coaches within the eight-team league. It certainly confused batters on this day, as eighteen of them walked away from home plate after hearing the umpire bellow, "Strike three." Four got on base, two by infield errors, one on a walk, and the other by being hit in the left side when a fastball got away. I hated hitting anyone and would always walk toward the first base line as the batter made his way to the bag and say, "I'm sorry. I'm really sorry." In later years, in high school, I'd get chewed out because getting hit was just part of the game and apologizing would show you had feelings, and pitchers were never to show any feelings of kindness toward a batter.

"Do batters ever apologize to you for getting a base hit?" queried my high school coach. He answered his own question. "Hell, no, they don't. So you never apologize for hitting them. It's just part of the game."

On July 16, three weeks from the first no-hitter, I threw another. Only ten on the team from Clyde struck out, but my teammates were nearly flawless in the field. I walked four, and a dropped fly ball by Danny in right field in the seventh inning allowed the only Clyde run.

As in previous summers with Billy, my new catcher—round-faced, pug-nosed Donnie Hazelett—and I clicked. Only five-six but about 146 pounds, Donnie was tough like Billy and projected that toughness garbed in chest protector, leg guards, and mask, squatting behind home plate and exhibiting a swagger that intimidated some of the hitters the moment they stepped into the batter's box. He loved the sight and sound of the ball popping into his mitt as a batter swung and missed and taunted hitters by yelling, "Come on, Pitch, fire that fastball in here!" and then getting the curve that he'd signaled to me. We were having fun together.

■ ▦ ■

Sunday, August 14, was a hot, humid Indiana day. Heavy rain had washed out the previous afternoon's final game of the season, so it would be played today. Our record of seven and two topped the league. The team's losses were June 11, the day my four friends and I didn't play, and one game in July when I pitched well enough but my team couldn't field balls cleanly and, as I told my Dad, "couldn't hit the side of a barn."

Our town and Pemberton had a historic dislike for one another, and it carried over to the schools' teams. In fact, in the two sports Barclay High School offered—baseball and basketball—the rivalry with our nemesis from the county seat was intense. That feeling carried down to the lower grades and was part of the talk of those who followed sports in both communities. I never saw or heard of fights, but hatred was in the air, faces, and body language of players and some fans, too. Pemberton's summer team was 6-3; a loss by us this day would result in them being cochamps, and neither of us ever wanted to be "co-" anything with the other.

I couldn't have been sharper. My fastball, curve, and knuckler were all on target, seemingly no matter where Donnie held his mitt. But their pitcher was nearly as effective. By the top of the ninth, we had mustered only two hits and a run. Pemberton hadn't gotten a hit or a run, but now had a runner on first thanks to an error. There were two outs.

There must have been two hundred people in the bleachers at our home field. Most were from Barclay, and I can remember everyone was standing and cheering for one team or the other. I admit to a bit of nervousness as I faced Pemberton's and the league's leading hitter. I always dreaded pitching to Ronnie Brimm. He batted right-handed and was nearly impossible to strike out because he protected the plate well and managed to get wood on the ball even if it was outside or high and inside. I started by throwing two consecutive knuckleballs for strikes. I could tell Brimm was upset. Almost two years older than I, he hated looking like a fool and slammed the top end of the wooden Louisville Slugger onto the hard-rubber home plate, scraped dirt back and forth with his right foot for leverage, and stared at me as though daring me to throw the next pitch. Crouched, Donnie signaled with two fingers, what he and I believed was the perfect pitch, a curve on the outside of the plate, a waste pitch that would be so tempting Brimm would go after it but miss. Or so we thought. The problem was my curve didn't curve, it came in straight although low and about three inches outside the plate. Brimm swung and lofted a high fly to right field. I held both arms in the air, ready to celebrate victory, and watched helplessly as the ball bounced off Danny's waiting glove, another error. By the time the ball was retrieved and thrown to the infield, the runner on first had rounded third and then quickly scampered back to the base as the coach screamed at him to "Hold up, dammit!"

Two outs, runners on first and third, and a one-run lead—I felt my composure slipping. The game should have been over. I'd done about everything I could from the mound. Fans were screaming.

Dusty Bailey, nearly as tough a hitter as Brimm but more prone to strike out and swing at bad pitches, was up next. With a runner on third,

Donnie and I both knew the knuckler was risky because of its unpredictability, although I had as good a command of it as I'd had all summer and Donnie hadn't let anything get by him all afternoon. "Strike!" yelled the umpire as my first pitch floated and danced slightly as it crossed home plate.

Bailey didn't swing. "We got him!" Donnie yelled, trying to antagonize our opponent, and signaled for a fastball. It got away from me and was high and outside, but Bailey swung anyway. I think the fans could now be heard all the way to Pemberton.

"Just one more, Pitch! We got 'em!" Donnie yelled again, glancing up at Bailey, hoping he was getting into the hitter's head. With two strikes, the smart thing was to waste a throw outside. Bailey expected anything but something over the plate. And Donnie loved doing the unexpected. In his squatting position, he held three fingers toward the ground. I bit the inside of my cheek to keep from grinning, went into my stretch to keep the runner at third close to the bag, and then threw. The ball moved ever so slightly right and left but with no rotation whatsoever and then dipped suddenly just as it reached home plate. Bailey stood frozen, the bat never leaving his shoulder. "Strike three!" bellowed the umpire. "Game's over."

Donnie sprang from his crouched position and ran toward the mound, arriving as the infielders pounced on me, knocking me to the ground. We were delirious. We'd won the league and by defeating our archrival. For a moment, we hadn't even thought about what else had been accomplished—another no-hitter.

I wasn't one to gloat. After an embarrassing display of "look what I did" after a win in the same league the previous year, Dad scolded me and told me never to do that again. Baseball, he said, was a team sport, and in team sports, the outcome is never about one individual, it is about all the players together. He would preach, "Although the words don't exactly match the letters, think of T-E-A-M as 'This Isn't About Me.'" To emphasize his point, he'd say, "If you pitch well and get credit for the win, did you win the game by yourself? Certainly not. Someone caught a fly ball; someone threw a runner out at first; someone got a hit to drive in a run. Even if you pitched a nine-inning game and struck out all twenty-seven batters you faced, someone had to catch the pitches you threw. So, even the most perfectly pitched game had to involve a teammate."

I did have the satisfaction, however, of having done what Dad asked me to do in June, dedicating myself to Billy's memory and being the best I could be. Perhaps Billy was cheering. I wanted to think so.

■ ▬ ▬

Although the Barclay High School baseball season wouldn't start until spring, Coach Steve Anderson called the first team practice for September 6, the day after Labor Day. Daily practices were held after classes ended through the middle of October. Boys who also played basketball were excused October 1 when that sport's official practices began. I was among them. My skills in basketball didn't mirror those I had in my favorite sport, but the coach liked the fact that at almost six feet, I was among the taller players, and he complimented me for what he said was "contagious enthusiasm" in trying to get better at handling the ball, passing, rebounding, and shooting.

On the fourth day of October, "Wait 'til next year" finally arrived for the Dodgers. They beat the Yankees four games to three and won their first World Series, resulting in delirium in Flatbush and a euphoric feeling for this member of the Miller household. I wasted no time making certain all my friends and Dad were well aware of the achievement. But there was a bit of sadness in the moment, too. I didn't have Billy to tease.

CHAPTER 13

My first personal observation of what Jackie Robinson had been dealing with—racial discrimination—came a month later, in, of all places, my home town.

My parents expected me to have a steady job, so I could earn my own spending money. Since Evansville College was a private institution, tuition, books, and room and board for Peggy Sue were expensive, and despite the fact both parents were employed, they wanted me to do my part. Besides, they reasoned, it was good for me to learn the responsibilities of being an employee in a nonfarm job.

During the 1955–56 school year, I worked Saturdays at Montgomery's General Store, aptly named because it carried a wide variety of products, such as cow milk strainers for farmers, bulk nuts and bolts and nails of all sizes, kerosene for lamps and lanterns, seed potatoes, and grocery items. Montgomery's slogan just below its name on a metal red-and-white sign above the front entrance was *"You Need It, We Got It."* The store would be my part-time employment until I went to college in 1958.

Owner Mike Montgomery taught me how to do it all—operate a simple cash register and count out the proper change to customers; operate an electric meat slicer with its whirling, razor-sharp steel blade and slice bulk cheese and meats, such as old-fashioned loaf, bologna, and pimento loaf, without taking a fingertip with it; scoop ice cream into cones from two-gallon containers—one scoop for a nickel and two for a dime; replenish products on the shelves, writing prices with a black marker on each item; sweep the floor; and so forth. It was great experience with a wide variety of responsibilities.

On a Saturday in mid-November, I was to the side of the glass-enclosed meat counter cleaning the electric slicer that sat on a large block-wood table. When I looked up, a hunter in his red-and-black plaid wool shirt, tan vest, and matching tan pants was standing in front of me, the first black adult I'd ever seen face-to-face.

It wasn't unusual for men from Evansville to drive to the Barclay area to hunt quail and rabbit each fall and winter because of the vast amount of open land, much of it belonging to coal companies that routinely posted "NO HUNTING" signs but didn't enforce the prohibition. Some farmers permitted hunting on their property, but most didn't.

Startled, because of the color of this man's skin, I didn't know what to say. Sensing my face had quickly become flush, I stammered, "How, uh, how may I, uh, help you?"

He replied politely, "Do you make sandwiches?"

"Yes, I, uh, we do," came my halting answer.

"Then I'll have four slices of salami, a slice of Swiss cheese, and mayonnaise, please."

As I retrieved the long roll of salami from the meat case, my hands trembled slightly, but I carefully cut four slices and then a slice from the long, square block of cheese while my customer walked through the aisles and selected a small bag of Chesty potato chips, a package of Nabisco Fig Newtons, and an apple from among the wooden boxes of fruit. I prepared the sandwich on white bread—the only type of bread available in the store in 1955—carefully encased it in white wrap paper, and handed it to him.

Later, I was embarrassed to recall I didn't even thank him, yet he had thanked *me*.

I watched from the store's large front window as the hunter disappeared into Butch's, a tavern across Main Street and four doors down from the store. Moments later, the man and two other black men, also wearing hunting clothing, emerged, and all three sat on a wooden ledge that protruded about eighteen inches from the face of the building and about two feet above the sidewalk. Local men commonly gathered there to wile away time drinking Coke, Royal Crown Cola, Double Cola, or a variety of other soft drinks purchased inside. Beer consumption wasn't permitted in front of the building. The hunters exposed sandwiches and other items from brown paper bags and began to eat. In that moment, I realized that although two of them had purchased their food from Butch's, they weren't allowed to have their meal inside; they were instead relegated to the ledge in front of the tavern. What Jackie Robinson had been facing in his life was evident here in Barclay.

In 1955, it wasn't uncommon for certain retail establishments in Evansville, Pemberton, and other cities in Indiana and throughout the South—especially restaurants, taverns, and lunch counters in variety stores—to have signs that designated where the different races could sit. There were "Colored Only" water fountains, "Colored Only" restrooms, and "Colored Only" seating areas. Butch's didn't have any signs—and there was none elsewhere in Barclay; owner Butch Burns just made it blatantly clear to blacks they couldn't sit inside and there was a ledge along the sidewalk if they wanted to use it. I knew in that moment I felt sorry for those men, and the impression would lead me to attempt to treat people of other races with as much respect as anyone else the remainder of my life.

<hr>

The most popular hangout for teenagers in Barclay was Maude's, a "greasy spoon" restaurant on the same side of Main Street as the general store and a block farther south. Maude Cooke was the proprietor, a kind, easygoing, grandmotherly type, who loved young people, but she could be stern. "No roughhousing, no bad language, no loud talk" was her rule, and she enforced it. Many a time, a long, see-through-your-body stare from Maude was all it took for us teenagers to promptly tone down our voices or clean up our language. We knew the consequence—the door to the sidewalk—and no one wanted to be known as having been kicked out of Maude's. Besides, teens genuinely liked and admired Maude, a slightly heavy, short widow in her fifties whose entire life revolved around the restaurant and making "her kids" happy. She and her late husband had had no children of their own.

Her specialties were cheeseburgers and hamburgers piled high with lettuce, tomato, onion, and sweet or dill pickles. She'd add mustard or ketchup, whichever the customer requested. Maude's burgers were simply the best, always dripping with grease. But grease was what made them so tasty. Other specialties were French fries, root-beer floats, and thick milk shakes. In the mid-1950s, Maude was on the cutting edge, so to speak, with the type of fries she served. Hers were thin, about half the width of fries a person would get elsewhere. Everyone loved Maude, who always wore a full-length patterned apron over her dress and a net to cover her medium-length dark hair. She'd fry the burgers, or sometimes a short-order cook named Dean Mobley would do it. Teens could joke with her and get teased back. She said she wished she'd gotten a million dollars every time someone remarked, "Maude, you're a cook and a Cooke," and then burst out laughing as though they were the first to ever think of the play on words.

Maude's was popular not only for the quality of food and the owner's personality, but also because it had a jukebox that played 45 rpm records. For a nickel dropped into a slot on the front of the multicolored plastic and chrome Wurlitzer jukebox that stood at one end of the restaurant, we could select one of a hundred songs by depressing one of the letters and one of the numbers on the front of the machine. For a quarter, six songs could be selected. P-9 was by far the most popular selection because "Heartbreak Hotel" had just been released by the newest singing sensation in early 1956. I think every one of us liked Elvis Presley. Not only did he have a great voice, but his music was also lively, and the performances, as seen on national television shows for the first time that year, were stunning and controversial.

Rock and roll was a new, upbeat form of music that was spreading around the nation when Bill Haley and the Comets' "Rock around the Clock" burst onto the national music scene in 1954 and became a sort of national anthem for young people. Maude's jukebox also contained country music ranging from Eddy Arnold to Hank Williams and the subdued tunes of Doris Day, Frank Sinatra, Tony Bennett, and other highly popular stars of their generation. But nothing—nothing—was more popular to our young crowd than rock and roll.

By 1957, Maude permitted jitterbug dancing in a small area on the light-yellow linoleum floor in front of the jukebox, with room for no more than five couples at the same time to dance comfortably until a slow song like Elvis's ultraslow "Love Me Tender" was played; then the limited space was packed with bodies pressed against bodies. Dick Clark's *American Bandstand* was now seen on national television at the end of the school day, and teens everywhere picked up on the jitterbug.

The high-schoolers in that Philadelphia television studio influenced not only dance but clothing as well. So it was common for girls in Barclay to wear full, plaid, pleated cotton skirts; white high-collared blouses; and white bobby socks with saddle oxford shoes, their hair in a ponytail or full and shoulder-length. Boys adapted to rolled-up denim jeans, white socks, penny loafers or black or white high-top gym shoes, and white T-shirts, and some were greasing their hair like Elvis, combing it into a ducktail in the back. Also popular were plain white dress shirts—cuffs neatly rolled back two times—with beltless jeans pulled down in front as daringly low as possible, just above the pubic line. I joined the trend until I overheard two elderly men sitting on a bench along a Main Street sidewalk commenting on it one day.

"Know why them kids wear them jeans so low?" one asked the other. Seeing a hunch of shoulders from his friend, he answered his own question. "'Cause they've got clap, gonoreral, or some other venorial disease. Cain't stand jeans touching their dicks."

That was enough for me. I didn't want the reputation.

Several of my friends fell in love with cars when we were in high school. By the time they were sixteen, some already had used vehicles and spent hours polishing or touching up the body paint or tinkering with the engine. Bobby's dad helped him buy a dark-green 1950 Ford pickup to which Bobby added fender skirts and a loud muffler. He loved driving down Main Street, stopping in front of his buddies gathered outside Maude's and the pool hall next door and depressing the clutch while revving the engine to elevate the volume of the sweet, deep-toned Hollywood muffler. "Man, that sounds cool!" someone would yell at him.

Since he always drove with his left arm resting in the open driver's side window, Bobby would flash a wry smile, point the forefinger of his left hand at the crowd, and shout back, "Fuck an 'A'!" his favorite expression to emphasize something he felt was good. He'd rev the engine again and yell, "Fuck an 'A'!"

On most nights, Bobby engaged in his little midstreet demonstration until business owners and residents who lived along Main complained to police, who were mostly successful in putting a stop to the antics. He reveled in getting away with an occasional demonstration, feeling he had "one-upped" the law.

Danny also got a car, a two-door, powder-blue and white 1950 Ford Crestliner that had been involved in a wreck in 1955 and its owner never had it repaired. The frame wasn't bent, but the passenger door, front right fender, hub cap, and hood had to be replaced. Danny's favorite hobby was working on cars, which he'd done part-time during the school year and full-time in the summer at Blake's Body Repair before he bought the wrecked car in '57. His dad helped him in the evenings and on weekends. Like Bobby, Danny inserted fender skirts on the Ford and purposely cut two small holes in the muffler so it produced a loud sound when he depressed the clutch and shoved down on the accelerator and then quickly let off it as he passed Maude's. Also, like Bobby, he made certain he knew where the police were before he'd be so daring.

I, on the other hand, had no interest in cars. My parents had a 1954 India ivory and Romany red Chevrolet Bel Air that featured automatic window and seat controls—*"More People Buy Chevrolets than Any Other Car,"* the company advertised—and I learned to drive it after turning sixteen, but that was the extent of my interest. I was preoccupied with baseball.

While I took good care of my health, a few friends smoked cigarettes—Lucky Strike and Camel were the favorite brands, although menthol-flavored Kool and Marlboro with something new called a "filter" were gaining in popularity. To show off, a friend or two would take cigarette tobacco from a red can of Velvet, dump it into a small piece of rolling paper, lick an edge, and make his own cigarettes. Never did any of them smoke in front of their parents. A few also drank beer and occasionally had a sip or two of whiskey. Ten High was a popular, inexpensive brand of bourbon. Falls City or Oertels '92 were the most common beer in their dads' refrigerators at home, or they'd get a friend of legal age to buy it for them. The latter wasn't a problem.

Drive-in restaurants were popular, especially the A&W Root Beer stand in Pemberton. While customers ordered curbside from "car hops," young male drivers typically wearing white T-shirts with the left short sleeve rolled to the shoulder to reveal their biceps, motored slowly around the restaurant, showing off their cars or themselves, sometimes revving the engines and letting the mufflers pop and crack. "Hey, Wayne, gittin' any tonight?" someone would yell from a crawling car as it drove by a friend parked with his date at curbside.

"Yeah, my right finger's in it now," came the smart-aleck reply from the driver's side, followed instantly by a closed-fist sock to the shoulder by his date. Since I didn't have a car, I engaged in none of that except to be a backseat passenger with a date or a buddy or two.

Actually, despite the fact I loved to stand in front of an audience and speak—which I would occasionally do at school—I was somewhat shy when it came to relations with girls. I secretly admired blond, pony-tailed Suzie McDonald but wouldn't dare tell her or even ask her out for a date. Since Barclay didn't have a theater, merchants sponsored a "free show" in the high school parking lot each Saturday night in June and July, a popular attraction for teens. Typically, if they didn't have a date, boys would sit together and girls would be in their own group, although they'd converse with one another before the movie began or after it finished. I wanted so badly to sit with Suzie but didn't have the nerve to ask if I could.

The parking lot was hard-packed gravel, so if a person didn't bring a blanket for padding, it wasn't the most comfortable place to sit. Merchants had a large film screen hung between two telephone poles at one end of the lot. A projector that had about two hundred feet of connected cords running from an electrical outlet in the school to the table where the machine sat in the parking lot, showed cartoons and the featured film. Of course, some mischievous teen would invariably unplug one of the cords in the dark night while the movie was being shown and plunge the lot into total blackness, and then one of the adults in charge of the event would take a flashlight and walk the cord to find where the connection had been unplugged. This was followed by a voice on the speakers mounted to the telephone poles beside the screen, "For the sake of all those who want to watch the movie, *please*, do not unplug the electrical cord. Anyone caught doing so will be escorted from the grounds and barred from coming here again," followed by snickers from the younger set and under-the-breath "Those damned kids" comments from adults. Prior to the cartoons, slides of sponsoring merchants' names were shown, accompanied by the announcement, "We wish to thank all these fine Barclay merchants for sponsoring the movies tonight. Please show your appreciation with applause." To which adults and little children would applaud and a few sarcastic teens would smack their hands together only once or twice and make some wiseacre remark.

I dated in high school but was never romantically serious about anyone. I had the typical sexual urges of boys my age and more than once was told by a date "Don't, Davie," when my hands roamed too much. It was never talked about, but there was a tacit understanding among teens that sexual relations were dangerous. A girl getting pregnant was a taboo that would mark her for years, perhaps life. It was common knowledge among older teens and young adults that a doctor not far away in Illinois would perform illegal abortions—"Using a coat hanger" was the rumor—but the procedure was said to be dangerous and you'd better not be found by authorities for having had one. Forced marriages almost always ended in divorce. Condoms were called "rubbers" or "fucking rubbers"—in the latter case, "fucking" was part of the noun—and almost no male teen carried them, scared to death his mother would find them if he did. To let other guys see a Trojan hidden in his wallet made one think of himself as "big stuff."

By the time I graduated from high school in May 1958, I'd compiled a three-year high school pitching record of 28–4, was captain of the basketball team my senior year, and served as class president that same year. Influenced by my Christian upbringing and a church event in October 1956, I was determined to show kindness toward others and to listen to other viewpoints but be resolute about beliefs I had. My favorite subject in high school was speech. I enjoyed standing in front of audiences and delivering whatever the material was that I'd researched and written with the silver-gray portable Smith Corona typewriter my parents gave me for my sixteenth birthday. I could take a position pro or con on a subject and state it with passion and believability.

The church event was a special Saturday evening youth rally at First Methodist attended by high-schoolers from several area churches. A charismatic young pastor was the special guest, and his message about the need to accept Christ as Lord and Savior and devote oneself to being not only a good person but also a wonderful role model resonated with me and nearly three dozen others to the extent that by the end of the service, we'd individually gotten up from the pews, gone to the altar, and committed our lives to God. "It was as though someone picked me up from my seat and led me to the altar," I said trying to explain the spiritual moment to my parents when I got home. They couldn't have been happier or more supportive, and we hugged as a trio in the living room. From that night forward, I would be more mindful of my actions and whether they met a higher standard.

My average of more than twelve strikeouts per game, two no-hitters in each of my junior and senior years, and my sizeable winning record garnered the attention of several colleges and universities, chief among them Indiana University, Purdue University, the University of Arizona, and the University of Southern California.

"Davie, I'd like you to come play ball for me," Evansville College coach Andy Ludlow said in front of my parents in the spring of 1957. "I can make you a much better pitcher, and if you develop as I think you can, you'll be prepared for the next level of ball after college." Coach Ludlow would spend hours talking with us that year and early the next. He'd pitched professionally for ten years but never made it to the majors. He was at first concerned about the crooked forefinger on my right hand but learned it might be the secret as to why I was so difficult to hit in high school.

The finger had been jammed in a pickup basketball game in the driveway of Bobby's house in the fall of 1956. The top joint was bent toward the middle finger, and Bobby tried to pull it back into place for me with limited success. By the time I finally went to Dr. Clark's office three months later, the deformity had set in, leaving him to shake his head in disgust. Dr. Clark looked me squarely in the eyes, shook his right index finger in my face, and lightly scolded me for not coming to see him earlier. "The only thing that can straighten the finger now," he said, "is surgery." I didn't like the thought of an operation, especially since the finger didn't hurt and I wouldn't be able to play basketball for weeks. As an option, Dr. Clark said the deformity should cause me no medical problems in the future, so I could just leave it as it was. That was an option I wanted to hear. My parents left the decision to me. Not having surgery turned out to be one of the best decisions I ever made.

As I grew physically and my fingers lengthened, giving me more control of the baseball, I became more and more confident that my special pitch would behave as it was intended. By the early part of my senior season, the ball was almost always dead—no rotation—and inexplicably, the bent finger somehow caused it to drop or dive toward the inside on a right-handed batter and away from a left-hander, making it almost impossible to hit.

In the spring of '58, I informed Mom and Dad and then Coach Ludlow that I would enroll at EC. Dad was disappointed that I turned down the offer from IU. He felt the experience of competition in the Big Ten

Conference would increase the chances of offers from the major leagues if I proved myself good enough. But he left the decision to me as an important life learning experience. Besides, my parents could afford the expenses not covered by the scholarship, and they knew I'd get a quality education in Evansville, just like their daughter was receiving.

Learning experiences were important, especially those that showed how harsh and seemingly unfair life can be. In December 1956, Jackie Robinson, the integrator of major league baseball, archetype for young blacks, hero of older ones, role model to everyone for how to play baseball with passion, and my idol, was traded, not just to another team but indignantly to the team's archenemy, the New York Giants. At thirty-eight, he was old by baseball standards. And he continued to be controversial, speaking out on race relations in America, especially the bitterness of whites toward blacks in the South. Instead of joining the Giants, he chose to retire and accept a position in the business world in early 1957.

In ten major league years, Robinson had fought loneliness, bigotry, and injustice while batting .311 and garnering rookie of the year and most valuable player honors. In the end, despite the historical significance of his entrance into baseball at the highest level, he was a commodity like any other player. The lesson to me was to always do your best no matter what you're attempting to achieve and realize that when you work for someone else, your future with them isn't something you can control and nothing is guaranteed unless it's written in a contract.

CHAPTER 14

The village that became Evansville was settled in 1812 when an adventurous Hugh McGary bought land on the north side of a large horseshoe bend of the Ohio River. Two years later, he named the settlement in honor of Colonel Robert Morgan Evans, who had served in the War of 1812. Indiana became a state in 1816, and Vanderburgh County was created by the legislature two years later. Evansville was chosen as the county seat.

Evansville College had its beginnings in 1854 when Moores Hill College was founded in southeastern Indiana's Dearborn County, across the bottom of the state from Evansville. Financial challenges led the college to relocate in 1919 to Evansville, whose officials had made a strong push with the Methodist Church to permit the struggling institution to be placed there. The college had been affiliated with the church since a year after its founding.

My scholarship in the fall of 1958 covered only tuition, not books or housing. But to have the $180 per quarter tuition provided by the private, liberal arts college was of major assistance to my parents. They had to pay the $12.50 per quarter student activity fee, $50 to $60 per year for books, and for my food and housing. I moved into a college-approved private home on Weinbach just southeast of the campus and walked to classes. Lodging was six dollars per week, and I was on a weekly campus food plan for $15, eating most of my meals at the school cafeteria.

College promotional materials informed me that a building boom had been launched after Dr. Melvin Hyde became president in 1955, and among the new buildings on campus in 1958 was Hughes Hall dormitory.

It was built to house men, but initially women lived there, and it was a big joke on campus when word got out that some of them had planted flowers in the urinals as a humorous relief from the stresses of academics. I wouldn't be able to live on campus for another two years, when a second dorm, Moore Hall, was opened for women, and men moved into Hughes.

When I enrolled, the size of the student body was approaching two thousand. Although I'd decided to major in marketing in the Department of Business and Economics, my first two years were required to be in the general college, where I had to take a combination of English, natural science, Bible or philosophy, physical education, social science, and foreign language classes. I chose Spanish, thinking it might be the easiest. My tuition covered the normal load of sixteen hours, and I knew I had to maintain at least a 2.0 grade point average if I wanted to keep the partial scholarship, so I studied at Clifford Memorial Library between classes during the day and in my house at night. Academics weren't particularly easy for me, but I didn't find them all that difficult either. I learned "*Como esta, usted?*" and "*Muy bien, gracias,*" and other phrases with relative ease, although I wondered if I'd ever put any foreign language to work in my lifetime.

Registration day for the fall quarter on September 17 was intimidating, as other students and I stood in long lines, trying to match our desires for classes with what was available after upperclassmen got first choices. Classes began the day after registration. During the first quarter, I got into the habit of attending college chapel service every Wednesday morning before class; it was a short religious service open to all faculty, staff, and students. As the first months of the school year progressed, I found myself migrating to the chapel late some afternoons, struggling with my class load and feeling alone and somewhat depressed. My talks with God in the chapel and in the quiet of my room were therapeutic—mind-clearing and tension-relieving. It was the first time in my life I'd been on my own and in need of an inner peace I believed could come from our creator. Slowly, I gained more confidence in how to study properly, something I didn't have to do in high school, as there'd been few homework assignments.

EC's school colors were purple and white. The athletics nickname had been the Pioneers until the mid-1920s when, legend has it, a losing, opposing basketball coach said, "You didn't have four aces up your sleeve, you had five." Purple Aces eventually became the moniker.

The baseball uniform I donned for the first day of practice that fall had a simple *Evansville* across the front of the shirt. "Wear this uniform with pride," a demanding Coach Ludlow bellowed when he gathered our team together on the infield. I would learn his bark was worse than his bite, but the way he expressed himself got the attention of everyone. He was taller than I and ruddy faced with a slight potbelly from too much food and not enough exercise since his years of playing professionally had ended. He had thick, coal-black hair and matching eyes that would penetrate anyone whose face he thrust his in front of, including umpires.

"Those of you who are new need to understand you're not playing for yourself but for your college. Anytime you think you're better than anyone else on this team, look down and see if it's your name that's stitched across your chest." Coach required us to look sharp, with clean uniforms even for practice. He believed the look of a team when it took the field could impact opposing players, and he used the image of the New York Yankees in their legendary pinstripe uniforms as his prime example. "When the Yankees take the field, they're already two runs ahead in the minds of their opponents because they just look that good," he opined. And known to use crude language from time to time, he demanded that caps be worn a certain way. "The bill on your cap has to be formed like a 'C,' just like Mickey Mantle does it. I don't want to see any straight bills on these caps. Anyone wearing a straight bill will look like a damned queer, and who the hell wants to be called that?" he'd declare and spit tobacco juice onto the infield grass almost at the same time.

Despite Coach's language, I was thrilled to be playing college ball and began working at all aspects of the game—batting, running, fielding, pitching. I relished being pushed into being better. All of us were to stay in shape throughout the cold, snowy winter months until spring practice began in February, which I thought was the ultimate oxymoron. Several of us played intramural basketball, but Coach Ludlow told us not to take unnecessary risks like diving for loose balls. Unlike many larger universities, the team couldn't afford a Florida trip to play several preseason games in late February or early March, so practice was held outdoors if the ground was free of snow and it wasn't freezing; otherwise, it was inside the National Guard Armory.

Evansville College's baseball field at city-owned East Side Park was much inferior to those of other universities that were interested in me, so in a baseball sense, my choice of schools was perplexing. There were bleachers for fans but no covered dugouts for the players, who sat on open-air benches. The outfield was not backed by a fence, so balls hit over a fielder's head could seemingly roll forever.

The fourteen-game regular season included nonconference and conference contests, and I got to pitch in nine of them, all but one in a relief role. I was really disappointed at not starting more than once, but if I'd been a veteran and some freshman started more than I did, I'd be hosed, so I needed to consider myself fortunate to play as much as I did. In my lone start, against Hanover College, I struck out the first three batters but then gave up two walks, two singles, and a double before getting out of the second-inning jam with my team behind 4–0. Coach Ludlow sat beside me at the end of the bench following the inning. "You're fine," he said. "You just got rattled when you gave up those two walks and got out of your normal routine. Calm down. Stay focused. Jimmy's an experienced catcher, so just rely on him to give you the signal and the location for each pitch. Learn to trust him, and don't try to win the game by yourself, because you can't do it. That's why there're nine players on the team." He smiled, patted the back of my neck and went out to third base to coach the bottom of the second.

From the third inning through the seventh, I was my old self, striking out nine and giving up four meaningless singles. Coach had seen enough apparently to be pleased. Although I sat on the bench the last two innings, I got the win because we scored five runs while I was in the game and Hanover got no more than the four in the second inning.

I realized after the season that Coach Ludlow's patience had helped me gain confidence that I could pitch, and pitch well, at the college level. In nine games, I threw twenty-seven innings, gave up twelve runs—but only eight of them earned—walked twelve, and struck out forty-four, most with the knuckler. My record was 3–1. Dad told me he couldn't have been prouder, and that added to my confidence. He attended all the home games and three that were away—Kentucky Wesleyan, Indiana State Teachers College, and Butler. Mom saw only the games played at home on Saturday afternoons, rushing to Evansville after her bank closed at noon.

I admit I didn't exactly excel in the classroom, but my combined GPA for the fall, winter, and spring quarters was 2.8 on a 4.0 scale. I wasn't in love with academics but realized they were a necessary evil if I wanted to get ahead in life. If I didn't make it in baseball for a living, I knew I needed some type of expertise for finding a job after graduation.

That summer, with Coach Ludlow's help, Bobby Hatcher and I got jobs on a highway construction crew, helping repave state roads in southwestern Indiana. Bobby was home from classes at Indiana State in Terre Haute, still undecided on what his academic major would be. We rode to work in his 1950 Ford pickup. What a difficult summer it was, reporting at 5:00 a.m. and often working until 6:00 p.m. with few breaks during the day but an hour for lunch. I carried my food in a silver metal dome lunch bucket, the one my father had carried to work in the coal mines every day. Mom had saved it and now her son had an opportunity to use it. The moment she gave it to me was emotional. She'd kept it hidden since 1944.

My highway job was mostly that of a "gofer," retrieving whatever any of the crew needed—tools from trucks, drinking water, lumber for making forms, and so forth. Afternoon summer heat could take its toll, and the philosophy of the crew boss about drinking water didn't help. "Don't drink a lot of water, or it'll make you weak. Take salt tablets instead." So despite climbing temperatures and dusty conditions, all of us on the crew drank little and learned to cope with our oftentimes intense thirst. Several of the men chewed tobacco to keep moisture in their mouths. I'd often get light-headed when I quickly stood up after being bent over but didn't think much of it. It wasn't until that fall during baseball practice at EC that I learned of the myth of the relationship of too much water to lack of strength. In fact, Coach Ludlow told us we should drink lots of water to keep ourselves hydrated and strong.

I could hardly wait for Sundays because it meant I'd be playing baseball and keeping my pitching arm in condition. With my college coach's permission, I played for Lamar in the eight-team amateur Lincoln Hills League, made up of several small towns not far from Barclay. There was also a semi-pro league in the area, but it contained players who were getting some form of compensation for their Sunday afternoon efforts and playing in it could cost a college player his eligibility. Coach Ludlow had to approve each of his players' involvement in any summer league, as he wasn't about to lose anyone to an eligibility issue.

My love affair with the game continued, but it wasn't long before a different kind of love caught me off guard.

CHAPTER 15

"Hi, I'm Anne," a slender, good-looking brunette said as she smiled and extended an arm across her body to her left where I was sitting to offer a handshake. I must have blushed, because when I shook her hand and introduced myself, I felt warmth in my face while my eyes met one of the prettiest women I'd ever seen. It was the first Wednesday morning college chapel service of the new school year.

Slowly withdrawing her hand but not taking her eyes off of me and turning her body slightly to the left, she said, "I'm Anne Keith. I'm just starting my sophomore year here. How about you?"

"I, uh, I am, uh, Davie Miller, and I'm a sophomore, too. Where're you from?"

"Oh, maybe you haven't heard of it. Pemberton. About twenty miles east of here. How 'bout you?"

"Well, I've certainly heard of Pemberton. I'm from Barclay."

"Barclay! Barclay was our biggest rival in high school. Matter a' fact, I didn't like Barclay when I was in school."

"Maybe because we beat you too often," I smiled and said with a hint of sarcasm in my voice. The truth is I played Pemberton in both basketball and baseball with some success but not as much as I was appearing to boast.

"What's your major?" she asked.

"Marketing. And yours?"

"Elementary education," she said as the chaplain cleared his throat at the altar, signaling the service was about to begin. It was the ultimate judging a book by its cover, but I already knew I liked what I saw in the seat next to me.

Our eyes met again and seemed to lock together as she said, "It was a pleasure meeting you," after the service ended.

"Me, too." I was the first to break visual contact, and as I began rising from my seat, I said, "I'm sure I'll see you around campus."

"I certainly hope so."

We shook hands, holding the grasp just a little longer than was normal. "Have a great day," she offered.

— — —

I was studying late the next afternoon in Clifford Memorial Library and was surprised by a light tap from behind on my right shoulder. Turning, I saw the smiling, lovely, slender brunette I'd met at the chapel and whose image had popped into my mind more than once since then. "Hello, Mr. Davie Miller of Barclay," she whispered.

"Why, hi," I replied lowly but with a bit of enthusiasm.

"Been studying long?" she whispered.

"No, just got here about fifteen minutes ago." I paused and then offered, "Why don't you join me?"

"Sure, glad to, but I promise not to bother you."

"Oh, you won't," I assured her as I motioned for her to take the wooden chair next to me at the small oak study table for four where I'd been studying alone. "I've learned to concentrate pretty well, so nothing much bothers me." But I knew "nothing much" did not include Anne Keith. I kept glancing over at her out of the corner of my right eye, unable to concentrate as my heart rate rose. Once she caught me peeking at her, smiled, and then turned back to her book.

"Would you like to grab something to eat?" I whispered after looking at my wristwatch and seeing it was nearly 5:30 p.m. She hesitated and then replied, "Sure, I'd love to. Where, the Union Building?"

"That's fine with me if it's okay with you."

"I was possibly going to meet a couple of sorority sisters, Michelle and Lindsey, for dinner, but we might run into them anyway. I'd told them I might or might not be there. They'll understand."

It was a warm late afternoon as we walked the short distance from the library to the student center where we proceeded through the short-order line at the Wooden Indian grill, pushing our service trays as we each ordered hamburgers, French fries, and Cokes. I guessed her to be about five-three, nearly a foot shorter than I was and perhaps about 110 pounds. Her slightly curly hair stopped at the top of the shoulders of her white cotton blouse with elbow-length sleeves. She appeared quite shapely as I could see the bra pushing out on the loose-fitting blouse. Her plain, straight, calf-length light-brown skirt revealed a very narrow waist. White bobby socks and black-and-white saddle shoes completed her outfit. But it was those eyes, those dark-brown eyes that matched her hair; her cute, perfectly formed simple nose; and that smile, oh, that lovely smile, that captivated me.

"Would you like some ketchup?"

"Sure. Thanks," she responded, taking the bottle and while shaking some onto an open spot on her plate, asked, "Tell me something about yourself."

I found out later, after we'd had several dates, that Anne was impressed that I appeared athletic in build, although she thought I was a little thin for my height, based on what she could detect under the short-sleeved, button-down blue, red, and white plaid shirt. I didn't wear my black hair long, but always parted on the left. She later admitted she was mesmerized by the "cute" dimple in my chin. She said my form-fitting khaki slacks revealed what appeared to be "a perfectly shaped" butt. I wore dark-brown socks and oxblood penny loafers. The college prohibited male students from wearing jeans, and female students were not allowed to wear slacks to classes, no matter how cold the weather might be.

"Well, there's not a lot to tell you. My dad's a schoolteacher at the high school in Barclay, and my mom's a vice president at one of the banks in town."

"A vice president? A woman vice president at a bank? She must be pretty sharp, because I've never heard of a woman being a vice president in a bank."

Gesturing with a French fry I'd picked up as she was talking, I said, "Guess I never thought anything of it. I grew up with her being there. I think she celebrated her thirty-fifth year a year ago."

"Which bank?"

"Barclay National. Anyway, I have a sister who's almost three years older than me, and she's not married. She's a teacher in Barclay." I paused. "That's about it."

"Well, are you in a fraternity or involved in any activities here on campus?" Anne countered, obviously wanting to learn more.

"No, no fraternity. Guess you'd say I was a GDI." I smirked. Anne knew GDI stood for the slang "God Damned Independent," and the thought made her smile, too. "I've heard pledgeship is really demanding, real time-consuming, and I wouldn't want to put up with all that stuff that happens to pledges, like swallowing goldfish, eating lard sandwiches with ketchup, and getting paddled."

The mental imagines appeared to make Anne almost gag, but she kept her composure and exclaimed, "Thank goodness sororities don't do those things to their members, or I wouldn't be in AOII!"

"Besides," I continued, "I play baseball, and it takes a lot of time throughout the school year."

"Baseball! You play for the Purple Aces?"

"Yeah, I got a scholarship to come here, and I really like the coach, so I'm glad I did."

"Then you must be good. What position do you play?"

"Pitcher" was all I said, not wanting to make any big deal out of it.

"I don't follow baseball, so when do you play? In the fall?"

I smiled at her lack of baseball knowledge. "No, we practice in the fall and have to find ways to stay in shape during the winter before spring practice starts sometime in February, and our games are in April and May."

"Well, I'll have to watch you play sometime."

"You'll have a long wait—about seven months."

I turned the conversation toward her, catching her having just taken a bite of her sandwich. "Now tell me something about you. I've done all the talking so far."

She held up her right index finger to signal for a chance to swallow, cleared her throat, and replied, "Well, my dad's a fireman in Pemberton, and I guess you'd say my mother's a 'homemaker.' Neither of them went to college. They're great parents, very loving, and since I'm an only child, they seem never to feel they do enough for me. I suppose I was spoiled when I was younger, but that's in the past. I certainly don't feel that way now, but they sure love their 'little girl.'" She smiled.

Anne explained that although her hometown was only about thirty minutes from the college, she wanted the experience of living on campus and had persuaded her parents to let her. It had been particularly difficult for her mother not to see her only child every day during the freshman year, but as time progressed, Jenny Keith adapted and "letting go" for the start of this sophomore year had not been traumatic. After all, Anne usually got home at some point each weekend, sometimes both days. She had a car, a 1954 Bel Air Chevrolet with a white top and black body that her dad, Brandt, had purchased prior to the start of her sophomore year.

"What about campus activities?"

"I have two Pemberton friends who pledged Alpha Omicron Pi a year before I did, and they urged me to consider the chapter, so I did, was chosen, and I really liked the girls there."

"But you don't have a sorority house, so where do you live and where are the meetings?"

"Most of us live in Hughes Hall and will move into Moore Hall when it's completed next year. Others live at home with parents. Our meetings are held in the Union Building, and we get involved in a lot of campus events, such as homecoming team competitions and Musical Madness. We'll have our spring formal later in the year. But being in the sorority isn't enough for me, and studying isn't either. So I hope to get involved in Union Board. At least I've put in my request, and I hope I'm selected. Where do you live?"

"In a boardinghouse on Weinbach, not far from campus; same place I lived last year."

Looking at the narrow, black-banded watch on her right arm—she was left-handed, I noted—Anne said, "Wow, it's almost seven. I need to get back to the dorm. I've got a ton to study tonight."

"Yeah, I do, too. Physics. I know I'm not gonna like that class. It might as well be spelled F-y-s-i-c-s, because I'll be lucky if I don't get an 'F.' I can tell already. I'm just not a sciences guy."

"Then why are you taking it?"

"My counselor recommended it as one of the natural sciences I need to have my first two years."

"Counselors! I'm not certain they know what they're talking about sometimes. I think they just recommend stuff so they can get rid of one student and go on to the next one waiting in line." She paused. "Tell you what I'll do. I'll help you with physics, if you wish. I had a physics class my senior year in high school and aced it—not meaning to brag—so I'm willing to lend a hand. But only if you want me to."

I didn't hesitate. "I'd love it." She held out her right hand and as we shook, said, "Then it's a deal. Just let me know when you need to meet about it."

I couldn't get Anne Keith off my mind as I struggled with physics in my room that night. I was shy about calling her for help but got up the nerve the following Wednesday morning at college chapel service. I'd thought about her often for a week and was dying to see her.

She was already seated when I arrived at the chapel. I was disappointed I couldn't sit closer than two rows behind her. It was my fault for sleeping too late and not being there when she arrived. After the chaplain ended the service by saying, "Go in peace," a wide grin swept her face when she stood and turned around and saw me. I said loudly, "I'll take you up on your offer to help me with physics."

"Great. When do you want to meet?"

The room was noisy, so Anne raised her voice. "Let's meet over there," she said, motioning with her head to a large area at the rear of the chapel.

"I'm available most weekday nights," Anne said when we were clear of the crowd.

"Okay, how about tomorrow evening after dinner?"

She frowned. "Well, you would happen to catch the one night I'm not available." Instantly, my heart sank. *Bet she has a date.* "I have a sorority meeting tomorrow at seven, so I won't be able to get with you. What about this weekend? You doing anything Sunday afternoon?"

Relieved to hear her excuse, I responded, "I'm going to see my folks Sunday for church and noon dinner, but I can easily be back here by midafternoon."

"That works well for me. I'm going to visit my parents, too, but I'm usually back on campus by about three. Where would you like to meet?"

"Clifford Library's fine with me. I bet we can get one of the small study rooms."

"Okay. I'll meet you at three thirty in the lobby. I have another sorority meeting at six thirty—we typically have our weekly chapter meeting then—so you and I'll have plenty of time to find out what you know and don't know about physics."

"I guarantee you the emphasis should be on 'don't know.'" I chuckled.

As the fall academic quarter progressed, our Sunday-afternoon study sessions switched to Monday and Wednesday nights and sometimes included dinner at the campus grill. I learned quickly Anne was smart. She reluctantly revealed she'd earned a 3.7 GPA her freshman year after having made all A's except for one A- and one B throughout high school. She'd been salutatorian of her class, edged out of valedictorian by a boy who got straight A's.

As she'd hoped, Anne was selected for Union Board and assigned to the Entertainment Committee, which was responsible for organizing parties for high school seniors who'd expressed an interest in EC and also planned All-Campus Sing and the campus Christmas party. She enjoyed volunteer work, because it put her in touch with more students than she'd meet otherwise, and it met her need to help others.

We began having formal dates besides our twice weekly study sessions. It was slightly embarrassing to me that I didn't have a car and she drove when we went off campus, but she seemed to think nothing of it. It wasn't uncommon for a student not to have a vehicle. Usually, she let me drive anyway.

A date typically involved going to a drive-in theater on South US 41 and/or dinner but only on Friday or Saturday nights. Weeknight dating, other than our study sessions, didn't exist. As a female student living in a dorm, Anne had EC-imposed restrictions. Women had to be in their rooms by 10:00 week nights and 11:00 on the weekend. Entrances to the dorm were locked sharply when the clock struck 10:00 or 11:00 and getting permission to enter required a call to the residence's office and a plausible excuse for being late. Males were never ever permitted inside the dormitory.

We enjoyed leisurely strolls among the buildings that branched out behind the administration building. Olmsted Administration Hall was a somewhat regal-looking building, Gothic in style with a stately center tower and constructed of Indiana limestone. It faced the main entrance to the campus along Lincoln Avenue. Trees of numerous species, including maple, oak, sycamore, and the official state tree, the tulip, grew throughout the campus.

A stone bench under a tall oak was our favorite spot to sit and talk on warm afternoons or early evenings. We loved mid- to late October when leaves changed from green to varieties of red, yellow, orange, and brown. I especially remember a late afternoon when the sun was slipping away for the day, casting Olmsted's huge shadow over us but allowing the upper branches of nearby trees to be bathed in rays. The two of us were at such peace. Imprinted in my mind was Anne's gentle, serene expression as she seemed lost in thought, her eyes focused on the kaleidoscope of colors as a slight breeze presented itself. She enjoyed poetry and verse, especially the writings of the late American naturalist John Muir. Without looking at me, she mused, "Muir once said, *'I wonder if leaves get lonely when they see their neighbors fall.'* You ever think about that?" She wasn't asking for an answer. I marveled at how bright she was and how lovely she looked.

We attended home football games from September through November and never missed a Purple Aces basketball game. EC would end up winning the National Collegiate Athletic Association College Division Basketball Championship that winter, the first of four over a seven-year period for the Arad McCutchan–coached powerhouse.

In the classroom, both of us had success, relatively speaking. Anne's GPA for the first quarter was 3.8, and mine climbed to 2.95, thanks to a B- in Physics. We celebrated with a bottle of some cheap red wine one of the older guys in my boardinghouse managed to buy for me. Since we rarely drank alcoholic beverages, it didn't take much to have us feeling a little tipsy and amorous in my boardinghouse room, but she was clearheaded enough to make certain desires were held in check.

I gained muscle from the conditioning program I'd been on and was in good physical condition when spring practice began for the upcoming fourteen-game season, despite the fact I hadn't had much of an opportunity to throw a baseball in December and January. Snow was on the ground for two weeks after Coach Ludlow held the demanding first practice in the basketball arena in mid-February. He cut no one any slack for being out of shape. You might not have thrown a baseball much, if any, during the past two and a half months, but you were expected to be in shape from a winter of personal conditioning if you didn't want to jeopardize your chance of making the team and risk losing any scholarship you might have. Running, running in place, jumping jacks, body twists, knee bends, and pushups were the regimen, along with light throwing for two hours each day for the first two weeks. Sundays were a day off. Coach pushed us hard, and I left each practice sweaty and tired, almost too tired to study.

In early March 1960, the eight pitchers and three catchers began working out in earnest outdoors. I was expected to be one of three starters, so I worked primarily with Jimmy Daub, a senior who had three years of college experience and would again be the starting catcher. Jimmy was gritty and the perfect build for a catcher, five-ten, two hundred pounds, barrel-chested, and solid as a brick. In fact, anyone making contact with him sliding into home felt they'd hit a brick wall.

Coach Ludlow worked with me on my pitching mechanics, but he relied on Jimmy to spend the hours necessary to get me fine-tuned. The two of us picked up from where we had left off the previous season, although I hadn't been one of the prime starters. He taught me more about pitching to spots instead of just throwing to the area of the plate. "You pitch, not throw," he'd admonish, having me pitch to the same spot time after time, then mixing it up, so I'd work on a variety of targets—high and outside, low and inside, a curve low and away, and so forth. I'd been doing this since Dad began working with me as a young teen, but Jimmy's expertise as a catcher provided a different perspective. "I can't get over how good your knuckleball is. You and I are going to have some fun this year."

The only playful negative about my battery mate was his love of the Chicago White Sox. As might be expected, Jimmy's favorite player was a catcher. On a 1959 American League championship team that had only one regular player who hit above .300 for the season, Sherm Lollar led the club in home runs, runs batted in, slugging percentage, and being hit by pitched balls. And he tied for the league lead in throwing out runners trying to steal. Anytime Jimmy said something positive about the White Sox, I'd respond, "Yeah, the Sox were good, but who beat them in the World Series?" The answer was the Dodgers. The question always irritated Jimmy, but the good-natured teasing served to strengthen the bond between us.

The year 1959 marked the end of the twelve-year career of my Dodgers pitching hero Carl Erskine, who retired June 15 because of arm problems and finished the season as a coach. He'd been outstanding, winning 122 games (.610), pitching two no-hitters, and playing in five World Series. I hoped he'd get inducted into baseball's hall of fame. He had a delivery I tried to emulate from the time I first saw him in a game on television late in the 1951 season. The right-handed Erskine threw overhanded as opposed to the normal three-quarters delivery of nearly all pitchers. In fact, I knew of only two other pitchers, Warren Spahn of the Braves and young Sandy Koufax of the Dodgers, who had a similar delivery and both were left-handed. Experimenting with the style, I found the downward path of the fastball made it more difficult to hit and seemingly faster. It even had a tendency to rise at the plate. The curve, what I had of one, also broke down instead of sideways from that plane. But it was the knuckleball that was especially affected; it was easier to throw, with more dance, and when it dove toward the ground at home plate, it was like the ball had fallen off a table.

My sophomore season could hardly have gone better. I started six of the team's fourteen games and pitched relief in four others, a record of 4–1 that was highlighted by a one-hitter against Southern Illinois in my second appearance. I struck out ten and walked only two, with none of the runners advancing past second base. Coach Ludlow told me major league scouts were especially impressed that among the fifty-one innings I pitched, four were complete games, and I struck out seventy-two while only walking twelve. My earned-run average (ERA) was a hugely satisfying 1.78. I tried not to think about the possibility of playing professional ball but believed it could be my future two years from then.

I still had a social life, although it was limited. Anne and I attended the college spring formal held at the Evansville Country Club as the school year was moving toward its conclusion. It was the first time I'd worn a tuxedo, which I rented, shoes and all, from a men's store in downtown Evansville. In my mind, Anne could never have looked prettier; she wore a full aqua blue, scoop-necked, chiffon dress and elbow-length white gloves. We attended the event with several of her sorority sisters and their dates and danced the night away, though I didn't have much confidence in my moves and professed a strong preference for slow music. Slowly, I learned to become somewhat uninhibited in gyrating to a new dance, "the Twist," and the more I tried the jitterbug, the more I liked it, too.

I moved into Hughes Hall that fall, sharing a room with fellow junior and shortstop Larry Kellum. The new Moore Hall for women opened that fall and was campus home for Anne.

She and I had dated throughout the summer and fell deeply in love. We spent as much time together as possible throughout the school year, attending athletic and cultural events—the Kingston Trio at the basketball arena, the municipally-owned Roberts Stadium, was the highlight. She'd been voted vice president of AOII with the expectation she would serve as president her senior year.

I was chomping at the bit for the upcoming baseball season to start. I worked hard at physical conditioning during the summer, played in an amateur league on Sundays, and worked demanding jobs on Uncle John's farm and in hayfields for several Barclay area farmers. Throwing/lifting bales of hay onto farm wagons helped build muscle, and I was now solid at two hundred pounds, having completed my upward growth at six feet three inches. Always hungry, I ate anything placed in front of me. My thighs were thick and legs strong, which would help me generate more power as I pushed off the mound's pitching rubber in delivering a ball to home plate. I continued working out in the moderately equipped weight room for athletes on campus, and by the time Andy Ludlow's mandatory reporting date arrived in February, I was more than ready to play and was told by Coach that I'd be his primary starter.

I'd spent hour upon hour pitching to my expected battery mate, P.T. Collier, throughout the late fall and winter. Paul Thomas Collier had been backup to Jimmy Daub the previous year, and while not as pugnacious or built as thick as Jimmy, he nonetheless possessed a gifted set of hands that rarely dropped a ball, including dancing knuckleballs that most catchers hated to handle.

I knew Mom and Dad were looking forward to watching me in every game, home and away, if possible. Fortunately, I didn't disappoint. In the season's first outing, against Southwest Missouri, I pitched a three-hitter, striking out eleven and walking one. The following Saturday, at Western Illinois, I did the almost unthinkable; I pitched a no-hitter. P.T. jumped on me and gave me a crushing bear hug when we met halfway between home plate and the mound only moments after the umpire called "Strike three!" on the last batter. We were immediately engulfed and driven to the ground by teammates who piled on in jubilation. Coach Ludlow and his assistants rushed from the bench as well and shook my hand, patted my back, or hugged me seemingly all at the same time as soon as I emerged from the pile of celebratory humanity.

I'd walked only one, but two other batters reached first by error, one on roommate Larry's inability to field a grounder that he took his eye off of and the other by third baseman Sam Franks's errant throw to first. None of the base runners reached second. The knuckleball danced, floated, broke, dipped, and dove the entire game, and fifteen batters heard the familiar call of "Strike three!"

"Davie, we're so proud of you!" Mom and Dad exclaimed with joyous expressions as did the young woman who had ridden to the game with them. Anne's hard kiss in front of my teammates left me blushing, and a few of them good-naturedly made snide remarks.

"He keeps his composure on the mound but not in the arms of a good-lookin' babe," Franks teased.

The ride home on the team bus was punctuated by loud talk and occasional whoops of joy as all of us woofed down McDonald's meals the team manager had purchased shortly after the game ended. I just smiled and accepted the adulation, remembering my father's years-old admonition that *"This Isn't About Me,"* and Coach Ludlow's annual exhortation that *"Evansville"* was on the chest of the uniforms, not the name of any player. About an hour after the bus left Macomb and players got quiet, tears welled in my eyes as I thought about Billy and how much fun we'd be having now, especially if he'd gone to EC and perhaps had been my catcher. As I prayed for Billy and gave thanks for my talents, the tears rolled down my cheeks.

The following day's *Sunday Courier & Press* had a large article about the game and a comment from sports columnist Kent Reibold that "baseball fans would be wise to attend some Purple Aces games and see this budding star in action." My coach's only comment the next day at practice was "One game does not a season make. You played well, but forget about it and keep working on your delivery and your curve. You need something besides a fast ball and a knuckler to make you special." I knew he felt I had potential to get to the next level beyond college, or even to be more effective while in college. What I needed was an effective curveball.

Coach Ludlow assigned one of his assistants, Wayne Mayer, to work with me because Mayer had played in the minor leagues for three years after pitching at Central Michigan. Although he was left-handed, and it seemed all left-handers were born with not simply curveballs but nasty curveballs in their genes, the mechanics of pitching were the same, and he was determined to help me develop that third pitch further.

Despite having three starting pitchers on our squad, I was chosen for game three as well. It was the first home contest of the young season and more than three hundred fans turned out, three times the normal crowd, many of them bringing folding lawn chairs because there weren't enough bleacher seats to hold everyone. I was aware of major league scouts in attendance, but they didn't make me nervous, despite the fact I walked the first batter and gave up two singles and a run. I settled down and didn't allow another hit through seven innings. Meanwhile, we scored three off of Purdue University's top pitcher. In the eighth, after getting the first two to fly out, I walked two and then forced the next batter to hit the improving curve and ground into a force out at second. I was replaced for the ninth inning as our guys held on for a 3–2 win. Three games, three wins for my teammates and for me. Even I will admit my statistics were remarkable: twenty-six innings pitched, thirty-four strikeouts, five walks, five hits, and one earned run, an unheard of ERA of .038.

After ten games, our record was 8–2, both losses coming when I didn't pitch. Coach had to be fair with all his pitchers, especially the other two starters, so I agreed with his decision to keep me out of some of the games. Game 11 on Saturday, May 13, two weeks before academic finals, was against our nemesis, Southern Illinois, who'd only lost three, and with me having been publicized as the starting pitcher and a crowd of more than one thousand expected to attend, the contest was moved to Gibson Park, home of the professional team in Evansville.

On this day, my nerves surfaced; it was not apparent to others, but I felt them when I took the mound to make my warm-up pitches. It was just as well I was unaware eight major league scouts were in the stands. I'd never pitched in a ballpark so large. The stadium's brick outfield wall was 320 feet down both the left field and right field lines and an even 400 feet in dead center. Even though it was also the largest crowd I'd pitched in front of, the fans seemed dwarfed by the size of the grandstand.

P.T. could tell during warm-ups I wasn't my old self, because the fastball didn't have the normal zip, and the curve was especially weak, hardly breaking at all. Old reliable was good, but the knuckler wasn't cutting the plate as it typically did. P.T. asked the home plate umpire for a moment to run out to talk with me before the first batter stepped into the box.

"Hey, man," he said somewhat loudly, holding his face mask in his left hand and looking me straight in the eyes, his face no more than six inches from mine. "This game's nothing special. It's just another game but a different setting. No big deal. You get it?"

Looking away, I responded, "Yeah, I get it," but I don't think my tone exuded much confidence.

"Well then, act like it. It's just you and me, pal, and seven guys behind us, so just concentrate on my mitt and my signals and we'll have a hell of game. Besides, pitch well and you might get some tonight." He grinned, as he motioned with his head toward Anne in the stands.

That he would make such a comment made me smile, and I responded, with enthusiasm, "Let's get 'em."

If the scouts had possessed radar guns, they'd probably have clocked my first pitch, a fastball down the heart of the plate, in the low to mid-90s. Dad knew who some of them were and told me weeks later he saw three of them shoot raised-eyebrow glances at one another. The fastball was followed by another just a notch slower but likely still about ninety miles an hour. The third pitch was unfair to the batter if he'd been told I had only two effective pitches. In came an unexpected sharp curve that P.T. had to backhand when it broke low and away. The batter swung and caught nothing but air. After just one hitter, P.T. and I both sensed this was going to be a special day.

I started off the next batter with another blazing fastball, and a late swing barely caught the ball on the end of the bat, causing a harmless foul to the right. Now smiling, P.T. extended three fingers just in front of his crotch, and the resultant dead, floating knuckleball started at the outside of the plate, and then dove down and inside to the right-handed batter, who swung and missed by a foot. No doubt anticipating another knuckler, he held the bat loosely, dug the ground with his right foot to get a firm position, and gave the appearance of being determined not to be fooled by the pitch. But he was fooled nonetheless. The fastball came in tight and on the inside, and although the batter sprang back—he'd been crowding the plate—the umpire called him out. Two up, two out on strikes.

Despite being the Salukis' top hitter, the six-five, 240-pound preseason All-American first baseman Clyde Voss was placed third in the batting order instead of as cleanup hitter this day. I assume his manager figured I'd be so tough to hit that he'd better give Voss as many opportunities as possible. Voss could hit the ball a mile. When he made contact, it seemed the ball would turn from a circle into an oval. Infielders, especially third basemen, lived in fear of a Voss liner that hit the ground about three feet in front of them or one that seemed to rise just as they were about to catch it at chest level.

The first pitch was high and outside, and Voss started to swing but laid off of it, perhaps as nervous about facing me as I was about facing him. The second was another fastball that he pulled away from, making contact on the inside of the plate, driving the ball deep and foul down the left field line. P.T. held down two fingers. My curve on the outside of the plate was a called strike, and my fourth pitch, which Voss probably guessed was coming, was one he could do nothing about. It floated toward the plate and dove under his swinging bat, making him look foolish, leaving him standing and staring at me as I walked from the mound toward the dugout, paying no attention to him.

What a start! I thought as I took my seat at one end of the bench and pulled a purple jacket over my right arm to keep the muscles from tightening. Unfortunately, I had little time to rest as we sent three to the plate and all three hit soft ground balls to infielders.

In the second inning, after striking out the first batter, I had control problems and walked the next. "Come on, Pitch," P.T. yelled from behind the plate. "Concentrate on me. There's nothing to this game. Just get it over the plate." With my back to the runner on first, I leaned from the waist to get the sign from my catcher and saw the right thumb pointed toward the inside of his right thigh. Southern Illinois head coach Charlie Hodges had the runner take a bigger than normal lead from first base, apparently preparing to try to steal second. P.T. noticed the extra step. I went into my windup, paused the ball at the waist, and then quickly wheeled and threw to first. It was a perfect throw just inside the bag, and the runner was out as he slid into the back side of Steve Clapacs's right-handed glove.

I could feel my shoulders sag when I let out a deep breath, knowing I'd escaped a potential jam. My next pitch was fielded on the second bounce to shortstop, and the inning was over.

Neither team scored until we pushed across a run in the bottom of the seventh, and when I took the mound to start the eighth, I'd allowed but one hit, a double, walked two, and struck out nine. Two other batters reached on errors, but no one had advanced past second. The partisan crowd stood applauding and yelling encouragement as all of us ran to our positions.

Southern Illinois pinch-hit for its starting pitcher to lead off the eighth, and the batter was retired by a fly ball to right field. The next hitter struck out on three straight pitches, a fastball and two knucklers, but Clapacs's inability to field a grounder hit to him at first put a runner on and brought up powerful Clyde Voss who'd had the only hit, the double in the fourth inning. Pitching from the stretch, I delivered a sharp curve that broke away from the right-handed-hitting Voss and caught the outside of the plate for a called strike. The crowd was on its feet, producing the noise level of a group double its size.

P.T. signaled for another curve. I peered over my left shoulder at the runner on first and threw to the plate.

I always had what baseball enthusiasts would call the perfect finishing position. In my follow-through motion, my feet ended planted almost squarely toward home plate, which enabled me to quickly spring toward balls hit slowly to my right or left. After releasing the ball, my right arm came down across my body with the hand finishing the motion just below my left hip and the glove hand at about chest level and facing the plate.

My intended curve ball hung.

Voss hit the ball with such force the line drive came screaming toward my head, leaving me zero time to react. The ball smashed squarely into my right eye, hurtling me backward and to the ground. I was unconscious. The remainder of this description comes from having talked with many who witnessed what happened, including my dad, Coach Ludlow, and my teammates. I lay motionless on my back, my head just behind and to the right of the pitching rubber, my face turned to the right toward the dirt, my mouth open. The cap with the Mickey Mantle-fashioned brim lay in the infield grass behind me.

After screams of disbelief, the crowd stood in stunned silence. Dad had a viselike grip on Mom's right hand with his left. Anne, to Mom's left, was then the only voice heard throughout the stands as she repeatedly screamed, "Davie! Davie! Oh, my God, Davie!" She started to run down the concrete steps toward the field, but Dad quickly reached across my mother's body and grabbed her and then stepped in front of Mom and pulled Anne into a bear hug, trying to console her, filled with fear himself.

Clyde Voss didn't complete his run toward first, making a sharp turn and dashing toward the mound instead. He was the first there but didn't do anything, not knowing what to do. Players, Coach Ludlow, assistant coaches, and the trainer rushed to me. Blood was oozing from cuts in the skin, and already the entire area below, right, and above the eye was swelling. The ball had struck with such force the imprint of the seam was in the skin covering the cheekbone.

The trainer wheeled and ran back to the dugout for an ice bag and towels. Coach Ludlow made certain no one but he and the trainer touched me. He took a clean towel, carefully slid it under my head, and then over it as the ice bag was placed on the ground, the covered, damaged face resting against it. Trainer Tim Fencl checked the pulse in my limp right wrist. There was one. And it was only slightly elevated. No one knew the extent of the injury. Their only certainty was I wasn't moving.

It wasn't quite ten minutes, seemingly an eternity to those in attendance, when an ambulance drove through the opened gate in the wall down the left field line. My head coach had ordered everyone except Fencl to move back so I could get plenty of air to breathe. Players stood with fear in their faces. Voss had begun to cry, softly, and tears rolled down his cheeks. He told me later that at first he was afraid I was dead.

One of the technicians on the two-man emergency crew pulled back the towel that covered the slightly sunken, bleeding area to access the injury, used a solution to lightly wipe the damaged area, stabilized my head, and ever so slowly, with assistance from his driver, Coach Ludlow, Fencl, and the two assistant coaches, moved me onto a stretcher and into the rear of the ambulance. Dad was now at the mound and had been given permission to ride with me to Vanderburgh Regional Hospital. Mom and Anne rushed to their car to drive there, Anne crying uncontrollably and my mother attempting to say something comforting, to no avail. Both feared the worst.

The college's athletics department contracted with a physician who was the chief team doctor for all sports. An emergency call to him and a brief description of the injury resulted in a specialist being summoned immediately to attend to me at the hospital.

Dr. David A. Eckhart was an oral and maxillofacial surgeon who specialized in injuries, such as blunt trauma to the mouth, face, jaws, and skull. He'd seen his share of such damage in twelve years of practice, injuries caused by fights, automobile accidents, baseballs, tennis balls, you name it. As always, his immediate concern with an injury involving the eye was the victim's sight.

After slowly regaining consciousness en route to the hospital, I now felt sharp pain while being wheeled into the emergency room; the eye was nearly swollen shut by the time Dr. Eckhart carefully examined it. I heard him say to medical staff gathered around me, "The force of the ball striking the face has pushed the eye back into its socket and the white of the bulb has completely filled with blood. The paper-thin orbital floor has broken from the pressure of the blow, and the bone below and to the right of the eye is no doubt fractured. Fortunately, the bone above the eye and the nose appear to me not to be broken."

After completing the examination, Dr. Eckhart spoke to me for the first time. By this time, I was more alert, although still fairly groggy. "Davie, I'm David, too. Dr. David Eckhart. And I specialize in injuries like this, so my team and I will take good care of you." I just stared at the ceiling having felt discomfort previously when I tried to move my eyes. But the pain was lessening. "We've started some medication to help get rid of that pain I'm certain you've been feeling. Dr. Pioch here will provide an anesthetic as soon as we get into the surgery room, and we'll take X-rays and find out exactly what's wrong and repair it. I promise. Okay?" I grunted in response. I was frightened and had a death grip on the metal sides of the cart, fearful of losing an eye. Nothing, absolutely nothing else was on my mind.

The surgeon continued to speak in a calm manner and said, "Oh, I want you to know your mom and dad and a young lady—I think someone said her name is Anne—are right outside in the waiting room, and they said to give you a kiss." He chuckled. "Well, I won't go that far—maybe one of the nurses here will—but I'll pat your shoulder on behalf of that supportive trio out there." He paused. "Oh, your ball coach and a few of your teammates are out there, too. They all said to give you a thumbs-up, so all of us here are doing that right now." I couldn't see all of the thumbs, but the thought made me feel better as I was being wheeled down the corridor.

▰ ▰ ▰

I was groaning and mumbling while coming out from under the anesthetic just over an hour after the surgery ended. Anne and my parents were at my bedside in the recovery room. At least they said they were. I have difficulty remembering much about it. "Hi, precious" is about all I recall. Mom said it as she softly stroked the left side of my head.

"Hi, Davie," said Anne, almost in a whisper.

"Hi, son" came from my dad as he, too, leaned over the bed. I managed a few mumbles but was soon asleep again.

I awakened in another hour; my parents and Anne, directly above me, were at first in a haze when I opened my left eye, but then the vision slowly cleared. "Looks like you've been in a fight," Dad teased, his head nodding toward the other eye, which was completely shut from swelling caused by the trauma of cowhide and the surgery that followed.

"Yeah, I have," I mumbled, the words more clear this time.

"The doctor says you're going to be fine," Mom interjected.

"But we might not be able to go dancing tonight," Anne teased, getting a sarcastic mumbled "Darn" in response.

I had little volume in my voice when I asked who won the game. Dad replied, "No one. The managers agreed to call it off because everyone was worried and lost any enthusiasm to continue playing." I wanted to react but felt no emotion at the moment. It was a bummer I was the cause of the cancellation. "Coach Ludlow and some of your buddies were here until you went into surgery. We'll tell them the results in a little while. I know Coach is anxious to hear."

Dr. Eckhart walked in. "How's my prize pitcher?"

Drowsily, I responded, "Not sure."

"Well, I'm sure of one thing …" I detected enthusiasm. "You're going to be as good as new, quicker than you might think."

I stared at him with my open eye, wanting to hear more.

He explained that in the one-and-a-half-hour surgery, he took bone from a small incision on the right side of the skull and reconstructed an orbital floor to get the eye back into its normal position in the socket. "I didn't detect anything unusual about the eye. Obviously, it was swollen," he related. "The zygoma was broken in four places. There was a slight fracture of the cheek bone, but I decided to let it heal on its own. Making slight incisions, I wired the four breaks in the bones below and to the right of the eye.

"I'm going to take the stitches out no more than a week from now. It'll take two to three weeks for the swelling to go down, and during that time, I'll have you come to my office maybe twice so I can monitor your vision and the hematoma, a big, dark-red spot that has covered all the white that's in your eye. *Very* normal for an injury of this magnitude. It'll disappear in time, and your vision should be absolutely fine as the healing process continues on its own." I was beginning to feel some emotion for the first time, hearing I hadn't lost my vision. Thank God. "There's nothing you can do to speed the healing. God gave us eyes, and for the most part, as long as we can avoid sharp objects, diseases, and things like glaucoma, they should give us great sight as long as we live." He paused, reconsidered, and then said, "Well, that doesn't mean we might not need glasses at some point," and smiled more broadly.

I'm certain my folks and Anne were surprised that in my condition, I would think about schoolwork. "What about classes?" I asked, knowing the academic year was coming to a close.

"You can go back to class as soon as you feel able. Within the week, I'd guess," Dr. Eckhart surmised. "Davie, it's going to take five to six weeks for those bones to heal. You had some broken ones around your eye, but they've been repaired and you should find no difficulty with them at two months most." Again, the doctor paused and then ended his remarks with, "You're a lucky young man."

Was I ever! No loss of vision and a healing process that wouldn't take as long as I would have thought!

■ ▧ ▥

I stayed in the hospital that night and was released to the care of my parents the next afternoon, slightly wobbly when helped to the waiting car after getting up from the wheelchair. It was a mostly cloudy day. I wore sunglasses anyway. Surprising to my parents and to me, there was no bandage, no covering of any kind for the damaged eye. The doctor said it was best to leave it uncovered as the healing process began.

I stayed in Barclay throughout the week, taking antibiotics as well as pain medication for the discomfort from the surgery and seemingly constant headaches. I needed help for something else, depression, but I wouldn't seek it from anyone. My folks checked on me by phone during the day, as did Anne every opportunity she got. Coach Ludlow did, too. He'd been concerned from the outset and contacted my parents often. Anne couldn't drive up to see me every night, but she made certain I understood how much she cared. No doubt I sounded awful on the phone because I was listless and mad—mad that I'd gotten hurt. On Thursday afternoon, I managed to contact each of my professors. All were aware of the injury since my coach had apprised them on Monday. With only another week until finals and with me missing this next-to-last week of classes, each professor graciously permitted me an additional two weeks to catch up and take my finals late.

I returned to class the following Monday but found concentrating difficult, having only one good eye to see out of and continuing headaches, although they were not as intense as those of the previous week. The pain in the area of the repaired eye was all but gone. I prayed for a change in my attitude and strength to deal with my physical situation. When finals ended for all the other students, my roommate Larry Kellum departed for the summer, leaving me alone in my Hughes Hall dorm room. The college was just as courteous as the professors, permitting me to live there until I had completed my studies. With no one around to interrupt me—except Anne, who would drive over from Pemberton from time to time and give me pep talks about believing good would come from having been injured—I had two weeks to concentrate in silence as I finished my academic work and took the finals.

﹡ ﹡ ﹡

The recovery period was almost exactly as Dr. Eckhart had projected. Full vision returned, the hematoma faded away, and by the end of June, I felt almost no soreness in any of the area surrounding the right eye. The only lingering reminder of the accident was an occasional headache. My attitude had improved greatly, thanks to prayer, reflection, and Anne. Dad accompanied me to an appointment with Dr. Eckhart on June 27.

"Davie, based on the results of everything I can determine about your eye, I'm releasing you except that I'd like to see you in six months, to make certain there've been no surprises. You've done a wonderful job of healing, and I'm happy for you," the surgeon informed me as we sat across the office desk from one another.

"Then I can play ball again?"

I was caught off guard at the lack of an immediate response. In fact, he sat there in thought instead. "I'm not going to tell you you can't play again, but you may not want to. You've healed well, and your eye and the bones are perfectly fine. In six months, the bones will be at ninety percent of prefracture strength. What I will tell you is this. There is a certain amount of risk if you return to playing, whether pitching, batting, or fielding. If you get struck in the eye again within the next half year, perhaps up to a year, there's the risk of more damage than before just because the area has been hit severely once. I can tell you that if the eye is traumatized within the first six months, then the eyeball may suffer great injury, which in extreme circumstances, might necessitate its surgical removal. What are the odds of that happening?" he mused as he tilted his head and looked at the ceiling and then back at me. "Probably not high. But since it *has* happened to you, do you want to take the chance that it could not happen again? That's not my decision to make; it's yours. But I want you to think about it." Dr. Eckhart glanced at my dad and then looked back at me.

I couldn't believe what I'd just heard; I was astonished. I'd not considered the possibility of not playing again. Dad broke the silence. "Dr. Eckhart, we're deeply grateful for all you've done from the moment Davie arrived at the hospital until now. My wife and I and Davie could never thank you enough. For him not to have lost any sight or not have lingering problems with the eye or the rest of the area that was injured ..." Dad circled the area above his own right eye with his right-hand index finger. "... is a miracle, and we couldn't be happier."

Dad looked at me and then again at the physician. "I know exactly how Davie feels in probably wanting to play ball again. He loves the game, as I do. I, too, was a pitcher but never in college and then only in summer semi-pro ball. So baseball's important to both of us. But," he said, and he looked back at me, "Davie's got a decision to make, and he'll have me and his mother to help him if he needs us." Looking back at Dr. Eckhart, he added, "We'll urge him to take his time and think this through, but we'll be supportive of whatever he decides."

The three of us rose from our seats, and my surgeon came around his desk, held out his hand, and said, "Davie, my best wishes to you. If you have any problems or concerns with your eye down the road, don't hesitate to get in touch with me."

I'm certain he was surprised when I moved past the outstretched hand and gave him a light hug. "Thank you, Doc, for everything." I was deeply appreciative but still dumbfounded by what he had told me about playing again.

The ride home to Barclay was quiet; neither Dad nor I said anything. I was lost in thought, and he probably didn't know exactly what to say. "Thanks for taking me, Dad," was the only remark I made when we got out of the car, and I walked ahead and to my room once we entered the house.

It was unfair of me not to have informed Mom earlier I wasn't going to be home for supper. She was preparing the meal when I came down the stairs from my bedroom. "I'm going to have dinner with Anne tonight. We're going to The Farmer's Daughter in Evansville for a bite to eat, then maybe to the South 41 drive-in. *The Absent-Minded Professor*'s on, and we thought it sounded like fun."

"Oh, I've heard from a couple of people in the bank it's got a lot of laughs," Mom replied. "Sorry you won't be eating with us." She paused. "Oh, I hear you got good news from Dr. Eckhart today. That's great."

"Who told you? Dad?"

"Yes, when I got home."

"What else did he tell you?"

"Nothing I can think of except you've been released."

        ■   ▨   ▨

"I don't know what I'll do," I admitted to Anne as we sat in my car at the drive-in restaurant after ordering from the curbside waitress. That spring, my folks had helped me purchase a used 1958 Chevy Impala. It had a red body with a white top and white sidewalls. "I hadn't even considered risk, getting hit again. I suppose it could happen. Wow, what would the odds of that be?" It came out as a statement, not a question.

"Oh, Davie, I know how important baseball is to you, but you've gotta think this through. What if the next ball, if such a thing ever happened, caused more damage?"

I got lost in thought and then turned to Anne. "Want to know the truth? I might be too scared to pitch again." She was surprised. "I've been having nightmares about getting hit. I've always known pitching is a dangerous position, but honestly, I never thought much about not being able to get out of the way of a line drive. I've been thinking a lot about it now. If I ever got to professional ball, the batters would be stronger than any I've ever pitched against. The balls they hit can be wicked."

I stared out the front windshield. "I was recalling the only other time I got hit while pitching. It was in a night game. The field's lights were okay, not great." I turned to Anne. "This guy hits a screaming line drive at me, and I didn't see it until it was almost upon me, headed right for my … uh … down here," I said, pointing to my groin. "I screamed just as it was about to hit me. The darned ball hit right here." I pushed my right leg to

137

the right and touched the top inner side of the thigh, just to the right of my crotch. "Man, was I ever lucky. Otherwise, I think it'd've killed me. As it was," I added, using my hands to demonstrate, "this entire thigh and the lower part of my abdomen here turned black and blue and stayed that way for days. I was almost afraid to pitch the next game, but as time passed, I forgot all about it."

Later, at the drive-in theater, Anne snuggled against me and kissed my right eye, and then we got lost in the hilarity of the movie. There was no more talking about the future, at least that night.

— ▬ ▬

"Coach, I'm not going to play baseball again," I said with all the nerve I could muster and swallowed; my heart was pounding. "This has been a gut-wrenching decision. I've prayed a ton; I've spent a lot of time talking with my parents, my girlfriend, and others …" I'd even "talked" with Billy. "I appreciated the long talk on the phone with you. I've considered that the accident was freakish. Playing baseball after college was my dream and what I worked so hard to attain, but in the end, I'm just too concerned about getting hit again here," I said, pointing with a trembling hand to my right eye. "The thought of possibly losing my eye overwhelms me. I can't get it out of my mind. I've thought of the prospect of laying out of ball for a year. If I was injured after that, the risk of it being more severe wouldn't be as great because the bones would probably be back at full strength, but I don't want to lay out and then try to come back again. Despite my faith, maybe I'm showing a lot of weakness. The nightmares of getting hit have been frequent. I know I'm letting you down and my teammates, too, but I believe this is the right decision for me. Please, forgive me."

My eyes filled with tears at the thought of making the admission to this beloved man and with the finality of what I'd decided. I lowered my head. He responded immediately. We were sitting in the dark wooden chairs in front of his office desk in the athletic department. It was July 17, three weeks from the day my dad and I met with Dr. Eckhart. "Davie, first of all, your decision doesn't surprise me. I sort of expected it. I figured the more you waited to talk with me, the more the likelihood you'd decide what you have." Leaning forward, he said, "Sure I'm disappointed, but not for me or the team—for you. I'm damned disappointed for you. I know how much you love the game. You have a special talent, and there's no doubt in my mind you can play pro ball. If I were in your shoes, I'd probably decide to play. But that's how hardheaded this old rascal is." He paused. "Let me tell you this. If I tried to talk you into changing your mind and you got struck, I'd never be able to live with myself. Besides being an outstanding ballplayer, you've got a lot of smarts. You're a good thinker, and you'll do well at whatever you attempt in life. I admire you, and I admire the decision you have made." I raised my head and blinked away the tears.

"You took a hell of a line drive. And the last thing you want is another one. Eyesight is about the most precious thing we can have."

"I wanted so bad to have another good season. But I've always known a career would end someday, and I'd need another profession. The last thing I'd want is for it to end with only one good eye." I looked at the floor and then back at him. He let me take my time in gathering my thoughts. "I have a huge amount of faith and believe God is there to provide strength and courage in trying to do your best. I don't believe he prevents accidents. The odds of me getting hit in the eye again are probably infinitesimal. But what played a major role in my decision was the fact I lost my best friend when we were swimming, as you and I've talked about in the past. I realized then how fragile life can be. Until that moment, I never thought about it; guess I believed we were indestructible. Call me 'chicken,' call me anything, but I just won't allow myself to play again. I felt in fairness to you, I needed to tell you as soon as possible. I understand I'll lose my scholarship."

For some reason, I thought of his facial expression as that of a reassuring, loving father. He had a slight grin. "Davie, you're not going to lose your scholarship." His statement surprised me. "Suspecting you might decide not to play, I went to the AD, and we both decided you'd keep the scholarship. Evansville College asked you to come here and use your talents on our behalf. You worked hard, played exceptionally well, and were injured on the job, so to speak. He and I agree we owe you the full four years of your scholarship. Besides, your B average for the spring semester was pretty impressive considering finals were taken during what had to be a traumatic time." He let me absorb his comments and then continued, "What I'd like to do, but only if you are comfortable at the time, is to have you assist me with the pitchers when they practice next spring. We'd do our best to remove as much risk as possible, perhaps have you wear a special protective mask of some sort. We want you to be part of the team. It would mean a lot to all the players … and to me."

My eyes welled with tears again. "Oh, Coach, I would *love* to be part of the team and help out. Absolutely. Oh, thank you, thank you." I wanted to hug him.

I returned home, more enthusiastic that I would still be on the team than that I'd retain the scholarship, although the decision not to play again continued to haunt me. I informed Dad as soon as I got there and then called Anne at Rita's 5 & 10 store in Pemberton where she had her annual summer sales job.

——— ——— ———

Our senior year seemed to fly by.

Working in the hayfields and performing other jobs at Uncle John's in July and August had helped me get back in shape after several weeks of inactivity. When I returned to school, I was ready for another season of baseball. *If only,* I thought.

Anne was energized by extracurricular activities, devoting significant time to Union Board and to her sorority. She was AOII president. Even though Greek chapters didn't have houses, they developed campus lawn displays in connection with Homecoming activities. Anne and her sisters thought theirs would win the sorority competition, but judges determined Chi Omega's was best. It was a huge disappointment. She and I attended the Homecoming dance featuring the Jerry Lewis Orchestra at the National Guard Armory and decided a new popular song, one I enjoyed dancing to because it was *slow*, would be *ours* for life, "Moon River."

She participated in AOII's routine in the annual Musical Madness, a skit that was good, but again, the judges decided Chi Omega's was better. *Those darned Chi O's!*

Coach Ludlow had me wear a mask similar to what catchers wore when I worked with pitchers that spring, with emphasis on the two freshmen, helping them with their pitching motion. I wasn't allowed to be anywhere near batted balls.

The squad struggled through the season, although Coach Ludlow had high hopes for the future of his first-year hurlers and one special recruit from Northern Kentucky who would enroll in the fall.

Anne continued to do well in the classroom and was headed toward a GPA of approximately 3.85 at graduation. Mine would likely be nearly a point lower, although I'd gotten good grades in the subjects that were of most interest to me, namely management, marketing, advertising principles, market research and analysis, and my favorite of all, speech. My greatest academic joy was being in front of a class and delivering a message about nearly any subject assigned by the professor. But public relations and marketing strategies held high interest for me as well, and early in my final semester, I set my sights on finding a job in PR or marketing and hoped it would be in the Evansville market.

June 4, 1962, was the day we'd worked toward for four years: graduation. The Miller and Keith families sat together in the stands of Roberts Stadium. During the three years we'd dated, I'd really enjoyed my conversations with her parents, and I believe she enjoyed hers with mine. Everyone got along well, and I'm certain the older adults hoped we two younger ones would become a permanent pair. As I sat there, half listening to the speakers, the day before my twenty-second birthday, my mind drifted to someone who'd been a special part of my life. I still missed Billy and probably always would. This was the anniversary of his death.

CHAPTER 16

With no future in baseball, I was lucky to have a job immediately upon graduation, starting the following Monday. Fred Alexander, owner of Alexander Fine Furniture (*"Buy Today, Get Delivery Today"*) on US 41 South in Evansville, was a supporter of EC athletics and a provider of summer job opportunities for student-athletes, mostly in the warehousing/delivery department. He said he was impressed with my reputation in the community and wanted me associated with his company, offering a position in advertising/public relations at a starting salary of $105 per week, which was not a large amount but graduates with degrees in the liberal arts couldn't command much in 1962. Although Alexander Fine Furniture was a significant competitor in the Tri-State area (Indiana, Kentucky, and Illinois), adding another person in advertising/public relations was a bit of a stretch financially, but Mr. Alexander said he saw in me an opportunity to spread the company name by having me get involved in community activities. Ever an opportunist, the sole owner of the firm was always on the lookout for ways to increase his sales. Competitors and others in the business community viewed him as an innovator.

On the day I accepted the offer, I learned a lot about the firm's history and its current owner. It was founded in an old warehouse building by Fred Alexander's grandfather in 1920. Fred's father worked with his dad and took over ownership when he died in 1938. Fred grew up in the huge metal-roofed, wood-framed store not far from the massive Ohio River Bridge that led to nearby Henderson, Kentucky, and had worked there on weekends and summers from the time he was twelve. Initially, he was an errand boy and also performed janitorial duties, which he didn't mind except for cleaning the small restroom shared by employees and customers just off the showroom floor and the other that was located next to the office in the warehouse. The building had a total of nearly twenty thousand square feet of space, but only a fourth of it was devoted to the display and sales area.

Eventually, Fred was strong enough to work in the warehouse, helping to handle large boxes containing furniture or big items, such as unboxed sofas. Despite the fact he loved athletics and being around the college scene, he had never been athletic and never participated in sports. His life had been work, work, and more work. He grew physically, and by the time he graduated from Evansville Central High School, he was permitted to help deliver furniture to customers' homes. The company had three delivery trucks, but one was primarily a backup, used only when Saturday or holiday sales volume warranted.

Fred didn't enroll in college. He had little interest in higher education, and his dad needed him in the company. The hours were long, six days a week. In 1955, Max Alexander turned the company over to Fred but came to the office every day and gave advice whether his son wanted it or not. Older customers loved seeing Max on the sales floor, and Fred realized his dad's value to the sales side of the business. By 1962, the showroom space had more than doubled, with more types and brands of furniture than ever before.

The responsibility for marketing, which was comprised of advertising and PR, had been in the hands of Ernest B Hittle, a crusty, sixty-two-year-old self-taught advertising veteran, since he joined the company in the early 1940s. There was no period behind the initial in his name. He would never talk about it with anyone, but rumor was the "B" stood for Ernie's feisty mother Beulah Mae's name. He was only about five-nine and of slight build, but his demeanor was such that no one would ever want to pick a fight with him or tease him about the rumor.

I guessed the gravelly voice was made so by years of downing straight bourbon or scotch and smoking cigars. Ernie had far more gray hair than his original black, and his face was carved with lines that showed he'd lived hard. He knew advertising well, or at least he thought he did. He was set in his ways, and the idea of having someone else on his one-man staff, especially a young person "still wet behind his ears," didn't sit well. And knowing that his new colleague had been what he considered "a college hot shot," which he told me, he had a preconceived idea that I had a big ego with little work ethic. But he knew the decision was not his and he would put up with this kid as best he could. In fact, "Kid" was the name he always used when referring to me.

"Kid, I'm gonna teach you a lot of stuff about advertising, and I'll make something out of you if you'll listen. Reckon you can?"

"Sir, I'm here to learn, and you'll never have to worry about me putting in the effort and hours to do so," was my attempt at assurance.

"Well, I'm not sure there's enough work for both of us, but you're here, so I'm gonna see what you're made of. Besides, Mr. Alexander wants you to get involved in the community, so I reckon you'll be gone a lot from this office anyway."

Through time, I found out Ernie was known in the local advertising profession as an after-the-workday hard-drinking regular at the Evansville Press Club bar. Divorced since 1949, he had little social life besides the Press Club and the Advertising Club of Evansville. With no college education, he'd spent two decades in the newspaper business, mostly in small cities, before joining the furniture company and taking over its fledgling advertising efforts in 1942. Fellow professionals regarded him as knowledgeable, dedicated, and outspoken. No one ever questioned where Ernie stood on any subject, and after he'd had a few shots of Kentucky bourbon, they knew never to ask a question unless they had plenty of time to get his often vulgarity-laced, long-winded answer. Veteran reporters and professional advertisers generally liked him; younger ones didn't have a lot of respect for him primarily because he was so opinionated. They thought of him as boorish.

The bulk of our company's advertising was placed in Evansville's two daily newspapers, one a morning edition and the other published in the afternoon. The firm didn't advertise in the joint Sunday edition because the store was closed. There was a tacit understanding among retailers and car dealers in Evansville not to open for business on Sunday. Ernie had cut his advertising teeth on newspapers and was uncomfortable in dealing with broadcast media, although the company advertised there, too, especially on television with Fred Alexander as friendly spokesman.

Ernie taught me how to lay out ads, using clip art provided by furniture manufacturers. Fred wanted a half-page ad on Wednesdays and a full-page one on Saturdays. For special events, such as "Christmas in July," which he pioneered much to the chagrin of area pastors, he'd request two pages side by side, called a "double truck" in the advertising profession. No one else, not even large department stores, placed such an ad solely for furniture. But Fred felt the attention gained was worth the expense.

Each Monday, he'd give Ernie the list of products and prices for the Wednesday ad and do the same Thursday morning for the weekend placement. Ernie moaned to me he wished he had more lead time before the ads had to be submitted to the newspapers. They were to be in by noon the day before publication. To make matters worse, Fred sometimes wanted a slightly different ad for the afternoon *Evansville Press* than was run in the morning *Evansville Courier*. But he wanted to see the results of Saturday and Wednesday sales before determining which products/ prices he'd select for the next ads. At least, when there was a double truck to be produced, he'd give the information to Ernie three days ahead of publication. The short deadlines had often caused Ernie to work far into the night, so now, although he had a neophyte on board, at least there was an extra set of hands to help get the work done.

━━ ▬ ━━

Fred decided Labor Day would be a great time to open his second store, a modern twenty-thousand-square-foot cinder-block and red-brick building with huge plate-glass windows that covered nearly the entire front of the structure on Green River Road on Evansville's east side. The showroom floor comprised more than half the building with the remainder devoted primarily to warehousing. It was a bold move for the company, but its profits had been good and Fred was determined to be the king of furniture in the market. While his father had not been a risk taker and was now mostly retired, Fred was the opposite. He told me his father didn't believe in placing price tags on the products. "If you do that, people are going to know what you want to sell stuff for," his dad'd declare. "If you don't show a price, you can quote anything based on what you think they can pay." More than once, the pair had strong arguments about pricing, and the day after Max Alexander fully retired, price tags appeared on every item in the store.

"You ever written a press release before?" Ernie inquired one August morning.

"Not a real one," I responded. "Just some examples in a class I took at EC."

"Well, you're gonna have your chance to write a real one. You prepare a draft and give it to me; then we'll talk about it."

It didn't take long after I joined the company to learn Ernie's strength was not news media relations, but with the "kid" on board, he now had an opportunity to execute the Grand Opening marketing plan using a combination of advertising and public relations he'd proposed to Fred. Ernie was good at devising and executing newspaper advertising plans. His direct verbal communication style left a lot to be desired with regard to building relationships with reporters. I labored over a typewriter at my desk in the small office just off the showroom floor, reviewing all the information I'd jotted down on a piece of paper as Ernie had somewhat hastily given it to me. Thank God I'd learned to type in high school and had written all of my major college assignments in that fashion. Ernie shared the room and had his own desk. There were also four green four-drawer metal filing cabinets, a table where ads were prepared, and shelves with books of furniture clip art and stacks of old newspapers that contained ads he'd intended to file but just never got around to. I hated the constant smell of cigar smoke in the poorly ventilated room.

I vividly recall how nervous I was as I began the assignment, using white correction fluid to remove errors as I typed. The old, gray, manual Remington Super-Riter typewriter was the one that had been used for years by Fred's secretary, who happily got a new machine when I came onboard. Using facts supplied by Ernie and developing a proposed quote for Fred, it took me an entire morning to prepare the draft that I submitted to Ernie just after lunch, placing in parentheses those items I was unsure about.

Alexander Fine Furniture to Open Huge Store

FOR IMMEDIATE RELEASE
CONTACT: Ernest Hittle

(date)   (telephone)

Alexander Fine Furniture, a fixture in Evansville for more than four decades, will open the city's largest furniture store, Labor Day, on the east side. The 20,000 sq. ft. facility, with an array and quantity of product never seen before in the Tri-State, will be opened with a ribbon-cutting ceremony at 9:00 a.m. that morning. Owner Fred Alexander, his wife, Mildred, and his father, Max, who has been a part of the company for 33 years, will participate in the ceremony.

The new Alexander Fine Furniture store will offer Broyhill, Thomasville, Henredon, Ethan Allen, and Drexel Heritage products that include sofas, beds, kitchen and dining room tables and chairs, end tables, coffee tables, easy chairs, and more in an 11,500 sq. ft. showroom at (address) Green River Road. The company has operated on Evansville's south side since its founding by Fred Alexander's grandfather, Earl, in 1920.

"We are proud of our new store and promise to continue our strong tradition of providing quality furniture at good prices each and every day," said Fred Alexander. "I'd like to thank residents of the Tri-State for their belief in our company and for their loyalty to my dad and I over all these years." He continued, "We will have special Sale prices for the first two weeks of the opening, including at our South US 41 store. And remember our slogan, '*Buy Today, Get Delivery Today.*'"

The public is invited to attend the ribbon-cutting. Coffee, cookies, and punch will be available while supplies last.

I laid the copy on Ernie's desk and waited for his comments and criticism. It didn't take long.

"What the hell is this?" Ernie nearly shouted from his chair as he held up the typed page of copy in one hand, smoke rising from a cigar in the other. "Kid, I thought you went to college."

"I did," I replied meekly.

"Did you take English?" he asked loudly.

"Certainly," I stated softly.

"Well, perhaps you'd better get some of your money back if you learned English like this," Ernie snorted. "I always heard you athletes were nothing more than a bunch of dumb jocks." The comment stung, but I kept my composure and felt Ernie was probably just being Ernie.

"First of all, when is a.m.?"

"The morning."

"Then if 9:00 a.m. is in the morning, why the hell would you use both 'a.m.' and 'morning' in the same sentence? That's redundant, a waste of words. It's either '9:00 a.m.' or it's '9:00 that morning,' not both. You get it?"

"Yes, sir," I replied, waiting for the next verbal blast.

"Now, you quote Fred as saying 'I'd like to thank.' I hate that phrase. If he would like to thank, why doesn't he just say he thanks? If he says 'I'd like to thank,' that's stating that he'd like to but he can't for whatever reason. You get my drift?"

I hadn't had time to absorb the comment but replied, "Yes," just the same. I'd think about it later.

Ernie wasn't finished being pedantic. "Here's another redundancy: 'Each and every day.' Don't you think 'each day' means the same as 'every day'? If something is done every day, doesn't that mean it is thus done each day, and vice versa?" I was standing in front of the desk, ashen-faced, angry not at the criticism but the manner in which it was rendered. Even if "Ernie was just being Ernie," his comments hurt anyway, especially the remark about athletes being dumb jocks.

"One more thing …" My grizzly mentor wasn't letting up. "My biggest peeve in the entire world is the misuse of 'me and I.' I wanna puke every time I hear someone say something like 'It was given to John and I.' Start listening carefully to people, and you'll find the vast majority, even people in the public eye, such as politicians, even supposed learned people, misuse 'me and I.' You've got Fred saying 'to my dad and I.' Fred just has a high school education, but I don't want us showing him to be a stupid idiot by using incorrect grammar."

Ernie was determined to drive his point home. "The rule of thumb is that if a preposition is in front of the subject, the word to use is 'me.'" As he placed the typed copy on the desktop for me to see, he pointed to the phrase and said, "Thus, you should have written 'their loyalty to my dad and me over all these years.' A good way of thinking about it is to drop the reference to 'my dad' so that the phrase is 'their loyalty … to me.'" Ernie paused. "You wouldn't say 'their loyalty to I,' would you?" He let the question sink in and then queried, "You following me, kid?"

"I think so."

To Ernie, this was probably another teaching moment. "Look, if I said, 'The opening of the store is a big deal for my dad and blank,' would it be 'my dad and me' or 'my dad and I'?"

"Me, because you used the preposition."

"Correct," he affirmed. "But if I said, 'My dad and blank are proud of our new store,' what would the word be?"

"'I,' because there was no preposition in front of the reference."

"Eureka!" Ernie exclaimed with sarcasm. "Go tell Evansville College to refund some of your money and give it to me. They didn't teach you any damned good English!"

As he rose from his chair, he slid the paper to me and demanded, "Now rework this draft and have it for me when I get back in an hour. And don't refer to 'punch' or 'coffee and cookies.' Just say 'refreshments will be available.'" As Ernie was exiting the office and starting down the hallway, I could hear him snort to himself, "Fuckin' 'to John and I,' 'for the people and I,' 'it's a proud day for my family and I.' I just wanna puke. Shit!"

— — —

I worked five and half days a week, which meant I usually drove to Barclay to be with my parents for Sunday worship service and then stayed for noon dinner. Anne was a frequent visitor, too. Sometimes, we went to her folks' house. My mother had never lost her touch for cooking delicious meals, which guaranteed I got one wholesome one for that week. Thank goodness because I hated to cook and ate entirely too much fast food or commercial canned green beans, corn, and peas with maybe lunchmeat sandwiches for supper during the week.

Anne's elementary school teaching position was rewarding in the sense that she loved being with children and helping them learn. Second grade at Dennis C. Pemberton Elementary School, named for the city of Pemberton's founder, was a big step for small children. In Anne's class of twenty-three, the seven- and eight-year-olds were learning the clock and hours and minutes and the calendar and days of the week. They were expanding their still-early reading and printing/writing skills, and fortunately, Anne possessed the patience needed to work with them. She and I seldom saw one another during the week but always on Saturday after I got off work and on Sunday.

I lived in a one-room apartment with a private bath in an old two-story house about a quarter-mile from the Ohio River and downtown Evansville. I didn't really want to live there, but it was all I could afford. Widowed Nancy Hilgedag owned the residence, which she said provided her with a small amount of income to supplement Social Security payments she'd received since 1954. A matronly sort, she kept the house clean and didn't bother her boarders. Loud music or other such noises were prohibited. There were no restrictions on the number of guests a person could have in his room, but no one could have an overnight guest. Mrs. Hilgedag was fond of Anne and looked the other way when she saw her enter the house with me on Saturday evenings. She really liked us and wasn't about to blunt any aspect of our romance. If she sensed what all went on in my room, it was never mentioned.

Although Anne lived at home in Pemberton, her parents were unaware she'd been engaging in birth control since her junior year in college, or they'd have been aghast. She began taking the Pill, getting her doctor to prescribe it. If her parents had known about it, they would have been privately admitting their daughter was engaging in sexual relations, and that was a subject even mothers and daughters didn't discuss.

Our earliest sexual relations during college, although not intercourse, had been in the backseat of my car at drive-in theaters, and we were always careful not to be caught by someone walking by. Once and only once did I dare sneak into her dorm room. To have gotten caught could have resulted in severe penalties for her—not expulsion but likely removal from all campus service organizations she was in. Since I didn't volunteer with any groups, perhaps I would have been placed on some type of probation. On the night I did sneak in, her roommate was gone for the weekend, and it was the most fantastic evening of my life. I'd never seen Anne nude before, and although I had an image of what she would look like without clothes, I was aroused by what I considered the perfection of her body's shape.

We slowly undressed one another after making certain the door was bolted and the window shades drawn. Only a small wall nightlight provided illumination. Neither of us seemed the least bit nervous at the prospect of being seen naked. From our forays in my car, we knew quite a bit about one another's body already. Neither of us spoke; we just explored with hands, fingers, and mouths. Our passions exploded in her bed.

CHAPTER 17

"Turn on your TV," Fred blurted as he rushed into our office. It was early afternoon, November 22, 1963. "The president's been shot!"

Typical for Ernie, "What president?"

"President Kennedy, in Dallas. A motorcade, I think. Just heard it on the radio in my office."

None of us said anything as Ernie turned on the small black-and-white television that sat atop a four-drawer file cabinet and then adjusted the attached UHF antenna slightly to get a sharper image on WEHT, channel 50, the CBS affiliate.

The three of us stood agape, eyes glued to the TV, not fathoming such a horrendous, world-shaking event could be taking place in the United States—in other countries, yes, but not here at home. Surely not.

Walter Cronkite gave updates as information became available. First, he told us that shots had been fired and the president may have been struck ... then that Mrs. Kennedy, also in the rear seat of the presidential convertible, had tried to cover her husband's wounds, which might have been fatal. Several minutes later, a visibly shaken Cronkite informed the nation the president had been assassinated.

As time went by, more details became known. The president and Mrs. Kennedy were in an open-air car with Texas governor John Connally in a motorcade at Dealey Plaza when shots were fired from a window in the Texas School Book Depository. The president was killed, and the governor wounded.

Vice President Lyndon Johnson took the oath of office of the president aboard Air Force One later that afternoon.

A few other employees crowded into the small office with us. No one spoke.

Then came a report that Lee Harvey Oswald had been arrested. Ernie broke the silence without ever taking his eyes off the TV set. "That son of a bitch. I'd kill him if I could. The motherfucker." He didn't have to. Jack Ruby did it for him two days later in the basement of the Dallas City Jail.

Practically everything except essential services, such as police and fire protection, were closed everywhere on the declared national day of mourning, November 25, the day of the president's funeral in the nation's capital. Anne and I had decided to watch television coverage in the quiet of my boardinghouse room. We held hands through the hours of mesmerizing coverage that ranged from a recap of all the events from the initial trip to Dallas to the funeral mass in St. Matthew's Cathedral to the burial. We didn't eat, didn't talk, didn't do anything except take an occasional potty break. She cuddled her head against my neck and was brought to tears at the sight of John F. Kennedy Jr., "John-John," his third birthday that day, dressed in a four-button coat, his little legs exposed, standing at attention and saluting the caisson that carried his father's body as it began its trip from the church to Arlington National Cemetery.

The two of us had been enamored with John F. Kennedy. Not old enough to vote when he was elected in 1960, we were nonetheless captivated by his youthful, striking good looks and charisma during the campaign against US vice president Richard Nixon. In fact, it was our infatuation with Kennedy that led us each to register as Democrats when we turned twenty-one.

My parents were split politically; Mother was a registered Republican and Dad a Democrat, each feeling their reasons were logical. Republicans were considered pro-big business and pro-bank, with Democrats the favorite of "the little man" in society. And the fact the teacher's union was pro-Democratic had made Dad's choice a no-brainer when he'd turned twenty-one and held a brand-new teaching degree. Despite their differences in political parties, my parents never discussed politics at the dinner table when Peggy Sue and I were growing up. From my teen years, I had absolutely no interest in anything to do with national or world affairs, social issues, or things of that sort, all the way through college, until I discovered Kennedy, the US Senator from Massachusetts, sometime in early 1960. When I was being reared in Barclay, I was like any other boy; I didn't care about anything but sports, mindless fun, and, later, girls.

CHAPTER 18

By the time I was twenty-six, my knowledge of newspaper advertising had grown tremendously, but I still had limited understanding of television commercials and their production because Fred pretty much turned that over to an ad agency. I'd also engaged in numerous public relations activities on behalf of the company, especially with the opening of two more stores, one in Mount Vernon to the west of Evansville, and the other on the north side of the city, and I'd branched out into something I fell in love with—public speaking. My salary was now $160 per week.

Three and a half years earlier, I'd joined the Fellowship of Christian Athletes and was able to take advantage of the baseball reputation I still had by speaking to youth groups in churches and at FCA events, not only in the Evansville area but also further into Indiana and in nearby Kentucky and Illinois. Most of my audiences were thirteen to twenty years old and almost always male. I never charged a fee, and any honorariums were returned to the sponsoring organization. Some of the engagements occurred during the day, but most were at night or on weekends. I was always billed as an athlete ("Former Evansville College Star Pitcher") first and assistant director of advertising and public relations for Alexander Fine Furniture second. The latter was important to Fred because parents, the purchasers of furniture, were often in the audience.

"You have an obligation to be a positive role model," I'd demand of my youthful audiences. Role modeling became my favorite subject because I believed it to be paramount to living the way God wanted us to live.

"There are too many examples of people who turn out to be negative role models in this world, ranging from athletics to entertainment to government to the business world. Don't join them. To be negative is one of the easiest things anyone can do. It takes almost no effort at all. But it takes *work* to live a life that's a good example for others to see, and you *must* do it."

As often as I could, depending on the setting, I'd take a corded microphone as far as I could down the aisles to get as close to my audience as possible. I reveled in youthful eyes that paid rapt attention. "When you're engaged in sports, whether it be basketball, baseball, football, tennis, track and field, wrestling, or any other, you're in the limelight. Others are watching you on and off the court or field of competition. On the court, you have to try your best to win in a positive way; off the court, you will be judged by how you conduct your life. If you choose to be an athlete, with that decision comes the responsibility of being a positive role model."

I relished talking about my close relationship to God, strong daily prayer life, and acceptance of Christ as Savior when I was a teenager, and my commitment to leading a life that was always as positive and helpful as possible. It was important to relate this, to show that even though I'd been considered a star athlete, it was my reliance on faith in God that helped me in school, on the baseball field, and in my daily life.

"Am I perfect as a result of this acceptance of Christ and this commitment to be good? Absolutely not. I stumble just like anyone else, but what's important is my *intent* to be good and my constantly thinking about whether I'm leading the type of life I should if I profess to be a Christian.

"I want to share with you something dreadful that happened to me. Just over five years ago, I was sailing along with a pretty good college career as a pitcher. My dream was to play in the major leagues. But one day, I couldn't get out of the way of a line drive. My right eye was slammed back in its socket, the bones around it broken. My career was over in an instant; my dream shattered. Luckily, I didn't lose my sight. My surgeon didn't order me to quit playing ball, but he made me aware that if I got hit in the eye again anytime soon, I could end up with severe problems. God had always given me strength to work hard and perform to the best of my abilities, but I did not believe—and do not believe now—that God prevents us from getting hurt. I think he does help us when we hurt.

"It would have been easy for me to sit around and mope and become a negative person. But who would have wanted to be around me? Instead, I engaged in prayer, seemingly sometimes for hours, asking God for physical healing and, more importantly, emotional healing, so I could carry on my life in a positive manner. I realized there was more to life than playing baseball and I had to find my purpose.

"The greatest role model ever was the most perfect person ever: Jesus. I urge you to try your best to be a very positive role model yourself." I'd pause, scan the audience, and then ask, "Do you realize that every day others are looking at you, watching how you act and listening to what you say?" Young heads would look left and right, and invariably, there'd be a few snickers, but I was convinced most of them had never thought about that before. "Yes, there are people who see you, and you influence them by what you do. Now, what if that influence isn't good? Think about that. You could influence someone to do something wrong just by the way you conduct yourself. I ask you to pray for strength and wisdom daily to withstand all the temptations to be something other than what you should be."

As time passed and I gave more speeches, I added material, challenging young people to be honest, of great integrity, and a witness for the highest of ethics. And I urged them to take their studies in school seriously.

While I wanted them to change their lives, a major change was just ahead for mine.

CHAPTER 19

"Mr. Keith, I'm seeking your permission to marry Anne." I was nervous when I made the request of Anne's father Brandt Keith as the two of us walked in his Pemberton neighborhood of modest homes on November 6, while Anne and her mother Jenny were washing Sunday dinner dishes. Perspiration had popped onto my forehead but not from the partly cloudy, nearly 65-degree day. Asking for consent was a courtesy practiced in the South, and I guess it carried over to Southern Indiana, because I never gave a thought to not inquiring. The Keiths knew their daughter and I were deeply in love and were hoping we'd marry, Anne's mother making certain their feelings were known to her. They wanted to become grandparents, and she was their only child. Privately, it bothered them she was almost twenty-seven and several of her friends who were anywhere from two to seven years younger already had children. In the 1960s, when parents and the to-be-married or newly married talked, the question was never "*Will* you have children?" but "*When* will you have children?" To get married and have children—the sooner the better—was an expected rite of passage.

I somehow found the courage to propose to Anne in my apartment the following Saturday evening. We'd never used the word *marry* in any of our previous conversations about the future, but each knew we wanted to be together forever. Our first date had been seven years earlier, and we had been dating only one another long before we graduated four and a half years earlier. Our discussions had included topics like whether we'd want to live in an apartment or a house of our own someday, how much money it would take for two people to live together, whether one of our cars needed to be replaced, and, of course, how many children we desired. Both of us wanted a house; our combined salaries were nearly $14,500 ($6,100 for her and $8,320 for me); our cars were in good condition so neither needed to be replaced; and as for children, we each wanted two, perhaps three.

Anne practically threw herself at me, wrapping her arms around my neck and breathlessly answering, "Yes, darling. Yes!" She held me with all her strength, almost cutting off my breath.

"I don't have a ring to give you," I managed to say, my voice barely audible from the strain on my windpipe. "We'd never really talked about it before, but I thought we should look together."

She released her hold only slightly while she pulled her head back to face me, and I saw the tears. Anne declared, "That doesn't matter. The ring can wait."

We awakened to a bright sun trying to burst through the drawn shades of my boardinghouse room on November 13. Our naked bodies were still wrapped together, having succumbed to sleep after prolonged lovemaking that followed long discussions about a wedding date, the type of wedding she wanted, and who the maid of honor, best man, bridesmaids, and groomsmen might be. We decided to skip worship service and just lie there until the last possible moment when we had to shower, get dressed, and drive to my parents' house for the scheduled Sunday noontime meal. It was customary for us to alternate between the Miller and Keith homes each Sunday, attend worship service with them, and then stay for dinner; only this Sunday, we'd be too late for church. Anne grew up attending Second Street Methodist in Pemberton, so the style and format of worship at First Methodist in Barclay was practically identical. The wedding would be at her church.

My folks were caught off guard when I broke the news after we finished the main portion of the meal and Mom was about to rise from her chair to get the apple pie she'd baked that morning. Peggy Sue was still unmarried, and as she was nearly thirty, parental concern she'd turn into "an old maid" had festered. Privately, they desperately wanted her to "find a man" and get married; most of all, they wanted grandchildren. After all, they were the only couple among their large set of friends who didn't have them, and they'd grown tired of being asked time and again when their children would get married and have kids. No doubt the first thought in each of their minds, although they didn't have to say it, and didn't, was relief. Finally, they would have a grandchild someday.

That relief increased the tears for my mother and made her and Dad's expressions of joy and happiness border on giddiness. Of course, they immediately began asking all sorts of questions about the wedding and the future, most of which we couldn't answer. Anne and I kept waiting for the "baby" question, but it didn't come, perhaps out of respect. Regardless, we knew it was top of mind.

The Keiths were just as thrilled later that afternoon, but not surprised since I'd sought Brandt's permission. "We are so, so happy for you!" Jenny exclaimed with a face that beamed and eyes that quickly moistened as she wrapped her arms around Anne and kissed her cheek while Brandt engaged me in a suffocating bear hug. He was about three inches shorter than I and powerfully built from constant strength conditioning that kept him physically fit for his job as a city firefighter.

"When's the wedding? Of course it will be here at our church, won't it? Who'll be your bridesmaids? Do your parents know this yet?" Jenny, a near replica of her daughter, asked in rapid succession, allowing no time for answers.

"Whoa, whoa, Mother," Anne declared, amused but thrilled that her mother was happy for her. "One question at a time."

As we sat back down in the living room of their brick and stone ranch-style house—Jenny and Anne holding hands on the sofa, Brandt leaning forward from an adjacent easy chair, and me sitting across from him at the opposite end of the sofa—Anne and I carefully answered as much as we could. We just hadn't had time to deal with every question that we or our parents had, so some questions remained unanswered.

There was plenty of time for the preparation; we were contemplating an October 1967 wedding, on a Saturday of course. Which date would depend upon the availability of Second Street Methodist and Pastor Thomas Bishop. Anne's best friend and fellow teacher Cheryl Winder would be invited to be maid of honor, Peggy Sue would be asked to be a bridesmaid, and I hoped Bobby Hatcher would agree to be best man. Beyond that, the remainder of the wedding party hadn't been decided.

"Of course, you'll want Debbie to be the flower girl, won't you?" Jenny stated as a declarative sentence, already beginning to exert a mother's influence on the decision-making. "Debbie" was Jenny's sister's four-year-old granddaughter.

"I don't know, Mother; I haven't thought that far ahead yet. Remember, we only got engaged about fifteen hours ago."

"We wondered why you didn't come home last night," Brandt stated, a devilish look on his face.

"I'm sorry, dear," Jenny responded quickly and as she softly patted the top of one of her daughter's hands, continued, "I'm just so excited ... for you, of course, and I'm getting carried away as a result."

"Oh, Mother." Anne now stroked her mother's hands in a reassuring way. "Don't apologize. Goodness, we're all happy, and we have lots of decisions to make. I'll certainly involve you in the planning, because you know more about weddings than I do." As she made the statement, Anne hoped she wouldn't regret it later. She'd heard mothers being mothers could become a wedding planning headache. And with eleven months to go before the ceremony, she knew she'd just have to endure any unnecessary intrusion of her mother in the process.

Knowing weddings were expensive for the bride's parents and that Jenny had never been employed outside the house, and without mentioning that Brandt provided the only income, Anne and I announced we wanted to share in the costs.

"No, I won't have that," her father declared forcefully. "You're our only child, and we'll pay for everything." As he glanced at Jenny and then back to Anne and then me, he added, "We want you to have as big a wedding as you wish to have. You're not to cut corners anywhere. A person gets married only once, so there should be no shortcuts, you understand?"

"We do," I answered. "Yet, we truly want to help with the expenses."

"I won't hear of it," Brandt proudly replied. "The two of you need to save all the money you can. You'll have plenty of expenses of your own later on: a house, furniture, children." There, he'd said it. In the very first conversation with his daughter and her fiancé, not the second or third or anything later on, but the *first*, he had said the "C" word. Jenny just sat there beaming.

An awkward pause was broken when I responded, "Yes, there'll certainly be a *lot* of expenses," followed by another moment of silence.

Not about to respond to "C," I glanced back at Brandt and then Jenny. Then Anne stated, "Well, just know that we're willing to assist in any way."

I quickly interjected, "Of course, my parents want to have a dinner for the wedding party after rehearsal. They're as excited as you are, and they have lots of questions, too."

■ ▩ ■

Fred Alexander was happy for me, pumping my hand over and over when I informed him of the engagement at work the following day. Even the often-grouchy Ernie shook my hand, smirked, and slapped me on the back, but as was typical for Ernie, he couldn't let the moment go by without saying something sarcastic. "Marriage can be great," he declared, "but you sure as hell are gonna lose your freedom." I didn't respond. I just smiled and nodded slightly, not wanting to get into any discussion where Ernie would expound upon all the negatives of marital life.

Planning and decision-making ruled all the time we spent together in the days and weeks that followed. Some weekday nights, we'd drive to one another's residence to talk in person; other nights, we'd talk on the telephone, causing me to amass large long-distance charges to the phone in my apartment. Fortunately, Second Street Methodist and Reverend Bishop were available October 14.

Requiring equal attention was a decision on where we'd live. We spent Saturday and Sunday afternoons that winter looking for an apartment. Our desire was to find a place somewhere on the far east side of Evansville, about equidistant from her school in Pemberton and my job on the south side. Both being of the nature to put all our energies into issues or challenges that faced us, we focused on finding the apartment as quickly as we could. During the first week of March, we made our decision. It was not an apartment but a two-bedroom duplex with a nice-sized kitchen and living room with wall-to-wall carpet, something I'd never experienced in a home, on the main highway that led from Evansville east to the small upriver town of Newburgh. The one-story structure was part of a modest development of duplexes built about fifteen years earlier. We decided we'd use the second bedroom as a study for her, as Anne always had lessons to prepare for school the following day. I didn't bring much work home, although I read industry magazines and literature about my dual profession of advertising and public relations and studied books devoted to public speaking.

Five months later, I got a phone call that changed our lives.

Bruce Wilson and his longtime colleague Gary McGlasson had

established their public relations and advertising agency in Evansville in the late 1940s and built it through hard work and quality service that got desired results for their clients. Wilson-McGlasson assisted clients with advertising needs, but the company's strength was public relations. Their clients included one of Evansville's major banks, a utility, and a wide range of manufacturing, retailers, and organized labor. It was the agency's responsibility to help clients build their reputations, and it had a reputation for doing its job well.

Wilson and I first met not long after I joined the Press Club, and he'd apparently been impressed with this neophyte's demeanor and the reputation I'd gained among the membership. As a graduate of Evansville College—which had been renamed the University of Evansville in 1967—Wilson had been aware of my athletic prowess on the Purple Aces baseball team. But it was the work ethic and ability to get my furniture company's name connected to community activities and in so many positive articles in the newspapers and television news coverage that he said led him to call me on Friday, August 11, and invite me to have lunch at the Press Club the following Monday.

Throughout the weekend, I was on pins and needles. "What could he want?" I asked Anne more than once, admitting I'd not had the nerve to ask Wilson for the intent of his invitation.

"I bet it has to do with the club, perhaps an office. You've been a member almost five years, and you've served on committees; maybe he wants you to be a chair or an officer."

"Could be. In fact, that's probably the reason. Or maybe he wants to invite me to get involved in a community activity. I've enjoyed my volunteer time with the American Cancer Society PR committee and getting to know Bob Dolson of his staff. Bob sure knows PR." I paused a moment before continuing, "Oh, well, I won't worry about it. No telling what it could be."

It wasn't unusual for me to have lunch at the Press Club in downtown Evansville, so when I left the office at 11:30 on August 14 after telling Ernie where I was going, my boss undoubtedly thought nothing of it.

"Great to see you, Davie," Bruce Wilson said, flashing a toothy grin and extending his right hand to greet me, the left hand holding his normal lunchtime friend, a martini with two olives and a twist. "Hope you had a good weekend," he stated while gesturing toward a corner table that offered some privacy from most of the reporters, other media staffers, and men from a variety of professions. Those in the media were "A" or voting members of the club, while persons in advertising or public relations were "B" members, and anyone else in a profession or politics who could pay the higher annual dues for "C" membership was eligible to apply.

Food was of average quality, but the club depended on it and the bar bills to supplement dues income. Veteran newspaper reporters were notorious for spending long hours at the bar. In fact, some columnists were known to write their best after they'd had a few drinks. Radio and television reporters didn't drink while on duty and would frequent the club if they got off work by the early evening. The older PR and advertising guys, and especially the "C" members, were the heaviest users of the facility and could be found there almost anytime between the 10:00 a.m. opening and midnight closing. Since female reporters belonged to Women in Communications, very few women were members of the Press Club, but all the service staff and the club manager were female.

Sadly, it was not uncommon for manager Frieda Walters to have to call a taxi about once a week shortly before the club closed to take home a member or two who had overindulged in their favorite spirits while trying to solve all of the world's problems with anyone who would engage with them. Frieda prepared drinks if the bartender called in sick, and her language could be as crusty as anyone else's. As with the other women on the staff, Frieda had to put up with dirty jokes and other raw comments that members made without any regard to being offensive. It was just part of the job and the times.

"Can I order you a drink?" Wilson inquired as we took our seats at the four-person table, me facing the open dining room, he across the table from me.

"No, thank you, sir," I replied, wanting to say I never drank during the day, but that could be interpreted as a put-down and I certainly didn't want to make my host uncomfortable.

"Well, good for you. I wish I didn't drink this stuff at lunch, but I always seem to have one. It's nothing but a vile habit. Never more than one, mind you, but one nonetheless." It was the truth, I learned later. Wilson always limited himself and, in fact, drank it so slowly often some was still in the glass when he left the table.

I was impressed with the agency president's attire: a solid, light-gray suit; medium-width light- and dark-blue-striped tie; white shirt with a thin gold bar threaded through small holes in the collar and behind the tie's knot; French cuffs monogrammed with a simple *W*; and gold cuff links. *French cuffs! Must earn a lot.* Wilson had a matching dark-blue handkerchief stuffed in the breast pocket, folded to a point at the top. He was the epitome of a suave businessman. I guessed him to be just under six feet tall, and his build indicated he worked out on a regular basis. His perfectly-groomed hair and his eyes were about the same color as mine, but he had a round face and sported a well-trimmed, thin mustache. He no doubt enjoyed some of the finer things in life because he made certain his silver link–banded Rolex watch was showing slightly outside his left arm sleeve. He wore a simple gold wedding band and on his right hand, a Masonic ring. I recognized it because Jenny's dad was a Mason at the Pemberton chapter. As usual, I wore a sport coat, this time a brown tweed with a white shirt and a solid dark-brown tie. Although I worked in a relatively small company, I was expected to wear a coat and tie every day.

After we ordered lunch—a BLT with French fries and a Pepsi for me and a thinly-sliced steak sandwich ("Medium well, please") with fries and black coffee for Wilson—he got down to business.

"Davie, I know you wonder why I asked you to meet me today, so I'll get right to the point." Pausing for only an instant, and looking me squarely in the eyes, he said, "I'd like you to come work for me."

Wham! There it was. No beating around the bush. No leading up to an offer. No inquiry as to whether I was happy with my job or what I wanted to do in my future. There it was, the cold, hard words: "I'd like you to come work for me." I was so caught off guard I just sat there, wide-eyed, my jaw dropping slightly to leave my mouth open with no sound coming out. Wilson gave me no chance to comment.

"I admire your work. I'm well aware of how successful you've been at Alexander's, and your good reputation in our profession is more than you may realize. Bob Dolson has spoken highly of you. I'd like you to be on my team, and I have an offer I think you'll like." Without any inquiry as to whether I was interested in leaving the furniture retailer or what I might want to do in the future, the always take-charge Wilson laid the offer on the table, glancing to make certain his voice wasn't carrying to the nearest table of members about twelve feet away. He'd smartly positioned himself so he was facing the corner of the room where I was sitting.

"As you may know, Davie, my agency is almost twenty years old. Gary McGlasson and I are both fifty and we've been quite successful; we have a strong list of clients and a quality staff of seventeen, and we're growing in revenue. Our future looks bright."

After pausing for a moment, he began to make the offer. "Ownership of the Dodgers' farm team here is unhappy with the size of crowds they've been drawing and want to ratchet up attendance next season. They have a pitifully small staff that handles PR, marketing, and ticket sales, and they need help, advice. So they've hired us—it hasn't been announced yet—and I think you are the absolute perfect person we could bring on board to handle this account. Number one, you know baseball. Number two," Wilson grinned as he said, "rumor has it you're a big LA Dodgers fan. Number three, based on everything I've observed and heard about you, you have the work ethic and PR abilities to potentially be a highly valuable member of our agency." Breaking from the seriousness of his comments, Wilson said as he grinned again, "Of course, you'd have to put up with Gary McGlasson's ravings about Southern Illinois." McGlasson was an alumnus of Southern Illinois University. Ever since 1961, the mere mention of the school had made me wince.

"As for salary, I'm guessing what I have to offer is a little more than what you're making now." Wilson didn't know what I made, but he and McGlasson had figured Fred Alexander couldn't pay a competitive wage to that of an agency. "Your starting salary would be twenty thousand a year with a guaranteed five percent raise after one year if you're doing the type of work we would expect and you're also happy being with us. After that, raises would depend on a variety of factors, including your progress and company revenues." I felt blood drain from my face. I couldn't believe what I was hearing. A salary more than double what I was making now! I must be dreaming.

Not giving me an opportunity to respond, Wilson offered more. "You wouldn't get a car from us, but we would pay mileage for every mile you drove yours while on the job and that includes any volunteer activities you engage in in the name of Wilson-McGlasson." There was more.

"Bob Dolson told me you're getting married in a couple of months. Although we don't give a week of vacation until after the first year, we'd be willing to let you have one for a honeymoon." Taking only the slightest of pauses, Wilson continued, "Finally ..."

Finally? There's more?

"... insurance. We don't have the greatest of plans, but it's a good one. Group insurance for health and life. It's something you've got to have, especially if you'll soon have a wife. The company would split the cost with you, and it'd be taken out of your paycheck once a month, although we pay our employees every other Friday." Wilson had been upbeat throughout his presentation and with bright, open eyes and an infectious enthusiasm, he inquired, "What'd'you say?"

Finally, I had a chance to speak. My head was spinning with thoughts.

What *do* I say? I thought, still overwhelmed by the rapid-fire offer, but smart enough not to shed tears or break into the biggest grin I'd ever had in my life, both of which I wanted to do at the moment. "Well, Mr. Wilson—"

"Bruce. It's Bruce. Just call me Bruce," Wilson pleasantly interjected.

"Mr. ... Bruce," I continued, "I must admit I'm startled." My heart was about to beat out of my chest. I'd become cotton-mouthed and reached for my glass of water, took a sip, swallowed, and continued, "I'm highly honored by your comments about me. And your very fair offer and the opportunity to join your agency ... well—"

Wilson interrupted again, "You'd also have your own office, but you'd have to share a secretary with others."

Own office ... secretary? This has to be a dream!

I settled down, and he answered immediate questions I had about the agency, the local baseball club, and the responsibilities I'd have. Wilson clarified that servicing the baseball franchise would be my main responsibility, but as with all of his staff, I could expect to have other clients as well. At the outset, however, I'd be given plenty of time to get my arms around the Dodgers and all the challenges they faced in attracting attendance.

My beloved major league Dodgers had played their last game in Brooklyn in September 1957. Ownership moved the club to Los Angeles to start the '58 season, a decision that angered Dodger legions in New York and thrilled their soon-to-be stalwarts on the West Coast. What made matters worse for New Yorkers was the Giants announced they were moving to San Francisco. The decision to take the Dodgers from

Flatbush had stunned me. *No more Brooklyn Dodgers? No more Ebbets Field? No more Carl Furillo banging into the right field wall? No more Duke Snider home runs? Impossible!* Admittedly, my interest in the team had waned slightly after Jackie Robinson retired following the '56 season, but I was still a fan.

Although the Evansville franchise was affiliated with the parent club, it was privately owned by local businessmen. The team played its games at Gibson Park, built in 1929 and named for Evansville native Pete Gibson who had a remarkable career with the Boston Beaneaters of the National League from 1886 to 1903. The ballpark had a capacity of five thousand fans, but the local Dodgers' lack of success on the field in recent years had led to a decline in attendance, much to the chagrin of the owners. The Dodgers played in the Trailblazer League, Double-A baseball two levels below the majors. It was an eight-team league comprised of franchises in Iowa, Illinois, and Indiana, and the Dodgers had finished at or near the bottom three of the past four years. Average attendance for the '67 season, which was thankfully coming to an end, was little more than one thousand. On the Saturday afternoon prior to my meeting with Bruce Wilson, the game between seventh-place Keokuk and last-place Evansville had drawn a paltry 327 fans.

"I know what my answer probably will be, but without seeming to be disrespectful, may I please have until tomorrow morning so I can talk with my bride-to-be tonight?"

"Disrespectful? Goodness, no." Wilson smiled. "Hey, I've been married thirty-one years, and the secret has been that my wife and I share in all major decisions—except what clothes she buys for herself." With that, he let out a loud laugh. "If you hadn't asked for a chance to think about it, I'd have wondered about you."

Getting serious, "We've got our work cut out," Wilson told me. "Although there's nothing better than winning to attract a crowd, it's our job to take the product and find a way to get more fans in the stands. It's that simple. Or should I say, 'that difficult?'"

"It's a great challenge, but it doesn't scare me," I declared, being careful not to commit to the job until I'd spoken with Anne. "I'll talk with my fiancée tonight and get back to you first thing tomorrow morning, if that's okay."

"That'd be great," he replied. "I want you to have a good discussion with ... Anne ... it's Anne, isn't it?"

"Yes, sir, Anne. Anne Keith. Anne's a schoolteacher in Pemberton, and the new year is about to begin, which is exciting to her. She's not only got school on her mind, but all the planning she's been working on for our wedding in October. But she seems to thrive on having lots of balls ... er ... uh ...challenges before her, so she'll handle everything well. We're a lot alike. We like challenges, and we love keeping busy."

As we got up from our seats, Wilson stuck out his right hand to shake mine and said, "I look forward to hearing from you tomorrow, and I hope it's good news. I can't tell you how much I'd enjoy having you join the Wilson-McGlasson team." Reaching into the right inside breast pocket of his suit, his Rolex now fully exposed, he pulled out a business card. "Here're my phone numbers at the office and at home. Call me tonight if you have any questions, or else I'll wait to hear from you tomorrow. I'm always in the office by 8:00, so call anytime after that."

"I'll call you just moments after eight," I replied. I was always in my office at that same time each day but would be late to work so I could make the call from my apartment.

I could hardly contain my emotions as I drove my two-door 1964 silver Corvair Monza back to the furniture company. "What the hell happened to you?" Ernie questioned as I walked into the office. "When did we start taking hour-and-a-half lunches around here?"

"I'm sorry, Ernie. I just got tied up in conversation and didn't realize what time it was until I looked at my watch. I won't let it happen again." It was an easy, truthful promise to make if Anne agreed on the job change. And why wouldn't she?

As luck would have it, Anne and I had prearranged to have dinner at 6:30 p.m. at Charley's Café in Pemberton, and I was to pick her up at her parents' house at 6:15. I arrived fifteen minutes earlier than that, catching her off guard.

"You're early," she stated with a look of surprise, but radiating a smile the moment she answered the knock on the front door.

"Your folks here?" I asked as I walked in and wrapped Anne in a bear hug followed by a hard, deep kiss, not wanting to let her go.

Breathless, she managed to reply, "No, they're not. They've gone to a program at our church. It's a dinner with a speaker from somewhere; I don't know where."

"Fantastic, because I've got something to tell you that you won't believe."

I led her by the hand almost hurriedly to the living room. "What? What is it?" she questioned as we sat on the sofa.

Squeezing her hands and then releasing them so I could gesture, I again said, "You're just not going to believe this."

In rapid-fire succession, I blurted without taking a breath, "I've been offered a job. It's with Bruce Wilson's agency, and it will pay two and a half times what I'm making now. Two and a half! Can you believe it? Oh, Anne, this is an incredible day."

"Davie, slow down," she pleaded softly, excited about my excitement and filled instantly with seemingly a thousand questions. I had tantalized her, and she needed me to calm down, go back to the beginning, and fill in all the blanks to the questions she could begin asking.

Trying to compose myself but still somewhat short-winded, I continued to nearly blurt the details. "Anne, Bruce Wilson offered me a job today. He wants me to join the PR staff of his agency and be responsible for the Evansville Dodgers … well … their marketing … well … advising them on marketing, so they can draw larger crowds to their games. I'd have my own office and use of a secretary. The company would pay car mileage; it has health and life insurance benefits; and, get this, I would make …" and I said it slowly while emphasizing each word, "… twenty … thousand … dollars … a … year … to start, with a guaranteed … five … percent … raise … after … one … year. Twenty thousand dollars, can you believe it?"

Anne sat there, as stunned as I had been when Wilson presented the offer at lunch.

"Davie, don't tease me. Tell me you're telling me the truth. Please, are you serious?" she pleaded, becoming as excited as I.

Looking her in the eyes, my face animated, I replied, "Anne, I'm dead serious. Bruce Wilson offered me a job, and I would make twenty thousand a year to start."

She threw herself at me, squeezing my neck with her arms. "Oh, I can't believe it." Releasing her hold, she pulled back and looking at me wide-eyed, said, "Now tell me all of that again, slowly."

I carefully repeated the offer and said Wilson wanted me to start in two weeks. It didn't seem fair to Fred Alexander to be given such short notice, but it was common practice in employment.

We could hardly eat a bite at the café as we talked about the offer, especially the salary. We quickly dismissed the idea of getting a larger place to live. My car was in good condition, and the two-door blue 1962 Ford Fairlane her dad had proudly purchased for her as a college graduation present had relatively low mileage. Each of us had been raised to respect the dollar, so we were somewhat frugal and agreed that saving as much of the combined $26,000 of our income as possible would become a goal. We knew we'd want our own house someday, and the cars would eventually need to be replaced. I now regretted we hadn't purchased a more expensive engagement ring, but the .5-carat diamond solitaire mounted on an 18-carat gold band that we got at Throgmartin Jewelers in Evansville, the same store where Dad had purchased Mom's ring twenty years earlier, cost $225, and that was as much as we'd felt we could afford at the time. The set included a plain gold band that I would slip on Anne's finger to seal our marriage in October.

At about three minutes past 8:00 the following morning, I called Bruce Wilson with the decision that Anne and I had easily reached.

"You've made my day … no, my month," Wilson responded enthusiastically. "You'll not regret this decision, Davie. You'll enjoy my … our … agency and the responsibilities you'll have. Helping the Dodgers won't be easy, but I know you're up to the challenge." I would become a staff member of the agency the day after Labor Day, five weeks and five days before the wedding. I informed Wilson that although I greatly appreciated the offer of a week for a honeymoon at the time of the marriage, Anne and I would not take one then because of her job. We would, however, like to go somewhere the week between Christmas and New Year's, if that was all right with the agency. It was.

"I'll see you September 5," Wilson said as we ended our conversation.

Now, for the tough part: I had to inform Fred and Ernie.

— —— —

There'd been no way to contact Ernie prior to an 8:30 phone call since he got to the office the same time I was to call Bruce Wilson. "I've been delayed, Ernie," I told him just before leaving the apartment.

"You sure as hell have," came the typical gruff reply. "We've got a lot of work to do today," he added, in an almost scolding tone.

"I'll explain as soon as I get there," I said and then hung up and with heart pounding, left for the office.

"Ernie, I need to talk with both you and Fred," I declared as soon as I arrived, my right hand in a pant pocket, to prevent it from trembling noticeably.

"Fire away," came the unemotional reply as Ernie looked up from his desk. Despite the fact we had worked together for five years, Ernie rarely showed any warmth toward me. He was always preaching and teaching, something I knew had driven me to become a more effective public relations professional than I'd have been if I'd worked under a much more forgiving and less demanding boss. Closing the door, I turned toward the desk and realized Ernie's grim face wouldn't make this any easier. "Ernie, I'm resigning," I announced straightforwardly, with no emotion in my voice or face. "I've accepted a position with Wilson-McGlasson," an agency Ernie knew well because of its longevity in the community and the profession.

Dazed, he stared for a moment. "The hell you say. Bruce Wilson? Why that old shit head, taking you away from me … us!" Ernie paused. "The hell you say!" Deflated, Ernie sat there and lowered his head.

"Ernie, the offer came out of the blue. I've loved it here. I've loved working with you. But Bruce Wilson approached me and made an offer I couldn't refuse."

"How much is he gonna pay you?"

"Twenty …" I caught himself and decided it was no one's business to know. "Much more than here, Ernie."

"Damn, those agency boys sure as hell pay a lot," he replied with a twinge of sarcasm. "But they should because they charge their clients a hell of a lot. Hell, they have to charge so they can afford their fancy cars and their fancy clothes."

"Ernie, it's not just the money, but the opportunity. You've taught me more than you'll ever know, and I think I've really grown here. But I'll have the opportunity to work with a variety of clients and grow even more. I'm not certain what I eventually want to do in this profession, but I know I seek different experiences."

"When you leavin'?" he questioned, the tone of his voice now one of resignation to the fact he would lose someone of whom he'd grown fond, although he'd never shown it or said it, and wouldn't. To do so would be displaying emotion, and Ernie wasn't about to allow a crack in his hard outer shell.

"The end of next week, Friday before Labor Day."

"Damn. Then you'd better go tell Fred." He stared at me with a forlorn expression as I opened the door and walked down the hallway.

Fred Alexander was disappointed. He revealed he'd privately targeted me to take over all his marketing efforts when Ernie retired, believing that not to be but two or three years away. He'd hoped that in heading up the company's advertising and public relations efforts, I'd bring in another young, energetic person who'd join me in developing a more vibrant marketing program than would be possible under Ernie. Even Alexander couldn't get Ernie to change from his set-in-concrete marketing philosophies that had become "old school" to the point the company's newspaper ads and sales themes basically had the same look as the year Ernie came on board. Fred said he was now kicking himself that he hadn't talked with me about the future, but it was clear he couldn't come close to matching Wilson's offer. I was relieved he offered congratulations, expressed sorrow that he would be losing me, and stated Wilson had made a wise decision.

"Very wise," said Fred. "He's a lucky man to get you, and you'll do well." He paused and then said, "I hope we'll stay in touch through the years, Davie. I'm really impressed with you, not just as a professional, but as a person. You'll never know the number of people who've come up to me over the years and commented about your personality, your demeanor, and your work in the community. It's been my fortune to've had you on my staff for five years, and I'll always be grateful and thankful. I wish I'd expressed that to you before now. I'm really sorry I hadn't." I swelled with pride.

"And there's something else you should know," he continued. "Ernie really likes you. In fact, it's more than 'likes,' though he wouldn't admit it. He and I've talked often about you, and without saying it to one another, each of us knew you'd leave one day. Heck, I can't offer the opportunity an agency or a bigger corporation can, but I'd hoped you'd want to stay. I don't blame you for wanting to go elsewhere. You owe it to yourself, and to Anne, to grab onto the bigger ring."

Work at the office the final two weeks was routine, although the atmosphere was eerily quiet as Ernie dealt with the loss he was soon going to experience. On my last day, Fred and Mildred Alexander had a catered lunch for the home office store staff and those management personnel who could break away from what were now five Alexander stores that included one in Owensboro, Kentucky, nearly forty miles slightly southeast of Evansville. Fred presented me with a gift of a dark cherry rocker and expressed his feelings well, thanking me for the job I did and wishing me well. He even invited Mildred and himself to the nuptials by boldly stating in front of everyone, "We're looking forward to being at your wedding."

Ernie said nothing at lunch even when Fred asked if anyone had anything they'd like to add. There was an uneven chorus of "You've expressed it well, Fred," when he made the invitation. I didn't realize it, but Ernie was struggling emotionally. Fred had told me after lunch I was free to leave anytime I wanted, as I had cleaned out my desk of personal belongings and taken some personal files from a metal file cabinet, all of which I placed in a tan cardboard box sitting on my chair. At midafternoon, I broke the uneasy quiet of the office by holding out my right hand and saying, "Well, Ernie, thank you for having me here." As Ernie looked up from his desk, saw the extended hand, and rose to shake it, I witnessed something I'd never seen and had thought I'd never see: Ernie's eyes covered by mist. *My God, he cares after all. He really cares!*

Ernie dropped his head for a moment, raised it, and began softly, something totally out of character for him, "Son ... er, uh ... kid ..."

Son? Son? Did he say, "Son"? Not Ernie, not hard, cold, irascible, sometimes crass, Ernie.

"I'm grateful for having worked with you. I hope you didn't think of me as too difficult to work with." He cleared his throat. "I know I'm set in my ways. I know I'm demanding. And I know I don't express myself in a very nice way sometimes ..."

What an understatement! I thought.

"But I always wanted you to do your best work, and I hope you'll look back and think kindly of me."

Realizing this veteran mentor knew he was losing an important part of his life, I struggled to keep my voice from breaking as I said, "Aw, Ernie, you've been great. You built a foundation for my professional life that I'll be grateful for forever. You taught me far, far more than you'll ever know. And I thank you immensely. I'll never forget you."

It appeared for an instant Ernie was about to come around his desk, but just as he started, he stopped, unwilling to let his emotions take him too far. "Here, I have something for you." He picked up an unwrapped, new hardbound book and handed it to me. "This might come in handy." It was *Principles of Public Relations & Cases I Have Known*, written by David Smith, known worldwide as a guru in the profession.

"Why, thank you, Ernie. I look forward to reading it and will treasure it. I really appreciate it."

After shaking hands one more time and flexing my fingers from Ernie's strong grip, I carried my box of belongings to my car, sat inside, looked at the outside of the building, and thought of the important years I'd spent there and then picked up the book and opened the front cover.

On the first page was a handwritten note: "To Davie—Never forget good grammar. Between you and me! Irregardless!—Ernie, September 1, 1967." "Me" had been underlined three times. A line had been drawn through the "Ir" of "Irregardless." It was a reminder that I'd once used the word when speaking with Ernie and was immediately challenged to find it in the dictionary. "There's no damned such accepted word," Ernie insisted. "It's another injustice to English that I detest. When people use 'irregardless,' they mean 'regardless.' He continued, "Think about it. 'Regardless' means 'in spite of.' I don't know what 'ir' means except that it is ir-ritating to me. So just say, 'regardless.'" I stared at the page and then looked out the window and smiled. Ernie was teaching to the last moment. Placing the book in the seat beside me, I started the car, pulled out onto US 41, and headed north, to a new life.

CHAPTER 20

On my second day on the job, Bruce Wilson took me to meet the local Dodgers administrative staff in offices behind home plate and high above the playing field at Gibson Park. It was the park where my baseball future had ended six years earlier. I grimaced when I looked out at the pitching mound. The entire exterior of the ballpark was dark-red brick, as were the columns that rose from behind the tenth row of seating to support the press box and staff offices. The columns blocked views and were an irritant for some of the patrons but nothing could be done about them. All seats were bench seating—wood painted dark blue—but with back supports. Infield and outfield grass was always a rich green, even in the dead of summer, thanks to the tender loving care of grounds superintendent Tony Edwards. In fact, the Dodgers' field had historically been considered the best in the league.

The club's chief executive officer's office had a view of the entire field. The dark-paneled office walls held frames of Brooklyn and Los Angeles Dodgers players who'd had stints with Evansville en route to the big leagues. President and General Manager Bud Stanley's pride and joy was a Branch Rickey-autographed black-and-white photo of Ebbets Field. In between it and a color version of the larger, more modern Dodger Stadium in Los Angeles was a black-and-white of the LA Memorial Coliseum, the unusual temporary West Coast home of the Dodgers from 1958 to 1961. Each of the numerous other photos showing Stanley posing with players, managers, and commissioners from various walks of baseball life sported an autograph "To Bud," followed by a few memorable words, all of which he could recite without looking while mesmerizing any guests who'd dare take a quick tour.

The office's prime feature was a large, dark mahogany desk with a high-backed black-leather chair. Four padded black-leather chairs sat in front of the desk and behind them, in the exact center of the room was a large octagonal dark wood meeting table with eight unpadded chairs. Off to one side and facing a twenty-five-inch diagonal television mounted on a shelf high in the corner of the wall opposite the desk was an all-leather black sofa whose three large-bottom cushions were cracking and showing signs of age. The smell of cigar smoke permeated everything. Bits of ashes were scattered over the desktop.

Bruce Wilson was proud of the fact he'd personally landed the account because he was aware a competitor had been working just as hard at wining and dining Stanley. He'd made no undue promises in order to secure the account, but Wilson convinced the club executive his agency would add someone just to handle the account and would use as many on staff as necessary to achieve the success the Dodgers needed at the box office.

"I've already heard a lot of good things about you," was Bud Stanley's first comment after we were introduced. I sat next to my boss and across the desk from the franchise president.

Drawing on what I would learn was an almost ever-present La Fendrich cigar even at 9:00 a.m. and slowly exhaling, the smoke wafting in his visitors' direction, he said, "I know nothing beats winning games and having a winning record to draw crowds, but we just don't have the horses on staff to develop whatever else it is that will bring people to games." Looking at me, he offered, "We welcome your ideas, your help, and we're willing to listen to everything you propose, I promise you that. Otherwise, the two of you and I wouldn't be meeting today. I also don't want to waste money, but I'm willing to spend it if there is potential we can sell more seats."

I broke in at the same time it appeared Stanley was going to continue, something Wilson would advise me later never to do. "When a client wants to speak, even to get what you might consider meaningless things off his chest, let him. You'll learn more, and you'll appear to be full ears with his interest top of mind. Remember, he's the client. He's paying the bills."

My interjection was "Mr. Stanley, I'll spend all the time that you and your staff want as I learn all I can about your product. I'll spend early mornings, evenings, weekends, whatever it takes, to learn and then present proposals in the belief they'll help all of us achieve the goals we establish." I brimmed with confidence, excited to be connected with baseball again. Judging by his facial expression, I thought Bruce seemed pleased.

"By golly, I think you've already given us a winner," Stanley directed to Bruce as he nodded toward me, blew more smoke, and expressed a slight grin.

"I have tons of confidence in Davie," Bruce replied, "and the others on our staff, too. We'll give you our best effort in everything we propose and do."

All I could think about at the moment was the cigar smoke. I'd endured it for years with Ernie, and now this. "Well, then, let's get started," Stanley replied. "I'll give you a brief overview of the situation, then introduce you to other staff, and, Davie, you can set up appointments with each of them."

Melvin "Bud" Stanley certainly understood baseball and what it took to turn a profit for his owners. He'd been with the club twenty-seven years, the last twenty-one as the chief executive. Thanks to him being a penny pincher, the financial situation had been in the black most of those years, but not the past three, including this season, which had been the worst. The owners, some of whom served on the franchise's board, didn't participate in daily management of the club, leaving that to Stanley, but they'd made it clear they were becoming impatient.

Stanley was balding—in fact, he was mostly bald except for a small amount of gray mixed with black hair above his ears and on the lower back of his head. He was paunchy, short in stature, no more than five-eight with a gravelly voice, ruddy complexion, and bushy, untrimmed, graying eyebrows. His sixtieth birthday had been celebrated with family and friends one week earlier. His biggest vice was the cigars, but he'd have an occasional drink of scotch, keeping a well-stocked bar for visitors in a glass and dark-mahogany credenza behind his desk. He never drank alone. Often, he'd speak without removing the stogie, whether it was lit or not, making it a challenge for visitors to understand what he was saying.

Historically, the ball club had performed exceedingly well, possessing winning records fifteen of the last twenty years. But the team finished at .500 in 1964 and hadn't done even that well the past three seasons. Attendance declined in concert with the won-loss slide, and this year had been the worst of the past four. Even a change of managers for the 1966 season hadn't helped, and Stanley revealed there would be another change for '68, but the announcement hadn't been made to the public. He didn't think the talent pool for the other clubs in the league had been that much stronger than the Dodgers' but conceded his pitching staff had been noticeably weaker. That was a matter to be taken up with the parent club in an effort to get better pitchers assigned to the Evansville affiliate next spring.

The historic winning record had ranked Evansville first or second in the league in attendance during the past two decades. Fans loved their baseball, despite the fact the team was not tied to either of the two major league teams that were favorites of area residents who enjoyed the game—the St. Louis Cardinals being number one and the Cincinnati Reds number two primarily because of the geographic closeness to southwestern Indiana. Sellouts at games hadn't been unusual in the past, with numerous standing-room-only crowds especially for key league playoff games. But average attendance hit 3,973 in 1963 and slid each year to a low of 1,217 this season.

"It's my duty to get better-quality players," Stanley declared, looking out the window toward the ball field below, not directing his comments at either of us in particular. "There's nothing you can do about that. I'm well aware that quality on the field increases the chances of winning baseball, and I'll have some serious talks with LA Dodgers' brass in an effort to make improvements in that arena." Then shifting his eyes to us, he said sternly, "But we've got to do more off the field to attract more fans, and that's why I hired your agency. I understand that ..." He paused. "What's that saying? That 'Rome wasn't built in a day'? Yeah, that's it. But we've just got to get more butts in the seats next season, and I'm all ears as to what you think can be done."

Without hesitating, Bruce interjected, "Bud, there's no reason we can't help you meet that goal, as long as we have your support and that of your staff. I'll leave it to Davie to talk further with you and with your key administrative players as we begin understanding everything you've done in promoting the club. Davie doesn't know it, but we've already pulled every newspaper ad you've had the past five years. He'll study those as part of the backgrounding we have to do." I was surprised, and impressed, by Bruce's revelation of the preparation already underway.

Bruce continued, "I'm glad to know you're willing to put more dollars to work in getting more fans. Some of that spending might be in the form of promotional costs, such as advertising, but some might be in lost revenue, such as offering family discounts. We'll generate a lot of ideas and distill them into a proposal to you. When do you want it from us?"

Stanley thought for a moment, looked at his desk calendar, and then replied, "I know this may seem like a terribly short amount of time to you, but what about October 18? That's six weeks from now."

Without consulting with Bruce, I replied, "When will you know who your new manager will be?"

"I suspect by the end of October," Stanley guessed.

"Then, let's shoot for our presentation to you on October 11."

Bruce was taken aback. His new account executive didn't even know what kind of staff support he had at the office and here he was promising a proposal a week earlier than Stanley had advanced. I hoped I hadn't been too brash. I knew I was a quick study. The only question was whether the agency staff could produce for me, especially the graphics people.

The club executive replied with a hint of a smile, "Bruce, I knew from the outset I'd like this young man." Stanley paused. "Then the eleventh it will be."

━ ▬ ▬

The following day, I was back at Gibson Park, interviewing staff I'd met the previous day. Bruce Wilson had told me he thought the meeting with Stanley had gone quite well and that I'd made a positive impression but he cautioned me not to overpromise on anything the agency might be required to do. He said I was to focus 100 percent on the Dodgers, that any work I would do for other clients would wait until later that fall. In fact, I wouldn't be assigned to assist other agency staff until Bruce was convinced the Dodgers' promotional plans were fairly well in hand, provided, of course, Bud Stanley approved of them and a time table for their implementation.

Key among the team's staff was public relations vice president Terry Simic. Simic was essentially a one-man department in carrying out his responsibilities for marketing, which included all promotions and ticket sales. He was stretched thin, almost to the point of breaking, especially with the decline in attendance, loss of profits, and pressures from Stanley who was reacting to the owners' unhappiness with the state of the club. He'd tried numerous promotions and wanted to try others but had met resistance from his boss. His renewed hope was that in hiring the agency, Stanley would be willing to spend dollars he'd so far been reluctant, or unwilling, to spend.

Simic and I looked at the list of promotions the club had waged during the past five years. I thought them fairly bland but didn't express an opinion, not wanting to appear like a know-it-all in only the first meeting with the client. After all, Simic had been trying his best under the circumstances. I needed him as an ally, not an opponent.

"Bud just hasn't wanted to spend much money the past three years," an obviously tired and somewhat exasperated Simic confided in such a way I knew he was asking me to maintain confidence.

"I understand," I replied, "and let me just say any references you ever make to Bud will be between you and I ... er ... me. I used to work for someone who didn't always want to make expenditures in advertising and other promotions I thought were necessary, so I know some of what you've been dealing with." Such an admission from someone ten years his junior had to be comforting to Simic and spelled the beginning of a close relationship. We would be "Davie" and "Terry" to one another, never anything more formal.

The two of us spent more than three hours discussing everything about the club, including management, the on-field team, team managers, promotions that had worked or hadn't, proposals that Bud had rejected, and the southwest Indiana baseball community. When we realized it was past 12:30 p.m., we decided to go to lunch at Pearl's, a neighborhood bar that served what many believed were the best breaded tenderloin sandwiches in the city. The meat stuck so far outside a hamburger bun it could have been cut in two for two meals. Inside the toasted bun were lettuce, pickle, and onion and so much mayonnaise it almost dripped onto the plate when a customer bit into the sandwich. Neither of us drank alcoholic beverages during the workday, but the bar was a favorite of Terry's because of its food.

At lunch, we discussed food offerings to fans at the ballpark. "Bud has always wanted to keep most prices as low as possible, not willing to gouge parents in the pocketbook," Terry offered, "especially for food that's popular with children. On the other hand, he feels it's okay to charge a little extra for beer, and that's where we're able to make some extra profit. The quality of the fried food is okay, not great." Ticket prices had been held steady for years; $1.50 for adult general admission and fifty cents for children. Reserved and box seats were fifty cents to a dollar higher.

Lunch was followed by four hours of separate meetings with other staff members, with the remainder interviewed all of the next day. My plan had been to learn everything I could about the franchise, and after two and a half days of talks with staff ranging from the general manager to the grounds superintendent, I felt I had enough to begin discussing a plan with Bruce and other agency staffers. I'd also asked Terry to let me borrow copies of as many promotions of the past five years as could be gathered.

After taking two days to decipher all that I'd learned and working through the weekend, not even having Sunday dinner with Anne or seeing my parents or her folks, I was ready for joint meetings with Bruce, two other account executives, and the chief graphics designer. Throughout an entire day in which lunch was brought into the agency's boardroom with its large, rectangular dark-oak table, I presented the information I'd learned from the Dodgers.

Bruce seemed blown away by the detail of the information that I'd gathered and by the way in which I presented it. But he didn't say anything about his impression, leaving that for another time. I laid out my initial thoughts about short-term and long-term goals and plans and asked for input from everyone. What would be presented to the Dodgers had to be an agency proposal, not Davie Miller's alone.

The week of October 8 was the biggest of my life. I would be presenting my/our agency's first major proposal to a new client only three days before my wedding. The stress should have been enough to weaken any man, but I was only twenty-seven, physically fit, and emotionally and mentally prepared for what lay ahead.

"Mr. Stanley and Mr. Simic," I formally addressed the two seated Dodgers' executives, "Mr. Wilson, Mr. Forbes, and I, along with other staff members of the agency team, have spent many long hours distilling all the information gathered from you and others on your staff and preparing what we believe is the very exciting plan we will present to you this morning. If you agree with what we place before you, we're convinced of short-term and, more importantly, long-term increases in the fan base for the Evansville Dodgers."

Standing at the end of the table, beside an overhead projector and in front of an easel that held various covered graphics, I exhibited a strong, firm voice and I'm certain my face exuded my confidence in what I was saying. I knew full well that while both men wanted an increase in attendance, Bud Stanley could hardly wait to see the bottom line—the price tag for all the elements of the package—and Terry Simic was anxious to see the details and what they meant to him in regard to more work. I sought to put each man at ease.

"There's undeniable value in the proposal you will hear and see, and be assured that Curt Forbes as our graphics director, I, and others will be much involved, or as involved as you want us to be, in working with Terry to make certain all of the approved elements are carried out this off-season, next season, and beyond." I looked for assurances that the clients were ready to listen with interest and then began.

Nearly three hours later, without a break for as much as the restroom but with numerous questions from the club's two administrators, the presentation was over.

"Gentlemen," the ever-cautious Stanley began, "overall, I really like what I've seen and heard. The plan's damned exciting, and while I have to do some close inspection of the costs in relationship to our expected revenues, I don't see a reason at the moment not to sign off on what you've proposed for this fall and winter and for next season. I have some reservation about someone being dressed up as a mascot, but I'll ponder on that before responding. And I might have some hesitation about a couple of the longer-term proposals."

He paused, looked at the excitement in Terry's eyes, and continued, "But I certainly know there's no need in approving the short-term plans without also agreeing to the bigger picture you've presented. So give me some time to think about all this and get back to you." I flashed a look of concern, which Stanley immediately picked up on. "Now don't worry. I gave you a pretty short window to study our club and make a series of proposals, so I expect the same of myself. How about Friday morning for an answer?" Smiling at me, he continued, "It'd be grossly unfair of me to have you worrying throughout your wedding weekend about whether I was going to approve anything or not." Everyone chuckled. "In fairness," Stanley stated, "I know Friday's a big day for you, Davie, so what if we meet first thing, say, 7:30 that morning? I'll have some coffee and doughnuts brought in, so we'll have something to put in our stomachs while we talk further about the proposal." Everyone agreed, and the session adjourned.

"Let's go to the Press Club for lunch," Bruce insisted in the parking lot when we three colleagues emerged from the ballpark. Since we'd ridden together, there wasn't much choice for Curt or me, but it would be good for all of us to digest the activities of the morning verbally.

In the passenger side of the front seat, my shoulders sagged from relief that the presentation was over. I was overwhelmingly pleased as to how well it had gone. "Davie, Curt," our chief executive said as he entered the driver's side and slid behind the wheel, "I am damned proud of both of you for how you handled our proposals this morning. You did a hell of a job. A hell of a job. I couldn't have done it better myself." We two junior colleagues beamed. "The presentation was clear, concise. The graphics on the overhead and the easel illustrated everything just as we had discussed in our planning meetings." Looking at me and then to the backseat at Curt as he started the engine, Bruce said, "The two of you worked really well in your planning sessions, and it was obvious you spent a lot of time together. I am proud of both of you. Damned proud."

Bruce could have announced a raise in salary for both of us, and it wouldn't have meant more than his praise. As he began driving, he declared boastfully, "I bet ole Bud will approve virtually everything we proposed. He's no dummy, and he knows his ass is on the line. He really doesn't have much choice other than to agree to a well-thought-out plan. If it fails, then we have to shoulder a lot of the blame. But if he can field a stronger team, in time, the promotions will get him and the owners what they want. There's nothing we can do regarding the club's profit-and-loss situation. Our sole goal is to get more fans in the stands over a period of time. We can do it."

━ ▬ ▬

I was floating on cloud nine when I picked up Anne for dinner. Despite the fact her mind was clouded with wedding details, she listened to how well I said things had gone. She couldn't have seemed happier. Actually, despite all the details associated with the wedding, all the planning was in place, the rehearsal and dinner would be in two days, and she would be Mrs. David Harold Miller in three.

■ ▩ ■

Stirring the sugar he'd spooned into his coffee, and clenching an unlit, new cigar in his teeth—*at breakfast!*—Bud Stanley told everyone to have a seat at the eight-person conference table in the middle of his spacious office. It was 7:30 a.m. I wasn't a superstitious person, or I might have worried about the date being Friday the thirteenth. Just as he'd said on Wednesday, and because he was so frugal, Stanley had only coffee and doughnuts available, but he kept small bottles of orange juice in a tiny refrigerator behind his desk, so Curt and I each accepted one to have with our pastries. We were so nervous we hardly ate a bite.

"Gentlemen," Stanley began. "I'm approving your plan." Terry Simic grinned, having already known the decision, but we other three sat there, waiting for the shoe to drop, and it did, but with a soft landing. "There's a slight caveat. I want to reserve the right to relook at the plan next July, which should allow time for changes in it going forward, if they're needed. We should know by July how successful we've been and whether we need to begin considering changes for the next off-season and regular season. Fair enough?"

Bruce was the first to answer. "Eminently fair, Bud. We couldn't agree more with the review date. Since the season begins in early April, I agree we'll have a good idea by July as to how the plan's working. There's really not much that could be done to impact attendance from that point 'til the end of the season in early September, because the promotions will have been set, but we'd know whether any drastic action is necessary. Regardless, our review in July would begin impacting off-season plans."

Our agency's design of action began with the announcement of the new team manager in late October and an accompanying media blitz with him being available for interviews by television and radio stations and newspapers throughout the Tri-State area of southwest Indiana, southeast Illinois, and a section of northern Kentucky just across the river from Evansville. From November through January, the manager and known returning players, especially the more popular ones, would be made available to area service and fraternal clubs, such as the Lions, Kiwanis, Elks, and the American Legion. A new slogan, *"Evansville Dodgers, the Tri-State's Team,"* would be blazoned in all promotional materials and news releases in an effort to tie the club to the broad region, reaching as many fans as possible. Once the 1968 season began, players with good grammar and diction would be required to be available to speak to school classes on mornings when there were night games at home, and the agency would take the lead in setting up the appearances, just as it would be responsible for working with service and fraternal clubs.

And, for the first time in its history, the team would have a mascot. *Buster,* a costumed blue-and-white (the team colors) duck, would be on the fringes of the playing field, in the stands during the games, and available to schools and at other tri-state sites prior to, during, and after the regular season. The duck was chosen because it was a popular fowl in the area and children were known not to fear it. There also was a very subtle tie to the name *Dodgers*—duck and dodge, if you will. A popular theory for why the moniker was chosen for the Brooklyn professional baseball club in the early 1900s was that Flatbush had many trolleys and it was not uncommon for people to dodge them—thus, *Dodgers*. An upright, costumed, friendly, happy duck who engaged in goofy antics on and off the field could be an attraction that would draw children and perhaps adults, too.

Promotions were planned for every home game, with an emphasis on "the family" on weekends. Group discounts, which had been offered for a decade, were made even bigger in an effort to attract service, fraternal, and civic clubs, with a deeper discount offered for school groups. Special ticket and food pricing for families would be offered on weekends and holidays, and pregame activities on Saturday and Sunday included "meet and greet" the players and coaches prior to the games and/or "how-to" clinics on the playing field, teaching children how to field, run the bases, bat, and throw. Newspaper ads throughout the season would feature profiles of the manager, coaches, and players with an emphasis on why each one enjoyed playing in Evansville. All radio broadcasts of the games would feature a recorded interview with a player, coach, or manager. Our plan seemingly left nothing to chance in an effort to attract fans to the team and thus to the games.

Saturday, October 14, was nearly a Pemberton Chamber of Commerce picture-perfect day. When the wedding ceremony began at 4:00 p.m., the sky was partly cloudy, slightly more clouds than blue, the air mild with the temperature hovering at 74 degrees. The fall season was just beginning to turn leaves near the church into their annual shades of earthy colors.

Anne was resplendent in the wedding dress she'd chosen, of course with her mother's help—whether requested or not. The full-length white peau de soie dress with lace appliqué featured elbow-length sleeves, a satin bow and train in the back, and a fingertip veil held in place by a small bouquet of white mums, similar to those carried by maid of honor Cheryl Winder and each of the four bridesmaids, one of them Peggy Sue. They wore simple elbow-length avocado-green brocade, full-length dresses with bows in the back, and their bouquets were a cascading mixture of white mums with green leaves.

Bobby Hatcher, the groomsmen, and I sported black tuxedos, black ties and cummerbunds, and black studs up the front of our stiff tux shirts. I was impressed with how sharp my buddy Bobby looked. He was good-looking but surprisingly didn't have a steady girlfriend. Of course, both mothers had purchased dresses for the occasion, a persimmon-colored one for Jenny Keith and cobalt-blue one for Mother, both midknee length, with matching pillbox hats. Brandt Keith wore a tuxedo for the first time in his life, renting one along with the other men in the wedding party. Dad wore his only dark-blue suit. He saved it for special occasions, wearing a combination of five other sport coats and suits in his closet for his teaching duties at school.

The altar was decorated simply with a large basket of white mums and a candelabrum with seven white candles on each side.

The planning was a huge amount of work for a ceremony that lasted only twenty-seven minutes, but the wedding couldn't have gone more smoothly. Reverend Bishop, who had jokingly shown up wearing an LA Dodgers cap at rehearsal the previous afternoon, pronounced us "man and wife" and then addressed the 117 people in the pews. "It is my distinct honor to present to you, Mr. and Mrs. David Harold Miller." With that, applause broke out, punctuated with a few cheers from the younger adults, while Anne and I began our slow walk hand in hand down the center aisle, grinning from ear to ear. To each side of the narthex was a set of stairs that led to the basement where we were joined by our parents to form a receiving line for all the well-wishers.

Sugar cookies and punch—a mixture of 7Up and fruit juice—were available until we newlyweds cut the four-tiered wedding cake and began the tedious task of opening more gifts than we ever imagined we'd receive, especially since a bridal shower had been held for Anne two weeks earlier. To the delight of all the women and the sheer boredom of the men, each gift was opened meticulously so the bows wouldn't be torn (belief being that you'd have one child for each ripped bow), and the name of the giver announced and dutifully recorded before the next gift was opened. One by one, all the gifts were opened; the process seemed to take forever, but Anne and I were truly grateful for the love being shown by relatives and friends. Proudly among them were all the grandparents and Uncle John and Aunt Ann. I deeply regretted that I rarely saw my Johnson family anymore. Fred and Mildred Alexander were there, too. Not surprisingly, Ernie was not.

Our wedding night was our first together in our new home. In 1967, unmarried couples didn't live together. To most religious parents, their children doing so would have been tantamount to sin. Anne and I didn't hold to such belief but out of respect for our parents, we had lived apart. Thus, I had moved into the duplex on Lincoln Avenue shortly after we signed the rental contract, painted the two bedrooms and the living room on the weekends, and purchased furniture at company-cost from Alexander's. Anne began moving her clothing into the residence during the two weeks prior to the wedding. We'd made love there numerous times but had not spent an entire night together there before October 14.

We called our parents on the phone late the following morning but otherwise didn't visit them, spending the day mostly in bed before making preparations that evening for our jobs the following day.

Anne loved teaching second grade. She felt the year she spent with her students was an extremely important one in a child's life. Her emphasis was reading, writing, and arithmetic. There was further work with the alphabet, which the children had begun learning in the first grade, and she expanded their reading abilities at a basic level, working with them to read without stopping to think about the words. She introduced cursive and taught the basics of addition and subtraction. Although she was in her sixth year of teaching, she pored through lesson plans each evening, wanting to make certain the following day would be filled with growth opportunities for each child. Anne was patient but firm in not permitting unnecessary noise or disruptions in the classroom. In return, children were basically responsive and felt kindly toward her. Her goal was to instill a desire to learn and see progress in each child. If love for her came with it, that was a bonus.

I loved my job, too. Within the first week after reporting for work at Wilson-McGlasson on September 5, I knew I'd made the right decision to join the company. Barbara Joachim, known simply as *BJ*, was a spirited secretary who always carried a smile and pleasant attitude and seemed to have the answers to any question I had about the company or people in the community. She'd been with Wilson-McGlasson only five years but had worked as a secretary at another company in Evansville for twenty years before it folded and was thankful to have found her job so quickly after that. BJ welcomed having a third account executive to serve as she wanted to be challenged with a large workload every day. I wasn't much of a typist and welcomed having someone who could prepare letters or news releases that I drafted either by hand or typed with plenty of X-ed-out words. BJ's desk sat just outside the doors of the offices of the three persons she served—Larry Frederick, Kathleen "Kathy" Williams, and me. Wilson-McGlasson had been a trailblazer in hiring Williams, not only because she was a female in a mostly male profession in southwest Indiana but also because she was black. There just weren't that many black professionals in any occupation in the region.

＊　＊　＊

On November 8—carefully chosen because Wednesdays were notoriously "slow news days"—at a news conference held at Gibson Park's home plate on a warm, sunny late morning, Tommy Pesky, his name synonymous with the fiery attitude he exhibited in eight years as a player with three different teams in the majors and ten years before and after that in minor league franchises, was introduced as the new manager. Promising to bring a new brand of on-field baseball to the tri-state, with risky base running and aggressive batting, Pesky said he was "a family man," who would establish a "family-like" atmosphere with his team, promising that each player would care about what the entire squad did, not what any individual accomplished. He was "a no-nonsense" manager who would not permit off-field actions that brought discredit to the team to go unpunished and hoped none would ever take place. He expressed the belief that "General Manager Bud Stanley and the parent club will give me a squad that has the capability of returning winning baseball to Evansville, something the tri-state deserves."

Pesky's introduction proved popular with the media. They loved his one-liners, especially broadcasters who lived for succinct, powerful, or entertaining answers. The evening's sportscasts devoted extra attention to the announcement as did the afternoon Evansville newspaper and the following morning's edition, too. Then Pesky went on the road to visit with media wherever they were located in the region. It would be a physically grueling week for him, but he knew first impressions were extremely important in the club's bid to begin winning the fans.

The plan that had been so carefully created by the agency and approved on October 11 was off to a perfect start.

CHAPTER 21

Anne and I had dreamed of a wedding trip that would take us away from the likely frigid Midwest in late December, and the large pay raise I received upon joining Wilson-McGlasson made it possible. On Thursday, December 21, we flew from Evansville to Chicago to Los Angeles to Papeete, capital of the South Pacific island of Tahiti. It was an extremely long day—we arrived nearly twenty-four hours from the time we arose in Indiana—but we'd been filled with excitement and knew warm weather and opportunities to sleep in the sunshine awaited us.

We took a taxi to the Hilton Hotel in Papeete where we slept about four hours while gentle breezes floated through our open seventh-floor window. Although this was finally our honeymoon, sex wasn't on our minds when we awoke and made plans to join an afternoon tour of the lush splendor of Tahiti with its white beaches and mountainous core. We wanted to see nature's beauty.

There was only one main road around the island, the largest of all of French Polynesia, as the tour bus fought traffic congestion while taking us and our fellow visitors to major tourist sites. At the Museum of Tahiti we saw one of English explorer Captain James Cook's ship anchors, which had been lost in a storm when Cook visited the area in the late 1770s. We stopped where a seventeenth-century Asian temple had stood but weren't enthralled with the menacing-looking stone statues that Polynesians had believed provided protection for them. From what, neither of us was certain. The temple had also been the site of sacrifices of humans to please the gods. But it was the beauty of the land, the rich green of the vegetation, and the enormous variety of flowers and blooms on trees that impressed us most. Our biggest relief came from the tour guide's statement that there were no snakes in the islands.

Following an afternoon in 85-degree heat, we picked up our luggage at the hotel and took a taxi to the port where we boarded our home for the next five nights, the luxurious cruise ship *South Seas*. Hugging and dancing almost like children upon seeing our well-decorated, yet simple cabin with sliding glass door that led to a private veranda on the fifth floor of the six-deck ship, we knew we were about to have the time of our lives with no duties, no worries, and no stresses, just sunshine, food, exploring different islands, lounging on the deck or beach, swimming in the ship pool or the sea, enjoying nonstop music throughout the afternoon and evening onboard, and being in our room in one another's arms whenever we wanted. It would be an idyllic week enveloped in South Pacific splendor.

Best of all, the ship had only 350 passengers, so we wouldn't be dealing with crowds typical of larger ships wherever we went onboard.

When we awoke shortly before 8:00 the following morning, the ship was docked at Raiatea, its port for two days. Breakfast instantly became a favorite, an immense variety of food along the seemingly endless buffet lines. It seemed every type of bread, juice, and meat was available for our choosing, along with soft-boiled, hard-boiled, scrambled, over-easy, or sunny-side-up eggs, as well as omelets with a wide range of ingredients. Certainly, the choices were far more appetizing than the octopus and eel among the options on our dinner menus the night before. As we took seats along one of the expansive windows of the dining room and looked out at the already brilliant sunshine dancing on the aqua-blue water of the enormous lagoon that lay inside the barrier reefs protecting the island, I thought, *This is living!*

We decided not to shop in the town of Uturoa where the ship docked because tours into the island were available and we wanted to take one. Like Tahiti, and like we would find all the islands to be, Raiatea was a lush tropical paradise with greenery draped over a rugged mountain protruding from the center. Bamboo, balsa, mango, and rosewood were everywhere one looked, as were spectacular flowers of an untold number of varieties. There weren't many inhabitants, and they depended upon tourism for their livelihood.

Polynesian myth had established that Raiatea was the birthplace of the world. A demanding hike took us and twelve other fellow travelers up Mount Tamahani, said to be the birthplace of Oro, the god of war. Here, the early inhabitants believed they could see the world—at least the world as they knew it.

The tour included a stop at a beach where our group of fourteen got out of open-air jeeps and into powerboats that took us to a tiny, uninhabited island—a motu—for snorkeling. Neither of us had snorkeled before, but after learning to keep our faces down and the end of the breathing tubes above the calm, shallow water, we had an adventure unlike anything we could have imagined. The colors, sizes, and species of fish provided a kaleidoscopic spectacle, nearly producing open-mouthed laughs as we tried unsuccessfully to reach out and touch them.

Exhausted, we showered and napped briefly in the lounge chairs of our shaded veranda prior to dinner, the extreme quiet of the setting and mild breeze combining for a peaceful atmosphere conducive to relaxation and sleep.

Fortunately, the ship would be at Raiatea all the next day, Sunday. Unfortunately, it was the Sabbath, so the shops in town were closed. We were disappointed, as it was something we hadn't realized, and irritated that the ship's crew hadn't told the passengers in advance. Just as well. It was an opportunity for Anne to keep her sunburned back out of the sun most of the day and relax, although both of us donned masks and snorkeled not far from the ship very late that afternoon.

Monday—another day, another island: Taha'a, Raiatea's close neighbor. One would never have known by looking that it was Christmas Day. There were no displays of decorated trees, ornaments, lights, and presents like back home in the United States, the sun and warmth of the day masking the holy day on the Christian calendar.

As we traveled with a tour group in open-sided but covered jeeps, we could see spectacular peaks rising out of the ocean in the distance, our stop tomorrow, Bora Bora. Like all the days on this trip, the high temperature would be in the mid-80s as the vehicles carried us onto dirt roads through rich green jungles that reminded me of World War II–movie battle scenes. Anne and I were fascinated by the abundance and variety of fruit—short, perhaps four-inch-long bananas; papaya; mango; breadfruit; and coconut. At one scenic stop, descendants of the Morai, dressed in traditional Polynesian costumes of grass or leaf skirts, flowers in the hair of the women, and wide colorful, patterned headbands on shirtless men, demonstrated the opening of a coconut and then offered everyone an opportunity to dip sliced pineapple and banana into the shredded meat inside, one of the most tasty treats Anne thought she'd ever experienced.

The vast majority of vanilla throughout all the islands of French Polynesia is produced on Taha'a, so the next stops were a vanilla bean farm followed by a pearl farm. The rich scent of vanilla made us long to taste some, but the beans weren't ready for processing. We'd never seen black pearls before, and Anne was fascinated. Pearls of various sizes that had been cultivated in the water and harvested were on display and for sale. It seemed obligatory that tour operators *had* to stop at commercial outlets, but then, we understood islanders depended on tourists' dollars for their living.

We took advantage of another opportunity to snorkel off a private motu in the turquoise water of the vast lagoon where our ship was docked and then in our room, shed wet clothes and fell into one another's arms without any regard for the drapes and sliding glass veranda door of our room being wide open. If someone wanted to peek around the dividers on the veranda, so be it. We could have cared less. We were deeply in love and oblivious to anything going on in the outside world.

Anne didn't say anything, but I could tell she was perplexed by my insistence on not joining the others for dinner in the large window-lined restaurant at the aft end of Deck 6. *After all*, I could read her mind, *this is Christmas! We should share it with others.* While enjoying wine prior to ordering our meal and with Christmas music playing softly on the dining room's speaker system, I sheepishly placed a small, blue, velvet-covered box on the white tablecloth in front of her. She stared at me and asked, "What have you done?" Then she looked down and slowly opened the lid. A shiny black pearl necklace lay before her. "Davie, oh, Davie, this is *beautiful!*" I moved behind her and assisted in hooking the delicate silver chain behind her neck. The single pearl glistened against the backdrop of her sun-reddened neck.

As she raised her hands to her shoulders, I held them and then bent and kissed her on the right cheek and whispered, "I found the perfect wedding gift for you."

She didn't know whether to laugh or cry or how to express her feelings. She demonstrated them later in our room.

Author James Michener wrote major novels about the South Pacific and Hawaii and once described Bora Bora as "the most beautiful island in the world." One look at it from a distance and then up close told us why. When we awoke, we opened the cabin's glass sliding door and were challenged to provide a proper descriptive of what lay before us—a lush, vegetation-covered, sheer-faced mountain with twin peaks that appeared to rise from the sea, a stunning, spectacular view. The numerous motu in the atoll surrounding the island had only one opening wide enough for a ship the size of the *South Seas* to pass through.

Bora Bora still contained US ammunition bunkers left over from World War II when the nation had five thousand troops maintaining a supply base. Tourists were warned to stay away from the bunkers because unexploded shells might still be in the area. No one ignored the advice.

Part of the pastoral afternoon was spent in the waist- to chest-deep warm water of the lagoon, snorkeling amid friendly stingray, reef sharks, and an endless variety of colorful tropical fish. It took nerve for us to lightly touch the stingray and shark but following instructions from our guides doing so was soon something most of us water adventurers didn't fear and certainly enjoyed.

The following day would be our last in this South Pacific paradise, a day on Moorea, perhaps the most beautiful of all the Society Islands. The ship anchored in the azure water of Opunohu Bay, providing clear views of the lush green island with jagged peaks and spires that included what many believed was the famous "Bali Hai," the fictional name given by Michener in his Pulitzer Prize–winning *Tales of the South Pacific* and made more famous by Rogers and Hammerstein's *South Pacific*. Leaning against the ship's railing, Anne said she could imagine the female haunting voice singing the song in the movie *South Pacific*, "Bali Hai may call you, any night any day. In your heart, you'll hear it call you, 'Come away, come away.'" It was easy to understand the call—the sugary white sand beaches; multihued lagoons; an abundance of thick, green vegetation; and sheer cliffs and peaks that included Mount Mouaroa—"Bali Hai"—which was formed by an extinct volcano.

Unfortunately for us, the call was to return to winter in Indiana, but an exciting future awaited, and we could hardly wait to enter it.

CHAPTER 22

Six months into the new year, Bruce Wilson and I sat down with Bud Stanley and Terry Simic to review the status of the local Dodgers and our promotional plans. The team was in third place in league standings, and thanks in part to a sellout crowd for a July 4 doubleheader with Davenport and near-capacity crowds the entire home stand of June 30 through July 9, average attendance was running almost a thousand more than at that time the previous year. The club's executives were elated, and thus so were Bruce and I. It was July 10.

"Damn, guys, what a hell of a week we had. Awesome crowds and eight wins out of ten games. Hard to beat that with a stick … no, a two-by-four," Stanley declared as he delivered a closed-fist blow to the dark-green felt-covered desk pad and blew out a ring of smoke from his La Frendrich cigar. He couldn't have been happier. "By God, I hope the parent club is noticing what the hell we've done with the better players they let us have this year, especially the pitchers. I told 'em, 'Quality begets wins, and wins beget fans.' When they assign good players to us, we'll do our best to develop them for a higher level, and at the same time, they'll help us win.

"And my promotional plan has obviously worked well, too."

Bruce didn't comment but glanced at me, and I saw the smugness of a wry smile on his face. He'd always told me, "Remember, it's the client's plan when things go well. We don't take credit. After all, if the client approves our plans, then he spends the money, and it becomes his plan. If things don't go well, he'll let us know that *our* plan didn't work. Doesn't seem fair, but that's the way the agency world turns, and you've got to get used to it."

To his credit, Stanley reconsidered his remark. "Dang, I'm too pumped up. Gotta admit it's the plan of all of us that's worked so well. If it weren't so early in the morning, I'd pour you a drink and we could toast one another. But the season's still got a long way to go, and I realize things can turn for the worse."

The review didn't take long. With all the numbers being so good, the four of us looked at the promotional schedule for the remainder of the season and decided not to make any changes.

The Dodgers were unable to climb above third place through the remaining games but were among the top four teams that made the playoffs. They lost to regular-season champ Terre Haute, who beat Keokuk for the title. But what happened in the stands was as important as the team's improvement on the field. Attendance averaged 2,398, nearly double the previous season. It was a remarkable turnaround. Overall income was higher than 1967 and no doubt Bud Stanley would be in better stead with the owners by the end of the fiscal year December 31.

Bruce was so pleased with the local Dodgers' situation, he gave me additional responsibilities. I was assigned to join Kathy Williams in servicing Central Vanderburgh State Bank and Larry Frederick who had primary responsibility for Hobson Chevrolet, the largest Chevy dealer in the region. But my president made it clear that nothing—even if it meant working nights and weekends—must prevent me from keeping my focus on the baseball club because the account was of prime importance to the agency.

■ ▓ ■

Domestically, 1968 was one of the worst years for internal relationships in the country's history. The war in Vietnam continued not to go well for the United States. Antiwar protestors demonstrated on college campuses and rioted in many cities. President Lyndon Johnson, whose war policies were the target of peace advocates, stunned the country in March by announcing he wouldn't seek reelection. Civil rights leader Martin Luther King Jr., a proponent of nonviolence in the pursuit of racial equality, was the victim of violence; he was assassinated by a white man in Memphis, Tennessee, on April 4, and only two months later, Senator Robert Kennedy, JFK's brother, was shot at a hotel in San Francisco after giving a California presidential primary victory speech. He died a day later. King's death led to riots in major cities. Outside the Democratic

National Convention in Chicago in late August, city police clashed with antiwar protestors, and scores were injured and arrested.

It was an agonizing year. Seemingly, the nation was falling apart. I had my opinions but except for talks at home with Anne, kept them to myself. I was conflicted. As a Christian, I didn't know if I should feel as I did about the war. I was a hawk, wanting the United States to use the atomic bomb if necessary to blast Hanoi off the map, not understanding why our country's leaders weren't doing more to try to win. At the same time, I didn't know whether I should want actions that could lead to the deaths of many thousands, perhaps hundreds of thousands, of people even though they were on the side of the enemy. No doubt my staunch private stance was influenced by the fact Bobby Hatcher had volunteered for military duty only a month after my wedding last October. Bobby would be one of four friends from Barclay who'd serve in Vietnam, the other three being called to duty after the national draft lottery was held in December 1969. It had been the first such lottery since 1942, and those born between 1944 and the end of 1950 were eligible to be called. I wanted the war over as quickly as possible.

I would not, however, present my views of the war to teenagers at the boys and girls clubs and churches where I spoke. If I was conflicted, why should I expose them to my inner turmoil?

Through the late 1960s and early 1970s, I spoke often to youth groups, additionally making occasional guest appearances in pulpits at Sunday-morning worship services in the Evansville area.

Anne and I had regularly attended services since the time we were married and had chosen a United Methodist church near our home as the one where we were most comfortable. The pastor's sermons made the Bible meaningful to everyday life, as opposed to the Bible-thumper–type sermons that preached the Old and New Testaments but never related them to current daily life other than to say a person was "going to Hell when you die if you don't accept Jesus."

The UMC was formed in 1968 when the Methodist Church merged with the Evangelical United Brethren Church, making it one of the largest denominations in the world. Anne became active in the church, taking a Bible studies class on Wednesday nights and serving on the education committee. She had an interest in teaching a children's Sunday school class but hadn't taken the step to volunteer. My job, which often included evening meetings or events with my clients, and my schedule of speaking engagements prevented me from being as active as she. Our faith and prayer lives were strong. While we didn't "wear our religion on our sleeves," as the saying went, we nonetheless tried through action and deed to live exemplary lives. We prayed prior to each meal together, even quietly and briefly in restaurants, and said prayers together in the evening or early morning before going to work, giving thanks for our talents and lives and asking for blessings on others. We were deeply in love and gave God credit for bringing us together and enriching us.

I was sought after as a speaker, especially by small United Methodist churches on Lay Sundays when ordained pastors stepped aside for a message from someone who didn't have a formal education in theology or religion but "walked the talk" in his or her daily life. Although I felt it an obligation to use my speaking talents, the joy of believing I was reaching audiences with my messages was the reward. My thought was if even one person changed his or her life for the better as a result of what I said at each event, I'd be thrilled.

Sometimes, while preparing speeches in the comfort of an easy chair and the quiet of our living room, I'd reflect on the handwritten letter I'd received from an admiring, aging Grandmother Johnson in 1968. Although she'd not heard me speak in person, at seventy-seven years of age, she was filled with pride over reports from others as to "how wonderful" they thought I was in the pulpit.

"Dear David," it began, the writing reflecting a bit of unsteadiness with the pen on the small off-white sheet of notepaper. She wouldn't use my nickname; she didn't believe in nicknames. "This has been a beautiful Sabbath Day. Your grandfather and I went to church this morning and two of our parishioners said they heard you speak at a community church event last week. They praised your abilities and your message. I want you to know I am so very proud of you as is Grandfather Johnson. That brings me back to memories of *long ago* when I spoke pieces. I too was a good speaker, spoke a piece at my commencement, and in churches. I wonder what the younger generation of Johnsons will be."

I'd smile at the thought of her kindness. Perhaps my speaking abilities came from the paternal side of my parents' union and this dear lady.

It may sound boastful, but I believed I was charismatic as a speaker, with hand gestures, facial expressions, and timely raising and lowering of the voice to make my points. I wanted to impress upon young people that even with all the temptations of life, this former athlete dared live the type of life he was urging them to adopt.

My standard title in speaking to either youth or adults was "What Role Are You Playing?" tweaking the message slightly for each audience.

"How many of you are baseball fans?" I'd ask and then look at the typical sea of raised arms. "My idol as a young person—not my hero but my *idol*—was one of the greatest baseball players who ever lived: Jackie Robinson, the first Negro to play major league baseball. But this worship of someone on earth was replaced by worship of the greatest role model who ever lived, Jesus Christ—the guy who would have worn a white uniform with 'number one' on the back and could have played any position. With his connections, I bet he could have thrown a heck of a knuckleball." The comment was assured to bring a laugh.

I typically cited Bible verses at this point. "Let me read two pieces of Scripture written by Saint Paul. The first is I Corinthians 12:4–7. I'm reading from The Living Bible," which had become my favorite by the early '70s, because it spoke in contemporary language.

"'Now God gives us many kinds of special abilities, but it is the same Holy Spirit who is the source of them all,'" I read. "'There are different kinds of service to God, but it is the same Lord we are serving. There are many ways in which God works in our lives, but it is the same God who does the work in and through all of us who are his. The Holy Spirit displays God's power through each of us as a means of helping the entire church." I opined, "Now, 'entire church' to me means 'others' no matter their status in life, not just people in your church.

"The second verse is Philippians 3:12. 'I don't mean to say I am perfect. I haven't learned all that I should even yet, but I will keep working toward that day when I will finally be all that Christ saved me for and wants me to be.'"

I challenged my audience. "My goal is that each person leave here determined to be a greater, more positive Christian role model in all you do. I'll speak to what that should be." I paused, surveyed the audience, and then declared, "I want to share a personal testimony with you.

"I had many role models when I was younger. My parents, grandparents, schoolteachers, Sunday School teachers. But my idol was Jackie Robinson. I had Jackie Robinson pictures, newspaper articles, and baseball bubble gum cards taped to my bedroom wall, and I lived and breathed the Brooklyn, now LA, Dodgers. Robinson was fiery on the field but had to suffer the indignities of the era, turn the other cheek for the good of his race, not fight back, and simply prove himself on the field. His election into baseball's hall of fame attests to his greatness as an athlete. And he's continued to fight against injustices after his career ended.

"Not everyone's agreed with his views on civil rights, but he's had the guts to speak out for what he's considered areas of life that need to be corrected or improved. And he's expressed that his religious faith—his Christianity—has been instrumental in the molding of his life." A mostly all-white audience hearing me placing a black person on a pedestal certainly got attention. No doubt, not everyone agreed with my choice of Robinson because not everyone thought that highly of the black race or of his sometimes controversial views. Segregation and discrimination continued to exist almost everywhere in America. What I sought to convey was the endurance of a man in withstanding all the personal attacks, and that human beings are not to be treated like that, by anyone of any race.

It was important to relate that while Robinson's example had been impactful on me "my greater role model became Jesus Christ, the one after whom we should pattern our lives; in other words, we should live lives of caring, humility, and serving/helping others, regardless of our age.

"Have you ever spent much time wondering why you're on earth? I certainly have. And I've come to the conclusion that the meaning of life is fairly simple. The essence of Christianity, I think, is to lead a life that is a great witness and to improve the world by using the talents God gave us. Adults use these in their professions and in community and church service. Young people use them in the classroom, extracurricular activities, and volunteer service. All ages use theirs by reaching out to people they see who are in need.

"But life's not simple. It's like a road—potholes here and there, a detour now and then, and sometimes you stray and cross over the center line. It's a real challenge to stay in the proper lane in life."

With adults, I'd relate to what I knew had to be on their minds. "I'm certain most of you, like I, have struggled at times in trying to determine what God wants of you. What does he want you to be doing with your life? What are the best uses of your talents? What community activities should you be involved in and how much time should you give to them? How much involvement should you have in the church? What about your job and all of its time demands? And don't forget your family, which too often we place last in the chain of priorities. Are you giving enough of your time and attention to them? I don't have children yet, but I realize that those of you who do find it a challenge to devote all the attention they should have from you.

"Finding the proper balance among community, church, job, and family is the great dilemma many struggle with throughout life. A friend and I have often discussed this: I want to get ahead in life through my job, but I want to have a great relationship with my wife and raise perfect children, while God challenges me to use my talents to work through the church and help others through my talents. Where's the time to do all this, and what is the perfect balance of those obligations of time?"

In an admission to older adults that I hadn't lived a long life yet, I'd say, "I know some of you may think I'm still 'wet behind my ears,' but I already believe there isn't a life-balancing formula. Finding the right balance in our lives is an ongoing, lifelong challenge for each of us. And the one thing we must start with is prayer, because through prayer, we open ourselves to God and seek what he wants from our lives and then live expectantly, expecting God to give us direction.

"Despite plenty of heartache, I've already been so lucky in life, and not a day goes by but that I don't thank God for all the good I am, the good I do, and the good I have. I fully recognize that *everything* good comes from God and that he has used me in so many ways. *Daily* I asked to be used for some good purpose, a request that's part of my moment of prayer as I begin each morning.

"There are opportunities daily for each of us to show our Christianity. We make conscious decisions throughout each day, and what we decide says much about our character."

I'd pause at this point, gathering strength for what I was about to say, fighting to maintain composure, because the story brought back such hurtful memories. "Allow me to tell you something very personal.

"As you know from the introduction several minutes ago—although some of you with awfully good memories may have known of me prior to today," which usually brought snickers from some adults and a big grin from me, "I was a baseball player. I became a better one than I would have been because of a tragedy the day before my fifteenth birthday. My best friend—someone who was like a brother to me—drowned when we and other friends were swimming in a coal pit near Barclay. I was horrified, devastated, as you can imagine. His death inspired me to dedicate myself to becoming a better ballplayer, in honor of him. In some respects, I believe it inspired me to become a better person as well. I know I spent a lot of time in prayer, asking for direction and strength to do the right things with my life.

"I was lucky and had a good high school career. It landed me a scholarship to the University of Evansville, where I was sailing along as a pitcher for the Purple Aces when tragedy of a different nature struck me. In a game against Southern Illinois during my junior year, a season in which I was pitching extremely well, a line drive off the bat of an opposing hitter struck me in the right eye. In an instant, what seemed like the prospect of a possible career in professional baseball ended. It was yet *another* time in my somewhat young life that I was devastated. Fortunately, I wasn't left with lasting visual problems, a brain injury, or worse. But based on information from my doctor, I decided it would be too risky to continue attempting to play. For weeks after that line drive, I suffered from depression—not clinical depression, but the kind that left me listless and not caring about anything. I would lie all day and night, day after day, seemingly destroyed mentally although physical pain from the head injury lingered as well. And what I did as so many do when we face situations of personal crisis like this, was to say, 'Why me?' In fact, we take it further, saying 'Why me, God?' as though he were to blame for what had happened.

"After too long of a period of self-pity, I decided this was a situation I couldn't resolve on my own. I turned to God and prayed fervently for answers as to what I was to do. As I was praying and, importantly, *listening for an answer*, God spoke to me. I decided I had an opportunity to be a witness, like I'm doing here today, to show that people can overcome terrible situations in their lives and make significant contributions in helping others.

"My attitude changed. And what happened? My college coach gave me an opportunity to do some instructional work with the pitchers. I had met a wonderful woman at UE; we graduated and later married. She has a strong faith herself. I'm now in a challenging, rewarding profession at a company that I greatly respect, and, guess what, I'm involved in professional baseball, not exactly in the way I had hoped to be, but I'm involved, as you heard in the introduction, as a public relations professional helping the Evansville Dodgers. I am the luckiest guy in the world.

"No matter your age, what kind of role model are you? Because you *are* one whether you've thought about it or not. You're one every day of your life, wherever you go.

"Think about this. There may well be people who look up to you—admire you—but you don't realize it. You may possess talents that others wish they had. Some may wish they could emulate your actions. At the same time, you may display actions that disappoint others.

"How do you conduct yourself in your daily life—in school, at work, in community activities, at home? Are you the same person in school, at work, in the community, and at home that you appear to be at church?

"Are you the type of person others want to be around, or are you the grouch, the always-negative person saying, 'we can't do that, we can't do this, that won't work, this won't work, nothing ever goes right for me, I hate my boss, did you hear the latest about' …—man, don't you just hate being around people like that? Nobody, nobody, likes to be around negative people. It is so, so easy to be negative; it takes practically no effort at all. On the other hand, it takes effort and a good mental attitude to be positive.

"My challenge to you is to set a positive example for others to follow. Think about it, if each of us did that what a better world this would be. Are you making the most of your life in order to improve the world and help others?

"I've been fascinated by the great Italian painter and sculptor Michelaneglo. I learned of him when I was a student at the University of Evansville and have seen his works in books and articles. He believed that the huge rocks and slabs of marble brought to him in his studio contained forms and it was his obligation to release them. He would chisel away at the marble or stone and reveal what, in his mind, was inside all along. As a result, he produced some of history's great works—among them the larger than life statue of David and the lovely, serene Pieta—Mary holding the limp, lifeless body of Christ across her lap.

"Like Michelangelo, we should continually chisel away to reveal more of us than we thought possible. We need to continually seek to improve ourselves and never become complacent."

"Saint Paul says, 'I strain to reach the end of the race and receive the prize for which God is calling us up to heaven because of what Christ Jesus did for us.' Christ challenges us to be different. By being the most positive Christian role models possible, and giving ourselves in service to others, we will be."

I was buoyed by reactions to my messages and inspired by them— either in the facial expressions I saw as I delivered my comments or by remarks from thankful well-wishers, some of them saying "the best message we've ever heard."

While I wanted people to think about the types of lives they were leading and endeavor to make changes for all the years ahead, I was taken aback by comments from an elderly woman following a Sunday-morning worship service at a south-side church in Evansville. Anne was with me that day.

As I stood in the narthex to greet those who desired to meet me, the short, slight, wrinkled-skin, gray-haired woman asked as she shook my hand, "You know how old I am?"

Always the diplomat, I said, "No, Ma'am. One thing I'm smart enough to do is never guess a lady's age," and smiled.

"I'm ninety-four," she stated with obvious pride evident in the tone of her voice and then added, "And I want to promise to you that from this day forward, I will do my best to lead a more positive life."

I was dumbfounded. Here was a person who'd lived a very long life, and yet at age ninety-four, she wanted to become an even better human being; she still wasn't satisfied with herself. Just as astonishing was the fact she said my message had inspired her to change her life. I'd never forget this moment the rest of my life. I thought about it as Anne and I sat in silence in our car in the parking lot, and my eyes got watery. I knew my ability to speak to audiences was a gift that I must continue taking advantage of.

— — —

In October 1972, Jackie Robinson died after years of dealing with heart problems and diabetes. He was only fifty-three.

CHAPTER 23

By late summer 1972, Anne still wasn't pregnant. My sister had a child, a girl, born in 1971, just over a year after Peggy Sue finally married at age thirty-two. Anne and I had made the decision the previous winter to start our family. At thirty-two, she was considered old not to have had children but enjoyed her teaching position so much she'd not wanted to get pregnant earlier. There'd been long discussions about the future, and although we would lose her salary if she stopped working altogether after the first child was born, my annual pay of nearly $28,000 was more than adequate to support us and make the mortgage payment on the three-bedroom ranch-style house we moved into on the western outskirts of Newburgh in 1971. I was anticipating a raise in salary for the following year.

Anne stopped taking birth control pills in December 1971, and we fully expected her to get pregnant quickly. But conception didn't happen right away; in fact, it wasn't taking place at all. Finally, in September, she made an appointment with an OB/GYN.

Richard A. Field had practiced obstetrics and gynecology since completing his medical training at the end of 1943 and joining a three-man partnership in Evansville. His first three years of undergraduate work had been at the Indiana University campus in Bloomington. He had earned his bachelor's degree in biology after successfully completing the first year of medical school. That's the way the educational system worked in those days. Three more years of study resulted in his MD degree, which was followed by a year of internship and, because of the war, residency of only eighteen months, all at the university's large medical center in

Indianapolis. He proudly displayed his framed diplomas and OB/GYN board certification on a wall of one of his two examination rooms.

To his younger patients, at fifty-six years of age, he had the trustworthy appearance of the fatherly type. His office was located less than a block from Vanderburgh Regional Hospital, where he performed all deliveries and surgeries. His partners and friends called him Rick, but he was "Dr. Field" to staff and patients and was as beloved as any physician could be, perhaps because of the deep, calming voice that came from his six-foot-five-inch, 220-pound frame. Despite his build, he was never considered intimidating, just the opposite, a big teddy bear. His black hair had begun turning a very light gray by the time he reached thirty and was now almost snow white. His demeanor and attitude always conveyed that he wanted what was best for each patient, and he took his time during each appointment to make certain every question from an often anxious woman was answered. In fact, his taking so much time threw the appointment schedule into disarray every day and drove his staff nuts. But every patient waiting patiently while she read magazines in the quiet of an examination room knew he would give her his undivided attention when he finally got to her.

It was midafternoon October 3 before Anne could get the appointment, so she left school after helping supervise the lunchroom during the noon hour and drove to Evansville, anxious both because she was concerned she'd not gotten pregnant and was seeing a new doctor for the first time. "I'm terribly sorry, but Dr. Field is running an hour behind schedule," the receptionist informed her with an expression of helplessness. Handing Anne a ballpoint pen, clipboard, and two-page form, she said, "We need you to complete this medical history, if you would, please. Return it to me when you've finished it."

As she'd been instructed, Anne had arrived thirty minutes early so that as a new patient, she could fill out the necessary paperwork. Now an hour-and-a-half wait before she'd see the doctor only added to her anxiety. But she'd had enough experience with physicians to know to bring lesson plans to work on while she waited. Doing so would save her time that evening.

It was nearly 4:00 when a nurse asked Anne to follow her to an examination room. It was simple in appearance. Light-green walls, two metal-framed, padded chairs in addition to the doctor's small wooden desk and chair, a small white metal table supporting an assortment of medical supplies—rubbing alcohol, cotton balls, and small wooden tongue depressors—and an examination table with metal stirrups. The nurse measured her height and asked her to step on the scale. She was five feet six and 120 pounds. Then she took her temperature and blood pressure: a normal 98.6 degrees and 130/72.

As the nurse was removing the cuff from Anne's upper left arm, there was a light tapping on the door, and Dr. Field began talking as he opened it. "I'm sorry to have kept you waiting so long," he said as he walked into the room, closed the door behind him, and extended his arm to shake hands. "I'm Rick Field." A white full-length lab coat covered his dark slacks, blue shirt, and narrow lighter blue tie. The lab coat was pressed and without wrinkles. Despite the otherwise neat appearance, his black shoes were badly scuffed. *I've never met a doctor yet who polished his shoes*, she thought. "Sally here and the other staff get real irritated with me for running behind schedule nearly every day, and I'm certain patients do, too. Please forgive me."

Anne told me his soothing voice, his dark eyes, and the sincerity of his expression put her at ease immediately. Just as quickly, she forgot he was more than an hour late.

As the nurse busied herself near the examination table, Dr. Field studied the medical history and asked Anne to give some details. "Put some meat on the bones of what I see here on paper," was the way he made the request.

Anne related that she'd been on birth control pills for about eleven years when she stopped taking them nine months ago with the intention of getting pregnant, but despite having intercourse every day of each ovulation period—sometimes more than once a day—she kept having her periods and was frustrated, no doubt a story Dr. Field had heard many times in his years of practice. Anne found him to be empathetic.

During the pelvic examination, Anne realized she was amazingly calm. Asked if she'd been experiencing any abdominal pain, she was truthful in telling the doctor, "No," but didn't reveal that she'd felt bloated and had lost her appetite. Her weight had dropped about three pounds in the past couple of months, but that didn't bother her because she'd felt slightly heavy anyway. "Have you been under stress in your job or your marriage or had any major life-changing events?" Dr. Field asked.

To this, she also responded negatively but added, "Except for getting uptight that I'm not getting pregnant."

After finishing the exam and telling Anne to sit up at the end of the padded medium-green examination table, Dr. Field told her, "I find nothing abnormal, so here's what I want you to do." He instructed her on developing a basal body temperature chart whereby she was to take her temperature each morning upon waking, before eating or drinking. "Plot the temperatures on this graph, so we can determine if you have the sustained core temperature elevation that demonstrates ovulation each month. Do this for two months and then see me. During your twenty-eight-day menstrual cycle, you menstruate about five days, and approximately fourteen days later, you should ovulate, then you are most fertile for about twenty-four hours. But having intercourse over a period of several days is the safest way to 'catch the egg,' so to speak."

Anne made a follow-up appointment for December 11. When she returned, her graph didn't demonstrate ovulation, and she knew her face and voice expressed disappointment. "It's important," Dr. Field said in an effort to calm her fears, "that you don't get overly negative or stressed about this lack of pregnancy. It's not at all uncommon for women to have difficulty conceiving, especially for their first child."

Seated next to her and looking her squarely in the eyes with a warmth and voice tone meant to reassure her and lighten the moment, he said, "Often we find in our profession that when women try the hardest to get pregnant, they fail. It's important you do your best not to think about it too much. Relax and thoroughly enjoy intercourse. Think only of you and your husband and the fulfillment you are giving one another each time you're in bed. Matter of fact, it doesn't have to be bed. Don't get into the habit of only having sex in bed and at night, and for goodness sake, don't just get right to the act of intercourse; enjoy touching, caressing, exploring as part of foreplay. Mix it up. If your ovulation period includes a weekend, there's nothing wrong with the living room sofa or any other place in the house at anytime during the day. Nothing. Have fun. Enjoy it. In fact, don't even keep a graph, then see me after two or three more cycles. If you're not pregnant then, I'll have a semen analysis—a sperm count—conducted on your husband. It may be that you're ovulating, but he's not producing enough sperm to fertilize your egg."

Anne's expected day of ovulation fell on New Year's Eve, and she forced herself to have two glasses of wine at the party she and I attended at a friend's house in Pemberton, with the hope she'd be so relaxed sex that night would be uninhibited and deliriously enjoyable. The alcohol worked. And despite a mild headache when she awoke the next morning, we had sex three times that day, once on the large rug on the bedroom floor.

But she menstruated right on schedule less than two weeks later.

In early April, I submitted to a sperm count. It was normal. "Anne, I'm going to prescribe something that I hope will stimulate ovulation," Dr. Field told her a few days later. Clomiphene tablets were to be taken for five consecutive days in her next menstrual cycle. July 10, still not pregnant, she was back in his office, having lost seven more pounds since October. She'd cried all night the previous evening. I'd been supportive of her throughout the year and a half she'd failed to conceive. Just as she'd described Dr. Field's demeanor, I tried my best to be calming, loving, tender, and soothing. She and I had talked often about the situation, and I made certain she understood I placed no blame and felt it was only a matter of time before she'd get pregnant. To her credit, her frustrations hadn't distracted her from the responsibilities of teaching her children during the school year, but this was summertime when there should be no excuse not to be relaxed and free of tension in the bedroom. The frustrations had finally boiled over the previous evening.

"Anne, let's look inside that body of yours and find out if it can tell us anything." As she described to me later, Dr. Field had decided to examine the fallopian tubes to determine if they were unobstructed and open. Carefully and slowly performing the pelvic exam, he felt an enlarged left ovary, about the size of a lemon. It should have been walnut-sized.

He removed his rubber gloves, walked up beside her, and gently placed his right hand on the gown over her abdomen. Looking at her supine on the table, he said, "Anne, I don't want you to be alarmed or overly worried, but I found your left ovary larger than it should be, and I want to examine it further."

Startled, her heels still in the stirrups, she abruptly raised and supported her upper body with forearms and elbows. "What do you mean, 'enlarged'?" she shot back.

"It's about twice the normal size, and we need to find out why." Her arms collapsed from the weight of the statement; her head sank back into the pillow, but she never took her eyes off him, disbelief in her expression.

Calmly, Dr. Field said, "I'd like to schedule you for further examination over at the hospital later this week. You'll need your husband with you, because you'll be under anesthetic during the test and I'll have to make a small abdominal incision—we call it an exploratory laparotomy—to find out what's going on in there," and he patted her abdomen. "I won't conjecture anything at this point, so please don't try to do so either."

Sitting at the kitchen table, Anne was staring into empty space when I arrived from work. She didn't even greet me when I walked into the kitchen; she just burst into tears as she sprang from her chair and threw her arms around my neck, squeezing tightly and not letting go. "Oh, Davie, I'm so scared. There's something wrong with me, and I have to have surgery this week."

"Surgery?" My hands lightly grasped her sides, and I pushed her back, so I could look into her eyes. "What do you mean 'surgery'? What's wrong?"

With tears streaming and fear in her eyes, she said, "Dr. Field told me one of my ovaries is greatly enlarged, and he has to find out why."

"But surgery, what kind of surgery?"

"Well, maybe it's not actually called surgery, but he said he has to make an incision in my abdomen, and I'll be out while he does it. If he finds something he doesn't like, he might go on and perform a hysterectomy! I'm so scared."

"When?"

"The nurse said she'd call me tomorrow morning but hoped the procedure could be scheduled for Friday, at Vanderburgh Regional. You'll have to go with me."

Friday? But I'm in charge of a pregame event for the Dodgers Friday. Immediately recognizing the selfishness of the thought and coming to my senses, I said, "Of course I'll be with you, no matter when you're scheduled."

We spent the evening engaged in small talk, as I tried to get her mind and mine off of Friday and the possibilities of what could be wrong with her. Neither of us slept well that night, and Anne didn't the next two nights either. Each of us prayed a great deal together and individually, asking God for good news.

We made the decision not to tell either set of parents about the procedure. Both couples were aware their children wanted to have a baby but were not cognizant the situation had grown potentially serious.

Finding me alone in the waiting room—it was Friday the thirteenth—a grim-faced Dr. Field broke the news. Then with me at Anne's side in the recovery room, he informed her as quietly and sensitively as he could. "I had to remove the uterus, tubes, and ovaries; they've been sent to pathology for study and we should have the results in about five days."

"Why?" Anne questioned. "Removed them, why?" Before he answered, she said, "You aren't talking about possible cancer, are you?" The thought had been on her mind for several days.

"It's my fear," Dr. Field replied, "but we won't know for sure until I get the lab results."

Instantly, both of us realized the desire to have a child was no longer an issue. A life was at stake.

Five days later, we received the news we never wanted to hear: ovarian cancer. In fact, we were told, the disease was most likely not confined to the tissues that were removed and had spread to the surface of Anne's internal organs. Chemotherapy would have to begin quickly.

Over the next three months, Anne had six intravenous chemo treatments in the hospital every two weeks. She was unable to teach but was optimistic for a cure, and her faith remained strong. "I can't wait to get back to my children," she said.

Both of us prayed often for a miracle, as did our overwrought families and friends. "God," I pleaded, "if you truly intervene in health situations, please, please, help Anne. May your power and that of man's medicine bring about a cure. She's such a caring person. She uses the talents you've given her to help little children and prepare them with some of the basics for life, and there are many hundreds or thousands for her yet to touch. I beg of you to give her that opportunity. I don't think you cause bad things to happen, but I believe with all my heart you bring about miracles. Please, please, give one to Anne." I prayed words like this often each day.

The senior pastor of our church provided frequent counsel to both of us, and the congregation had Anne on its daily prayer list. My parents and Anne's visited us or called often. Even Coach Ludlow telephoned on occasion to extend his best wishes. Coach never forgot me, nor I him. I'd seen him numerous times since graduation.

Chemo was difficult for my wife. I hated to watch her vomiting, dry-heaving, struggling with pain, and overall feeling horrible at times. Within a month, most of her hair had fallen out, and she wore a scarf if we went outdoors. Then she'd have some good days, and there was hope, but the wretchedness of the side effects returned shortly after each treatment. My agency told me to take all the time necessary to be with Anne. Her mother moved in with us for about ninety days, devoting herself to providing all the assistance she could. Jenny was strong in faith and character. I don't know how I could have survived without her.

Three months after her last chemotherapy treatment, Anne returned to Dr. Field, complaining of abdominal swelling; she attributed it to eating too much, which was paradoxical to me because she seemed to have little appetite and her weight had decreased further. Finding nodules when he examined her again, Dr. Field knew the cancer had recurred, and he and Anne were dealing with an aggressive tumor.

Within two months, she was dead. It was March 21, 1974. Anne Jennifer Miller was only thirty-three years old.

CHAPTER 24

In the torturous days that followed, I struggled not only to deal with my own grieving but also to provide comfort to Anne's emotionally ravaged parents, who'd lost their only child. And I found it exceedingly difficult to do so. I was consumed with dark emotions, turning on God, blaming him for not saving my wife. My frequent talks with our creator in the otherwise deathly stillness of my home were filled with anger. "My mother had been widowed at twenty-nine, and now me at thirty-three. I lost a father, my best friend, lost my baseball career to injury, and now my wife. What more do you want from me?" I'd shout at God at times, cry for long periods, kick furniture, slam a fist against a wall. The faith I'd expressed in numerous public settings had reached its ultimate test. And I wasn't doing a very good job of sustaining it. Fortunately, I wasn't much of a consumer of alcoholic beverages, so I didn't turn to the bottle to drown the agony.

The owners of my agency reached out by phone almost daily after telling me to take as much time off as I needed, not to come back to work until I felt ready. Perhaps they didn't *know* how I felt, but they sensed I was as emotionally low as one could get and wanted to make certain someone was talking with me. My family and Anne's kept in touch by phone, but I didn't want to see anyone just yet. On the seventh day following the funeral, there was an unexpected visitor.

I'd kept the curtains on the front picture window drawn, so the living room was dark when the doorbell rang in the middle of a gray afternoon. "Just wanted to come by and see how you were doing and find out what help I could be to you," Andy Ludlow said when I opened the front door.

"Coach, what a surprise." Hesitating and then thinking it was probably the proper thing to do, I said, "Come on in." Actually, I felt myself perk up a bit when I saw his friendly look and heard the soft voice of this man I'd admired ever since we met after a Barclay High School baseball game when I was a junior. My admiration grew when I learned it was Ludlow who may have saved me from more serious injury, even a permanent disability, when he was among the first to rush to the mound after I was leveled by the line drive. Upon seeing the severity of the injury, he took charge and yelled at the trainer to rush back to the dugout for ice bags and a handful of clean towels and an assistant coach to call an ambulance. It was Coach who made certain towels were placed under and around my head while the trainer ever so carefully kept the eye covered with cloth and an ice bag against it. All the while, this wonderfully caring man kept stroking the uninjured side of my head, uttering assurances that I would be okay. "Hang in there, son. Help's on the way, and we're gonna make sure you're taken care of quickly. You'll be just fine." Later, I recalled none of that as I recovered, but fellow players, assistant coaches, and the trainer made certain I was aware of my head coach's actions. I would always be indebted.

As I escorted my baseball mentor to the kitchen, he said, "I've purposely not called you since the funeral because I figured you needed time alone and maybe you were getting more calls from well-meaning people than you may have wanted." I opened the Venetian blinds of the kitchen window and then flipped on the lights when I realized the exterior light wasn't illuminating the room enough. Seeing Coach Ludlow's face made me feel better already.

"Yeah, well, I've had a lot of calls, but no visitors." Glancing at the floor, I continued softly and monotonously, "Not because people haven't wanted to come by, it's just that I didn't feel like seeing anyone." Now looking at him, I said, "But I could stand some perking up. I think I've wallowed in my bad feelings long enough. A week's a long time to agonize alone." Tears filled my eyes. I looked away.

He sensed the moment, reached out, patted my shoulder, and flashed a slight grin with etched wrinkles that ran out from the edges of both sides of his closed lips. The trademark smile in his weathered face said more than he could have placed in words. I saw the expression when I looked up, pulled my right forearm across my eyes to wipe away the tears, tried to force a pleasant look, and asked him to have a seat at the kitchen table. I sat in an adjacent chair.

"Boy, this has been tough," I exclaimed, barely audibly, again facing the floor. "Anne was so vibrant. We had such a great marriage and so much fun. She loved her career, and both of us really wanted to have children." I paused, glanced up, and then looked back down. "I know I'm not supposed to say 'it's not fair,' but it's not." Coach Ludlow was an active member of the FCA and had heard me speak to youth groups several times, accompanying me as a fellow member on a couple of programs. Even though he was an avowed Christian, he could let loose with a few well-chosen less-than-nice words at umpires or his own players in the heat of a ball game. But I had never met a finer man.

"Davie," he began, softly but firmly, "you're somebody really special." My eyes shot wide open as I looked at him, completely taken aback. "You've had so much heartache in your life, yet you've persevered at every step. You are an unbelievable role model, not just to young people but even to me. You 'walk the talk.' There are teenagers out there who admire you and think they'd like to be just like you. And I guarantee you there are peers and persons of older ages who believe the same thing."

Without pausing for any comment, he continued, "You know, I don't know that God *took* Anne or didn't try to save her. Yeah, there are preachers and others who believe he takes people from this earth and those who think he doesn't intercede in illnesses. Not that you've asked me, but I don't think God is the type who just takes people. School is still out for me on whether he acts on people's prayers by saving others from dying. Yet I believe in miracles because I've prayed for them for friends that have had horrible illnesses, and although doctors said there wasn't any hope for them, somehow they continued living and were cured. But I've prayed for others, and they didn't make it. Does God choose to let some live and others not? I don't think so, but I'm not a theologian, so I'm not smart enough to have an intelligent answer. My faith is pretty simple: God put us on earth. We live, and eventually, we die, some of us far too early. The important thing is to know that there's an ending for each of us someday, and we need to make the most of our lives with all the abilities God has given us. If we do, we'll go to heaven forever, and you'll be with Anne again. It's that dad-gummed simple to me."

He paused, cleared his throat, and continued, his voice becoming louder the more he talked. I listened intently. "Let me say one more thing. I'm not in your shoes, so I have absolutely no idea how you feel. My brother died when I was seventeen and he was nineteen. He had leukemia. I'm sixty-four, and my parents are dead, both from lingering illnesses. But let me just leave you with a thought. You have really been doing something special with your life. Now continue to do that for Anne. You can't take on the lives of two persons, but you can be determined to continue being a great role model, and maybe there's a way you can even reach younger children, like those Anne taught. You know, they're impressionable. They won't understand big words when you talk about life, but you're intelligent enough to know how to speak at their level. And I'm not talking about just making speeches but getting involved in community service, perhaps with a social agency where you can do some one-on-one assisting.

I felt a change in me. He'd lit a spark. "You're right. I needn't sit in this house and continue moping. Anne wouldn't like it, and she certainly would want me to do something special with my life."

We continued sitting there, staring at one another, and then he broke the silence. "Well, I want you to think about what I said. You've got a lot to offer, and I'll always be here for you if you'd like to talk more." My wonderful mentor paused, and I could tell there was something special on his mind. "There *is* something I'd like you to do for *me*. I'd like you to come to some of my practices and games when your work schedule will permit it. We're working hard to get ready for the start of the season. I want the players to get to know you. They're aware of you 'cause you're a legend in our program, and it'd mean a lot to me if you'd be willing to give them your thoughts at team meetings from time to time, sort of like pep talks. Would you be willing?"

Brightening, I quickly responded, "Sure, Coach, I'd love to." His bear hug as he left the house made me realize how fortunate I was to have such a friend.

CHAPTER 25

poured myself into my job, working long hours and on weekends, part of the remedy for dwelling on life without Anne. I hadn't eaten well and lost several pounds until I got ahold of myself after the talk with Andy Ludlow. I decided I *had* to take better care of myself.

I made the decision to live for Anne just as I'd been challenged. I had strong emotional support from family. My parents, Anne's, my sister, and the Miller and Hutchison grandparents were in touch with me often but, unfortunately, not Grandmother Johnson. Grandma Dorothy, now approaching her mid-80s, suffered from "hardening of the arteries," a term often used to describe one's loss of memory, especially short-term memory. Widowed in 1972 when Grandpa Charles suffered a heart attack at their farm, she lived in her home with Ann and John who'd operated the farm with minor help from his dad since the mid-1960s. Grandpa signed over ownership of the property to John in 1967 with the promise that he and Grandma could still live in their home. Ann and John moved there in the summer of 1973 when it became obvious Grandma no longer had the mental capabilities to be trusted to care for herself.

Mom was a source of inspirational thought and made herself available as often as I wanted to talk with her. Dad did, too, but Mom had retired at the end of 1973 at the age of fifty-eight, with forty years of service to the bank and had lots of time on her hands. She had risen to senior vice president and got along well with the president who had succeeded Chester Brummett when he'd retired a decade earlier. Mom and Dad had earned a good living, put their children through college, and felt secure in what was in their savings account. Her bank pension payments had begun immediately. Both parents would apply for Social Security payments to begin at age 62. She wanted to have more time to be of service through their church, and Dad strongly supported her decision to leave the bank. He would be sixty in 1974 and intended to teach at least five more years.

Their lives together had been a blessing to both. While Mom had dealt with more heartache than he, and her face showed the strain, Dad had mostly maintained his good physical condition through the years, although a slight paunch was evident. He was as handsome as ever—perhaps even more so with the gray that had sneaked into his hair.

I thoroughly enjoyed my talks with Mother, getting her advice on dealing with personal tragedy and learning about her life with my birth father and the period of years when I was very young, too young to recall much. My dad graciously always found excuses to leave the two of us alone, knowing why I wanted to be with her.

I had now been at Wilson-McGlasson nearly seven years, and they'd been successful ones. The Dodgers' account was considered a flagship property for the agency. The team had twice won the regular season title and the playoffs once. Average attendance set a record of just over 4,100 for the 1973 season. Ownership was thrilled with Bud Stanley's performance, and so he was thrilled with the agency's and mine.

The relationships I developed with colleagues Kathy Williams and Larry Frederick while assisting them with their accounts were excellent. Both were nearly forty, hard workers, and talented as public relations specialists. Frederick was a patient mentor to me, helping me learn the automobile business, and Williams, who held both business and marketing degrees, was considered a whiz at understanding financial institutions and providing quality PR guidance to the powers that be at her banking client.

The challenge to help his client was particularly difficult for Larry. The country was in an economic recession, and automobile sales were plummeting. Arab oil-producing nations had not only raised prices but had also instituted an embargo. This led to an energy crisis in the United States that resulted in government-imposed oil rationing and many service stations having no fuel to sell early in 1974. Gasoline prices jumped from the high thirties to more than fifty-cents per gallon. Year-round daylight saving time was imposed, and highway speed limits were capped at fifty-five miles per hour, all in an effort to force fuel conservation throughout the year. The stock market continued its downward spiral, which had begun early in 1973. Inflation became a major problem, and interest rates rose, as did unemployment.

The problem for Hobson Chevrolet was the manufacturer of its cars made large ones, gas guzzlers, like the Bel Air, Caprice, and Impala. Americans now wanted vehicles with much better fuel efficiency. Smaller cars and trucks produced overseas became more popular, and until the Big Three auto makers in the United States—Chrysler, Ford, and General Motors—could produce compact vehicles, the industry was going to suffer. With Frederick taking the lead, he and I devised a strategy of "if we can't convince them, we'll help them"; in other words, keep the name in front of the public via advertising but devote most of the company's television and newspaper funds to giving tips on energy conservation on everything from vehicles to the home. The theory was that other dealers would cut their ad budgets. If Hobson could continue a presence but with an emphasis on helping the consumer rather than wooing him, when the recession ended, the public would give more consideration to purchasing from Hobson than others because of the favorable impression that had been made.

With sales down, income was down, so the dealership laid off several salesmen. But owner Edward "Eddie" Hobson (*"Your Friend for Life"* said his company's slogan) believed strongly in having a significant presence in advertising and reduced the budget only slightly. At the same time, he agreed with his Wilson-McGlasson strategists to build his firm's brand by getting involved in supporting community events, shifting some of its promotional funds there. It sponsored "Family Night" at a Dodgers game in June, was title sponsor of a downtown Evansville street fair as no-cost entertainment to families, and took the lead in working with the public school system to encourage elementary children to brainstorm ideas for energy conservation in school and at home. The student judged to have the best idea in each school was awarded a pizza party with twelve friends, paid for by Hobson, and the student named the overall winner in the city was given a $500 certificate of deposit provided by—who else?—Central Vanderburgh State Bank. For me, the involvement of the three clients I assisted was a perfect marriage.

Despite the record year of 1973, the local Dodgers were convinced they needed to have far more family promotions coupled with discount prices in 1974, in answer to societal economic woes. The strategy worked, as cash-strapped or cash-concerned families looked for low-cost entertainment.

—   —   —

"You've got to join us," Larry Frederick declared again at the start of the workweek the fourth week of May. "It'll be a lot of fun for all of us," he said, referring to a new slow-pitch softball league that had been formed among area advertising and public relations agencies, radio and television stations, and the newspapers. The rules were simple: each team was required to have at least two females on the field at all times, and all players had to either work for the league members or for a client. Any team getting caught playing a "ringer," such as a friend of a friend of an employee, would be automatically expelled.

I admit I'd gotten the itch to play ball again a week earlier after Larry first planted the seed. His timing couldn't have been better. I'd given a pep talk to the UE baseball team just days prior to that, and my juices had begun to flow. Sure, I could get struck in the eye again, but the injury had been so many years ago—thirteen—there was no more risk for damage than there'd been prior to that game with Southern Illinois. Any fears were long gone. My initial thoughts were to tell him, "Yes."

"Great. Simply great. I needed a left fielder with a strong arm; in slow pitch, so many balls are hit there," he responded and slapped me on the shoulder when I answered in the affirmative. "You'll be glad you played. Slow pitch is a fun game, and it'll be good for you to get onto a ball diamond again."

The ten-team league's games were played on Tuesday and Thursday nights at a four-diamond complex in a flat plain on the city's west side, near hilly municipal-owned Helfrich Golf Course. Privately owned, the facility featured well-lit ball fields, sanctioned umpires, and beer, the latter the drawing card and decision-maker when league organizers looked at the few complexes in the city that could host their teams. Games were rotated, so that if a team was scheduled to play on Tuesday one week, it would play on Thursday the next, beginning June 11. Rules on decorum were strict, and umpires were expected to enforce them: no cursing, no metal spikes, no arguing umpire calls, and no beer drinking during your game.

I was amazed at how easy getting back into the groove of fielding, throwing, and running the bases was. I hadn't thrown a ball in years, so I was careful not to put too much strain on my arm during the first couple of weeks of practice. No sense ending up with a bum arm before the season even started. I was just as cautious with my legs. While I'd jogged some on the streets and roads in my neighborhood over the past couple of years, sudden bursts of speed in running bases could pop a hamstring quickly. I had no concerns about being able to hit the large softball. I should have. Rules required the ball be pitched at a height ranging from six feet to twelve feet. I constantly overswung, as was typical of someone who had played baseball, trying too hard to hit what appeared to be a simple underhanded-tossed target, sort of like hitting a hanging Mexican piñata with a stick at a child's birthday party. But it wasn't all that simple at first. With instruction from teammates who had slow pitch experience, I proclaimed I'd "got the hang of it" before the scheduled first game.

The summer of fun was as mentally therapeutic as it was good for me physically, despite the ugly scabs I seemed always to be dealing with from sliding into bases in the shorts I wore. I missed Anne terribly, but the games got my mind off of nighttime loneliness and provided an outlet for my emotions.

CHAPTER 26

The nation's long war in Vietnam came to an end with the fall of Saigon in April 1975. My four friends who fought there had long been home, all of them impacted by their experiences and not for the good. Ralph Dunigan had two tours of duty and was embittered by his inability to find a job. Stevie Carter continued to have nightmares about the horrific fighting at Khe Sanh, which cost him two fingers on his left hand. Joel Rennick would not let go of the fact there was no homecoming or that no one seemed to care he'd risked his life for their peace.

But it was Bobby Hatcher whom I worried about most. Like Ralph, Bobby had served one tour in Vietnam and then volunteered for a second. It wasn't, however, a sense of duty that led him to go back for more; it was the easily attainable supply of drugs. War does that to some people, makes them easy prey for the seductive influence of mind-altering narcotics. For Bobby, the best friend I ever had after Billy, nothing worse than an occasional beer or sip of bourbon had ever entered his body after high school. By 1962 when I graduated from college, I'd never heard of drugs and wouldn't have known the smell of marijuana smoke wafting in the air from someone wearing too much perfume. But the intensity of serving in the army in the A Shau Valley had gotten to Bobby about three months after he was shipped to Southeast Asia.

The valley in northern South Vietnam, west of Hue and northwest of Da Nang, earned its nickname "Valley of Death" the hard way; it became a major battlefield as North Vietnamese forces used the Ho Chi Minh Trail to get supplies and material through the valley and deeper into the south. Scores of men on both sides of the conflict died there.

Fellow soldiers introduced Bobby to marijuana, a minor drug in comparison to what he would try next. Marijuana was soothing and not terribly addictive, he thought, as he found solace during combat missions and while relaxing back at base camp. But by the time his first tour had ended, he'd gotten hooked on heroin. And he couldn't wait to get back into action, but not for the combat.

When I saw Bobby back home for a break between tours, there was something unusual about him. His speech was sometimes slurred—which was unusual for my normally quick-talking friend—and at times, it seemed he couldn't keep his eyes open. But I dismissed all of it as the need for some good R & R. When he returned to the States following a second year in Vietnam, he definitely wasn't the Bobby of old. His speech was noticeably slower and often slurred; his eyelids drooped almost all the time, and he had lost a lot of weight.

"Got to ask you, what's wrong?"

"Whadaya mean, man?"

"You don't look so hot."

"Well, I'm fine, man. Jes fine. Life is *good*, man."

Man? What gives with this "man" stuff?

Growing up, we had been so close we each knew what the other was thinking, so I didn't hesitate to pose the question. "Bobby, what's wrong? You've changed, so don't try to hide anything from me."

"Hey, nothin's wrong. I'm just fine, man. You've no idea what hell I've been through, but I found peace and I'm fine."

"Well, I don't think you are, and if you don't want to talk about it, that's fine. But I'm here for you. I want you to know that."

"Thanks, man. All I gotta do now is find a job and make some dough."

That had been in 1970, and during the next two years while living at home with his parents, Bobby struggled with his dependency, finally seeking help from a live-in rehabilitation clinic in Louisville, Kentucky, about one hundred miles east of Barclay. He was in and out of the clinic and struggled to maintain employment. He wore his hair long, looked gaunt, and his once 190-pound frame was down to 165. I forced him to talk with me, and finally, he unloaded his struggles.

"Man, you've no idea what hell I went through in Nam," he finally related. "But I won't blame the drugs on anyone. They were cheap and easy to get. I got hooked, and I can't get off them. I've tried to some extent, but I need them for living."

"Bobby, there's more to living than being high all the time. Life's full of fun and great opportunities. Look at yourself; you're wasting away. You're robbing your parents of their retirement savings by not having a full-time job. I beg of you, kick this habit, and I'll help you find a job. We'll stay close, just like the old days." I brought up prayer, but he'd have nothing to do with it.

"God, what God? Hell, there's no God in my life except my drugs. They're my source of strength."

"But they're not, Bobby. They're the source of ruination." I related how God had given me strength and that I was such a better person because of my faith. In the summer of 1974, I shared with him how I was determined to live in Anne's memory, and it was because of prayer that I decided to dedicate myself to helping people of all ages in any way I could. "Bobby, kick the habit and become a spokesman for living a clean life. You would be one heck of a role model, especially to young people who either have experimented with drugs or were tempted to try them. You could save a lot of lives."

By the fall of 1975, he was experiencing problems with his kidneys and his inability to remember was noticeable to anyone who spent much time in conversation with him. I'd failed to get through to him in any meaningful way.

CHAPTER 27

Physically, I got into great shape except for an occasional migraine. The first I'd ever had came during a night softball game in July of 1974. I was in left field when it sneaked up on me. I was looking toward the infield, and it seemed something was in my left eye; I kept blinking, trying to clear my vision. I'd close my eye and rub it with the top of my forearm or fingers, attempting to make whatever it was go away but to no avail. Suddenly, as I looked up to follow the path of a fly ball, I saw it as a weirdly shaped object coming toward me. Part of it was out of focus; the other part had more than one edge. At the last moment, I jerked my head to the right, the ball barely missing my body before hitting the ground and rolling well behind me. The runner scored an inside-the-park home run by the time my throw reached the infield.

"Hey, what was that all about?" Larry asked when we got back to the dugout.

"I've no idea except I've got blurred vision in my left eye." Suddenly, I was scared and for a moment thought the problem was related to the injury of more than a dozen years ago.

"Hold your head back while you sit there, and I'll get an ice pack," Larry directed.

I recalled nearly a year later when I had the second one that the visual was the same as at the ball diamond. With my eyes open, half of the vision in my left eye was gone. When I closed them, I saw a beautiful multicolored prism in the left one, something that reminded me of a Picasso painting. It started near the center and had brilliant, earthy shades of brown, yellow, and blue. During the next thirty minutes or so, the prism slowly moved to the left and finally disappeared as though exiting the far side of the eye. But the artistic experience was replaced by an intensely dull headache that lasted for hours. I took aspirin, but it had no effect. Physically, I was wiped out. The second episode made me decide on an appointment with my general practitioner.

"I think you've had migraines," Dr. William Ellingwood told me. "From what you've described—the loss of sight, prisms, and then terrible headaches—it is a classic migraine."

"What causes them?"

"There's no good science on them, unfortunately. It's inexplicable as to why they come on. The prevailing thought is stress is the primary cause, but I've had patients who've experienced them in good times and bad—in other words, good stress and bad stress. You've certainly experienced both the past year."

"Could they be related to my head injury in '61?"

"Could be, but not necessarily. I'm going to prescribe Imitrex in pill form. It's usually effective for those having migraine experiences. Take one at the onset of the migraine and then another thirty minutes later if necessary. Imitrex should clear up the visual problem, but there's no guarantee you won't have a severe headache afterward. Unfortunately, those seem to come with the territory."

"What if I get more migraines?"

"If they become more frequent, such as three or more a year, we might consider having an MRI conducted."

"What could that show?"

"Well, I don't like to speculate," he replied, knowing one answer was a tumor on the brain. "Just don't worry and don't conjure up all sorts of possible causes, or you'll drive yourself silly. As long as you only have one, possibly two, migraines a year, as much as you don't want to experience them, I wouldn't be too concerned. Imitrex should do the trick to help you get some relief quickly. Also, you won't necessarily have headaches after each episode. But if you ever become too concerned, be sure to get another appointment with me."

▬ ▨ ▬

The good news from '75 was the nation's recession officially came to an end, although America would not recover quickly.

There wasn't a day I didn't think about Anne. Her framed photos were on the nightstand next to my bed, on a table in the living room, and on a ledge between wall-mounted cabinets above the counter in the kitchen. I spoke to her from time to time, relating challenges I was facing at work.

Not until approximately two years after Anne died did I have a date. I just hadn't been interested in a relationship with a woman. My secretary BJ urged me for weeks to meet an "extremely cute" cousin of hers. Finally, I relented. She *was* "cute," and she also exhibited the promised "bubbly personality." But BJ failed to mention she was nearly five by four, not exactly my type. We had a nice time at Lechner's, a quality restaurant downtown on the top floor of the seven-story Bennett Building that faced the Ohio River, but nothing clicked for me, and I didn't invite her out again.

I enjoyed interactions with women at work, at clients' offices, and on the softball team. Some thought I was flirtatious. Perhaps I was and didn't realize it. Friends didn't know how to broach the subject of dating, so they took the easy way out and didn't mention it. I dated many times over the next several years but always compared each woman to Anne, and none had her qualities.

One thing I realized, and it bothered me, was I would likely never have a child of my own. Oh, how Anne and I had wanted to have children! I couldn't wait to have a son who would grow up to be a ballplayer. The two of us would spend hours playing pitch and catch. I might even coach or be an assistant coach on his team. I'd teach him how to throw a knuckleball, and perhaps he'd be the professional player I never had an opportunity to be. Perhaps. But that possibility was likely gone, and it was a depressing feeling.

Then it struck me when I wasn't expecting it.

CHAPTER 28

I was blindsided by the feeling I got the moment I met eyes with Dr. Diane Johnston when she walked into her optometry examination room and introduced herself. I'll never forget the date: March 16, 1981.

I hadn't had a feeling like that since I'd met Anne, and only twice before, once when I had a suffocating crush on classmate Phyllis Summerville that began in the seventh grade, though I'd never had the nerve to tell her or ask her for a date. I kicked myself throughout high school for being so shy. The other secret passion was my sophomore social studies teacher Miss England; it arose at a time testosterone was rearing its head. I also had a crush on another Phyllis, of the McGuire Sisters, the popular singing trio I saw often on television. But that was a typical teen-lusting-after-older-woman situation that would remain only in my imagination.

"Mr. Miller, I'm Dr. Johnston, Diane Johnston," she said with a lovely but not overly strong Southern drawl, shaking my hand as I started to rise from the dark-gray simulated-leather exam chair where I'd been waiting. "Don't get up," she said. My heart was fluttering.

"Tell me about yourself," she inquired as I scooted back into the chair, and she took a seat at a small desk about five feet away, to my left.

"There's a lot to tell." I smiled. "Where should I begin?"

She laughed. "I'm sorry, I just need to know what brought you here." She never took her eyes off of me except for what I noticed was a quick glance at my left ring finger. I'd already glanced at hers, too, and saw nothing on it but thought perhaps she removed her rings during her workday.

"I've been having migraine headaches a couple of times a year for the past seven years and decided on my own perhaps they were due to some eyesight problems. Frankly, I can't remember the last time I had my eyes examined, so I thought I'd get an appointment." Pointing to the area of the right eye, I said, "I was struck here by a baseball twenty years ago and was afraid maybe the damage back then has caught up with me, although my surgeon at that time released me as having no visual problems. I saw my GP after my second migraine, and he said not to worry about them unless they were more frequent than a couple a year. Oh, maybe there's been a year or two where I had three, but nothing has changed much. Even if my eyesight isn't the cause, I need it checked anyway."

"Well, first, thank you for coming in to see me. It's important that all of us have our eyes examined on a regular basis, especially as we get older—not that you're old." She smiled.

"I'll be forty-one in June."

"Well, then, if it's been quite a long time since your eyes have been checked, I'm glad you're here." I loved hearing the drawl.

Diane Johnston was a brunette, and I guessed her to be about five-six or five-seven, somewhere in the range of 115 to 120 pounds, with a well-proportioned figure and penetrating eyes, the color just like mine. She wore a powder-blue knee-length lab coat, with *Family Optometry* stitched in dark-blue just above the left breast. I'd noticed two University of Alabama diplomas side by side on a wall while I was waiting. One was an undergraduate degree, the other for optometry.

She looked once again at the medical history I'd filled out on the office form, double-checking that I took only one medication, the Imitrex, as needed. After rising to turn off the room light at the wall switch, she paused. "It would appear you're in reasonably good health since you only occasionally take one form of medication."

"Excellent, actually. I keep active, work out on an exercise machine at home or at the YMCA, play softball in the summer, and try to watch what I eat."

"That's great. It's vital to take good care of your health." She paused.

"I'll start with a few simple tests," she said, moving toward me, only a small light on the front wall giving any illumination to the room. While she checked the pupil function with a small but bright light—somewhat like a penlight—and the movement of each eye, she asked for more information, including my profession and my efforts to maintain good health. Obviously, it would have been unprofessional for her to inquire about my personal life, and she didn't.

"I'm an account executive at an ad agency here in Evansville and have been there over thirteen years. The clients I spend most of my time with are the Evansville Dodgers and Hobson Chevrolet."

"Try to hold your eyes steady," she requested and then asked, "Are you a baseball fan?"

"Yes, I've been a lifelong Brooklyn and Los Angeles Dodgers fan."

"Well, I love baseball, too, having grown up in Alabama and having had a father who enthusiastically cheered for the Atlanta Braves, so I became a Braves fan, too. Tell me about your injury."

"Broken bones around the eye and the floor of the socket," I responded, finding it difficult not to move my head as I did, "but I healed somewhat quickly. Since I decided not to play anymore, I turned to exercise of a different sort—machines, which I've used on a somewhat regular basis and jogging. I'm not married, so I can spend as much of my off time as I wish working out."

"Now let's find out how well you can read from a distance," she said and illuminated a chart on the front wall. Handing me a small black cover paddle, she told me to cover one eye with it and read the lowest row possible of the eight rows of letters. The line I chose turned out to be the 20/20 row, which I read without difficulty. Then I did the same while covering the other eye.

"Very good," she assured me.

Holding a card version of the chart, I struggled slightly with the smaller lines.

With me still seated, Dr. Johnston screened my visual field, asking me to tell her how many fingers she was displaying at various points in front of me or along the periphery of the eyes.

"I'm going to use a phoropter to determine whether you need eye-glasses. It's got a series of lenses."

"Looks like an alien's face," I joked. She smiled but had probably heard similar comments a thousand times.

"Place your chin here," she said and pointed as she moved another device toward my head. This time, she used a lamp to look at the front of each eye and then conducted an eye-pressure test.

"Now's the part most patients don't like, but I need to dilate your pupils, and I'm going to start simply by placing a drop in each eye."

As she proceeded, I inquired, "So you grew up in Alabama?"

"Yes, Tuscaloosa. After high school, there was no choice but the University of Alabama. Well, there was a choice, but it seemed everyone in town went to the campus there, so I did, too. Ever been there?"

"No, I haven't."

"Well, it's beautiful. Buildings among old, tall trees. Just lovely. I really enjoyed it. Then I went to UA's optometry school in Birmingham."

Leaving the subject, she said, "It'll take about twenty minutes for full dilation, so I'll complete some paperwork." After turning on the ceiling light and while working at the small desk, she inquired, "If you don't mind me asking, what brought you here?"

"Well, like I said earlier, I was having some occasional migraines."

"Sorry. Poorly worded question. What caused you to come to this particular office?"

"Oh." I chuckled. "I should have known what you were asking. Yellow Pages. I didn't ask anyone for advice; I just looked under optometry in the Yellow Pages and something drew me to your name. There's no explanation other than that. Well, the small slogan under your name: *Nothing Is More Important than Your Sight.*" I assumed that meant the doctors here would have their customers' interests as their most important goal."

"Doctor," she replied. "There's just one of us—me."

Rising from her seat, she said, "I need to check on another patient, so I'll be back in about fifteen minutes. Meantime, just relax while your eyes do the same."

I relaxed so much I was startled when she returned, realizing I'd drifted to sleep. "Now let me look into those eyes," she said with such pleasantness her voice was almost intoxicating. "Look past my right ear as I look at the right eye," she requested and began moving a small bright light about, so extreme in its brightness, I could hardly bare it.

"How long have you been here?" I asked, not moving a muscle except the facial ones I used for the question.

"Four years. Came here from Talladega, Alabama, after having been in a partnership there."

"But Evansville of all places!"

"Evansville's nice. I really like it here, and my daughters do, too. They love their elementary school."

Growing bold, I asked, "What's your husband's profession?"

"I'm not married. Divorced. That's why we're in Evansville."

"I'm sorry. I shouldn't have asked. It was none of my business."

"Goodness, don't be sorry. I don't mind being asked." She offered no more, and I didn't ask.

After finishing the test, she donned a headset with an attachment and said she wanted to look at the peripheral retina. "Look up ... look to the right ... now down ..." and so forth she ordered until she removed her gear and walked to the wall switch where she turned on the lights.

"Good news, Mr. Miller." She smiled. "Your eyes are normal. The visual symptoms you described in conjunction with migraines might be neurological in nature. Your eyes aren't causing them."

"That's great. Then no need for glasses?"

She moved in front of me. "No, not for now. You're borderline on needing glasses for reading, so I recommend you see me in another year but no glasses for now."

Another year! I want to see you long before that.

We shook hands, and it might have been my wishful imagination but it seemed our grips lasted a little longer than normal. Our eyes held their focus on one another for a moment before she glanced down, let go of my hand, and thanked me for coming to her office.

Driving back to work, I knew I *had* to call her; I *had* to find an excuse for a call. For two days, she remained on my mind. The thought of her was controlling my life, driving me crazy. Finally, my heart rate elevated, dry-mouthed, I could see the ever-so-slight quiver in my right hand as I pushed the numbers on the phone in the privacy of my office. It was Wednesday, shortly after 10:00 a.m.

"Family Optometry," came the cheery salutation.

"Hello. My name's Davie Miller. I saw Dr. Johnston on Monday morning. Could I speak with her?"

Concerned, the female receptionist asked, "Oh, is there a problem, Mr. Miller? Is everything all right?"

"Well, uh ..." I paused, trying to think of exactly how I'd rehearsed a response, "yes, I'm fine. This is primarily a personal call, nothing urgent, and I'd be glad to leave my number if I may."

"Dr. Johnston's with a patient at the moment, but I'll give her the number when she's finished. She's got a pretty busy schedule today, so I can't promise when she might get back with you."

I gave her my private office number, wanting to provide my home one, too, but decided that might seem far too personal. "I'll be in my office until probably 6:00, then back tomorrow morning at eight."

It seemed the longest day of my life. I worked on client business, but my mind was directed to the agonizing anticipation of a ringing phone. In fact, every time it rang and it wasn't her, I tried not to be rude to the caller. At seven minutes after five—I would also remember this forever—I was alone in my office, the door closed, and the phone rang. "Davie Miller."

"Mr. Miller, this is Diane Johnston. I'm sorry it's taken me so long to get back to you, but I've been on the go all day and this is the first moment I've had to call. I hope everything's okay?"

Challenged by a mouth of cotton, fortunately, I'd taken a sip of water from a glass on my desk the moment she began to speak. "Oh, yes, everything's just fine." I thought my heart was going to beat out of my chest as I spoke quickly, "Dr. Johnston, I hope you won't think this horribly rude, but I wondered if you would have any interest in going to dinner with me someday after work or just meeting for a drink." Without so much as a pause, I continued, "Perhaps you consider it inappropriate to do so with clients. If so, or if you're in a relationship, then please forgive me for calling you." My right hand held a pencil, and I realized I was marking aimlessly on a small pad of white paper on the desktop. How I got those words out, I'll never know. Then I thought I'd pass out while waiting for her response.

"First, it's Diane. Second, I don't consider you rude. Third, I'd love to."

I failed to respond immediately, and it seemed like an eternity passed while I dealt with engulfing euphoria. "That's great. What shall it be, dinner or a drink?"

"I'm not much of a drinker, but let's meet some late afternoon and I'll get my mother to watch the girls after they get out of school."

Her mother? What's she doing in Evansville? Must be visiting. I didn't ask.

■ ▓ ■

The late Friday afternoon meeting for drinks—I had Coca-Cola, she a Diet Pepsi—evolved into dinner after all. Each of us was intrigued—in fact, fascinated—by the other. We'd agreed to meet (actually it was her idea) not far from where she lived on the west side of Evansville, in the vicinity of the Indiana State University regional campus.

Elizabeth's had quickly become a popular "in" place among the younger adult crowd in Evansville. Owned by Elizabeth and Kyle Sinclair, the money to build and open it came from his inheritance, but he insisted on the name, believing it would stand out in the growing crowd of restaurant choices, because almost no one ever placed a woman's name on a dining establishment. Both of them worked the crowd every night, and it didn't hurt that at fifty-three, she was, to use the term of young men, "stacked." Elizabeth Sinclair, "Betty" to her closest friends, was drop-dead gorgeous, and she played the male crowd by wearing dresses or tops that revealed her significant cleavage. The breasts were naturally hers, not surgeon-assisted. They were part of the restaurant's attraction.

We met in the dimly lit bar area of dark wood and soft, black-leather chairs surrounding small, round knee-high tables of fake dark marble. The wicks that rose from small, circular, clear oil-filled glass bases burned on each of the tables. Tall stools lined the bar.

At her urging, I related my life story in brief. She was profoundly sorry about Anne. I apologized. "I seem to have done all the talking. What about you?"

"That's fine. I asked in the first place," she replied. "Well, I'll be brief, too. I met my former husband when we were students in optometry school. We married just over a year after getting our degrees and took the foolish chance of opening a practice together in Talladega—Johnston Optometry. As we were approaching graduation, we'd found out about an older optometrist who wanted to sell his practice and retire. We thought it a perfect opportunity. Talladega was okay, and my husband, being a NASCAR fan, thought it heaven on earth. But it was a mistake. We had a good marriage and produced two wonderful daughters, but working together every day and taking our work home at night was too much. We'd argue about the business and then ..." Her voice dropped, and she looked at the floor. "... I found out Mark was seeing someone, a patient. I was mad and heartbroken. We separated immediately and were divorced as quickly as the judicial system would permit it.

"My mother had family up here—she'd been born and raised around

Princeton—and they made me aware of an almost identical situation to what Mark and I had encountered in Alabama, someone wanting to retire, so here I am."

"And that's why your mother is here, too?"

"As it turns out, yes. Daddy died while I was in optometry school. After I came here four years ago, I urged Mother to move up here to be near me and her granddaughters and what family she has left in the area. It turned out to be a blessing for her and for me. She gets to see a sister, cousins, nieces, and nephews she'd rarely seen over the years of living in Alabama, and she's an instant sitter of my daughters whenever I need her. I hardly have to ask. Mother lives only three miles from us in a small home of her own."

"How old are your girls?"

"Almost seven and almost nine. Jillian was only two when we moved here. Both she and Lydia—that's my mother's middle name and mine, too—attend the same school, and Mother watches them every day after school until I get home. Lucky, aren't I?"

"You sure are."

We realized we wanted to talk more, wanted to learn so much more about one another, so while I was inquiring with the dining room receptionist about a table for two, Diane went to a pay phone and called her mother.

I watched her intently during dinner, captivated by her striking good looks; there was not even a blemish on her face. She had perfectly formed, pure-white teeth, and the warmth of her smile and the pleasantness of her voice made me wonder how some jerk could leave her for someone else. Had I become the fortunate forty-year-old victim of "love at first sight"? If so, what a coincidental pun considering her profession?

Time flew that evening, an hour in the lounge and two hours at dinner. Diane carefully inquired about Anne, our marriage, and my life without her. I wanted to know more about her life in Alabama. "I kept Johnston after the divorce. My maiden name is Habig, but I thought if I went back to it, I would just complicate things here with me being Habig and my daughters being Johnston. It would be unfair to them to have to explain that all the time."

Surprisingly to each of us, on this first-ever evening together, it was obvious we felt comfortable asking about the other's dating lives. "I've dated some the last five years but never anyone seriously," I revealed.

"Well, I haven't. After the divorce, the girls and I soon moved up here, and I had no interest in men for a long time. One thing I've learned is that an unmarried, nearly forty-year-old with two children is not an attraction. But I dearly love my daughters, and they've been my source of strength through some difficult times. And my dear mother has been, too. She still is."

Before we parted, I said, "I was so very nervous about calling you Wednesday, afraid you would think it inappropriate for me to do so. I'm glad I did. I had a wonderful time tonight."

"I'll let you in on a little secret," she said with a look that made me melt. "I was hoping we'd see one another again."

CHAPTER 29

"Mother, I'd like you to meet David Miller," Diane said a week later when I stopped at her house to pick her up for dinner. "Davie, Thelma Habig."

I bowed my head ever so slightly and smiled as we shook hands. "Please to meet you, ma'am. I've heard a lot about you."

With a slight drawl similar to her daughter's, Thelma replied, "I hope it wasn't all bad," and smiled.

I gave a slight chuckle. "No, ma'am. I assure you it was all good."

Diane had told me her mother had a habit of coming to conclusions quickly, judging books by their covers. I hoped she liked the cover standing in front of her.

"Where're your daughters?" I inquired.

"They and their good friends Haley and Alyssa are playing at Cousin Nicole and Drew's house and should have been home by now. But it's only 6:30, and they'll likely be here by seven," Diane replied. "Mother, make certain they brush their teeth before going to bed. Jill won't unless you tell her to. And, I don't care how late they stay up on a Saturday night, but I know you're not a night owl, so I won't have to worry that it will be too late," she added flashing a wry grin.

"I'll have you know I sometimes stay up until 9:30, young lady," Thelma retorted and winked at me.

▬ ▬ ▬

Our dinner dates became more frequent, and in April, we attended an Anne Murray concert at Roberts Stadium. We both enjoyed her music,

245

which was a cross between our two favorites, country and pop. The performance came two weeks after the seventh anniversary of my Anne's death, and I was torn with emotion, almost a guilty feeling, listening to this other Anne singing "I Just Fall in Love Again." I'd certainly done that. And I felt Diane had, too. It was a comforting feeling.

Diane was fortunate in that her "ex" paid monthly child support but made no demands to see his daughters. It was an unfortunate situation for the girls though. They'd been without a father in their lives for more than four years and had seen him only twice, though they never went to Talladega to spend any time with him. Their mother found it difficult to accept that a man could divorce himself not only from his wife but, in effect, from his children, too.

We made love for the first time in her home, exactly two months date-wise after my appointment at her office. It was a Sunday afternoon. The girls were with their grandmother who'd promised to take them to Mesker Zoo. They'd been there several times and seemingly never tired of going.

The raw display of our lust swept the family room of the ranch-style house and then her bedroom as years of pent-up emotion from not having been entangled with a person of the opposite sex were unleashed. Seeing her nude for the first time, I thought hers the most perfectly formed body God could have made, similar to Anne's. She seemed likewise consumed by the sculpture of my broad shoulders and toned torso. We lay afterward, her head on my hairy chest, a sheet pulled to our waists. As she slowly stroked my flat stomach, I toyed with her exposed right ear, and she spoke. "It's been five years!" She didn't have to explain.

"Then I guess we were saving ourselves for one another," I replied.

She raised her head, looked lovingly at me, and responded, "It was well worth the wait."

Without warning, we heard the sound of a key entering the lock on the front door and then the doorknob being turned. Diane bolted from the bed, pushed the bedroom door closed, rushed to her closet for a robe, and pulled the door closed behind her when she entered the hallway leading to the living room. "Jill's sick!" I heard her mother exclaim, as she and the two girls entered the house. "Sorry to have come home so early, but I thought it best to get her here and to bed." I cracked the bedroom door slightly and noticed her mother, obviously having seen my car in the driveway, flash a sheepish grin as she looked at Diane's robe and then her disheveled hair.

Her face flushed, Diane squatted and hugged Jillian. "Oh, honey, I'm sorry you don't feel well. Tell me what's wrong."

"I threw up near the monkey cage. My tummy hurts, and I don't feel well."

"Let me feel your head," Diane responded, placing her lips to Jillian's right temple. "You're warm, so I suspect you have a little bit of fever but not a lot. Let's go back to your bedroom, and I'll put you to bed." Looking at Lydia, Diane said, "Lyd, you can sleep with me tonight," and then seeing her older daughter start toward her bedroom, she blurted, "Wait! Not now! You, uh, you can get some things out of your room to play with in the living room until it's bedtime." I'd quickly eased the door shut and held a foot against the bottom of it.

The quartet moved down the hallway, past Diane's room, and into the bedroom shared by the girls. Diane told me later that while she helped Jillian get out of her clothing and into bed, Thelma assisted Lydia in selecting some dolls and games. Pulling the covers up to her daughter's neck, Diane said, "Just lie here and try to be comfortable. Be sure to call out to me if you need anything. I'm not going to give you anything to eat or drink right now." Then suddenly realizing Lydia wasn't in the room, Diane told me she wheeled and bolted into the hallway and was aghast to see her own bedroom door open.

"Mommy, you didn't make your bed today," Lydia called out from inside the room. Rushing the several feet from one bedroom to the other, Diane found her older daughter standing at the foot of the bed. Diane related she was horrified at the prospect of Lydia seeing me and wondering at the same time where I was. *Is he in the closet, under the bed, in the bathroom? Does he have any clothes on? My God, what if she sees him?* Thoughts were flying through her head, she said. She was frantic.

Then her mother walked in and calmly whispered into her ear. "Don't worry, sweetheart. I just saw a car back out of the driveway."

"Her wry smile said a thousand words," Diane told me. She said her shoulders sagged and she whispered, "Thank God," to Thelma.

Within an hour, she'd called me at my home. I was laughing. "I'm sorry. I shouldn't laugh. I hope Jill isn't quite ill."

"She'll be fine. Probably too much hot dog, soft drink, and cotton candy. Mother always gets the girls anything they want. I suspect she'll be fine by tomorrow morning."

"I was laughing at the situation, about almost getting caught. Wouldn't we have had red faces?"

"How in the world did you get away?"

"As soon as the four of you walked down the hallway, I grabbed my clothes and dashed into the bathroom to put them on. Then I carefully opened the bedroom door, tiptoed quickly across the living room, carrying my shoes, hopped into my car, and left, hoping no one would see me."

"Mother did, but she just smiled about it. She's a sly fox, my mother. Never worry about her. She's so happy for me she can hardly stand it." Diane paused, and I felt the sensuality of her whisper. "I *have* to see you again. *Soon.*"

▬ ▓ ▬

Over the next almost two months, we were together nearly every day immediately after we got off work—sometimes having sex in her office after the staff left—or nearly every evening and on the weekends, her girls quickly growing accustomed to seeing and enjoying me. They seemed to drink in my kindness. Lydia was the type who never met a stranger, but Jillian displayed little-girl shyness the first couple of times she was around me after we were introduced at a restaurant where the four of us had brunch. She soon warmed up to me, and it wasn't long before she was sitting on my lap with Lydia on the sofa at my side when I read children's short stories to them in their home. Reading to children was one of the pleasures of my life, as I'd been serving as a volunteer reader to first- and second-grade children in an elementary school near downtown Evansville for several years, something I'd decided to do in Anne's memory.

Inevitably, the subject of baseball came up. "Would all of you like to go with me to a baseball game someday?" I asked one evening. "I know the Dodgers team here real well, and I'd love to take you." Looking at the girls, I offered, "I can even introduce you to some of the players and probably get an autographed ball for each of you."

There was little reaction, which was disappointing to me, but their mother said, "We'd love to, wouldn't we, girls?" to which she saw continued stares until she added, "We can get soft drinks and peanuts and Cracker Jacks," a statement guaranteed to get a "Yeah, let's go!" response.

"I've got the perfect game for us," I said. "The Fourth of July. There'll be fireworks afterward. Clowns will be there as will silly *Buster,* the team mascot. You'll like him. I'll even make sure you get to meet him."

— ▬ ▬

The evening game was a sellout, as the Dodgers were holding on to first place by two games and continuing a streak of ten years of breaking season attendance records. Attendance in 1981 was running 8 percent ahead of the previous year's. I had four tickets down the third base line, three rows up from the field and just to the right of the home team dugout. I didn't realize how risky it would be to take two young girls without much knowledge or interest in baseball an hour ahead of the start when, with fireworks, they'd be there about five hours. *Buster* came to our seats and hugged each of the girls although Jillian, not being certain about him, tried to shy away. Clowns representing the Shrine Circus were in the stands and on the field during pregame practice, and one of them, Curly, gave both girls balloons that he twisted together to look like animal characters. I got shortstop Javier Sanchez and left-fielder Will Junkins to autograph balls they handed the girls while introducing themselves. "Wow, isn't that something—your own baseball!" I exclaimed, disappointingly eliciting little reaction. My work was cut out for me to make them fans of baseball, assuming their ages might have as much to do with it as anything.

By the time Diane's mother and I held a surprise fortieth birthday dinner for her, inviting her staff and friends to a private room at Elizabeth's on August 17, the night before the milestone, I felt I'd known her for years, she'd shared so much about herself.

Diane Lydia Habig Johnston was born and raised in Tuscaloosa. Her father was a professor at the University of Alabama and a staunch fan of Crimson Tide athletics, especially football. To most supporters—and there were many thousands—the coach could have been *Saint* Bear Bryant, he was so revered. Dr. Christian Habig—Diane was born while he was earning his PhD in economics at the university—joined the faculty in 1942. Just a month shy of his twenty-second year there, he died of a massive heart attack in the classroom. Diane's mother had no career of her own, having devoted herself to raising her only child. But Professor Habig had invested wisely in stocks as well as in the financial services company

Teachers Insurance and Annuity Association–College Retirement Equities Fund. TIAA-CREF was a massive national organization that specialized in helping those in academics invest and save for retirement. Altogether, Thelma was left with an estate of more than one million dollars.

Diane grew up as a tomboy, roughhousing with boys her age, but always upset they wouldn't let her try to play baseball with them. "You're a *girl!*" they'd exclaim. "Girls can't play ball. They throw like sissies."

She had been as skinny as a rail during childhood and until she began developing a bust and adding weight by the time she was thirteen. The "tomboy" had turned into a prized catch for any midteen boy; by the time she was old enough to drive a car, she was considered the most attractive girl in her class.

Although her parents strongly but inwardly wanted her to go to UA, they told her she could go anywhere she wanted, even a private college. She began applying the spring of her junior year and had acceptances by late that fall from Harvard, Stanford, University of Michigan, University of North Carolina, and UA. Despite only two Bs throughout her first three years of high school, she decided to pass up more prestigious schools in favor of her hometown university, primarily because several of her closest girlfriends were enrolling there.

She could never recall why she chose optometry for a career. For some reason, she was drawn to the sciences and excelled at chemistry, biology, and physics while earning her bachelor's in chemistry. A summer internship with a Tuscaloosa optometrist friend of the Habig family, between her sophomore and junior years, sparked a keen interest in the profession. The thought of helping people with what she believed was the most precious sense they had led her to the decision to pursue the career. It was at the university's medical center in Birmingham that she earned her optometry degree and met her future husband. I knew the rest of the story.

Often, we spent hours talking politics, world affairs, economics, entertainment, religion, you name it. She was engaging and bright, well-read. I'd always heard it was dangerous to talk politics and religion with someone you admired, so I was cautious.

Although I still considered myself a Kennedy Democrat and she was more conservative, our discussions never got heated. We'd fallen too much in love to risk letting political views ruin a great thing.

She'd been raised a Southern Baptist. Her mother had become a member of the Baptist Temple in Evansville, and Diane and the girls attended there irregularly. "Something was missing," she told me, referring to the ministry. So she and her daughters had tried different churches. Within a few visits with me, she felt she fit in well at the United Methodist where I belonged, my far eastside church home ever since Anne and I had married. I'd rarely missed a Sunday-morning service and had finally served on several committees, currently Pastor-Parish Relations.

We attended area cultural events—live theater, concerts, and the symphony—thoroughly enjoyed movies, and of course watched the local Dodgers on occasion because I needed to be there from time to time. My agency account was still vitally important to our company.

———

Eighteen months after we met, we were married in a private ceremony, attended only by her daughters, her mother, and my parents. Mom and Dad loved Diane, just as they had Anne. And to have two more grandchildren, even though only by marriage, was icing on the cake. They and Thelma got along well and enjoyed spending time together. She thought Barclay to be a "cute" town and welcomed opportunities to visit their home. I deeply regretted Diane and her mother never got to meet my grandmother Johnson who'd died two years earlier at age eighty-nine, having lived the final two years of her life in an Alzheimer's unit at an assisted-living center in Pemberton. It is a sad disease and prohibited her from recognizing me for nearly four years before she passed away. Grandma had been such a vibrant woman in her prime, full of wit and spunk. Being of similar disposition, Thelma would have especially enjoyed her.

A regional airline carrier took us to Chicago's O'Hare the following day. We dreaded having to go through one of the world's busiest airports since we'd heard so many horror stories from friends who'd dealt with the crowds, but we awakened at 3:30 a.m. for the approximately one-hour flight that left Evansville at 6:00. Our direct American Airlines flight to Maui was on time and left seventy-five minutes after we arrived at O'Hare, but the twelve-hour honeymoon journey to the main airport at Kahului on Lazy 8-shaped Maui via a switch of planes at Honolulu left us exhausted.

When we arrived, it was 4:15 p.m. in Maui—a four-hour time difference from Southern Indiana—and by the time we picked up the powder-blue Volkswagen convertible we'd reserved from the Hertz rental facility and drove an hour along the Pacific coast to Kapalua at the far northwest of the island, we felt like zombies. Had it not been for the picture-perfect, sunny, blue sky typical of Maui, and the awesome view from our Bay Villas window at Kapalua Resort, we would have crashed into bed without removing our clothing or unpacking our suitcases. But our exuberance at being there, the amazing beauty of the island, the picturesque and almost indescribable setting of the sun as it slowly disappeared between neighboring Molokai and Lanai, and of being Mr. and Mrs. Davie Miller for less than forty-eight hours kept us going, until our bodies hit the proverbial brick wall and we could go no longer. We couldn't even manage sex in the most idyllic of settings.

I awoke first, at 4:30 a.m., the time zone difference being too much of an adjustment in one night and tried unsuccessfully to go back to sleep, tossing and turning for a half hour until I felt a hand touching my left hip from behind as I lay on my right side. The hand teasingly descended, immediately eliciting a warm hardness despite the fact I was still somewhat groggy. Slowly, I turned onto my back, and my lips found hers and the heat of her mouth. Her tongue explored while she moved her body over mine, and I was soon inside her. It was the beginning of a week of exhilarating love and exploration.

■ ▪ ■

Our villa was perched above the craggy lava rock shoreline shaped by nonstop waves from the glistening Pacific, which sometimes pounded violently in contrast to its name, but the ocean in front of us this day was placid. Brilliant, lazy, white waves crested not far from shore. Our U-shaped third-story honeymoon romance palace had one bedroom with a king bed, two bathrooms, a living room and a kitchen, all in an advertised 1,250 square feet. Sliding glass doors led from the bedroom and the living room to an open-sided lanai with two lounge chairs and a small glass-topped table with its four chairs. Water was everywhere we looked, changing at times from dark blue to greenish to aqua to emerald. The setting reminded me of Anne and some of the scenes we saw in Tahiti, and I became melancholy just thinking about her.

A twisting, mostly rocky path along the shore led up to a deluxe hotel. On the nearby hillside lay a heavily sand-trapped, tree-lined golf course that sloped toward the ocean and was abutted along the top side by more villas that offered views even more stunning than ours.

Diane described Kapalua as "heaven on earth" although she had hardly begun to see much of Maui. The resort was colored lush green, punctuated by palms and the tall, narrow, cone-shaped Cook Pine. There seemed an endless variety of flowering bushes and trees, the blooms in numerous shades of red, yellow, and purple. Both adopted our favorite as the tall orange-flowered African tulip tree found throughout the resort. The daily high temperature was about eighty-five degrees, and the wind was always present but calm. Mornings, we awoke to "vog," volcanic air pollution from the big island of Hawaii southeast of Maui, creating a type of smog that gave way to sun and blue sky during the afternoon. Sunsets behind the two nearby small islands were spectacles, if the typical late-afternoon light cloudiness gave way.

Although never cutting short our time in bed, we were active out of doors throughout the week, snorkeling off a catamaran at crescent-shaped Molokini, driving the six hundred curves along the northeast coast to Hana, visiting Charles Lindberg's grave a little further down the coast from the town, taking the steep, curvy drive to the highest point in Maui, the ten-thousand-plus-foot peak of Haleakala, a dormant volcano that had last erupted two or three hundred years ago, driving into the richly green, quiet, almost serene Iao Valley, one of the rainiest places on earth, walking the long hotel-lined beach at Kaanapali and hand in hand exploring the shops along Front Street, which paralleled the waterfront in the most popular, although small, town of Lahaina.

Diane was fascinated with the Hawaiian alphabet, comprised only of five vowels and eight consonants, one of which looked like an upside-down apostrophe. As we drove through towns or villages, she'd attempt to sound out names in the proper manner and often got so tongue-tied both she and I laughed out loud. Reading from a tour booklet, she said, "It says here that King Kamehameha I ..." She tried five times to pronounce it the way she thought it to be. "... was the first of five monarchs to rule the Kingdom of Hawaii from the late 1700s to the late 1800s, and he united the Hawaiian islands. But get this, Davie." She paused as she studied the name of the first king's great-grandfather. "The great-grandfather of the first monarch was ..." She again paused and began counting the letters. "... Well, I can't begin to pronounce it, but it has twenty-three or twenty-four letters. Can you believe that? Twenty-three or twenty-four depending on whether you count that little squiggly mark I see." And she began listing them, "K-e-a-w ..." until she had spelled Keaweikekahiali'iokamoku. "My God, it would have taken his people half their lives just to try to pronounce his name," she said and began laughing so hard her sides were hurting and tears had rolled down her right cheek. The pure joy and happiness in her face made me feel so at peace.

Our daily dress was shorts and T-shirts, no matter where we went, even fine restaurants. We found time most days to lie on one of the beaches and soak up the sun, always protected by breezes from the nearby mountains or the Pacific. On the last afternoon, sitting in a rented beach chair with my feet in the water at Kapalua Bay, I held her hand and mused, "You said earlier in the week this is 'heaven on earth.' Well, if I were to die and go to heaven and God said to me, 'Welcome to Maui,' I'd be happy." It was a blissful time.

￭ ▦ ￭

During our tightly packed week, we even managed to squeeze in the one-hundred-mile flight from the small hilltop airport near Kapalua to Honolulu, where we spent the day in almost utter silence, absorbed by the sadness of what had happened at Pearl Harbor on December 7, 1941.

Not one to have biases against people of other races, I surprised myself by developing one on that day of visiting museums with their wall-mounted, captioned, black-and-white photos and watching movies of the horror of the surprise Japanese attack. Not one of the boatload of visitors to the USS *Arizona* memorial said a word on the brilliant white, narrow structure straddling the width of the sunken ship that continued to hold the remains of hundreds of US sailors and amazingly still leaked oil, which could be seen on the surface. People were openly talkative at the historic USS *Missouri*, the huge battleship that had become a floating museum of sorts. It hadn't been at Pearl Harbor those forty-one years ago—in fact, it hadn't been built yet—but its place in history was secured by being the ceremonial deck for the signing of the Japanese surrender in Tokyo Bay in September 1945, ending the world's costliest war. I thought back to what my mother had told me about the hardships Americans endured during those four years of war and the lives of the many thousands of our military that were lost, and shook my head. I was angered.

Diane mused how the Japanese visitors to Pearl Harbor must feel. I opined they must not have feelings of remorse, because they, and other "Orientals" I assumed were Chinese, were so "damned pushy," cutting into lines, brushing shoulders with others as they rushed to get from one place to another. Such feelings and expressions were out of character for me, but the emotion of everything I saw overwhelmed me.

Diane told me to keep my thoughts to myself, "No sense starting an incident here of all places!" Finally, at the end of the flight home, I'd had enough.

We were seated midway back in the thirty-passenger plane and after seat belts were permitted to be unbuckled, an older man—I guessed him to be in his seventies and Japanese—barged from the rear of the plane, down the aisle before the door had been opened and before others in front of him had risen from their seats. He stopped momentarily next to me, and I, filled with emotion from Pearl Harbor's displays and the behavior of some of the foreign guests, lost it. I threw my right arm out into the aisle, across the front of the man. "Stop right there!" I commanded with a volume that caused heads to turn. Bolting from my seat and looking into the face of the man from no more than three feet away, I said, "Your people lost the war! Now show some respect. Get back!" and pointed toward the back rows. Horrified, Diane grabbed my right forearm and squeezed so hard the nails of her fingers dug deep into the skin. I turned to her and in return received a stare that could have penetrated steel. The target of my scorn hadn't understood a word of what I'd screamed, but he certainly understood the demeanor and its related intent. He stepped backward about three feet, letting Diane and me get into line.

Diane muttered, "Davie, I can't believe you did that. I can't believe it." No doubt my face had been ashen, and I could feel it change to crimson at the admonishment from my wife, but I wouldn't look back at the much shorter, thinner, older man behind me. Despite Diane's feelings, I was the recipient of several low-volume "Way to tell him off" type of remarks from passengers standing in front of me. I showed no further reaction; I wanted to but knew I'd have a wounded wife to deal with anyway once we set foot on the ground. Exiting the ramp and walking toward the terminal, I looked at her beside me and saw the penetrating stare hadn't ceased. My outburst had been far out of character and not in line with the treatment of another human being that I'd espoused in my church speeches. At the moment, I wasn't ashamed. I had just been overwhelmed by the thought of the senseless world war, the thousands of people who had been killed, and the seemingly disrespectful way I thought many of the Asian visitors to Pearl Harbor conducted themselves on this day.

"Sir," I heard a female voice behind me. "Sir?" I turned. It was a young Asian woman just in front of the older man and a woman beside him. Almost rushing to me, she said, "Sir, I apologize for my father. He was wrong to do what he did." She was almost bowing as we stopped on the tarmac. "I live here, and my parents are visiting. They live in a Japanese culture of so much population they feel they have to push to get anywhere. I'm afraid it's just a part of their lives, and they don't know to turn it off when they're out of their country. Please accept my apology." She turned to her father and spoke in Japanese, to which he placed his hands in a prayerlike position, bowed to me, and uttered something in his language. "He says he is deeply sorry for his actions and hopes you will not hold his display of rudeness against his daughter, him and his wife, and his country." I was speechless, so humbled by the display of remorse by a man I had belittled, all I could do was bow in return.

Breaking the silence when we got into our car at the airport parking lot, Diane said sarcastically, "Well, 'Mr. Role Model,' 'Mr. We Must Show Respect to All People,' I think you've just eaten a piece of humble pie." I felt the sting. It was deserved. I knew she meant no malice, and nothing more was ever said about the matter.

CHAPTER 30

After six months of living in Diane's two-bedroom home—I'd been fortunate to sell mine and make a handsome profit—we moved into a relatively new two-story, three-bedroom house that featured an extra room for an office and a cathedral ceiling and wide fireplace in the great room. Tall white wooden columns graced the front porch. The gray stone, brick, and white wood structure was in a hillside neighborhood of similar houses just off State Road 62 a few miles further west of where we'd been living. The location just inside the county line from neighboring Posey County was still convenient to her mother's house and to Diane's office. It meant a further drive into downtown where Wilson-McGlasson was located, but that was no big deal. And best of all, the girls would still be going to school in Vanderburgh County.

The house was more expensive than the ones we'd owned, but there would be no problem meeting the monthly mortgage payments. We'd gotten the most favorable rate possible from Central Vanderburgh State Bank, and our combined income would allow us to live quite comfortably, although Diane didn't make as much as people would think for a person in her profession.

My salary received a boost when I was unexpectedly made a vice president and offered a partnership in the agency a year and a half later. It was October 1984. I'd been there seventeen years.

"Davie, I have a new, major account for you, and for us," Bruce Wilson informed me in late November from across the desk of the agency president's office. "Latimore College." My heart sank. "I know what you must be thinking, 'What in the world are we doing taking on *that* institution as

257

an account?' It's a fair question. I realize their reputation isn't particularly healthy, and that's part of the reason they approached us. Both Gary and I had four meetings with them before making the decision. We did so in large measure because we felt *you* were *the* person who could handle the account, especially their egocentric president." I knew Stephen Wiseman only by reputation, and there was nothing exciting about having to work with him.

Only his very closest friends were permitted to call him Steve and only in private. To all others, it was Stephen or Dr. Wiseman or Mr. President or President Wiseman, depending on where one stood on the scale of rank. It was his requirement. Stephan F. Wiseman, PhD, EdD, the former in philosophy, the latter in higher education with an emphasis on administration, felt the sun rose, shined, and set on him. To him, life was all about him; it evolved around him. It was an opinion not shared by many, not even his wife. He was larger than life, and it was a tacit requirement to cater to him, respect him, and acknowledge his presence, title, accomplishments, and absolute rule. As a result, he'd had numerous clashes with the faculty. Even though his was a private liberal arts institution whose records of proceedings were not made public, reports of his difficulties with the faculty often found their way to the media anyway.

Latimore College was located on a hilly, wooded campus in far north Evansville. When founded by millionaire industrialist Calvin Latimore in 1919, the college was in a rural area. But as the metropolitan area grew, the institution eventually became part of the city. Originally an all-male school, it began accepting women in 1937 and now had a student body of six hundred, 62 percent men. The college proudly promoted its 12:1 faculty-student ratio. The campus was considered one of the prettiest in Indiana, with the layout of the dark-brick buildings among stately oak, maple, and ash well-planned from the inception. In addition to Emily Latimore Hall, the administration building named for Calvin's wife, there were three classroom buildings, four dormitories, the library, a student center, and the president's small two-story house. A physical education/ recreational sports/gymnasium facility lay at the north end of campus, and there was a men's basketball team that had been participating in NAIA (National Association of Intercollegiate Athletics) competition only since 1970. No other intercollegiate sports existed. Latimore College was affiliated with the Southeastern Baptist Church of America of which

Calvin Latimore had been a staunch supporter and member. Therefore, drinking alcoholic beverages and smoking on campus were prohibited. Dances at social functions were not permitted until 1970.

The year 1970 was significant in that it was the third year of the presidency of Edward Thompson, a Baptist layman, the first nonordained president in the college's fifty-one-year history. He was more liberal than his predecessors, believing the institution could only survive if it loosened some of its deeply conservative social hold on the student body. His strategy worked, because in the second year of his presidency, there was a 2 percent increase in enrollment, followed by a 1 percent gain at the beginning of his third. The enrollment increase broke a slight downward trend that had begun a decade earlier.

Thompson was replaced in 1978 when he left to assume the presidency of Salisbury College in North Carolina. The replacement was Stephen F. Wiseman. Make that, *Doctor* Stephen F. Wiseman. He was a head case from the outset, and at least one-third of the nine-member board of trustees wondered within three months why in the world they'd hired him. The fact was, he got attention for the college and enrollment had held stable for his first three years before starting down again. Was the decrease the $21,500 price tag for attending Latimore, the restrictions on social life, the negative publicity the president had been receiving, or something else? Finding out and making recommendations for correcting the cause or causes was the challenge for Wilson-McGlasson.

Wiseman had been hired after being away from college administration for a year. The circumstances under which he'd left the presidency of Corning College in Iowa were suspect, although he and a college news release both said he felt he'd achieved all he could and wanted to seek responsibilities elsewhere, hopefully within higher education.

"We might be able to help with the reputation of the college," I responded to Bruce, "but not that president. No one's going to change him. I just hope he doesn't do more harm to the school than he already has." Bruce was understanding. He and Gary McGlasson had expressed misgivings to one another before making the final decision to add Latimore to their list of clients and realized the president would be their biggest challenge. They felt I could handle the account well, and Wiseman had assured them he would be fully cooperative in listening to advice and giving it a thorough review. They knew he couldn't be trusted 100 percent.

But, to the trustees' credit, a $450,000 three-year contract with Wilson-McGlasson was approved with the option for either party to extend. The college had a strong endowment, so nearly a half million dollars was a drop in the bucket.

"Do you hold an advanced degree?" Wiseman smugly asked at the first meeting he had with Bruce, Gary, and me in early December. Wiseman already knew the answer, but it was his immediate attempt to establish rank with this junior person assigned to him. The college executive was only ten years older than I, but in Wiseman's mind, his superiority and acumen far exceeded any numbers in years.

"No, sir, a bachelor's, in marketing."

Bruce quickly inserted, "Mr. Miller is one of the top public relations minds in the city, in the state for that matter. His more than twenty years of experience in the profession and achievements of his clients speak volumes."

"I see." The smugness continued from an all-too-proud holder of two doctorates. "And you went to the University of Evansville," Wiseman continued, with a raised eyebrow; it was more of a statement than a question. Without giving me an opportunity to reply, he quipped, "Not bad for a larger private institution, but a little too large for my taste, although the president there and I get along well. At least we haven't had any major disagreements in meetings of presidents of the state's private colleges and the universities and those here in the Evansville region."

As he talked, I sized him up. Probably about five-ten and not a bad shape, although he had a slight potbelly that I'd noticed behind the rarely unbuttoned dark-gray suit jacket as we were standing. The hair was the blackest I'd ever seen, and then I realized it had been colored. *Colored! Stephen Wiseman colors his hair! The mustache on his narrow face and his thick eyebrows, too. What an egotist!* When Wiseman finally offered us seats and turned to walk to his chair behind the desk, I noticed the mostly balding spot at the crown of his head. He'd combed hair over it and tried to hold it in place with spray, but if he thought people hadn't noticed, this was one battle Stephen Wiseman was losing. He couldn't control everything.

An assortment of pipes was in a desktop stand, so I assumed he smoked. His stuffed-shirt appearance was enhanced by a bow tie. *A bow tie! Nobody wears a bow tie anymore, for God's sake.* But Stephen F. Wiseman did, always with heavily starched white shirts with traditional collars, never button-downs. The attire was what he thought helped to set him apart. It did.

Not letting up, he continued directing comments at me, as though the agency's two top executives weren't in the room. "Let me tell you a bit about Latimore College and the challenges I ... er, we ... think we face. You may know some of it from your two bosses here ..." It was another dig at me not being at the level of Dr. Pompous sitting across the extra-large cherry-wood desk from me—and Wiseman launched into a pontification on the achievements and weaknesses of the institution, although "weaknesses" is my word, not his.

Reversing declining enrollment was the challenge. The causes, the president admitted, weren't known. But he had begrudgingly agreed that a perceptional survey among current students and those in high school and junior high/middle school was among the tools the agency could use with the college paying the cost beyond the annual monetary agreement for Wilson-McGlasson's services.

I was given permission, for which I was thankful, to interview faculty and staff in individual, private meetings with none of the names of the persons chosen to be linked to my findings. My partners and I had already decided that community leaders' opinions, opinions of executives of other institutions of higher learning, and those of parents of current and potential students would also be sought. The costs of obtaining this information would be borne by the agency, but we weren't making Wiseman aware we were going to conduct those interviews. Finally, we would speak privately and confidentially with any of the colleges' trustees who were willing to weigh in.

The challenge was enormous, almost mind-boggling to me. And as Bruce and Gary had already advised the president and the trustees, turning around a reputation would take years. It wasn't like the task of selling televisions and appliances for an advertised price and having people come in that day to purchase. Convincing prospective students and their parents that Latimore College was *the* place for them would take time and money. But first, the root or roots of the problem had to be identified. We also stated it would take at least six months, but we'd shoot for only six months, June commencement, as the maximum to conduct all the research. Our recommendations wouldn't be ready until July, too late to have any impact on the 1985–86 fall semester. Wiseman and the trustees understood and accepted the time line.

Fortunately, I was permitted to give up the lead account role with the Evansville Dodgers but would remain in an advisory position for my colleague who was named to oversee the relationship with the franchise. A different set of eyes would be good anyway. Bud Stanley had retired five years earlier, and I'd gotten along well with the new general manager, but after so many years of being connected with the club, it was good that someone else would take over. I would also take on a lesser role with Hobson Chevrolet. All the time I could muster for at least the next three years would be required for Latimore College.

It took Bruce and me and the opinion research firm we hired nearly four weeks to finalize the research instruments that contained the questions we wanted to ask current and prospective students and parents. Privacy laws wouldn't permit the college to give its students' names and addresses to the agency, but the school would do the mailing with instructions that no names or addresses were to be placed anywhere on the long questionnaire or the return envelope. The envelope was addressed to the research company.

Selected high schools and junior high/middle schools in a broad twenty-one-county area of Southern Indiana—87 percent of the student body came from within that region—were asked to cooperate by presenting survey forms to students/parents who in turn were asked to complete them on a voluntary basis.

Meantime, I was given a list of all faculty and staff and their campus addresses and office telephone numbers. Bruce said he would interview selected community leaders, who included business and bank executives, heads of school districts and nonprofit agencies, and a few others. Of course I knew Bruce wouldn't do it all by himself—he'd get other agency staff to assist him—but it was thought that one chief executive interviewing another would produce the best results. Even Gary got involved. He volunteered to interview college presidents, which turned out to be the easiest task. None would talk with him on or off the record. So he was given another assignment: talk with as many trustees as are willing to speak, all of it off any written record.

Faculty were all too eager to be interviewed. In fact, my challenge would be to limit the interviewees to a manageable number. Staff were more reticent, but I was successful in obtaining enough permissions to make the resultant findings indicative of overall feelings.

"The answer is the president's a jerk," was the candid opening reply from Professor Willard Bell, head of the faculty council. "All the significant problems of this institution can be traced to one person, Stephen F. Wiseman."

I quickly inserted, "Now, remember, Professor, we're trying to understand why enrollment has been declining at Latimore, so how does the president's relationship with the faculty council relate to that?"

"You don't understand? It's not just his relationship with the council but with the faculty overall. Add to that his relationship with students, especially student leaders. I assume you have them on your list."

To my embarrassment, I didn't. *How in the world could we have forgotten them?* To hide the faux pas, I replied assuredly, "They'll be interviewed."

Bell, a professor of history, continued, "It's a morale issue among faculty. We're treated as second-class citizens, subservient to the wishes of our exalted leader. 'Exalted' only in his mind, I might add. It's been a constant battle for us ever since he came here. And when faculty feel unappreciated and unheard, it affects their performance in the classroom. Word gets around among students on campus and in the community that faculty are uncaring, and there goes a once-proud reputation. Blame it all on Stephen Wiseman." Bell didn't let up, and his frank opinions were exactly what I wanted.

"Faculty have a voice. The president hears but doesn't listen. The same for the trustees. He's got them in his hip pocket. And you know what? The funny thing is our issues are not salary. Isn't that a switch—a faculty not necessarily wanting more money? Our issues have to do with having better teaching aids in the classroom—modern electronic equipment to help reach a student body that has grown up in what is fast becoming a visual world. With classroom facilities that aren't as old as Methuselah. They are so out-of-date it isn't funny. We've fallen way behind other schools of higher learning in the region in all those areas, and in the most important issue of all, faculty governance. We strongly feel we should have the ultimate decision in regard to admissions standards, curriculum, and the awarding of degrees. But Wiseman controls all that because of his hold on the trustees."

As we finished the enlightening interview, I stated, "I want to repeat that your answers will be merged into the overall findings and not attributed directly to you. In fact, the list of faculty who are interviewed will not be released to the president, the trustees, anyone."

"I could care less about my comments being known. I've got tenure, so no one's going to touch me. Besides, it's my obligation to speak out if it's going to help this wonderful college. I've given twenty-seven years of my life here, and I love this place. I sometimes wonder whether the subject I teach is going to have much impact on my students' lives, but it's my duty to teach and to do it well. Students are wonderful, energetic, wanting to learn. To get accepted here, one has to have a high GPA and SAT, so our admissions selectivity ensures some pretty bright young people. That makes teaching fun, at least for me."

During my exhausting six weeks of interviews, I heard the same themes from the other faculty I interviewed, including the deans of the four schools at the college—arts and sciences, business, education, and religious studies—a typical lineup at small religion-based colleges and universities.

Staff, on the other hand, had entirely different concerns for the most part. Salary was number one, followed by benefits. There was a mixture of other opinions, but the most common mirrored what worried Professor Bell, a lack of understanding—seemingly a lack of interest—by the president and trustees as to what concerned the staff, and thus a decline in morale. Almost unanimously, staff said the shift began not long after Wiseman came on board. As with faculty, staff said morale impacted how students were treated, beginning with the admissions office in its dealings with prospective students.

I got help from agency colleagues, who took on the interviewing of student leaders. My hands were full.

By late March, everyone had completed their assigned interviews. Distilling the information was my challenge. I was tired. Diane and the children noticed it, and she urged me to slow down, get some rest. I'd suffered another migraine, and this one left me feeling worthless the remainder of that day. But I wouldn't rest. There was too much to do in a somewhat rigid time schedule the agency heads and I had set. Results from the computer-form surveys of students and parents would not be known until June 1—at least that was the deadline given to the research firm. The goal was to have a presentation ready for the trustees by approximately August 1. It was ambitious.

I was not prepared for an unexpected development.

CHAPTER 31

On the second Saturday in August 1985, the three of us from the agency and the trustees met privately. By prior agreement, the three-hour session didn't include the college president. Anything pertaining to him would be left to the trustees to deal with.

I'd been running on fumes, but adrenaline had me pumped for this day. There was another source of excitement for me as well, something only Bruce, Gary, and I knew, and it came from a shocking telephone call I'd received at home the previous evening.

"Is this David Miller?" the muffled voice inquired after I picked up the ringing phone and answered, "Hello."

"It is."

Sounding as though he were speaking through a handkerchief or something similar held over his mouth, the caller asked, "Is you the David Miller who's conducting a review of Latimore College?"

"I am." My interest quickly piqued.

"Then you'd be wise to learn about some sex that's been taking place in the president's office."

"What? What are you talking about?"

"That's all I'll say 'cept a student's involved," and with that, the line went dead.

I just sat there in the great room of my home, astonished, phone in hand. *What was that all about? Sex involving students in Wiseman's office? My God! Was it true? Was this a disgruntled employee out to get the president with some made-up story? The person's grammar wasn't indicative of a faculty member, unless he was just trying to throw me off.*

"Who called?" Diane asked, looking up from her copy of *Optometry Magazine*.

Sidestepping, I said, "Oh, no one. Just a call from someone with some additional information for our research." Rising from the recliner, I said, "Excuse me, but I've got to call my partners regarding this presentation." I was holding the thick package of findings and recommendations I'd been studying for the next day's revelation.

"But it's late, almost nine o'clock," Diane said, looking at the dark-oak octagonal-faced pendulum clock mounted above the mantel of the fireplace.

"Believe me, they won't mind," I responded, knowing that what I was about to tell Bruce and Gary erased any possible concern about the hour of day.

From my home office at the other end of the main level of the house, my conversations with the partners had them flabbergasted. We agreed not to discuss the matter further until after tomorrow's presentation. Then we'd sit and talk about how to proceed with the additional information.

▬ ▬ ▬

The trustees, especially the six who strongly supported Wiseman, were dismayed by the findings. In a nutshell, almost everything related back to the president. Community leaders didn't like working with him, because he was an egotist in the extreme. There was an air about him that virtually no one respected. Faculty felt he held little regard for them when, in fact, a college's reputation typically began with its academics. Student leaders had the same opinion, one of them snidely calling him "Iron Fist Steve."

As for the trustees, all nine had agreed to talk but strictly off the record. Nothing could be attributed to any individual. Their overall views could only be summarized. As expected, Wiseman's backers voiced support for him, although everyone mentioned his ego and how it could be or was a problem. All admitted he was very difficult to persuade to consider matters that were not at the top of *his* agenda.

Board chairman Horace Sanderson tended to straddle the fence in regard to the president, and Bruce could tell he might be open-minded about some changes. Sanderson had been chair of the formerly all-male, all-white board for ten years but had served on it for seventeen. It was still all-white, but Marilyn Armstrong had been invited to break the mold a year after Wiseman arrived. She was the sole owner of a highly successful blind and drapery manufacturing company in Evansville and had met the president when her retail store was asked to select new drapery for his campus home. His interest in her being on the board was purely monetary. She had big bucks, and he wanted some of them for the college. When it came to any issue, she always sided with what he asked of the board.

The strongest of those who held negative opinions of Wiseman was Irwin Nass, a millionaire farmer from near St. Meinrad, a tiny town about an hour northeast of the college. Nass was seventy-three and had served the board nearly as long as Sanderson. At just over three thousand acres, his was one of the biggest farm operations in the region, devoted entirely to wheat, oat, and soybean. He was still active with the farm, but two sons, who had both earned agriculture degrees from Purdue, now ran it. Nass's wealth, however, didn't come strictly from raising grain. He was a major stockholder in Immigrant Bank headquartered in Dale, about ten miles from his home, and the bank had been hugely successful since World War II, serving a wide radius from Dale, mostly the German-ancestry families who lived throughout the rolling hills of that area. Interestingly, Nass was the only board member who hadn't earned at least a bachelor's. His education came from a keen intelligence about matters of life and the college of hard knocks and hard work. The other thing different about him from the other board members was he was Catholic, a Catholic working with Baptists. But it mattered not to him or to his colleagues. Nass believed strongly in a religion-influenced education, and that was why he'd accepted the invitation to join the board in 1970.

Nass didn't like Wiseman from the get-go. He much preferred persons who were down-to-earth, like he was. He thought a leader should be kind and supportive of others, not a "pompous ass" (his description of Wiseman). If you wanted Irwin Nass's opinion, you'd get it, and there would be no pussyfooting around whatever the subject was. Nass felt the president to be an enormous detriment to the college, and he was willing to look for anything that could lead to dismissal.

The most revealing results, and perhaps the most harmful, were the attitudes of the younger undergrads and high school juniors and seniors. Theirs were not directed at the president or even the price tag of tuition but at what they considered a stodgy college reputation. Younger society's social attitudes had changed, and the college hadn't kept pace. All of this had coincidentally collided at the halfway mark in Stephen Wiseman's tenure. Restrictions or prohibitions involving dorm hours, alcohol, smoking, dress, and entertainment, such as rock bands, were considered anti-modern-day-student. But the students were also concerned with the conditions of classrooms and the attitudes of professors and admissions staff.

I led the presentation with the use of overlays on an overhead projector which displayed the information on a large screen that descended from the ceiling at one end of the trustee boardroom. My partners sat near me at that end of the long, dark-oak table. Only the nine trustees and the board secretary, a trustee staff position, comprised the audience. The results and questions and answers took two hours, and recommendations with more Q & A took another one and a half, thirty minutes longer than had been planned. Our agency trio was buoyed by the reaction, especially the many head nods when recommendations for improvement were given.

"We have a few recommendations in regard to the president himself." Bruce stood and addressed the trustees. Pages rustled as members thumbed through their agency-provided documents, looking for whatever pertained to Wiseman. On purpose, there was nothing on the matter in print except in the chairman's packet. No chances were being taken that one of the other members would sneak something to the president. "Actually, and most confidentially, we're not certain he can change who he is. The matter of his demeanor on campus and in the community is something the board will have to deal with. We do, however, strongly suggest some actions of what he *can be* on campus."

The image on the screen changed with the heading "Recommendations—President Wiseman." "Number one," Bruce pointed to the screen with a small laser penlight as he started down the list. "The president needs to hold regularly scheduled meetings with student leaders, to seek their opinions or just hear what they have to say about anything that's on their minds and *truly* listen to them. Number two ..." and he continued through a long set of recommendations that dealt with everything from faculty relations to physical facility changes to student social governance.

Gary then stood and took over the presentation. As I had done with

Bruce, I assisted by placing one overlay after another on the projector's horizontal face. "Finally, we have a significant marketing plan to present to you." The images on the screen showed a well-laid-out plan with time line, all aimed at changing the college's image. There were short-term recommendations and longer-term ones that went past the third year of the agency's contract, a subtle way of saying "We want to continue doing business with you after our agreement is set to expire in late 1987." Of course, we weren't absolutely certain we would want to work with the college past that date—the decision would depend on how cooperative the trustees, and especially the president, had been—but it was good to reserve the possibility by planting a seed now.

▬ ▬ ▬

The three of us had driven separately to the campus but agreed to meet for a drink afterward, Bruce's favorite way of celebrating a successful presentation to a client. Each of us ordered a beer and wondered aloud what the trustees might decide during their afternoon conversations, especially in regard to approaching Wiseman with results and demands. Would they have the nerve to confront him with the most candid of findings about his demeanor and leadership? Would they present him with requirements for change? What would be his reaction? How would his larger-than-life ego take all of it? What would happen if he bristled and refused to accept both the results and the trustees' comments?

But there was potentially a bigger issue, one unknown to anyone except we celebratory three at the bar table. How were we going to proceed with what little I'd been told?

"Guys, this could be as serious as anything we've ever been privileged to know," Bruce said with a tone bordering on astonishment. "Obviously, we don't know if it's true, but it's a package of dynamite if it is."

"Regardless," Gary responded, "we can do nothing more than make the trustees aware of the information, if that's what we want to do."

"I don't know," I interjected, speaking as softly as the other two. "Maybe there's a way for us to check this out before going to the trustees." After more discussion about pros and cons, we agreed to think about it over the weekend and get together Monday morning immediately following the regular 9:00 a.m. all-account-executive meeting.

When I got home, I was brimming and the restaurant dinner Diane and I had arranged earlier in the week was mostly a one-sided conversation with me talking nearly nonstop about what had taken place at Latimore, not mentioning the information discussed with my partners at the postpresentation celebration.

In bed, I went through the motions of pleasing Diane, totally exhausted from a day of emotions. The phone rang. The backlit digital clock on the bedside stand beside me displayed 11:17 p.m. Diane was in the bathroom.

"Mr. Miller?" It was the same muffled tone of the previous evening.

"Yes."

"How'd the meeting with them trustees go today?"

"What meeting?"

"I ain't educated, but I'm not a fool either," the mystery man retorted calmly.

Swinging my legs over the edge of the bed and sitting up, I asked, "Who are you?"

"It don't matter. Jest wondered if you told them trustees what I told you last night?"

"Well, let's just say I'm interested in knowing a lot more."

"Don't know a lot but enough to get old Wiseman in hot water."

"You mean the president?"

"Yep, that's him."

"How can I find out more? I've got to have some direction."

"Let me think about it. You'll hear again." Click. With that, the line was dead.

Diane had walked back into the bedroom during the conversation and was putting her gown on when the call ended. "What was that all about and at this hour of night?"

I twisted to look at her. "Craziest thing, and I hate to say it, but I can't tell you." I continued to look at her, trying to think of a better excuse. "I have no idea who called. The same person as last night. He has some information relating to our Latimore project and …" Pausing again, I gathered my thoughts. "I love you deeply, sweetheart, but the information is extremely sensitive and confidential, and I just can't tell you about it."

Getting into bed, Diane replied, "And I don't want you to. I have doctor-patient relationships, too, and I can't talk specifics with you, so I truly understand." We kissed and said, "Good night," and within moments, she was sound asleep. As tired as I was, it would be another mostly sleepless night.

▬ ▬ ▬

Sunday was the longest day possible. I hardly heard a word of the sermon, mulling over and over what I'd been told by the mysterious caller. *"Sex ... in the president's office." "... to get old Wiseman in hot water."* How could I learn more? What should Bruce, Gary, and I do? The thoughts and questions were driving me crazy. Fortunately, my exhausted body fell asleep while I was watching television shortly after 7:30 p.m. Diane woke me just as the closing credits for the 9:00 program were being shown and steadied me as we walked to the bedroom. The following morning, I didn't even remember removing my clothing and collapsing into bed.

I ate almost nothing for breakfast and heard almost nothing during the meeting with the two senior partners and all the account executives at the regularly scheduled Monday morning meeting. My mind remained fixated on the scant, enticing information from the clandestine caller.

CHAPTER 32

We found out later Irwin Nass had been kicking himself. He'd had damaging information about Stephen Wiseman at the time Wiseman was being considered for the presidency but withheld it, hoping what Wiseman was said to have done and his subsequent firing—despite the Iowa college's news release saying he'd decided to step down—would cause him to change his ways. Being caught in an affair with one of the two female members of the college's board in his office was bad enough. But when the trustees received undercover information about an affair with a faculty member, it was the final straw. Wiseman was lucky to avoid divorce. Why his wife didn't file for it, no one on the board understood.

Nass had learned of the confidential information from a close Iowa farmer friend, who'd served on the Corning board. Most of the trustees were farmers, and this member, like Nass, couldn't stand Wiseman's egotism. Less than half a year into Wiseman's reign at Latimore, Nass knew he'd made a horrible mistake in not taking his secret information to his colleagues.

"I've got someone I can go to," Gary told us when we met at 10:30. "And I think I can use him, to get his opinion of how to proceed. Irwin Nass. He and I really hit it off in my interview with him."

"But what do we tell him?" I asked. "We've got scant information to go on. None of it says the president himself has been involved in something in his office. Thus far, we know only that allegedly something has taken place there and that whatever it was, if true, could embarrass him."

"I agree with Davie," Bruce backed me up. "We've got to be damned careful not to implicate someone in something we don't have all the facts about."

"The caller will get back to me, I'm certain," I stated with confidence. "Let's sit on this a few more days. I'm sure I'll get another call, and I bet it will be sooner than later."

Bruce concluded the meeting with "I agree. Meantime, I hope we hear back soon on our proposed plan of action. I'm anxious to get started."

It was Gary, not me, who received an evening call at home this time. And it wasn't the mystery caller. It was Irwin Nass. "How'd you like to learn something about the farming business?" he asked.

Not certain the offer was the actual reason for the call, Gary told us he replied, "I'd love to. I grew up in the city and have always had a lot of admiration for farmers, but I know little about all you do."

"Great," his elderly caller responded. "How 'bout Friday? Make it late morning, and my wife'll have an old-fashioned farm lunch for us out under one of the big maples next to the house."

"Sounds good to me. Ten o'clock? I'll need directions."

"By the way," Nass added, "this visit should be just between us." Gary said he understood perfectly. Nass didn't want anyone on the board or elsewhere to become aware. It was, after all, improper for him to reach out on his own to someone the board had hired.

"Oh, off the record, you and your colleagues should be hearing from Horace Sanderson tomorrow. I think you'll like the news."

Nass's tip was on target. Shortly after arriving at the office the following morning, Bruce got the call. Could he and his partners meet with Sanderson at the trustees' office on campus that afternoon?

At the outset, Sanderson said just enough for us to understand Monday's trustees' meeting with Wiseman hadn't gone well. The president had challenged some of the results, didn't like some of the recommendations, and was belligerent about almost every criticism of him by the numerous and varied survey results. He indicated community leaders "didn't have the intelligence" to understand him. But Sanderson wouldn't comment further. He considered it a personnel matter protected by employment law.

"Our board met all day and into the evening yesterday, discussing your findings and recommendations. I can tell you we were and are utterly pleased with your work. Of course, we didn't like seeing a lot of the results—especially disappointing, almost disheartening, were all the negatives from community leaders. And we had no idea our college's reputation is what it is among those of our future—the prospective students and their parents. So, we made some difficult but necessary decisions, not all supported by our president, I might add. But of course they're our decisions." Looking at the material in front of him, Sanderson listed them.

"First, we approved funds for modern audio and video equipment for professors to use in the classrooms. Second, our classrooms will be modernized in other ways as will our dormitory rooms. Third, we will continue not permitting smoking on campus by students, faculty, staff, or anyone. It's the right thing, to ensure Latimore remains a smoke-free environment. We will no longer prohibit the consumption of alcoholic beverages by those twenty-one and older but only in private, never in public areas. The severe penalties for underage drinking here, which may include expulsion, will remain in effect. Our weekly morning convocations will continue to occasionally remind students of the pitfalls of alcohol and drugs. Dormitory hours for men and women will be abolished, effective with the upcoming academic year. We will relax the college's dress code, and we'll form a committee of students, faculty, and staff that will vote on all requests for outside entertainment including concerts.

"Additionally, we'll hire a specialist in guest relations and provide mandatory training for staff at all levels on how to interact with our visitors or telephone callers, the most important of which are prospective students and parents. The specialist will head an initial three-person staff to conduct the training and develop an ongoing program. Faculty will be invited to participate. The director of admissions has been placed on notice that he and his staff will become far more "customer friendly," if you will, or else. The first contact prospects have with our college is often the admissions office. A poorly handled telephone inquiry or an attitude of indifference toward visitors can determine whether Latimore remains on someone's list of possibilities. We want to stay on that list!

"We'll promise to all staff a review of salaries and benefits but will make no promises beyond that. I haven't a clue as to what the outcome of our review will be, but it will be fair and we'll make certain staff know exactly *why* we decide whatever it is we conclude. Finally, we will open up dialogue with the faculty in regard to their views on faculty governance."

Setting aside the material he'd been reading from, Sanderson addressed us face-to-face. "Actually, there is one more thing, and it relates to my opening remarks. This is said in utmost confidence." He paused to scan our faces. "The president has been told to make some major changes. In fairness, we need to give him time because they involve personal habits or attitudes that have been a part of him for a long, long time. Something I will mention is that we want him to establish a culture of outstanding relations with students, including regularly scheduled meetings with student leaders whereby he keeps them up-to-date on matters of the university and listens—you heard me—listens to what they say. As time goes by, I hope you will see change for the better taking place in him."

The remainder of the two-hour meeting involved decisions regarding the marketing plan our agency had proposed. It had been approved almost as presented but included one surprise. The trustees wanted to bolster the tiny campus relations staff that was responsible for media relations, promotional materials for the admissions office, the internal campus newsletter, and community relations. "Tiny" was hardly the word for the PR staff's size. It was one professional and a secretary. The director, Cynthia Moynihan, had nearly been worked to the bone. The addition of two professionals to serve with her would be a godsend because the Wilson-McGlasson plan would place a great deal of additional work on her staff's plate. She'd have a strong ally and partner in me and members of my staff, too.

███ ▒▒▒ ███

In giving a summary to Bruce and me later, Gary McGlasson said that on Friday morning, as he exited I-64 onto SR 162 and drove along SR 62 toward St. Meinrad, he felt revived by the scenery. He related he'd dressed down from his normal professional attire and felt much different, good, in his blue jeans, Evansville Country Club golf shirt, and Titleist cap on his six-foot-six frame. Gary was an imposing figure, every bit of 250 pounds with sandy-brown, wavy hair and dark eyes. He'd played basketball in college but never exercised in the decades since, and it showed. His wasn't the biggest metropolitan area in the world, but he felt he spent too much time there, not venturing out to the small towns and rural areas that surrounded it. The pastoral settings of rolling hills, farms that dotted them, and the bounding of a deer near a cornfield off to his right as he neared St. Meinrad reminded him of what he'd been missing with too much of his life. Turning south from the town, about two miles later, he drove onto a gravel road and just over a mile to the Nass homestead.

Irwin Nass was waiting and waved as Gary swung his Jeep Grand Wagoneer into the driveway. He greeted Gary with a strong handshake. "I knew you were coming. Saw the dust being kicked up on the road from the kitchen window. Didn't pay for you to wash your car before coming here if you did. Hope you had no problems finding this place."

"None whatsoever. Your directions were perfect."

Nass didn't dress any different than for any other day of the year except Sundays and the times he had meetings at the college or his bank. He wore overalls, a faded print shirt—usually long-sleeved—and work boots, plus a green-and-yellow John Deere cap that had a large spot on the bill where he apparently always grabbed it with dirty thumb and forefinger when removing it after he'd been working. Nass's hair had turned white years earlier, and while his hands were rough and tan from a life of farming, Gary had noticed previously the nails were always clean and trimmed.

"Come on in for a moment," the host directed, motioning toward the house. "I want you to meet Iona before we take a walk around." Iona Nass was a year older than Irwin. While he'd been born and raised there on what became their farm, she was a rural native from just east of Ferdinand, about seven miles away. Her maiden name was Rademacher, pronounced the German way with the "a's" sounding as "ah" just like the "a" in Nass. They'd been married fifty-two years.

One would never know Irwin and Iona had a lot of money. Their two-story white, wood-frame home was simple in decoration. Two two-seat swings hung on the wrap-around front porch with its painted grey concrete floor. Gary guessed Irwin to be about five-nine because he dwarfed his host, and Irwin had a little more fat on his bones than he probably preferred. He wore short sleeves that day, and his white arms looked solid from years of farmwork that often required strength. The backs of his hands showed numerous sun spots, and when he turned them over, a person could easily see the maze of lines that ran throughout his palms. His fingers were thick.

Gary hadn't been on a large farm complex before. He counted eight steel grain storage bins of different sizes. Irwin proudly proclaimed they could hold nearly 400,000 bushels if all were full. A system of metal tubes funneled the grain from large trucks that hauled it from the fields to the barn lot. There were no cattle. "Once tried raising beef but taking care of them was too much trouble," Nass offered. The barn and numerous other buildings held what to Gary was an amazing variety of farm implements, from massive combines to tractors to fertilizer tanks. But he thought all likely necessary for a farm as huge as the Nass family's.

"Our two boys are out in the fields, or I'd introduce them to you," Nass said as they finished their walking tour and sat down at the redwood-stained picnic table. It was a typical hot, humid August day in Indiana, and both wiped their faces with handkerchiefs in the shade of large, wide-spreading maples. Three oaks that Gary guessed were one hundred feet tall were nearby. Iona had warm washcloths and a towel for them to clean their hands.

"Lord, you have blessed us abundantly, more than we ever deserve," Nass prayed, not asking Gary if it was all right with his guest. Irwin was a deeply religious man, and in his mind, praying was something a person was to do. God needed to be thanked, whether you were rich or poor. You had life, and you needed to show your appreciation for it. "We thank you for this meal Iona has prepared and ask that you bless it to our bodies, so we will have strength in our service to you. Amen." With that, both raised their heads and saw the beef stew; homemade rolls; fresh vegetable salad of lettuce, radish, carrot, and celery; and another of Iona's specialties, cherry pie, sitting before them.

Passing the stew after first dipping three large spoonfuls onto two slices of homemade white bread on his plate, Nass began. "I'm gonna call you 'Gary,' if that's all right with you, and I want you to call me 'Irwin.' None of that formal stuff out here." A hint of a breeze picked up, a welcome relief. "I'll be honest with you. I didn't ask you to come all the way here just to see my farming operation."

It was as Gary had suspected. *This may get interesting*, he thought, immediately excited about the prospect. "I think I can trust you," his older host continued and then looked him straight in the face. "Can't I?"

Without flinching, Gary answered back, "You bet you can. I have some pretty high morals and principles, and one thing I would never do to a fellow human being is break a trust. Besides, I like you, Irwin."

Nass gave a slight smile to his towering guest on the other side of the table, took a mouthful of stew, and began talking as he was chewing. "Well, I felt we got along well in that interview you had with me, and there was something about you that said you were okay." Then he began.

"I try to be a Christian, but pardon me, Wiseman's an asshole. A pompous, pontificating, 'look at me and all I've done and all that I am' asshole." Continuing to eat and not letting up, he said, "My fellow trustees know it, and even those that have been his biggest supporters are beginning to see the light. Wiseman's in trouble. He's been told to shape up or ship out. Without saying it to him, we're willing to cut bait and let him swim with what we'd owe him under his contract, not that we want that to happen, mind you. But he *has* to change. My fondest hope would be to find a way to get rid of him without having to pay him." Gary wanted to supply some ammunition but didn't have the damaging facts—not yet anyway.

Nass went on to share the entire meeting between the trustees and their president. None of it was particularly startling to Gary. He'd expected Wiseman to dispute findings, especially those that related directly to him. But there was more.

"Just gotta get this off my chest, to share it with someone, and I know I can trust you. Maybe you can give me some advice," Nass told his junior guest. He revealed at length all he'd been told about Wiseman's adultery in Iowa. "What should I do with this? Seems a little late now to tell the board about it."

"Wow, you're holding a bomb, Irwin. My initial reaction is to agree with you that now is not the time to act. The past is past. And you've no indications he's been guilty of similar behavior here, I presume."

There was a long pause, an almost uncomfortable one, as Nass pondered, and then he said, "Well, let me say there have been rumors of indiscretions here but nothing to put a hat on."

"You're kidding," Gary responded, as a statement, not a question. "And where do the rumors state these indiscretions have taken place?"

"In his office."

Gary's earth shook. Looking directly at his host, he asked, "Irwin, did your source suggest where any of the sex took place in Iowa?"

"Sure did. He was caught doing it with a faculty member on the sofa in his office late one night. Damned fool failed to lock one of his office doors, and a secretary who'd returned to the office to pick up some materials for an early morning report she was to have for the president unwittingly caught them. He later secretly paid her to keep quiet, and it worked for several months until her conscience got the better of her and she told her pastor. To make a long story short, the president, married female professor, and secretary were all permitted to sign statements that they could resign in totally separate actions in exchange for trustee guarantees none of what they did would ever be made public. The conduct of Wiseman and the faculty member was certainly considered unbecoming conduct and on college property; the secretary was guilty of accepting a bribe."

"Your trustees ever consider bugging his office here?"

"You mean his phone?"

"No. A video bug."

"That'd be illegal as hell."

"There's risk in it. But if you recorded something and confronted him, what's he going to do? Sue you? Sue you for catching him having sex in his office with someone other than his wife?" Gary could see the machinery of Nass's mind grinding several thoughts. He broke the silence. "Something for you to think about."

■ ▩ ▨

Bruce and I had been on standby, awaiting a possible call to meet the following day. Diane wasn't all too happy she and I couldn't make definite plans for the weekend with the girls, but I assured her that if a meeting was called, it would be extremely important. Bruce and Gary wanted a full weekend off just as much as I did. The call came from my partner's mobile phone as he was driving back from St. Meinrad at midafternoon Friday to Bruce first and then me.

The Saturday morning meeting at the agency was filled with the specter of tension after Gary told us everything he had learned from Nass, and the three of us considered possible steps to be taken. "So, what we know is there are rumors of sexual improprieties and two late-evening phone calls to Davie that we believe suggest someone knows something more than rumor. The question is how do we proceed from here?" Bruce summarized.

"I'm certainly disappointed I haven't heard more from my source," I responded. "I thought sure I would by now."

"I'll tell you what I think," Gary declared.

"What?" Bruce asked, studying his partner.

"I think I should get back to Nass, tell him what little we know, and recommend the board get a private investigator involved." Two heads nodded haltingly in agreement, both minds thinking through the implications of the comment.

"I like it," Bruce declared. "Let's do just that."

"Me, too," I interjected. "We owe it to the college to do something. Going through Nass makes him the guy to run with this matter, and for all anyone knows, we stay out of it. We're not privy to anything."

Following a picnic lunch and long afternoon in the hot sun at Mesker Zoo, the final Sunday before school began for the girls, I was snoozing in my favorite easy chair in the great room while Diane was in the girls' bedroom upstairs, answering Jillian's call for a glass of water. The phone rang, startling me. "I've got it," I responded to Diane who'd yelled down, "Can you get that?"

"Sorry I ain't got back to you in awhile." It was the muffled voice again. "I've been thinkin' over the situation, and I'd like to talk with you." Silence. "But with guarantees. I cain't lose my job over this."

"Go on."

"I know something you should know. I just got to tell you."

"When can we meet?"

"How 'bout tomorrow? I get off at one and could meet you off-campus somewhere, but it's got to be a place where no one knows both of us."

"One would be fine with me. I'll take an early lunch, and maybe we could meet at Conly Park."

"Lunch? I get off at one o'clock in the morning."

Oh, my God, I thought.

"Won't that work for you?"

Not a silly question, I decided, from someone apparently accustomed to the late shift. "Why, uh, sure, that'll work for me." *Diane will think I've lost my mind when I tell her.* "Where?"

"There's an all-night diner near Diamond and 41, *Jugg's*. I often go there after work, so it's a good place to meet. But bring nobody and nothin' with you—no camera, no recorder, no paper. I know what you look like, and if I see you with anything, I'll leave immediately."

"How will I recognize you?"

"I'll do the recognizin'. Just sit in a booth in the back corner. Likely won't be nobody back there. I'll find you."

"Davie, is everything all right? You're not in any trouble over something, are you?" Diane responded when I informed her of the call and the need to meet someone in the wee hours of Tuesday morning.

"No, no, not at all, sweetheart. I'm perfectly fine. It's the same caller I've had three times now. I'm sitting on something potentially explosive in regard to our Latimore account, and I'm about to get more information. I'm so, so sorry I can't tell you more, but someday, you'll understand if the facts come out like I think they will. And don't worry. I'm certain I'm not at any physical risk in meeting with the person." Diane trusted me explicitly and knew not to ask more.

■ ▨ ▰

Bruce and Gary agreed the following morning not to proceed with Nass until after my clandestine meeting with the mysterious caller. They also agreed to the full terms of the man's demands. There would be no hidden camera, no hidden microphone, and neither of them would watch from out of sight. We couldn't afford to blow the lead.

I saw him approach, a black man in dark-blue work slacks, like the type I'd seen on blue-collar employees at the college. He wore a clean white crewneck T-shirt and had a blue-and-white Dodgers cap pulled down to semihide his face. I knew it to be an Evansville Dodgers cap, so the man was possibly a fan. It was 1:17 a.m. I was into my second cup of coffee, already enough to make me hyper and unable to sleep yet again that night. The information I was about to get would ensure it.

The man stopped at my table. "Mr. David Miller?"

"Yes, sir, that's me."

He slid into the booth, his back to the door, and tilted his cap so I could see his face. He didn't offer to shake hands. "You guarantee me you have no one with you, and there is nothin' that'll record us?" he said as he quickly glanced behind him.

"Yes, sir, I guarantee you. No, sir, I have nothing with me. It's just you and me."

I studied his face; there was a bit of gray stubble on the chin, probably one of those guys whose beard grew quickly during the day. The hair that showed beneath the sides and back of the cap was mostly gray, but I got the feeling from the tilted cap, there was little or no hair on top. I guessed my boothmate to be in his sixties, probably early sixties. His skin was somewhat light and the voice tone and facial expression indicated a person of kindness. At first glance, he didn't appear to be tall, maybe no more than five-eight and not overweight.

"I've got some information I need to tell you. But you have to promise you'll never connect me to it. How you handle it will be up to you. I've prayed and prayed over this and know I have to trust you to protect me."

"Sir," I began, not knowing what name to call him, "I'm a Christian, and I have high ethics and morals and would never do unto a fellow man what I was asked not to do."

My guest began to speak but was interrupted by the waitress who'd recognized him when he walked in the door and automatically brought an empty coffee cup and cream. "Hello, Wilbert." She smiled, her familiar greeting indicating he was obviously a frequent customer. "You need anything else?"

"No, thank you."

"Your wife and grandkids doing well?"

"Yeah, they're all fine. Thanks." As she left, the man now known only as Wilbert, reached for the pot of coffee already on the table, poured it and some cream into his cup, and began in a hushed tone.

"I was cleanin' offices in the administration building late one night, about three weeks ago, toward the end of summer school. Must have been about ten when I entered the president's greetin' area. Was by myself, dustin', straightenin', dumpin' papers from the secretary's trash can into a large container I wheel from office to office. It was quiet, real quiet. Nothin' unusual for that time of day. Then I heard noise from inside the president's office. That was followed with what sounded like grunts and groans, which startled me. Made me fear somethin' bad was happ'nin' in there. There's two doors to his office, one leadin' to the receptionist and the other down a back hallway to a private toilet, sort of an escape path if he ever wants ta hide from someone. I tiptoe to the nearby door and ever so slowly crack it open, not knowin' what might be goin' on. Two people were on the floor, on a big carpet in front of the fireplace. I was scared, almost frightened. Looked like they were wresslin'. Then I realized, they weren't fightin'. They was a-havin' sex, and they didn't know I was there."

He paused, and I could tell he was having difficulty in forming what he wanted to describe next. I let him take his time. "Well, sir, Mr. Miller, one of them was … the president."

"The president … President Wiseman?"

"Yes, sir, Mr. Miller. It was him. I knowed immediately it was him. He was on top."

I saw the face blush with the words. "And do you know who was with him?"

"Yes, sir, a girl."

"A girl!" I exclaimed, struggling to keep the volume of my voice from rising as I looked around to make certain none of the other customers heard him.

"Yes, sir. It was a student. I seen enough of her face I recognized her. Seen her on campus over the years."

"How do you know she might not be a graduate, not that it matters a great deal?" I realized it was a dumb statement. It certainly mattered a lot if the president had sex with a student.

Wilbert studied my face and then replied, "She's a cheerleader … for the basketball team."

"Good God," I replied in a hushed tone and then just sat there, staring at my informant across the table. "Are you absolutely positive they were engaged in sex? I assume you mean sexual intercourse."

"No doubt in my mind, sir. Her dress was pulled up, panties on the floor beside her. His pants were down at his knees, and he was humpin' away, and they was makin' lots of sounds." Another blush.

"Did they see you?"

"No, sir. They was so busy, they had no idea I was there. I pulled the door closed without makin' a sound, made sure I didn't leave no cleanin' rags or anything there, grabbed my trash cart, and got out. I was shakin' so bad I left the building as fast as I could. Lordy, I still shake when I think about it, especially when I go to that office every night, prayin' I won't hear somethin' like that again."

"Have you?"

"No, sir."

We sat in stillness, and then Wilbert spoke, pleading. "Mr. Miller, I cain't lose my job. I'm not educated. Didn't even graduate from the old Lincoln High School. I'm only three years from retirement. My wife suffered a slight stroke seven years back and cain't work. She still gets treatments, rehab for her left arm and leg, and we've got nothin' but my job and Social Security to keep us goin'. I've been sick about what I seen. Sick because somebody needed to know, and yet I didn't know how to go about it without maybe losin' my job. Then I seen where your company was workin' with the trustees, and I recognized your name. Been a baseball fan all my life. Love them Dodgers. And I knowed you played for Evansville College. I was at a church meetin' once, a Lenten breakfast, and you was the speaker. I liked what you said, and when I was prayin' and wonderin' what to do about what I seen, I knew you to be a good man, someone I could talk to and trust."

I felt tears forming, overwhelmed with the internal torture this kind man had been going through and the huge risk he must have felt he was taking. It would not be a risk with me. I would handle the information with delicacy, protecting Wilbert whatever-his-last-name-was.

"Mr. ... er, sir, I guarantee you and your name will never be associated with what you've shared with me. I will protect you while finding a way to do something with it. You have my promise, one Christian to another. If there's ever anything else you need to share with me, you can do so without fear. I don't know your name; I will not try to find out; I will not try to find a way to call you. But you will know how to reach me."

Wilbert slid out of the booth, stood, extended a hand of friendship, quietly said, "From one Christian to another," thanked me for the coffee and my time, and turned. I watched as the brave, small-statured man with pulled-down Dodger cap exited through the restaurant door. Perhaps I'd never see him again, but I certainly would never forget him.

▬ ▬ ▬

"Irwin, I have something we need to talk about," Gary McGlasson told him in a phone call on Thursday, after he, Bruce, and I had spent hours discussing what to do with the information we had. The next morning, he was back at the Nass farm, sitting at the same picnic table as the previous week. Iona had prepared a pitcher of lemonade, and the rose glass container sweated onto the wood tabletop, leaving a ring when Irwin picked it up to pour glasses full for him and his guest. The weather bureau had predicted 90 degrees for the afternoon, so both men were glad they'd chosen to meet at 9:00. They sat in shade.

Gary gave us the details later.

"Irwin, you were more than kind to share some very confidential information with me last week, so turnabout is fair play. I didn't withhold any facts from you last Friday, because they weren't facts at the time. They still aren't necessarily, but it's information my partners and I want you to have. What I'm about to tell you is for you to use as you feel best, but I—we—will urge you to do something with it. It almost makes me sick to share this because of who all it involves."

Gary went on to tell Nass of late-evening telephone calls to me by a mystery caller. Gary wouldn't reveal anything about the person. He said he and his partners had decided to give Nass everything they knew while doing everything they could to protect their source whom they felt was bona fide.

"Earlier this week, Mr. Miller met with the individual. What Davie was told is that the person saw President Wiseman having sexual intercourse with a woman on the floor of his office, late one night about a month ago."

"You are absolutely shitting me!" Nass exclaimed, slapping his open right palm on the top of the picnic table. "My God, you are shitting me!"

"I'm not, Irwin. I didn't drive all this way to tell you a Friday morning joke." Nass looked at him, mouth slightly open. "It gets worse, Irwin. The woman was a student. The source is unequivocally certain. Says the girl is a basketball cheerleader."

"Well, that seals that bastard's fate," Nass asserted, jumping to an unknown conclusion, now exposing a wry smile. "Tell me more."

"I can't. The source told no more. If you trust me as you've said you do, you'll have to trust that what I told you is what we were told and that we'll do everything to protect the informant. We will not jeopardize that individual in any fashion."

"But how can I get the trustees to act on Wiseman if I can't give them more information?"

"Start with Sanderson. You share what you were told about what went on in Iowa and remind him of rumors the trustees have been hearing about Wiseman at Latimore. Then tell him what I have given you and let him know that under no uncertain terms will my agency divulge the source. But you—the trustees—can't fire Wiseman over this latest secondhand information. If Wiseman has been bold enough to engage in sexual activities in his office at least once here and in Iowa previously, he'll do it again. Maybe he's been doing it a lot. Maybe it's a fetish. Maybe he gets an extra charge out of having sex in the office, and maybe he hasn't been forgetful in not locking the door. Perhaps that's part of the game he plays, the rush.

"Remember me suggesting a video plant in his office? I was serious last week and am even more so now. If I were the trustees, I'd hire a private detective who could carry out the operation, then act when Wiseman is caught on tape. Of course, the legalities of this will have to be checked out with an attorney, maybe not the college attorney because she might be in Wiseman's hip pocket. As I said before, he's not going to sue you if he's caught. He's not about to have extremely embarrassing information about him come out in public through a lawsuit. You trustees catch him, and you might get your personal wish, Irwin, Wiseman leaving without getting a dime of his remaining contract paid in exchange for his resignation and a trustee commitment to privacy."

Striking the top of the picnic table with the bottom of a closed right fist, Nass declared, "We'll get him. Mark my words. We'll get him." Gary told us he enjoyed the moment, the sight of determination in the face of the old farmer who knew he held potentially damaging information like a barn cat holding cheese for the unsuspecting mouse. It was very likely Wiseman was not a wise man after all.

CHAPTER 33

The marketing plan with its public relations and advertising aspects began rolling out in early October, but it was hardly enough to have much impact on spring semester enrollment. The college's hiring machinery ran at a different pace than the agency preferred or expected, thus adding two professionals to the school's PR staff was taking too much time. It would be almost Christmas before the last of the pair came on board. My staff and I were guiding aspects of the plan and produced a new family of promotional brochures for the admissions office, but it was the college relations office's responsibility to carry out the plan itself and the time line was behind schedule already.

Late in the afternoon of April 11, 1986, Latimore College issued a brief news release to the media. Under the heading, "President Stephen F. Wiseman Resigns," one simple paragraph quoted trustee chairman Sanderson as stating the president had "sought permission to resign immediately to seek other interests, including the possibility of returning to the faculty at another institution. He is considering options." Later in the same paragraph, the chairman was quoted, "Dr. Wiseman's request was acted on with regret by the board of trustees." Missing from the release was the typical "we thank him for his service" type of comment.

It was normal procedure in the public relations profession to issue news releases about negative items late on a Friday, purposely being too late to be included in afternoon newspapers. Area papers had small staffs for the weekends, so it was practically guaranteed no one would follow up on Saturday, certainly not on Sunday. By the time any press reporter looked into the development on Monday, it was likely not to develop into a significant story. Latimore was not a major college, and since television stations didn't have any reporters specializing in higher education, the resignation got little more than a mention in the early evening and late-evening newscasts on Friday. The Saturday morning Evansville newspaper had a small article based strictly on the news release.

My partners and I had received no warning a development was to be announced. That we didn't concerned and irritated us. After all, we were being paid a large amount to advise the trustees and the college. But we surmised the nature of the release was such that the conservative chairman didn't want anyone to know anything until it was made public. Gary couldn't wait to talk with Nass. He didn't have to wait long. He told Bruce and me that just as he and his wife were preparing to leave home for dinner with friends, the phone rang, and she shot him an evil glance when she heard him say, "Why, hello, Irwin. With all due respect ..." he begged off talking at length, and the two agreed to speak by phone at 8:00 the following morning.

"We caught him, by God!" Irwin exclaimed on Saturday. "Thanks to you. It was your idea. With only the knowledge of the trustful vice chairman and me, Sanderson hired a private investigator, who did a great job of planting two video bugs in the office. But nothing happened. We were beginning to think either your source was no good or Wiseman had stopped his late-evening calisthenics. Wednesday night, it happened. Boy, do we have some good porno." Nass laughed. "That little student sure as hell is built well. Man! We watched Wiseman lock both his doors and test the drapes to make certain no one could see in; he turned off all the lights except a small table lamp, and both of them stripped, started their lovemaking on the sofa, moved to the big floor rug at the fireplace, then to the *desk* where she laid on top. That old bastard sure is a stud; I'll say that for him.

"When confronted by Sanderson early yesterday morning, we were shocked he didn't make a scene. Old pompous, egotistical Stephen F. Wiseman was reduced to the level of a whimpering puppy." Irwin laughed out loud. "Oh," realizing he'd left out some details, he continued, "the trustees met Thursday afternoon after Sanderson and the vice chair had viewed the video the PI gave them. All the trustees watched the tape, then discussed what to do and made our decision. Sanderson had done a great job hiding the spying process from the other trustees, fearful one of the Wiseman supporters would alert the president. By the time all of us watched, even they could do nothing to help their beloved leader," he said with sarcasm. "You'll be interested to know the student—the cheerleader, she's twenty and a junior—won't be disciplined. Not certain what we could do to her anyway, maybe 'conduct unbecoming.' Of course she doesn't know about the video and won't unless Wiseman tells her. If he does, she'll have to live with fear the college might do something to her. She probably suspects something since he suddenly resigned only a couple of days after their latest tryst.

"As for Wiseman, under the watchful eyes of two campus policemen, he started cleaning out his office yesterday morning, and I'm certain we'll see a moving van at his house soon. The search for a new president will begin right away. Meantime, as the news release said, executive vice president Joe Cummins is the interim. He didn't want to be but agreed under our pressure. We hope the search doesn't take long, and I doubt Cummins will be a candidate. Can't imagine the tension in the Wiseman household. Wonder what he told his wife?"

━ ▦ ▬

The search took only three months. And the trustees did something historic for Latimore. They hired a woman. None would have predicted it at the outset, and they didn't set out to do it, but Janet Garrett, provost at the three-thousand-student Hall University in Tempe, Arizona, was their unanimous selection. Garrett, fifty-one, was considered a rising star in higher education in America's West. She'd earned all three of her degrees including an EdD in administration from Stanford after growing up in Albuquerque and graduating at the top of her high school class. She'd held posts at colleges in California, New Mexico, and Arizona before becoming provost at Hall in 1982. Garrett was known to be an innovator and was admired by students for her presence throughout campus, attendance at student-organized events, roundtables with student leaders, and informal evening gatherings with selected groups of students at her home. She was a divorcee with no children, so she devoted all her energies to her responsibilities. A direct opposite of Wiseman, she was charming and down-to-earth. She was a listener.

Garrett met with Bruce, Gary, and me at the outset of her second week on the job. It was August 11. All three of us liked her immediately.

Vivacious, with a sparkle in her eyes, she was an excellent communicator. Although diminutive, there was an air about her that said, "I'm in charge," but not in a threatening way. One could quickly discern she was intelligent. A brunette, Garrett had eyes to match and a smile that could make men crumble.

"I've studied the marketing plan approved by the board a year ago," she informed us. "I like it, almost all of it. It's obvious some was based on who the previous president was, so you'll need to relook at those aspects." We nodded in agreement. "I'm a go-getter. I don't like grass growing under my feet or under any plan that's been approved. Thus, I'll do all I can to ensure the total public relations effort moves forward and on schedule. Consider me an ally."

A breath of fresh air!

"One other thing, I love public speaking. So tweak the plan to include appearances for me in front of all the important groups of people—community leaders and high school students and parents—that you think necessary. We've got an image to turn around here at Latimore, so let's get to it."

I relished the opportunity to work with the new chief executive and was buoyed by her enthusiasm and what appeared to be street smarts. I knew, as did my partners, the next couple of years were going to be enjoyable.

My personal life had been busy that summer as well. Both girls played in softball leagues, much to my delight. Lydia, fourteen, was becoming the spitting image of her mother. Jill, twelve, was tough as nails. They were stepdaughters, but I was in love with them and treated them as my own. I felt their love, too. They'd hardly known their blood father. I'd become "Dad" or "Daddy." Diane's mother continued to be of major help by ferrying the two to practices. Diane and I, and Mrs. Johnston, too, never missed the games, one always held on a weekday evening and the other Saturday morning. League play ended in mid-July, which left room for a vacation trip before school resumed in late August. We sneaked it in immediately after the softball season, as I knew I'd be swamped with work once Latimore's new president took office. The trip to a cabin at Walloon Lake near Petoskey in Northern Michigan was a welcome respite from the dreadful heat of Indiana. Actually, it wasn't the Hoosier temperatures as much as it was the combination of temperature and humidity.

The girls weren't the only ones playing ball. I continued playing for my agency team in the media league and loved every minute of it, except the hip bruises and scabs that formed on my knees and arms from headfirst sliding into bases in softball shorts. It was dumb to slide I knew, but once I got on base, my competitiveness wouldn't allow me to do otherwise if there was going to be a close play. Whenever I'd make some comment at home about my soreness, Diane would just turn her head and walk away saying, "Don't complain to me. You have enough intelligence to know you're not a kid anymore. If you slide and get hurt, I don't want to hear about it."

Thank goodness I was in decent shape for the unexpected that was coming.

CHAPTER 34

"I have a big surprise for you, and you've got four and a half months to get ready for it," Diane said excitedly as we sat in Evansville's swankiest restaurant, The Blue Oyster, downtown, just off the river. We were observing our seventh wedding anniversary two days early, September 16, 1989. She flashed the widest grin I'd ever seen on her, and her eyes sparkled with the anticipation of her news. "It's a combination anniversary and early fiftieth birthday present."

Curious, I responded, "But I won't be fifty until June."

"I know, but there's a special reason to give it now."

Handing me a white business-size envelope on which she'd printed "HAPPY 50TH," she beamed as I held it in front of my face, studied it with a raised left eyebrow, and tore open the sealed flap. "Welcome to Spring Training," the headline on the contract I pulled from the envelope said. Frowning as I glanced at my smiling wife and then back to the form, I began reading. "You're kidding!" I exclaimed. "You've absolutely got to be kidding!"

"I'm not," came the giddy reply. "You're going to Fantasy Camp with the Jacksonville Phoenix." I was overwhelmed.

Fantasy Camp was an opportunity for men and women of any age and ability to spend a week with former major league baseball players and current major and minor league coaches in the organization. The only prerequisite was a person's ability to pay the $4,500 price tag.

It meant a week of playing games against teams of fellow campers and learning to throw, hit, run, and slide, just like a youngster being taught by an adult—a week of the sorest muscles any of the participants could ever imagine, capped by a game of campers playing the coaches and former players, some of whom were still able to hit the ball a mile even if their bodies had fallen out of the shape they had been in during careers that had a wide range of years.

I had long gotten over any fear of getting hit in the eye again. The years had done that for me. The risk was no greater than it had been prior to my 1961 injury.

I couldn't have received a bigger surprise. I'd heard of major league baseball teams conducting fantasy camps but never considered going because of the cost. For just an instant, *we can't afford this* crossed my mind, but just as quickly, I recognized that we jointly had annual earnings of approximately $200,000. Of course, we could afford it.

The Jacksonville Phoenix became a team when the American League expanded to include it in 1985. Jacksonville was Florida's largest city in population and land area, and progressive governmental and business leaders combined to wage a campaign to establish and get the franchise accepted by the league. Their efforts began in 1979 after young oil tycoon Benjamin Goldfarb agreed to put up the money for majority ownership. Goldfarb, a native of Jacksonville, whose wealthy, now deceased, steel-industry parents moved there from Pittsburgh in 1946, had been looking for ways to invest some of his inherited and self-made multimillions. Majority ownership it was, to the tune of 79 percent.

The Phoenix, named for the mythical bird that rose from the ashes, had its home in Duval County Stadium, a fifty-three-thousand-seat facility built in a public-private partnership, the public part being taxpayer dollars, the private portion mostly Goldfarb's. Phoenix was chosen as the nickname in a public contest because Jacksonville had risen miraculously from the ashes of one of Florida's greatest disasters, a fire that destroyed the city's business district and left thousands homeless in 1901. Construction of the stadium began in the fall of 1983 and was completed in time for the opening game one and a half years later. It was fast-track construction at its finest.

"Good thing you play softball, so you're partially in shape already," Diane teased. "I can imagine you'll use every muscle in your body, some you didn't know you had; thus, as I said, you've got just over four months to get ready for it."

My reaction was kidlike. I wanted to yell out, to jump in the air. I was, for a rare time in the years Diane had known me, practically speechless. I did rise, however, and move around the table to give her a bear hug and a hard kiss. I was beaming. "My God, sweetheart, I don't know what to say. I'm absolutely stunned, just stunned. How in the world did you ever think of this? How did you know about it?"

"I asked your dad for some ideas, and he suggested Phoenix camp. He knew all major league teams had them and that you'd love being around some former players for a week. He strongly suggested I give the present to you now instead of next June. For one thing, your body's younger than it will be then," and she laughed out loud as I was taking my seat again. "But the other is the February camp is special because you're likely to see some of the players who report to spring training while you're there. I'm sure you know more about that sort of thing than I do, but Matt thought it important. There's a fall fantasy camp in November, but he and I both agreed that would be too quick for you to get in shape."

I could tell Diane was *so* proud of herself, her feelings evident as I sat across the candlelit table. I hoped I'd shown my appreciation and wanted to ask so much more but realized this night wasn't just about me. It was *our* night, and I needed to devote my attention to her. The past seven years had been wonderful. It was a perfect marriage, not unlike Anne's and mine. Diane seemed always to want to please me. Perhaps it was because she'd been the victim of a guy who'd found someone to replace her and in effect walked out on her. But I knew I was similarly attentive to Diane and joined her equally in caring for her/our daughters. We reminisced over a bottle of cabernet sauvignon—a rarity, as we seldom had a drink. I presented her with a silver David Yurman bracelet, which was expensive but not quite half the cost of her gift to me. Yurman was her favorite jewelry. Our celebrating continued at home, beginning the moment we entered the house. It didn't matter how we acted, the girls were spending the night at Grandma's.

▬ ▬ ▬

I worked out in earnest over the next several months, hoping to be prepared for the February 8 start of camp. I did push-ups, sit-ups, and a series of other aerobic exercises at home, used equipment at a YMCA to increase upper body and leg strength, and ran along the state highway near our home after work and on weekends, concentrating on short bursts of speed, until winter weather set in, and then I ran on the indoor track at the Y. I also shot baskets in the facility's gym, dribbled while weaving and bobbing as I ran down the floor, and threw a tennis ball against the wall, practicing moving right and left as I would to field baseball hot grounders. Agency colleague Terry Koriath and I spent hours over those months throwing baseballs to one another at Gibson Park—permission granted by the hometown Dodgers—and then in an industrial warehouse owned by Terry's father.

"I can't believe you can still throw a knuckleball!" he exclaimed, nearly getting hit in the groin when one of my spinless pitches suddenly dove below his glove.

"Well, I've always thrown it for fun playing pitch and catch during softball seasons, so I guess I kept the grip and motion intact." In actuality, I was surprised at my ability to control a baseball after not playing the game for almost thirty years. It was a lot easier to throw a knuckler with the larger softball.

As the week went by, my excitement grew. Camp wasn't far away.

CHAPTER 35

During the February 8 flight from Evansville to Atlanta and then to Jacksonville, I permitted myself to wish I'd been going to Vero Beach and the fantasy camp at Dodgertown where I'd be with Duke Snider, Carl Erskine, Roy Campanella, Clem Labine, Tommy Lasorda, and other heroes, but just as quickly, I knew the thoughts were selfish and I was so thankful to Diane for getting the opportunity to participate anywhere.

Three other campers and I were picked up by a Jacksonville Phoenix van with the logo of flames and a large, intimidating, wide-winged bird on each of the vehicle's sides and driven less than an hour to Sailors' Village, spring training home of the Phoenix adjacent to their huge open-air concrete-and-glass stadium. My excitement was somewhat like I'd felt as a child anticipating gifts at Christmas. Staring out the window as we traveled, I thought of Diane and how she must feel at this moment, so happy that she'd made the opportunity possible. The others and I engaged in small talk, no doubt each of our minds thinking more about what lay ahead than having much interest in the other three. The driver turned the van onto Shipyard Avenue, and there it was, in all its glory, our temporary baseball Mecca.

Sailors' Village, aptly named for the hometown Class A Jacksonville Sailors minor league team, which got its name from the US Navy's huge presence in the area—thousands of active-duty personnel at three naval bases and thousands of retired military, mostly Navy, lived in Jacksonville and the suburbs. It was located on the city's south side, near the intersection of Interstates 95 and 295.

The treeless complex featured six well-manicured baseball fields, a building housing batting cages, an area devoted to pitching mounds, another section with outdoor batting cages, an office building, and a clubhouse. A small ballpark, Goldfarb Field, a name announcers had to take their time to enunciate, seated 5,320 for minor league games. Players lived in villas laid out in such fashion they could easily walk to the clubhouse.

Carrying my soft-shelled athletic bag that contained toiletries, casual clothing, underpants, athletic supporter, socks, glove, and spikes—the pair that was new when I began the 1961 season at EC and surprisingly was still in good condition—I checked in at the main office and was assigned a villa that would be my home for the next seven days.

"Hi, I'm Richard Jacklin," the pleasant face greeted me as I entered my room. "I'm your roommate."

"Davie Miller. Pleased to meet you," I said, as we shook hands.

"Isn't this something?" Jacklin exclaimed with the same enthusiasm I felt at the same moment. Displayed on our queen-size beds were several items the Phoenix had provided, including two team logo T-shirts, socks, and a cap. We'd been told our uniforms were in our lockers at the clubhouse and if our sized burgundy cap with a white J outlined in black on front didn't fit, we could exchange it. All the campers had been required months earlier to fill out a size form for uniforms, T-shirts, and cap.

"You played a lot of ball?" I inquired.

"No. Never," came the eyebrow-raising reply. "Never played in my life, even as a kid. I grew up in Manhattan, and my parents made me study and learn to play piano. Seems that's all I did."

We sat on the sides of our beds, facing one another. I saw a very skinny man, almost emaciated, I thought, with sunken eyes and a sharp nose. His straight hair was light in texture, and there wasn't much of it. The strands were uncombed, and I suspected he didn't bother trying. His well-manicured fingernails and thin hands appeared never to have encountered any heavy work.

"I'll give you a brief history of Richard Jacklin, and it's Richard, by the way, not Rick. I earned all my degrees in New York, including my MD in psychiatry. I've practiced in Miami for nearly thirty years. For my sixtieth birthday, my wife and three grown daughters surprised me with this trip since I'm a baseball fanatic and they thought it would be a great experience for me to be here. I'm certain it will, but I'll probably be the laughingstock of camp." I didn't know how to respond, because I had no idea what type of talent or abilities any of the other men had—make that "and one woman," Sylvia Meade, who was with her husband, Nate, from Staten Island.

━ ▬ ▬

It was minutes prior to 3:00 p.m. when Richard and I walked to the clubhouse nearly in the center of the complex of villas and bordering one of the diamonds. Locker room, training room, dining room, and cocktail lounge were all housed there. The day's printed schedule called for an afternoon of leisure or field activity, meaning anyone was welcome to go to one of the two diamonds available for informal practice or just hang out and not do much of anything. Both of us agreed we wanted to start throwing the ball or engaging in whatever was available outside the clubhouse.

The locker room was a series of dozens of wire lockers hooked together in rows. Each had a camper's or instructor's name attached above the front opening. "MILLER 42" read the small placard hanging on mine. Inside hung two uniforms, one white, the other gray, both identical to what the Phoenix players wore. In large print on the back of each uniform was "MILLER" and below it the large numeral 42, both in burgundy. I was overcome with emotion, seeing *my* name, *my* locker, and *my* boyhood idol's number—42, Jackie Robinson's number—on *my* uniforms. That the Phoenix permitted each camper to choose his own uniform number had been a surprise when I received the information form in October. But if someone, or several, wanted to wear Ted Williams's #9 or Mickey Mantle's #7, as an example, they could. None of the former Jacksonville players had achieved a career of that magnitude, so their numbers wouldn't be popular. Tears welled as I stood there, the moment indelibly imprinted in my mind.

"I'm Carlton Oliver," broke the spell. I wheeled and behind me, four lockers down the row, was Carlton Oliver, once an outstanding third baseman who'd retired after the '87 season, ending a sixteen-year career that included twelve with the Dodgers, one with the Cubs, and three with Jacksonville. I managed to respond with my name but didn't know what else to say, awestruck to be in the presence of a former player I'd admired for years. "Glad to have you here." Oliver smiled. "You'll have a blast."

Finishing dressing, Oliver said as he parted and looked over his shoulder, "See you at the diamond."

As an expansion franchise, Jacksonville had selected its players in a variety of ways, but mostly from a draft whereby each American League team produced a list of unprotected players from which the Phoenix could select. In addition, free agents were fair game if contract terms could be worked out. And in two cases, the club talked two recently retired players into returning to the game. Most of the team had been journeymen who were either so-so in talent or in the declining years of their careers. As a result, the Phoenix had found little success on the field, but Jacksonville area fans were fanatics about their team, and thousands walked through the turnstiles for every home game. Ownership was pleased with attendance but not with the won-loss records. It knew, however, that building a team from scratch would take years, lots of patience, and money.

I fumbled with the buttons on my gray uniform shirt, anxious to get outside. The instructions said first-timers were to wear gray for practice while veterans donned white. It was a caste system from the outset, but it didn't matter once campers got to the field. Everyone was cordial. Or almost everyone. I soon found out a few of those who had participated previously in these camps thought they were hot shots.

While some of the players were throwing balls back and forth, others were taking infield practice or shagging fly balls. Clyde Tempel, a once hard-hitting first baseman and among the National League's leading batters until he twisted a knee after fielding a grounder and making an awkward move to get the runner five years ago, was at first. After loosening up off to one side of the field, I got behind three others at shortstop, and we took turns fielding grounders and throwing to the muscular, apparently still-in-great-shape Tempel who effortlessly caught the balls with his outstretched, large glove. I could have pinched myself that I was throwing to *the* Clyde Tempel. Then I took turns at second and third and in the outfield, fielding grounders or deep flies hit by a coach for the major league team. Sylvia Meade was there, too. *Boy, could she ever field ground balls.* At second base, the distaffer rarely bobbled one, even hard ones hit right at her. Her throws to first were a relatively short distance, but she had nothing like a "girl's throw," her motion challenging that of several of the men. No doubt it was better than my roommate's.

"Those of you who're wise," Coach Billy Kennedy advised loudly as practice ended, "will head for the training room. I don't care how good and loose you feel now; I guarantee you'll be sore as hell tomorrow, and stiff. We've got our parent club and minor league trainers on duty to rub you down, put ice bags on you, or do whatever to take care of you." I went straight there and was surprised to see many others head straight to the showers or their lockers to change and then go back to their rooms. I knew from experience how important it was to get an ice bag on the throwing shoulder. In fact, I'd done it at home after games all the years I'd been playing softball.

"Here's a rookie, guys," cried out one of the assistant trainers for the parent club, to which his colleagues yelled back in a chant, "Rook, rook, rook, rookie" when I walked in the door.

"Be sure to tuck a hot tamale in his armpit when you put the ice bag on!" another shouted from across the room. Everyone laughed. I grinned.

A bag of ice was molded to my right shoulder and wide tan gauze wrapped under the arm and around the bag to hold it in place. "You'll feel nothing in less than ten minutes," I was informed. "We'll keep the bag on fifteen to twenty minutes, and tomorrow, you'll feel good as new." Sitting there on the training table, I watched other campers getting a variety of services that included back, neck, calf, and hamstring massages. Ice bags on body parts were evident everywhere.

"Didn't you go to the training room?" I asked Richard when I got back to the room and found him lying on his bed, watching TV.

"No, didn't think I needed to, I didn't throw that much. Stayed in the outfield and didn't get many hit to me. I just concentrated on running a lot."

"You really should run over to the training room. It'll relieve you of soreness tomorrow morning."

"Aw, I'll be okay."

"How'd you like being out there?"

"I loved it. First time I'd ever worn a glove, and I was surprised I could catch balls as well as I did. Of course, I dropped a lot of them and trying to field ones hit to me was a circus. I bet some of those guys wondered why the hell I'm here." I saw the boyish excitement in the doctor's face, and I was happy for him.

Almost everyone was dressed in golf shorts and shirts or T-shirts when they arrived at the clubhouse lounge for "happy hour" preceding the first dinner together. Campers and instructors alike moved about the room introducing themselves to one another, one big happy family ready to spend a week together. "Davie Miller, I'm Guy Bolyard, camp director for this group of wannabes, wish-they'd-beens, or actual former stars of one brilliance or another." Bolyard was a classic among the veteran campers. A friendly, tell-it-like-it-is type of guy who wanted nothing better than for each participant to thoroughly enjoy the week and not get hurt.

"Glad to have a fellow Hoosier here." The graying Bolyard smiled as he patted me on a shoulder. "I grew up in Fort Wayne, then went to IU. Joined the White Sox in forty-eight, played, then scouted until I retired. I've headed this camp from the outset, three years ago."

"Mr. Bolyard, it's great to be here. A thrill, actually."

"You'll be surprised to know, I remember you from many years ago." I *was* surprised and showed it. "I became a scout in sixty-one and Indiana was part of my territory. You were on the list of players our club was watching. Matter a' fact, I was in the stands the day you got leveled. Damned sorry about the injury. Damned sorry. I think you had quite a career ahead of you. I hope you've had no major aftereffects from getting hurt."

"No, sir, none at all." I was filled with pride at his compliment.

Bolyard patted me on the back. "See you at calisthenics bright and early tomorrow."

My welcoming experience in the dining hall was something to behold. No doubt campers would be treated like kings if the first night's meal was indicative. The buffet line included entrée choices of prime rib, fried grouper, baked chicken, and pasta, always pasta regardless of the other choices at evening dinners. Campers, current staff, and former stars sat together in unassigned roundtables of eight. Who one sat with was the luck of the day. Whether one would rub elbows with former major leaguers like Carlton Oliver and Clyde Tempel or "Joe Schmoe from Nowhere, USA," depended on where an empty chair was found.

The dinner hour was filled with the buzz of excitement, jokes, storytelling—some former .250 lifetime hitters talked as though they'd led the league in batting year after year—and people getting acquainted with one another. The grizzly, slightly built, totally gray-haired Bolyard took the stage and offered welcoming remarks and then ran through the schedule for the week and gave a profile of the participants—107 of us, ranging in age from thirty-four to seventy-three. Some of the campers had been there all four years. After tryouts that involved pitching, fielding, and batting, six teams would be chosen in a draft among the managers, each of whom was a former major league player.

■ ▒ ■

Sleep didn't come easily, but I slept soundly when it did and was startled by the alarm from the clock I'd brought with me. My roommate began complaining of a stiff throwing arm and sore hamstrings and got an unsympathetic "I warned you" in response. After a breakfast offering of seemingly every type of food one could consider for the early morning meal, although I was careful not to overindulge, I headed for the locker room, donned my gray uniform, and went to a large grassy area where Jacksonville head trainer Clyde Williams was about to lead stretching and warm-up activities. It was a pleasant morning, neither hot nor cool. Then it was off to tryouts for the rookies.

One-third of the first-timers were sent to the batting cages, one-third to the pitching mounds, and the final third to one of the diamonds. I was assigned the latter. Under the watchful eyes of the former major leaguers and the current major and minor league managers and coaches, other players and I fielded ground balls at various infield positions and caught fly balls hit to the outfield. A horn sounded, and everyone rotated. It was my turn in the batting cages. I was never much of a hitter, and although batting against a stationary throwing machine should be easier, I showed my lack of talent. Former Cardinal great Juan Alvarez offered tips to all the hitters, instructing us on proper weight shift and hand-arm rotation when we swung. I wanted to laugh when I saw Richard Jacklin in an adjoining cage but realized I wasn't any better making contact despite having a more seasoned swing than he.

The morning of work ended with pitching tryouts for my group. Every player was required to show what skill he had, regardless of any prior experience on a mound. I was loose and felt great. My first offering, a fastball, snapped the glove back on the minor league coach squatted behind the plate. There's a distinctive sound that only people in baseball know the meaning of—when they hear a ball strike the leather of a catcher's mitt with authority, somewhat akin to a golf ball hitting the sweet spot of a driver. Heads turned. Six mounds were in use, but coaches' eyes shifted to the young guy wearing #42 with "MILLER" on the back.

Another fastball, then another. Bam. Bam. The sound of the ball slapping leather. Mickey Katter, former National League All-Star and World Series pitcher, who had an outstanding record with the Phillies in the late '40s and early '50s, an invited special guest of the Phoenix, was standing behind me. In his Southern drawl, Katter said, "Dang, boy. Impressive. That's enough fastballs. Save your arm. Show us what kind of curve you have." There wouldn't be much to see. I never had much of one. After a half-dozen pitches, Katter asked, "Got anything else?" I didn't reply, just motioned to the catcher that I'd throw a knuckleball. My first delivery was as good a knuckler as I'd ever thrown, the ball perfectly dead, and when it neared the plate, it dove, hit the plate, and bounced up into the catcher's groin. Good thing he was wearing protection, but the collision of ball and cup hurt anyway. He signaled for someone else to take over and limped away.

The managers and coaches would have a draft of players after the morning of tryouts. Therefore, each was careful not to make any comments to others for fear he'd call attention to someone he wanted on his team. But I sensed a group gathering behind me.

Knuckleball after knuckleball bobbed, weaved, danced, and dove. Raised eyebrows were predominant. I learned from Guy Bolyard later it was a rare display of pitching by an amateur in fantasy camp. No one said a word to me when the tryout ended, except a fascinated-appearing Katter who asked, "How old are you, son?"

"I'll be fifty in June." Katter just shook his head as everyone headed to the clubhouse. The Alabama native's last season in the majors was 1954 when he pitched at the almost unheard of age of thirty-nine. His specialty had been the banned spitball in which he'd secretly apply a substance before he threw the ball, causing it to act erratically en route to the catcher's mitt. But Katter had more than one pitch while achieving a winning record in his eight seasons with the Phillies—24–6 in 1949—so he knew when he saw someone special.

I grabbed a turkey-and-cheese sandwich at the deli-style lunch setup in the locker room and headed for an ice bag. Players were talking, wondering whose team they'd be on. Most didn't care; they were just happy to be there. By the time I'd finished with the ice treatment and downed another sandwich, chips, and an apple, the teams were posted on the locker room bulletin board. As I stood searching for my name, I felt a pat on a shoulder. "You're my starter," Jack Watson told me. "In fact, you were the number-one draft pick as I got the first selection." I was dazed. Not that I was on a team or that I would get to pitch, but that I would be managed by *Jack Watson*, as outstanding a right-fielder as the game ever had. Watson spent most of his years with the Red Sox but also played for Cleveland, San Francisco, and Jacksonville. "Our game's at 1:30, so be ready."

My stomach was now in a knot, and I wished I hadn't eaten the extra sandwich. I had to be ready to pitch and to do so for Jack Watson. It was an overwhelming feeling, almost scary.

While Watson had a potential star as a pitcher, he also had Richard Jacklin. The Miami doctor was among the last available for the draft. Everyone had to be on a team and had to get an opportunity to play, regardless of skill. Whenever he was inserted in a game, Richard would always be placed in right field, the premise being that fewer balls would be hit there.

When my team of real-life lawyers, business executives, doctors, blue-collar workers, educators, and one PR executive took the field, I felt at ease and at home back on a pitching mound. My physique rivaled that of younger players, quite unlike the potbellies and excessive weight among the others.

"Strike!" called the umpire when the first pitch was thrown. "Strike two!" followed. The key in fantasy camp games was to get the ball over the plate. That sounds obvious, but not all who attempted to pitch were skilled at it and too many "ball four" calls could make a game extra long and a manager frustrated. I wasn't the only one with pitching skill, but the camp was not blessed with an abundance. "Strike three."

Watson let me pitch six innings before taking me out with an 8–0 lead. He said he planned to use me as often as possible during the week. As former competitors at the highest level of baseball, each of the managers hadn't lost their zeal to win, and earning bragging rights as the overall champion of the five games was important to them.

━ ▬ ━

I pitched in three of the next four games. Word got around the camp, so whenever I was on the mound, people who weren't involved in other games gathered. Batter after batter could be heard muttering after striking out, "Damn, he must've been a pro," "Not fair," "Did you see that knuckleball?" and similar. Sylvia Meade gave me the finger in jest when I got her out on a knuckler, but I didn't use it against her the next two times she batted. She actually grounded to third once. I almost felt guilty for striking out men who obviously had little talent for hitting, especially the older ones. But I wasn't about to let my team down, especially warm, congenial Watson, whom I admired. Even at my skill level, I still got instruction from my one-week mentor. "Keep those shoulders down when you deliver the ball. Keep them down and level," he'd advise. Whatever the manager told me to do, I'd try it.

Evenings at camp were special. Following the nightly premeal reception hour and dinner, awards were handed out to the player on each team judged by their manager as being "Player of the Game." I received the first one for my team. Watson, being fair, as he should have been, chose four others after the following games. Then former major leaguers mounted the dining hall stage and regaled their audience with stories of times past. Subject matter varied from night-to-night along the lines of "Who was the toughest hitter you ever faced?" "What game sticks out in your mind more than any other?" "Who was the best player you ever saw during your day?" and so forth. The post-dinner programs could have gone on for hours, they were so entertaining, and informative, but there had to be an ending. After all, there was another game to get ready for tomorrow.

My team went undefeated in its five games, and I was practically unhittable. I didn't know it at the time, but privately, Watson was asked by Phoenix staff what he thought of the knuckler. "One of the best I've ever seen at any level. Maybe it's that crooked finger that has a lot to do with it, but I wouldn't want to face him. He's made a fool of a lot of guys this week, even some of those in their thirties and forties still playing some type of amateur-league or semi-pro ball. Several of them are pretty good hitters, but not against him!" He told me about the conversation later.

Highlighting the week was the annual campers versus Phoenix game in Goldfarb Field. Fans, many of them tourists or "snowbirds" from Canada spending the winter in Florida, filled every seat for their chance to see former major leaguers. Every camper was given an opportunity to take the field for at least one inning and to bat once, thanks to a rule that their team was given six outs per inning. The former greats got the standard three.

As the starter for the league champions, I took the mound in the bottom of the first, completely at ease and full of confidence. Three strikeouts later, I got an ovation from an appreciative audience. An assortment of fastballs and knucklers had batters guessing, with two of them taking called third strikes—both final pitches being nasty knuckleballs. The home team's bench was abuzz.

There were so many of us on the camper squad that pitchers were to play only one inning. Guy Bolyard gave me two. He confided in me between innings the crowd would have booed him out of the stadium if he hadn't. The home team had a mixture of former players and current managers and coaches, some of them outstanding hitters at the major league level, and they weren't in the batter's box to halfheartedly attempt to hit. It would be embarrassing to lose to the campers; besides, fans loved seeing them hit home runs just like they did in their prime. Didn't matter. In two innings, I struck out five of the six I faced. One of them hit a grounder to second for an easy out. It was an astonishing feat, striking out five *professional* baseball players.

As the game progressed—I struck out in my only at-bat—Bolyard approached me. "Someone wants to see you." The camp director turned the game reins over to his assistant while he and I took the concrete steps that led from the dugout up to the burgundy chair-backed bleachers and then down to a grassy area behind them. "Fred Marshall," the executive-appearing man in white dress shirt and striped burgundy and black tie behind the extended arm said. "I'm the Phoenix general manager. You put on quite a show over there," he said, nodding his head to the left, toward the stadium field. "In fact, I'm told you put on quite a show all week."

Bordering on bewilderment, I took the compliment somewhat in stride. "I had fun. Sure was glad to have been here all week. It's been a dream from the time I arrived." Marshall and Bolyard looked at one another and smiled.

"How'd you like that dream to continue?" the GM inquired.

Frowning, I said, "Not sure I understand."

"I'll be honest," Marshall responded. "We'd like to see you pitch against some of our roster for spring training." My breath shortened, a quizzical expression developed on my face. "I don't know what your job situation is back home in Indiana, but if you could stay here a few more days, we'll give you an opportunity of a lifetime." Now I was dumbfounded. "What do you think? No charge to you. We'll pick up all expenses, pay you a thousand a day, and give you a first-class ticket home at the end."

Not certain how to respond, I said nothing at first and then managed, "Wow. I don't know what to say. You want me to pitch in spring training against the Phoenix?" I glanced at Marshall and then at Bolyard, who was smiling from ear to ear.

"Sure do," the Jacksonville executive responded. "We'll let you stay in the villa you're in now with one of the catchers who'll be reporting tomorrow when the campers leave. You'll wear the uniforms you have, and we'll make certain you're well taken care of, including complete insurance coverage in case anything happens. Of course, the company would want you to take a physical even though you've played all week and appear to be in great health. It's a routine procedure required even for the professional players."

My mind was swirling with thoughts. "Well, I need to talk with my wife and my partners at the ad agency. This might not go over well with them—uh, not my wife, the partners."

"I fully understand," Marshall replied. "I've thrown a curve at you, and I know it's asking a lot; actually, maybe I should say 'offering' a lot. And let me say both of us realize there's risk in this. I'm aware of your injury of almost thirty years ago, and the balls hit here aren't anything like those in college or fantasy camp. You'll have to take that into consideration. Guy will take you to an office where you can make your calls if you decide to stay. I hope you do."

"How long do you want me to be here?"

"Another week if you can spare it."

"Guy, I'm stunned," I said as Bolyard and I walked to a two-story office building not far from the stadium.

"Don't blame you. I would be, too. But what an opportunity. I'm telling you you've impressed a hell of a lot of people this week. Stay another week, and you'll have quite a story to share with your grandkids someday."

Before I picked up the phone, I sat at the office desk and pondered. What an opportunity! Risk? Certainly, but I'd pitched all week, and risk just wasn't a concern in my making a decision. The call to Diane was cautiously enthusiastic. I wanted to share my excitement as I truly felt it but didn't know how she'd respond; I was apprehensive she'd nix the idea. My fears were abated. She was as happy as I was, if not more so.

"Davie, I'm so proud of you. What a wonderful opportunity, something perhaps no one has ever been able to do. If you're at peace with your decision, go for it. Enjoy it. Have fun."

Next came the call with trepidation to Bruce Wilson. But I got the same result. "In fact, I might fly down to watch you. Regardless, we'll handle your accounts for another week. The good thing is this is February and not a lot's happening in regard to Latimore."

CHAPTER 36

"Jerry Wilkes," my new roommate introduced himself when he entered the villa room late Thursday morning, athletic bag slung over his left shoulder. All the fantasy campers had begun their trips home that morning. "You a new coach here?"

I laughed. "At my age, you'd think so, but they asked me to stay after the fantasy camp I attended this past week."

"To coach?"

"No. Unbelievably, to pitch."

"Pitch!" Wilkes exclaimed, skeptically sizing me up from head to toe.

I smiled. "Sounds preposterous, I know. But I had a good week on the mound, and they asked me to stay."

"How old are you?"

"Old enough to almost be your father. Forty-nine. And you?"

"Twenty-seven. Graduated from Miami of Ohio and was drafted by the Reds, then traded to the Phoenix in a six-player deal after last season. Am anxious to prove I belong here."

"You're a catcher."

"Yeah. How'd you know?"

"The general manager said I'd be rooming with one."

"The general manager? *The* Phoenix general manager? *The* Jacksonville Phoenix general manager?"

"Yes," I said, attempting not to make a big deal of the matter.

"Man, you *must* be something special."

I gave a five-minute synopsis of my baseball and professional background and details about fantasy camp. "For my age, I pitched well. The knuckler was good all week, so I got the surprise offer to stay another week and pitch against you professionals. Still can't believe it."

"What'd'you think they'll have you do? Pitch batting practices?"

"I suppose so."

Wilkes, a specialist at catching knuckleballs, although none of the Phoenix pitchers had one, found out he was personally assigned to catch me in batting practices that began that afternoon after I took the physical and was cleared to play. Phoenix manager Sparky Malone believed players should bat on the open field as well as in cages from day one, so I got the assignment to go with Wilkes to diamond 2, since the cage was on 1. Having played for a week, I was in better condition than most of the professional pitchers and so was ready to face batters who were supposed to have conditioned themselves throughout the off-season but hadn't had much opportunity, if any, to practice hitting back home.

I now was nervous, never having faced the likes of a Bob Tomlin or Chris Skirvin, major league veterans I knew from reading the sports pages or occasionally watching games on TV over the years. Tomlin had come to the Phoenix two years earlier after ten years with the Reds and Angels. He could hit the ball so hard it seemed to flatten. Skirvin, a fellow outfielder, was an original Phoenix and had averaged over .300 since joining after seven years with the Braves. Both came to diamond 2 after taking their swings in the cage. They knew nothing of me, assuming I might be a new minor league coach. A few infielders and outfielders were on hand to get some initial practice in fielding hit balls.

"Who's the old guy?" Tomlin asked Wilkes while stepping into the batter's box.

"Name's Davie Miller," the catcher replied and said nothing more. My first pitch, a fastball, was drilled into left field; my second ended in a drive to the fence between left and center. Sparky Malone had ordered us battery mates not to let up, to throw the best stuff. He didn't want to baby any of his players, and each of those returning for a new season knew they had to be in shape at the outset or else. Wilkes signaled for a knuckler. I delivered.

Tomlin started to swing, held up, and then swung, missing the fluttering ball by a foot. "What the fuck was that?" he spewed, looking down at Wilkes who was holding the ball and smiling with the expression of a cat who'd caught a mouse.

"Oh, just a little pitch from some old guy on the mound," he said, emphasizing the descriptive "old guy."

"Signal for another," Tomlin commanded. In came the pitch, he swung, and the ball bounced harmlessly foul off the end of the bat. "Damn," the tall left-fielder declared. "Haven't seen anything like that except from Charlie Hough."

After mixing up my pitches to Tomlin, I faced Skirvin. "What's he got, and who the hell is he?" the left-handed hitter asked as he passed Tomlin en route to the batter's box.

"Oh, just the usual," Tomlin lied, struggling to keep from laughing.

"Who is this guy?" Skirvin said to Wilkes as he stepped in.

"Just some guy I guess they brought in to pitch for today," he said, feigning ignorance. "Pretty old to be here, I'd say."

"Well, bring it on," Skirvin replied. "I was hittin' damned well over there in the cage, so let's see what I can do here."

My first pitch was a fastball lined into right field; the second drilled to the left, right over third base. A third fastball was a high fly to the left. Skirvin never got the bat off his shoulder on the fourth, which dove at the plate, and Wilkes reached and caught it in the tiny webbing of the mitt. "What the hell?" the batter said, getting nothing but a smile through the facemask from the squatting catcher. I followed that knuckler with another, just off the outside of the plate. Skirvin's swing caught nothing but warm Florida air. "Hell, I've not seen anything like that!" the center-fielder exclaimed. He stepped out of the box and yelled at me, "You've got a hell of a pitch … sir." I smiled, but, still nervous, didn't hold it long.

When I reached eighty pitches thrown to eight batters, Jacksonville pitching coach J. R. Martin summoned me to the sideline. "No sense overstressing the arm. We want you to pitch a lot this week, maybe not much if any tomorrow. I'll say this for you, if your knuckler was like that in college, you would've had one tremendous career here in the majors, and I'm sorry you didn't have the chance. God gave you a gift with that pitch." Nodding his head toward a group of players, he continued, "You should hear the grousing among the guys who faced you." Martin chuckled. "The word's already gotten around the team about your knuckleball. Don't be surprised if some of the pitchers ask you to work with them." My eyebrows shot upward, showing my surprise. "It's okay with me if you do," the coach assured him. Nearly blown over by the compliments, I couldn't wait to give Diane the news when I made my daily call that evening.

I was given Friday off but told to be ready to pitch practice Saturday morning. Warming up at 10:00, I knew this was going to be another good day.

A small stand of bleachers, big enough to hold approximately three hundred spectators, stood behind home plate. After loosening up down the left-field line, as I walked to the mound to throw a few more warm-ups and then face my first batter, I heard "Go get 'em, Davie!" from more than one person in the stands.

But concentrating so intently on what lay ahead, I didn't pay much attention until a lone voice yelled, "Just do it, sweetheart!" I knew instantly it was Diane. I stepped from atop the mound and walked a couple of steps toward home plate, my face reflecting the absolute surprise that had hit me. Behind the screen, I saw a beaming Diane pointing to the others standing with her—Bruce Wilson, Gary McGlasson, and their wives, Jo and Michele. I could have been pushed over with a feather.

Not knowing what to say, my spell was broken instantly by, "Hey, we're here to play ball. I've got a living to make," from Zack Long, a burly, unshaven thirty-something veteran third baseman, who had no time for the niceties of life.

To put it mildly, I was pissed as I returned to the pitching rubber. My first pitch was anything but what Long expected, a nasty knuckler that his bat just missed, if you count a mile as "just missed." Long was now in a foul mood. "Hey, this is batting practice," he shouted at me, "not a rehearsal for tryin' to make the team. Shit!"

I responded with another knuckler, and Long stepped out of the box toward the mound. Wilkes grabbed his right arm. "Don't do it, Zack. This is just batting practice, and he's a teammate."

"Some asshole teammate!" Long replied as he stepped back into the box, tapped the end of his bat on the plate, and prepared for my next delivery. It was a fastball that must have missed my head by no more than two feet when it came back on a clothesline faster than I'd sent it toward home. I'd had practically no time to react. I hadn't heard Diane's bloodcurdling scream, "Daay-vee!" This, indeed, was the big leagues. For a moment, I wondered if being there was complete foolishness on my part. Long scowled. He could have cared less about any club general manager experiment with this old fart facing him from sixty feet and six inches away. As he said, he had a living to make.

Both of us settled down, and I threw a variety of fastballs, weak curves, and knucklers. Long left the plate after about fifteen pitches but didn't take his eyes off the guy who'd now become his opponent as he walked to the sideline and muttered something to teammates who'd watched the entire episode.

None of the other hitters reacted similarly when they had their turns at the plate, each getting an opportunity to take ten pitches, only two managing to hit a knuckler fair. At about the magical eighty count, J. R. Martin yelled to me that I'd thrown enough for today and told me to go see my friends.

Although it was already 82 degrees, I picked up my jacket lying against the fence far to the left of the third base line and inserted my right arm, to keep it even warmer. Then I walked to the right side of the bleachers and into the arms of my wife and friends who'd made the surprise trip from Evansville to watch me fulfill a dream of playing in the big time.

"Davie, I'm *so* proud of you," Diane exclaimed after giving me a big smack of a kiss.

"We are, too," Bruce commented.

"Sure are," Gary added. About that time, someone yelled, "Watch out!" Everyone behind home plate ducked instinctively as a foul ball landed to the left of the bleachers.

"We'd better get away from here," I advised. Motioning with my covered right arm, I said, "Let's walk over to the clubhouse where we'll be out of harm's way."

"I'm shocked!" I exclaimed, holding Diane's hand as we walked. "I can't believe you guys are here. When'd you come down?"

They were all giddy. Diane breathlessly explained it was "Bruce's idea," and they agreed "it would be a blast to surprise you" so they flew down the previous afternoon and spent the night at a motel not far from Sailors' Village.

"After all," Diane continued, "this will be the only time we'll get to see you in the majors," and we all laughed at the preposterousness of what was taking place.

"Yeah, I'll be home next Thursday evening, but meantime, I'm having a blast," I responded with boyish enthusiasm.

— —

While I showered, the five others strayed toward the batting cage at diamond 1, the two men mesmerized at seeing big-league ballplayers only a few feet from them. Having been told by my manager to take the afternoon off, I showed my special visitors around the clubhouse, taking Bruce and Gary into the locker room, and then all of them over to my villa so they could see what had been my home away from home for more than a week.

"Smells like a jock's room!" Bruce sniffed in jest. "I smell wintergreen someone's been using on their muscles."

"Yeah. It's my roomie. His hams and quads have been a little sore from squatting so much behind home plate." They laughed.

In no hurry to leave the complex, the six of us loitered around the ball fields, soaking in the Florida sun, far different than the snow and cold of the Midwest they'd left behind for a couple of days, and watching all the activities of the afternoon. At dinner, I regaled them with stories of the week at fantasy camp, every word of my initial conversation with general manager Marshall, and the two days of spring training I'd experienced before they arrived. I was like a kid, enthusiastically spewing forth detail after detail.

"You'll have to write an article for the *Courier* and/or the *Press* when you get back!" Bruce exclaimed. "We can get that handled for you. Plus, I'll make a call to the sports editors first thing Monday morning to make them aware of what you're doing. They might want to send someone for your last days here or at least interview you on the phone." He paused and reflected for a moment. "This is a *big deal*. Selfishly, it's great publicity for the agency."

Gary chimed in, "The University of Evansville needs to know about it for their alumni magazine. I'll handle that."

After dinner and forty-five minutes with Diane in her motel room, I was driven back to my villa. "I'm so very proud of you," Diane told me as we kissed good-bye while she squeezed my neck in a hard embrace. Then the car headed toward the Sailors' Village exit.

— —

"Davie, Fred Marshall wants to talk with you," Sparky Malone told me after batting practice Wednesday morning, which, as far as I knew, was the last time I'd ever pitch to major leaguers again. My extra week in Jacksonville was to end with a trip home the following day.

Still in uniform and sweaty, I walked to the two-story brick office building and was greeted by the general manager's secretary when I entered the reception area on the second floor. "Mr. Marshall's expecting you, Mr. Miller. Go right on in."

"Day-vee," the GM drew out when the door opened, and I saw the smoke-filled, combination light- and dark-oak room that served as the club executive's spring training office. A thick leather couch and matching large burgundy easy chairs with an unusual inlaid, Phoenix bird-shaped glass-top coffee table in between the furniture sat off to one side of the room. Two smaller, upright chairs with padded burgundy-leather cushions were in front of the large solid-oak desk. Marshall leaned across it to shake hands and motioned for me to sit down. Smoke from a lit cigarette rose from a clear glass ashtray on the right side of the desk. I hated cigarette smoke, but at least the window air conditioner was breaking up the column as it blew cold air into the large office.

"I hope you've enjoyed your week with us," Marshall began.

"Have I ever, Mr. Marshall! It's been a dream come true, and I thank you for the opportunity." I was met with yet another surprise.

"How'd you like the dream to continue?"

My forehead formed a deep frown, considering how furtive I thought the general manager was being. "What're you talking about?"

"About you pitching some more with us." The furrow in my brow deepened. "About you coming down here and pitching in an exhibition game." I didn't reply, as flabbergasted as the moment I'd received Marshall's inquiry during the camper-Phoenix game. "Surprised, huh?" Marshall grinned. Still no reply. "Yes, I'm talking about you pitching in a Grapefruit League game." Grapefruit League was the name given to exhibition competition among major league teams headquartered for spring training in Florida.

"Well, you got me, Mr. Marshall. I certainly never expected anything like this."

Marshall had a reputation for innovation in promotion.

"Why me?"

"Because you are something else, Davie Miller. God-given unbelievable. No one in our organization has ever been around anyone like you. Nearly fifty years old with a combination of pitches, especially a knuckleball that is drop-dead something to behold."

"But, Mr. Marshall, I've got a job, a career, and I can't jeopardize it. You and I both know I'm not going anywhere baseball-wise."

"You've wanted to play professional ball at the highest level ever since you were little, haven't you?" Marshall calmly queried.

"Yes, sir, since I was a young teenager, but that all ended a long time ago."

Marshall seized the moment. "Then I'm offering an opportunity of a lifetime, a chance you never dreamed could happen, an opportunity to pitch in a major league game, albeit an exhibition. What'll you say?"

Unconvinced but mostly concerned about my job back home, I repeated my earlier question, my head swimming, "Why me, Mr. Marshall?"

The GM didn't respond immediately; he just stared out the window while gathering his thoughts. Then he turned to me and replied, "I'll be honest with you, Davie. I'm a promoter. I love to fill the stands. I love to introduce non-fans to baseball and to offer our loyalists something special. It's good for the game. And I, uh, we make money off of every fan whose butt is in the stands during spring training. We only charge a couple of bucks for them to attend, but they buy concessions and purchase merchandise in the souvenir shop. That's where we make the money. Can you imagine the turnout, the publicity when it's announced you'll be pitching a week from Saturday against Detroit?" The thought of appearing in a game against the Tigers, or any team, was beyond my comprehension.

"A thousand thoughts must be running through your head," Marshall continued after seeing his hoped-for prized possession sitting there staring into space. "Here's the deal. You fly back to Evansville tomorrow and return to your job. Fly down here Saturday, pitch batting practice Sunday, and return home that evening. Stay in shape all next week by working out and pitching wherever you did all that before you came to fantasy camp. The game on March 3 is at one o'clock here at Goldfarb. I'd like you to get here early enough that Friday to throw some, just to make certain you're ready the next day."

He paused. "There's more, in case you're wondering." He chuckled. "All this has been cleared with Sparky Malone. He's not 100 percent keen on the idea, but he appreciates all the attention you gave to his pitchers and thinks a couple of them have found a new pitch in the knuckler. He's willing to let you pitch three or four innings on the third, since it's the first exhibition game." I wanted to hear more.

Marshall grinned. "Your boss knows about this."

"Bruce Wilson?"

"Yes, I spoke with Bruce Wilson by phone this morning, and he's ecstatic. Our small corporate jet will take you home this afternoon, fly you here for this weekend, and then we'll send it back March 2 to pick up you, your wife and children, Wilson, and as many as five others and provide local transportation, housing, food ... you name it. How's that and fifteen hundred dollars for this Sunday and five thousand for the exhibition game sound?"

I thought I'd died and gone to heaven. "More than I could have ever dreamed possible," was all I could muster and not with a lot of vocal volume. I was simply overwhelmed.

I called Bruce just to make certain the general manager had been honest about contacting him and then placed a call to Diane's office. She was with a patient and had about as much difficulty as I initially in comprehending what had been offered when she called back as I packed what few belongings I would take with me on the plane. All my baseball paraphernalia were to be left in the villa and would be clean when I returned on the weekend.

"Davie, this must be a dream. Tell me it is."

"Certainly, it's a dream come true, sweetheart."

"You've got to contact your dad."

"Don't worry, I will. It's my next call. I want him and Mom to come down, too. It will be as great a thrill as he's ever had in his life. I can hardly wait to see his face when he walks into this complex."

CHAPTER 37

I threw well in batting practice that Sunday in Jacksonville and each late afternoon the following week, pitching to Terry Koriath in his father's warehouse until slightly more than a dusting of snow melted to permit a return to Gibson Park. As a reward, Terry got to make the trip to the game along with Diane, the children—who had their principal's permission to miss classes that Friday—Dad and Mom, Bruce, Gary, and Greg Glass, a sports reporter for the *Evansville Courier*. I'd wanted Andy Ludlow to join us, but he was too ill from the effects of a stroke he'd suffered four months earlier. The plane was abuzz with excitement, which only grew when we arrived in Jacksonville. Their luggage was taken to a hotel not far from Sailors' Village, and we were whisked to the baseball complex. I showed everyone the villa, since only Diane, Bruce, and Gary had been there previously, and then the group was escorted to the stands behind diamond 2 while I dressed for my warm-up activities.

"Davie, you've no idea how proud I am of you," my seventy-seven-year-old gray-haired father said the following day as he hugged me and patted me on the back just before he and the other eight in our group left me at the clubhouse entrance and walked to Goldfarb Field. Tears welled in his eyes, and he didn't mind that I saw them.

"I know you are, Dad. And I want you to know this moment would never have come had it not been for you. You taught me the pitch that got me here. Without a knuckler, I'm just another pitcher and I'm Davie Miller sitting back home in Evansville. I owe all this to you."

Dad's shoulders, which had been drooping from old age, suddenly sprang up straight, and he beamed while a tear rolled down his cheek. "No, son. You're here because of *you*. I might have taught you something, but you're the one who worked his butt off and persevered. No one deserves this more than you."

"I'm dedicating this effort to you, Dad. Remember that when you see me on the mound. I just hope I don't embarrass you, and myself, with some lousy performance. But I feel good, so let's see what happens."

Fred Marshall had spared no expense in promoting the game. One would have thought it was the first regular season encounter for his club with all the advertising and public relations efforts that were expended. Baseball purists derided him, and several national baseball writers criticized him for being "another Bill Veeck." Veeck was a promotional genius and owner of the Cleveland Indians, St. Louis Browns, and Chicago White Sox from the late 1940s to 1980. Among his wacky publicity stunts to draw fans were a batting appearance by dwarf Eddie Gaedel in a 1951 game (he walked on four straight pitches) and the reactivation of Minnie Minoso at age fifty-four and again at age fifty-eight, so he could have a few at-bats each time just to claim appearances in four and then five decades of baseball. Marshall was not quite of the same ilk but loved the media attention, whether good or bad, as long as it drew fans to the stands. His experiment with me worked.

The March 3 game was oversold. Marshall must have slipped the fire marshal some greenbacks to allow a standing room–only crowd. My entourage had seats behind the home club dugout, so I could see them when I walked from the mound after each of my half innings of pitching. I tried to convince myself this was "just another game." My excellence at mind control had always served me well. It had to again on this day, or I'd wilt. My batting practice experiences had me accustomed to facing big leaguers, and, as I had done every morning of spring training, I prayed for strength and calmness and thanked God for the talent and the opportunity to be there. I knew Detroit had the worst record in baseball in 1989 but was expected to improve. To me, it didn't matter whether they were the best or worst; they were still a major league team, and I was an aging amateur who now had professional status merely because I'd been paid to appear.

The crowd was in a frenzy, anticipating this commoner being given an opportunity to pitch in the majors. Fred Marshall's promotions had them primed. The Phoenix's fire-red-feathered, uniformed mascot bounced back and forth atop the home dugout exhorting the crowd to cheer. They rose and applauded when I took the mound to warm up and now were ready to scream at my every pitch.

Weak-hitting shortstop Felix Lopez hit the first pitch, a fastball, into right field, just beyond the reach of the Phoenix second baseman, and the crowd quieted immediately. Was this older man on the mound just another promotional stunt that wasn't worth all the hype? Were they in for a letdown of major league proportions? Squatting behind home plate, Jerry Wilkes motioned for me to stay calm. "Just pitch to me, partner!" Wilkes yelled through his catcher's mask. He signaled a knuckler and wasn't disappointed. Tigers' second baseman Toby Greenspan stood there and watched as the ball danced slightly as it floated past him, belt high.

"Strike!" bellowed the umpire. Greenspan nervously took several practice swings. I got the sign, stretched, looked over my left shoulder at Lopez leading off first, and threw. The curve on the outside edge of the plate was hit toward second. Two throws later, from second to short to first, the Phoenix had executed a double play. I was relieved. So was the crowd. No doubt Dad was a nervous wreck.

"Come on, Daddy!" my daughters yelled as I looked in for Wilkes's sign. I'd noticed Willie Walker in the on-deck circle but hadn't watched him make his way to the plate. If I had, I'd have seen a thick-necked, stoutly built, six-footer who strode with confidence, the same self-assurance he'd displayed when he'd led the league in slugging percentage and RBIs the previous year. He also hit twenty-four home runs, among the AL's best, led by Fred McGriff's thirty-six for Toronto.

Wilkes called time and met me at the base of the mound. "Nothing but knucklers, nothing but knucklers. We're giving this guy nothing good to hit because he can drive the ball so hard it'd go through your body and still climb over the center field fence. Got me?"

"Gotcha." Five pitches later, two of them fouled off, Walker was out on strikes and the crowd stood cheering wildly as I walked toward the dugout, refusing to acknowledge the reception. "Way to go, Davie!" my Evansville family and friends yelled down to me as I approached the dugout steps. I looked up, gave a faint smile—my dad flashed a thumbs-up—then I disappeared below the concrete top.

The Phoenix scored twice in the bottom of the first giving me a bit of a cushion for my second trip to the mound. Detroit was sending up its powerful fourth, fifth, and sixth hitters, but they went down in order, one on strikes and two on knucklers they drove mildly into the ground to infielders. The crowd was beside itself and so were the Phoenix and Tigers radio broadcast teams, knowing they were witnessing history.

I was reached for a home run in the fourth when I hung a curve that 1989 .227 hitter Greenspan blasted over the left center wall. The second baseman had hit only one the previous year, and I knew it. I was now mad at myself, and that was good. I always pitched some of my best ball when I was. Detroit wouldn't get another hit.

Manager Malone had planned to take me out after three innings, but when Jacksonville's best pitcher in 1989, Lew Wright, began warming up in the bullpen, the crowd booed, not him but the possibility I would be removed. Malone relented and wasn't disappointed. I got a standing ovation at the end of the fourth, and the crowd's roar surely could be heard five miles away. The players in the dugout pushed me back outside to offer a tip of my cap in acknowledgement, although I was somewhat embarrassed to do so. I paused for just a moment to smile at my family and friends.

Jacksonville play-by-play announcer Ted Gordon: "Folks, can *you* *believe* what we just witnessed? Forty-nine, nearly fifty-year-old Davie Miller has just done the impossible. Never a pitcher in professional baseball, he pitched four innings against the Detroit Tigers, allowed two hits, one run, no walks, and struck out five. Amazing, absolutely amazing."

"Yes, it was, Ted," piped in analyst Duane Zacker, a former pitcher himself. "A lot of people criticized Fred Marshall, but I think they saw he knew what he was doing. It might have been a one-game experiment, but it's a memory none of us here today will ever forget."

I was overwhelmed with accolades from my temporary teammates, getting high fives, back pats, and compliments from one after the other. All were happy for me, and a couple whispered to me they wished I were on the team for good.

Despite the warm early March temperature, I pulled a jacket over my right arm as I sat on the bench to watch the remainder of the game and cheer for my team. "Better get some ice on that arm," came the comment, and as I looked up, I saw Marshall coming down the dugout steps. "You've got more to pitch."

Confused, I frowned and forced a smile. "'Fraid I can't be used again today, Mr. Marshall."

"Not today but two weeks from now," he declared, catching me off guard as he seemed always to do. The GM motioned to the end of the bench, and I scooted over there. Lowering his voice, Marshall said, "We've got three more Saturday exhibition games, two of them here at Goldfarb. How'd you like to play in the ones here?"

No doubt my facial expression reflected my bewilderment. "Mr. Marshall, I'd love to, but these guys aren't going to like it. They're all trying to make the team, and they don't want a distraction like me being around."

Holding up his opened right hand, he said, "Now, now, don't worry about these guys." Motioning toward the players with his head, he added, "None of them's competing against you. I guarantee they're as thrilled about you being here as the fans are. What'll you say? I know you're having fun, and I also guarantee that group of nine Hoosiers sitting up there is enjoying every minute of it. I was watching your dad and, boy, is he ever proud of you. I thought he'd shake my hand off when I congratulated him just before walking down here. They'll all be invited back. Same deal as today, except I'm going to double your pay for each of the next two games."

"Ten thousand?" I exclaimed and then realized I might have repeated the figure too loud.

After looking to make certain no one was listening, "Ten thousand," Marshall affirmed quietly and then let me sit there and absorb the details. "I'll see you after the game, and we can talk about it some more."

After the sixth inning, I walked out of the dugout and motioned to Diane to come down to the small metal gate that led from the field to the stands. "You won't believe what Mr. Marshall is proposing to me."

"Davie, I'd believe anything after today," she said, reflecting the enthusiasm and exhilaration she felt. I had to talk quickly before the inning began, and she said she'd share the news with the agency partners. After the top of the seventh, I was to look up to her in the stands. If she flashed her white teeth, all was okay. If her mouth remained closed, it meant I would have some selling to do with Bruce and Gary.

I fretted, and to my chagrin, the half inning took nearly thirty minutes to play as Detroit sent ten players to the plate. As soon as the last batter popped out foul to Wilkes's sub at catcher, I tentatively walked up the steps and to the side of the dugout. As I emerged, I heard a cheer and saw the ennead from Indiana standing and clapping, each one of them displaying toothy grins from ear to ear.

CHAPTER 38

I was now off for two weeks as the Phoenix wouldn't play their next Saturday exhibition game at home until the seventeenth. There'd be another on the twenty-fourth, and then the season opener was scheduled for Monday, April 2. The fourteen days gave Fred Marshall time to put his promotional genius to work without taking away from the attention he needed to give to the upcoming season. Spring training games were one thing, filling fifty-three-thousand-seat Duval County Stadium was quite another.

I was besieged with media requests for interviews when I returned to the office on Monday. In fact, no sooner did I finish with one radio interview than BJ gave me a note that another station was on the line. Two Evansville television stations wanted me live on the noon news, so I worked out an agreement to talk with one at 12:07, the other at 12:22. The third TV station in the market scheduled both Diane and me live at 6:16 p.m. Newspapers called from all over the United States, headed by the *New York Times* and *Sporting News*. ESPN devoted several minutes to my story at intervals throughout the day. Unfortunately, Latimore College would have to wait until tomorrow, because I simply had no time to devote to the job that made my living.

The lack of time for Latimore didn't bother Bruce or Gary in the least. They, too, had their share of media interviews, and they ate it up. Even Diane was swallowed by the attention tsunami and thrilled to see references to Family Optometry in numerous reports. Both local newspapers developed features about me and my family, the longest being that of *Courier* reporter Greg Glass, who'd accompanied my family and friends on the trip to Jacksonville. His article focused on the relationship I'd had with my father, detailing how it began with the Christmas presents of a baseball and a fielder's glove more than forty years ago and evolved through childhood and my teen years with father teaching son the elements of pitching, especially the weird-acting knuckleball.

Sports Illustrated did a feature about great knuckleball pitchers through the years, noting that the slower speed of the erratic pitch and less stress on the arm led to long careers or men being able to pitch well past the normal retirement age. Hoyt Wilhelm pitched twenty-one years and retired just shy of age fifty; Phil Niekro twenty-four years and forty-eight; his brother Joe, twenty-two years and forty-four; and Charlie Hough twenty-five years and forty-six were examples. Thus, it was understandable that I could still pitch at nearly fifty, but what wasn't was the fact I was an amateur and I'd been out of baseball for twenty-nine years. I was considered "the epitome of a phenom."

I eventually got back into the daily groove of serving my clients, none of whom felt they had been neglected the past few weeks. Latimore was in the throes of getting ready for spring semester events that included a student musical, a student variety show, school and departmental honors programs, and finally baccalaureate and commencement. Campus PR staff and I worked with admissions on a new set of promotional materials to be unveiled in the fall as efforts geared up to get high school seniors to place Latimore on their list of colleges to consider for the 1992–93 school year.

■ ▨ ▬

Each afternoon at 5:00, Terry Koriath and I went to Gibson Park to practice. We only had about an hour of good daylight, but that was plenty so as not to tire my arm. On March 16, the Phoenix corporate jet was at the Evansville airport to pick up its special set of passengers—Diane and me, Dad and Mom, Bruce and Gary and their wives, Terry, and to be fair to the local print reporters, a sports reporter for the *Evansville Press*, Charlie Kinman. I wished I could have included my sister and her husband, but there just wasn't room on the plane. Diane's mother kept the girls for the weekend at her home.

I started and pitched quite well for three innings against a split squad for the Atlanta Braves. The Braves' other half was at their home park in Kissimmee playing the Phillies. The game at Goldfarb Field was sold out, standing room–only, and noisier than two weeks earlier, if that was possible. Cheering at my every pitch and giving me a standing ovation each time I came off the mound, the crowd and its energy pumped me up. Up until the fourth inning, I felt great, just as though I belonged in the pros. In the fourth, however, my head started hurting. It was an intense headache, but nothing like the migraine I'd suffered at work earlier in the week. I'd made BJ promise not to tell anyone while I closed the blinds, turned off the office lights, swallowed an Imitrex tablet with the glass of water she brought me, closed my eyes, and laid my head back in my padded black-leather desk chair. As usual, the prism in the left eye disappeared in about a half hour, but I had a dull feeling the remainder of the afternoon.

My concentration was off, and before I knew it, I'd walked the first two batters and hit the third. Sparky Malone came to the mound. "You okay, kid?"

"Not really. Head's pounding and I've lost concentration."

"You know what? You gave me three great innings. Striking out six Braves is an outstanding feat. Hell, they couldn't touch that danged knuckler." He chuckled. "I've had Madden warming up anyway, and I think he's ready, so you go take it easy on the bench and start thinkin' about next Saturday. I plan to start you again." Reluctantly, I handed the ball to my skipper and grim-faced walked to the dugout, head bowed, disgusted with the way I'd performed the past fifteen minutes. The crowd showed me they felt otherwise, with prolonged applause as they stood after witnessing another memorable performance.

Diane sensed something was wrong but said nothing about it to anyone. Afterward, accepting congratulations from numerous well-wishers, I simply said I'd just lost my control and offered no excuses. In our motel room, I admitted to my wife that I'd had a migraine during the week and my head had started bothering me during the game, but there were no visual prisms like those associated with my previous migraines. "Guess it's all the attention and related tension that I didn't realize I had."

"Davie, I sure worry about you. You've had enough migraines over the years maybe you should see a neurologist."

"Naw, I don't have that many in a year—usually only one or two—so I think it's just all that's been going on the past few weeks finally caught up with me."

Fred Marshall told me not to worry about the fourth inning and to take pride in the fact I'd been so outstanding for three innings. "You're in a category by yourself, Davie, and never forget it. Not to have pitched a game in two weeks and then come here and perform like you did was amazing. Go home, rest, and get ready for next Saturday. I know it'll be another great day."

■ ▩ ■

Saturday, March 24, was a picture-perfect day in Jacksonville—not a cloud in the light-blue sky, wind blowing in toward home plate but so light it would have practically no impact on a ball's flight to the outfield. The third standing room–only crowd to see me pitch in three games was mostly in short sleeves as the temperature had broken into the seventies at game time. Television cameras were everywhere, having taken the small amount of space reserved for them near the press box and fanning out down the left and right field lines. A platform was even constructed atop the press box, but it could only hold three cameras and their operators, and Marshall prayed the roof wouldn't cave in from the weight. The GM had told me he was thrilled that in my two previous games, concessions and merchandise had sold exceedingly well. He expected to make a lot more money today.

I achieved something against the Astros that day that sent reporters scrambling to call in early stories to their newspapers or broadcast stations—three innings of no-hit ball that included seven strikeouts. The two balls that were hit were both to the right side of the infield, one to second and the other to first base. Marshall wanted me to go another inning, but by prior agreement with the manager, I was removed. With spring training ending in only a week, the regular pitching staff needed to get in as much game experience as possible.

A large contingent of fans from southwestern Indiana was on hand, thanks to Marshall agreeing to offer a charter flight. His gamble paid off. The plane was packed. All 212 of them (including Peggy Sue and her husband, Wade) were seated in a reserved section, just past the home dugout and extending toward left field. Were they ever a raucous group, waving white towels with "MILLER 42" on them and screaming at my every pitch.

The ovation I received when I walked from the mound for what I believed to be my last game appearance in a major league uniform was deafening for such a small ballpark. The players wouldn't let me enter the dugout until I'd removed my cap and waved while making a pirouette to acknowledge all the fans. If I'd ever had a bigger smile, I was unaware of it. In fact, my facial muscles began aching from holding it so long. Diane was blowing me kisses, and I saw my dad holding his clasped hands above his head, shaking them in jubilation.

Player after player congratulated me. Big Dale Alderfer gave me a bear hug that took all my breath, and Teddy McClain's handshake felt like it had broken my right hand. I sat there through the remainder of the game filled with the satisfaction of someone who'd climbed Mount Everest. *What a way to go out.*

After the game, opposing manager Ben Lamm and three of his players, one of them star pitcher Bud Fletcher, came to my side of the field to offer their congratulations. Fletcher, who'd toyed with a two-fingered knuckleball, wanted me to demonstrate my grip and said he'd fly me to Houston to work out with him if I'd be willing. The other two players had struck out against me and said I had the nastiest pitch they'd ever seen.

There were so many comments from so many people my head was swimming, but at least it wasn't hurting. It was an excitement I'd never thought possible. It was as though this was the silver lining in the dark cloud of my injury in 1961.

Diane and the others from our special group came down the bleacher steps onto the field. "I am *so, so proud* of you, Davie Miller," she whispered in my left ear as she wrapped her arms around my neck. I saw the tears on my mother's face and moistness in my father's eyes. For an instant, I thought about Anne and Billy and how happy they must be up above me.

"Davie, could we see you for a moment?" I heard Sparky Malone say from behind me as I was accepting more well wishes. Turning, I saw Malone and Fred Marshall together. Diane was the only other one who heard the question above all the chatter. "Bring your wife and let's go down there." Marshall pointed into the dugout. I looked at Diane, shrugged my shoulders and raised my eyebrows in a questioning fashion, and then took her by the arm and followed the Phoenix pair down the steps.

"Have a seat." Marshall pointed to the bench. He and Malone continued to stand. It was the first time Diane had ever been in a dugout, and she glanced around to familiarize herself with it. All the hulls from sunflower seeds and ugly dark stains from tobacco juice made her shudder. I could tell she thought it "gross."

"Davie, we've just witnessed history. Not certain exactly what history except something no one in this park had ever seen before!" Marshall exclaimed. "You should thank God for what you possess."

"Oh, believe me, Mr. Marshall, I do, every day."

"Let me tell you, you are good for baseball. You represent the dreams of millions of young boys who aspire to make it here to the big leagues and the former aspirations of adults who wish they had. There are older and younger adults who'd pay you a million dollars to trade places with you." I smiled and glanced at Diane, who reached over and patted my right hand as it rested on my thigh.

"I'll cut to the chase," Marshall declared. "Sparky and I invited you down here for one reason. The team's opening game is a week from Monday here at home." He motioned with his head toward Duval County Stadium, which could be seen towering in the distance over the right-field wall. "We want you to start the game for us."

It was a thunderbolt-of-lightning statement, an improbable offer that left me, and Diane, bewildered, dazed, stunned—you name it—something Marshall had a habit of doing. I was incapable of an immediate response.

I sat there, my face twisted in disbelief, mouth slightly open, shaking my head slowly, trying to get a grasp on the enormity of the offer. Slowly, I lifted my head and looked at the Phoenix pair. "You want *me* to be the starting pitcher for Jacksonville in the first game of the American League season?" My head remained rigid, mouth agape, eyes glazed but shifting back and forth from one man to the other, as I awaited the answer.

"That's exactly what we're saying," Malone replied.

"But the players, the pitchers, what will they think?" I stammered.

"Don't worry about them," the skipper answered.

"And don't worry about the American League or Major League Baseball," Marshall added. "You're good for the game of baseball. It will be a one-game contract, nothing more. You'll start the game and pitch as long as Sparky here thinks you're effective. After all, it will be the actual season, and we don't want to take any unnecessary chances of losing the game."

Diane and I looked at one another, held our stare, and then I broke it with, "What will other teams think? What will the public think? What will the media think? I don't want to be the butt of jokes or criticism or ridicule." It was a heartfelt concern, and the two executives knew it. Marshall was the first to speak.

"We can't guarantee there'll be none of that, but we do know that the public and the game of baseball realize you are something very special, and for you to be given an opportunity to represent the hopes and dreams of millions, the good vibes, the good press will far outweigh the negative. If we didn't offer this to you, I guarantee there would be public outcry that you should be given a chance to play, not that anyone would think you should start but at least you should be on the team opening day. What'd'you say? I'd really like to play you."

I looked at Diane for some response as my expression began to lighten. I saw the answer in her eyes. With trepidation and keeping my glaze locked on hers, I responded, "It would be the thrill of a lifetime." I then turned to Marshall and Malone, and my face broke into a huge smile.

"Fantastic," Marshall replied as he slapped his hands together. "I'll work out a contract for you to sign this afternoon. Meantime, this has to be highly confidential. I'm sorry but neither of you can tell anyone. I mean *anyone*. I have to handle the announcement very carefully after I contact the commissioner's office and the president of the league. No idea what their response will be. Guess we'll see how good a salesman I am. Even if they don't approve, I'm going to do it anyway and be prepared for the consequences."

Diane and I walked hand in hand up the steps to our waiting family and friends, wanting desperately to tell them what lay ahead, but we were bound to secrecy. If all went according to plan, they'd find out after the contract signing or at least sometime that evening.

— — —

I undressed in the locker room at the clubhouse, continuing to accept accolades from fellow players. I stood in the group shower, closed my eyes, and held my face to the stream of water as my body relaxed, but my heart tried its best to beat out of my chest. I was awash with euphoria.

As Diane and the others waited outside and talked with fans and players who recognized them, I slowly dressed. "Mr. Miller, Mr. Marshall on the phone!" the clubhouse manager yelled as I sat in a chair near my locker, pulling on my socks.

"Davie, it's Fred, can you come over to the office as soon as you're ready?" Without waiting for a response, he interjected, "Oh, and bring your wife, too."

Diane and I told our group the truth: that the GM wanted to see us and we hoped to be back soon. We were taken by a waiting golf cart to the office building.

It was no surprise that Marshall had the club photographer and Malone on hand. Handing me a one-page sheet as Diane and I took seats at the small conference table in Marshall's office, the team executive said, "Here's a simple contract you should read over. In brief, it says the Jacksonville Phoenix baseball club will hire you for five days, from next Thursday, March 29, through Monday, April 2. The reason is we need you here to get ready for the game and for all the publicity that will naturally come your and our way. From the moment you sign the contract, you'll be fully covered by life and health insurance, and you'll be paid twenty-five thousand. Not bad for five days' work, huh?"

I shot a glance of disbelief at Diane and then continued reading the contract, although I actually didn't focus on the words.

A series of photographs was taken, different angles of me pretending to sign the contract with Marshall—Malone seated beside him and then standing behind him—and others with Diane also in the scenes. While this was going on, the Phoenix PR director entered the office and showed Marshall the draft of a news release. The executive made a few pencil edits, said, "Go with this," and handed the sheet back to the director.

"We'll announce this at six," Marshall said, looking at his watch. "That'll be in time for the local news. As you know, this is going to spread like wildfire, so be prepared to have your lives turned upside down for another week or so." He smiled. "Sorry, but that goes with the territory of being somebody special." We all laughed—well, almost all. I feigned my elation. I was numb.

At my request, a limousine took the ten of us from Evansville to a private room at Nance's, a notable seafood restaurant where I could break the news to everyone at six. It was a good thing Mom was seated; she nearly collapsed. *Press* reporter Kinman had the scoop of all scoops—my personal announcement and all the attendant reaction. Even those who didn't drink—which didn't include Bruce or Gary or their wives—took a sip of red or white wine from the bottles of pinot noir and chardonnay that had been preordered courtesy of Fred Marshall. In fact, as usual, the club picked up all of the party's expenses for the weekend.

Where my group and I stayed in Jacksonville was a closely guarded secret, again thanks to Marshall. But an enterprising local newspaper reporter posing as a staff member from hotel housekeeping surprised me when I answered the knock on the door, half-dressed from the initial phase of an amorous night. Instead of being rude, I agreed to meet him in the lobby for an exclusive interview in exchange for a promise not to reveal my whereabouts to any others in the media. I felt I could probably trust the reporter as far as I could toss him, but there seemed to be no other choice.

Diane and I spent some time in prayer that evening. We often prayed together at home and felt on this night we needed to jointly give thanks for an opportunity that no human being had ever been given before. We asked that we be given the strength to be humble in all our interactions with family, friends, and the public, in-person and via the media, especially during the next seven days but in the future as well, when this fairy tale was over.

Our group was mobbed by media when we deplaned the private jet in Evansville the following afternoon. And I might as well have stayed in Jacksonville for what little work I got done Monday through Wednesday. I, sometimes with Diane, was live on national networks' sports and news interview programs. High school coach Steve Anderson and college skipper Andy Ludlow, now eighty, in failing health, and confined to a wheelchair at an assisted-living facility in Evansville, were visited by media and asked about their impressions of me as a younger man and now. Neither took credit for my prowess on the mound but praised my work ethic. Ludlow knew how low I had fallen emotionally after Anne's death but never mentioned it.

As luck would have it for the Rotary Club of Evansville, one of the city's top civic organizations, I was available to speak as an exclusive substitute at its regularly scheduled meeting at noon on Tuesday. Two radio stations carried the address live. The mayor presented the key to the city to me. In my message, spoken without notes because there was no time to prepare them, I thanked all those who'd played any role in molding my life, expressing special appreciation to Coach Ludlow, the University of Evansville, and my pastor. I even snuck in a soft-sell reference to Diane and Family Optometry.

"I know this is a secular setting, but I owe everything I have ever achieved to God. I never blamed God for the injury I sustained here in college. I always thanked him for giving me baseball talents beyond what most people have. Perhaps because of that injury, I'm in the position I'm in now. And I thank him for keeping my head on straight in years when I thought I was something special."

I surveyed the crowd of men and women as I stood behind the small tabletop lectern whose sides I lightly gripped in the middle of the wide dais. Lowering my voice, I said, "I'm nothing special now." The room was quiet. "For whatever reason, I've been given this unique opportunity, and I'm as confused about how and why it's taken place as anyone else might be, especially those who follow the game. But I know the faith I've had virtually all my life has sustained me through thick and thin, and I promise to carry the pride of Evansville with me when I step on that mound six days from now. Thank you." The 317 people in attendance rose, and the ovation was so loud I thought I was back at Goldfarb Field.

"Darling, you were wonderful today," Diane said when she greeted me at her mother's house where we were going to dine with Thelma and the children. "I heard your speech on the radio." The girls had hardly seen their father the past couple of weeks, and they were filled with questions, the main one pertaining to school.

"No, you can't miss classes. I'm terribly sorry, but with your mother and me going to Jacksonville very early Thursday morning, it won't be possible for you to join us. I'll make certain the broadcast of the game is recorded, and we'll bring a videotape for you to look at when we get home Monday night. There'll probably be a lot of coverage by the television stations so you can watch the local news with Grandma that evening. A deal?"

"A deal," they responded with a total lack of enthusiasm. I hated our decision. It was robbing our daughters of a unique opportunity, but we felt it best for them to stay in school and not be subjected to all the media attention and scrutiny in Florida. Regardless of how well I played, we and the girls would have our own celebration Monday.

Tuesday and Wednesday were whirlwinds as well, but nothing like I was about to face back in Jacksonville. With one exception, the same entourage as the previous week entered the hangar used by passengers of private planes, and I was met by a reporter crew for one of the local television stations. It was an example of another enterprising journalist, this one having received information from an anonymous source within the Phoenix as to the location and time our Evansville group would be arriving. I had told my party before we landed, "Hang onto your hats! We're in for a lot of attention the next five days."

My new guest was the person to whom I gave the most credit, besides my dad, for helping me grow as a pitcher. Donnie Hazelett had replaced Billy as my catcher after the tragedy of 1955 and became part of the magic of that summer's no-hitters. I'd never forgotten. Donnie was already fifty and had morphed from five-six and 146 pounds to five-ten and about 235 pounds. He worked in the mines near Barclay, and his feelings about being singled out for inclusion in my limited group were beyond his capability to express in words. It was his biggest shining moment in life, and I made certain to call attention to him in various interviews and speeches over the course of the fantasy in Florida.

I would have loved to have had another special guest, Bobby. But even if I could have talked Fred Marshall into letting me bring another person with me, Bobby was in no shape to be around almost anyone. His body was wasting away, now completely controlled by drugs. Despite all my efforts over the years, he remained hooked.

Media attention seemed nonstop, and the number of cameras at Duval County Stadium when I practiced Friday and Saturday and then Sunday was something to behold. I was even a sensation in Japan. Several photographers from Japanese papers covered every move of their hero, Akio Hayashi, Jacksonville's second-year, twenty-one-year-old, fleet-footed right-fielder. Both Terry Koriath and Donnie, who had problems squatting because of his size, caught ceremonial pitches in their street clothes strictly for photo ops Friday morning. Their involvement in my life was a nice sidebar.

CHAPTER 39

Monday, April 2, dawned but with the sun hidden by clouds that had dropped light rain on the Jacksonville area throughout the night. It was going to be a humid day, the most perfect conditions I could have hoped for. I never understood the reasoning, but the knuckleball always reacted at its worst—meaning, at its worst for batters—in atmospheric conditions like this. Television stations' meteorologists were predicting an unusually warm day for early April, 78 degrees by the 1:10 p.m. game time, but mostly cloudy, little wind, and 77 percent humidity. The women in my group resigned themselves to the fact it would be a "bad hair day."

I was surprised I was asleep when the alarm in my Sailors' Village villa sounded at 6:30. I'd tossed and turned all night, getting little sleep, no doubt from the stress of the upcoming day but also because I'd had a dull headache I couldn't shake until I finally took three aspirin at 2:15 a.m. I was groggy, not the way I wanted to start such an important day in my life. My manager had requested that I stay at the villa and not with Diane, so I wouldn't have any distractions. I'd kissed her good night, heard her say "Love you deeply," replied "You, too," and said good-bye to my parents and friends before departing their hotel by limousine for the villa at 9:00 p.m.

The club sent a car to pick me up at 9:00 a.m. and take me to a private players' entrance at the stadium. Following leisurely light stretching in my room and an attempt at some breakfast in the clubhouse, I was waiting outside the villa, clothing and toiletries stuffed in a burgundy leather Phoenix logo bag, when the plain car arrived. It would be the last time I'd be at Sailors' Village unless invited back as a special guest sometime.

There was a tinge of sadness to the thought, but my mind quickly jumped to what lay ahead.

For the most part, I was kept away from the media so I could concentrate on my preparation. The chief trainer gave me a rubdown, massaging the right shoulder and arm all the way to the fingertips. I donned my uniform minus the top, wore a burgundy T-shirt with a small, white #42 over the heart, and walked through the players' tunnel that led to the back of our dugout. Batting practice was underway, so I stayed to the seating side of the field when I emerged and walked to left field. The gates were opened at 10:00 so fans were streaming in to watch practice and hopefully find players who'd be willing to give them autographs along the wall that separated the stands from the field. A few cheers went up when I came out of the dugout, but I didn't acknowledge them; I was not ignoring them on purpose but because I was concentrating so intently I hardly heard them. Media had been instructed to leave me alone until the end of practice, and then they could have me for fifteen minutes, no more. I walked to the outfield and warmed up by jogging near the wall from the left foul line side to the right, seeing the distance signs of 335, 375, 400, 375, and 335 as I loped. I was reminded it had been built as a "hitter's park." Fans loved runs, especially home runs. The outfield grass was damp, but I could tell the infield was perfectly dry thanks to a tarp that covered it until batting practice had begun.

Earlier, I couldn't have been more pleased by the reaction of the players in the locker room. Instead of showing any jealousy or disdain for Fred Marshall's one-day experiment, they demonstrated the opposite. Bob Tomlin and Chris Skirvin, my very first batting practice "victims" of a few weeks ago, stopped at the training table as I lay on my stomach during the massage and offered encouragement as did Zack Long who'd gotten mad at me the first time we faced one another in practice. "You're damned good, Davie, and I'm really happy for you," the third sacker commented. "Give 'em hell today. Just remember, nothing gets past me if they hit it my way." He patted me on my bare shoulders and headed to the field. The young Hayashi, who had become a friend, stopped by, uttered something, smiled, and left. I hadn't any idea what he'd said.

Forty minutes before the scheduled start of the game, the part of the crowd who saw "MILLER 42" on the back of the uniform of the man who stepped from the dugout to walk to the bullpen along the left field line, greeted me with light applause and yells that grew slowly and then intensified, as more and more fans recognized my presence. I turned toward those nearest me and smiled. Then I spotted Diane, my parents, and the others, sitting together about seven rows up from the dugout, and waved as I received her blown kisses. We'd not talked that morning as I was all business and Diane and the group knew to leave me alone. After all, we'd celebrate after the game, regardless of how well, or poorly, I pitched.

At 1:03, the crowd went wild when our Phoenix players ran to their positions and I slowly made my way to the mound. Following the National Anthem, which was sung by a Jacksonville high school baseball player with a gifted tenor voice, my head was bothering me again, but I'd taken three more aspirin and tried not to think about it, focusing instead on Jerry Wilkes's mitt as I threw my warm-up pitches. Infielders and outfielders were practicing as well while public address announcer Chuck Fischer introduced each of us. By the time Fischer's booming voice said, "And on the mound ..." the entire crowd was on its feet and all but drowned out his announcement of "Daaaay-veeeee Millllll-errrr." The crowd was delirious. I hated it. I just hated long, drawn-out pronunciations of names by stadium announcers. It had become a trend with one announcer after another seemingly trying to outdo the others. *Sophomoric.* Something that small-town high school PA announcers would do, and did.

Wilkes caught the last warm-up pitch and threw it to second, and the home-plate umpire bellowed "Play ball!" The 1990 American League season was underway.

Amazingly, I hadn't thought about the opponent, not given one iota of thought to it, until I turned on the rubber atop the mound to face Wilkes after receiving the ball from third baseman Zack Long, who repeated, after he spit a half mouthful of tobacco juice on the ground, "Give 'em hell. Nothing gets past me." As I looked toward home, I saw *pinstripes* in the batter's box. The pinstripes of Babe Ruth, Lou Gehrig, Joe DiMaggio, Mickey Mantle—pinstripes of the New York Yankees. Never mind that the Yankees hadn't appeared in a World Series or won the American League or even their division since 1980, they were still *the* New York Yankees.

Whether it was the look on my face or the fact my battery mate wanted to talk with me anyway, Wilkes asked for time and ran out to the mound, his face about two feet from mine. "You and me are gonna have fun. You with me?" Without waiting for a reply, he continued, "As far as you and I're concerned, this is just spring training batting practice. You're gonna focus on my target and nothing else. You're gonna throw knuckleball after knuckleball but maybe send something inside just to keep them awake. Okay?"

Breaking out of a brief stupor, I tried to smile and couldn't. I replied, "Okay," anyway.

"In fact," Wilkes commanded, "start out high and inside, but don't hit him." He slammed the ball into my glove, wheeled, and waddled briskly back to the plate.

A crowd that exceeded the fifty-three-thousand capacity was on its feet, many of them wearing the specialty "MILLER 42" uniform tops they'd bought at the stadium gift shops. Every one of the nearly one thousand who'd arrived on four charter flights from Evansville wore them in their section in left field.

I turned my back to the plate, rubbed up the ball in my hands, and uttered a short prayer. Mentally, though a speck dull, I was ready. As I was instructed, my first pitch to Yankee second baseman Bucky Crabb was a fastball high and inside, almost too inside. Crabb jerked his body back and staggered to keep from falling to the ground, his batting helmet falling off in the process. Recalling high school Coach Anderson's admonition of years ago never to apologize to a batter, I took the throw and walked back to the rubber. Two more pitches, both floating, bobbing knuckleballs, and the count was two strikes and a ball. Wilkes called for a low inside curve, figuring the scouting report had told the Yankees I wouldn't attempt a curveball. Crabb was off stride but caught the ball hard enough to send a grounder between third and short. Fans gasped, but true to his word, Zack Long didn't let it get by him and threw to first for the out. The crowd rose to show its appreciation for a good play.

I refused to look at the stands, all three decks filled with jostling burgundy shirts. I was nervous enough as it was. I tried to spit, but nothing was coming out of my mouth. I'd have given my weekend salary for a cold bottle of water at that point. I turned so the Yankee dugout couldn't see me, took a deep breath, told myself to calm down, and readied myself to pitch.

Yankee third baseman Mike Crow, like Crabb, noted for his glove and not his bat, opened the year in the second spot. He'd mostly batted eighth in 1989, but, unusual for most third basemen, he had speed, and skipper Barney Westerman was determined to find a more effective lineup at the plate this year. Crow was told to be aggressive, but the knucklers baffled him and he watched three go by, two for strikes. I tried to waste a fastball outside, but Crow swung and caught it just enough to send it spinning back into Wilkes's mitt, a reaction so quick it showed why signing him last fall had been an intelligent move.

The crowd was in a frenzy. The prideful Yankees had two outs and no one on base against a guy who could have been elected mayor of Jacksonville if balloting had been held at that moment. I had begun to relax but then recognized the terror that was scraping dirt and digging his spikes into the ground to my left of the white-topped, hard-rubber plate. Emilio Calderone, a Venezuelan discovered by the Yankees eight years ago in a small summer league one hundred miles southwest of Caracas, had come up through the club's farm system. He played left field, perfect for a left-hander since his glove hand would help him reach for balls hit down the line, not having to back-hand them like a right-hander might have to do.

Calderone had hit .298 the last season, and he, too, had speed. Westerman wanted to get players on base for his power hitters in the fourth, fifth, and sixth positions. But Calderone had some power as well, hitting eighteen home runs and driving in eighty-two in 1989. He was built like a bull with a thick neck, shoulders, and chest and massive forearms for his five-ten height. He never shaved on game day, so the blackness of the stubble on his face enhanced his menacing appearance. The scouting report said it was difficult to get fastballs by him, and if you didn't have a good curve, don't try it. By prior agreement, Wilkes knew I would throw only knuckleballs. If Calderone drove one over the short wall only 335 feet straight down the right field line, so be it. He would get nothing better to hit.

The first knuckler broke right just as it neared the plate. Calderone started to swing. The crowd booed when the umpire called it a ball, and the third base ump affirmed the batter had held up when Wilkes appealed the call. The highly partisan crowd's booing continued as I delivered. The Yankee left-fielder took a vicious cut, but the ball sank below his lightning bat.

I took my time. One thing I'd learned in my years of playing ball was to take extra time when the game was tense and the batter appeared anxious. I'd been told: "Pick up the rosin bag behind the mound; rub the ball extra long; be in no hurry to throw the next pitch; add to the batter's anxiousness." I bent forward from the waist and peered as though I was getting a sign, but Wilkes did nothing more than twiddle his fingers to make it look like he was calling for a certain pitch. This time, the knuckler, as perfect as I'd ever thrown it, thanks in large part to the humidity, came straight at the batter, then broke down and away from him. Calderone never moved his bat forward. "Steeeriiike!" shouted umpire Jerry Reynolds as he wheeled to his right and threw his right arm out in front of him. Reynolds was given to theatrics, which crowds loved if the call went their way.

I held the ball, turned my back to the plate again, and looked at the digital scoreboard high above the stands in deep center, seeing two lights illuminated under "Strike," one under "Ball," and two under "Out." Confident, I muttered, "This is it," turned, and bent for my signal. Wilkes called time.

"Changed my mind," he said when we met near the mound. "Waste one. I mean really waste one, a fastball far outside. Don't worry, I'll be ready to spring and get it. If it gets away and he doesn't swing, so what if it goes back to the screen. No one's on. We've got this sucker set up for the pitch after this one. Believe me. We've got 'em."

The pitch was about as hard as I could throw and at least two feet off the plate if not three. Calderone didn't bite. Now I didn't want to take time. It might not have been the prettiest pitch I ever threw because the knuckler dove to the ground *before* it reached home plate, but Calderone was chomping so hard to get his bat on whatever was thrown he swung and missed as the ball hit the dirt and bounded toward Wilkes. Before the left-fielder could even get out of the batter's box and start toward first base, Wilkes tagged him.

Chants of "Miller … Miller … Miller!" resounded throughout the stadium, and I glanced at a beaming Diane and my father standing and clapping next to her while I made my way to the bench. High fives greeted me. "Marvelous," "Awesome," "Way to pitch" echoed throughout the concrete dugout as I took a seat and pulled on a jacket. While the team struggled against the Yankee starter, my head was hurting again. "Got any aspirin?" I yelled at the trainer who responded with a cup of water and two small white tablets. The headache had become severe, but I said nothing about it.

Our team quickly went down in order and players hustled out to their positions to start inning number two. I slowly removed my jacket, grabbed my glove, and walked to the mound. My first warm-up toss was basically that, a light pitch to loosen the muscles. It was far left of the plate, and Wilkes back-handed it. The next was also wide. "Come on, buddy, hit the mitt. Time to get going again!" Wilkes yelled as he threw the ball back to the mound. I signaled a knuckler, but it spun, highly unusual. The next was no better and outside the plate to the right. "You okay, partner?" Wilkes yelled, growing a bit concerned.

"Okay," I responded but didn't enunciate clearly and was now having some problems with vision. The remainder of my warm-up tosses were mostly guesses as to where the plate was. Diane no doubt noticed the look on my face when I turned her direction for a moment. I felt almost as though I wanted her help and didn't know what to do.

"Play ball!" plate umpire Reynolds commanded. The first pitch sailed high, so much so Wilkes had to spring to catch it. Diane found out later he'd been concerned and thought about calling time-out. He wished he had. Instead, he signaled for a knuckler, I wound up, brought my left knee up in the usual fashion, and started my motion forward. As I did, it seemed the inside of my head exploded. The force of my delivery continued, but the ball sailed about thirty feet into the air and far to the right of home plate as my body slammed to the ground. My memory ended.

CHAPTER 40

As his wife, I recall scattered laughter came from those who thought Davie had caught a cleat in the dirt. One fan was heard telling another, "How embarrassing! He might not wanna show his face." When Davie didn't move, it was as though someone had thrown a giant switch to silence all sound within the huge open-air structure.

He lay motionless on the infield grass, his face contorted, his neck bent so that his chin was nearly wedged against his chest by the force of the fall. It seemed the world stood still for an instant, as no one on the field or in the dugout moved, and then the freeze frame of life was jolted as players rushed to him, Wilkes throwing the mask from his face and joining them. Trainer Nick Lawless burst from the dugout and soon bent over Davie's head, his face almost touching Davie's. He was yelling something into my husband's ear. I could tell there was no response. It was obvious Davie was unconscious. By this time, Sparky Malone and others had reached the mound.

The manager was obviously alarmed and said something to Lawless, but the trainer looked up at him, didn't answer, and quickly turned back to Davie.

Lawless said something, and three of the players rolled Davie onto his back. From my vantage point, I could see Lawless placing fingers against one side of Davie's neck. As a health professional, I knew he was checking for a carotid pulse. Then he yelled something at the manager, who motioned, and in an instant, team physician Dr. Gregory Keeley burst from his seat in the stands and ran toward the mound.

Although all the players in the dugout and those in the field formed a circle to try to block the fans' view, I could see Dr. Keeley doing chest compressions on Davie while an assistant trainer performed mouth-to-mouth breaths. Many of those seated in the two upper decks no doubt saw everything and were overcome by a sight none of them had ever witnessed on a ball field. Everyone stood throughout the stadium.

I didn't scream or yell. Matt and I had grabbed one another almost immediately when Davie fell. I buried the left side of my face into Matt's chest when my husband didn't get up and squeezed tighter when I saw Davie wasn't moving. Mary June held her hands to her mouth and murmured tearfully. It was the second time she'd witnessed her son lying prostrate in a baseball game.

The Phoenix always had an emergency medical crew stationed in their vehicle outside the stadium. Within moments, the ambulance drove through an entrance in right field and sped toward the mound. By the time the technicians reached Davie, Trainer Lawless had administered an electrical shock with a portable automated external defibrillator, and I saw Dr Keeley inject something, probably epinephrine, all to no avail. The paramedics loaded Davie into the ambulance and would continue working on him en route to the hospital emergency room.

The silence of the massive crowd was broken only by sounds of weeping women and men. The players returned to the dugout, no doubt the word among them foreboding. The grim-faced public relations director was sent to my seat to ask me to follow him. He said nothing else. I insisted that Matt and Mary June accompany me. Matt steadied his wife with an arm around her waist as they walked. The crowd wouldn't be told of Davie's condition until after the game.

The hush remained as the three of us were guided down a series of steps and a hallway to the locker room. Out of respect, the stadium television cameras didn't show us on the big screen in center field. The door was opened, and several men, including the team doctor, were standing together, the blood gone from their faces. I was informed that "everything possible had been tried medically for Davie but ..." and Dr. Keeley didn't have to finish the sentence. My screams could be heard through all the stands immediately above me—bloodcurdling, agonized screams of denial that seemed to continue for several minutes. Other crying and sobbing filled the room as well. With tears streaming down his face and his chest heaving, Matt did his best to control and support me, and Mary June, too. One of the coaches caught Davie's mother just as he saw her knees buckle.

CHAPTER 41

There was a pall over major league baseball all that week. Players wore small black armbands displaying the number 42. US flags were ordered at half staff throughout professional baseball.

With my permission, it was announced Davie died of a brain aneurysm, an aneurysm in a blood vessel that burst. Doctors said it could have developed over a long period of time. Perhaps it was related to the head trauma he suffered in 1961; perhaps it was not. The Phoenix had been cautious. Due to his age and following the requirements of the insurance company, before he was permitted to play in spring training, Davie'd had a physical including an EKG to check his heart. But no routine physical examination would ever have revealed the aneurysm. Why he had an aneurysm and why it burst when it did, no one could be certain. More people die from them than live for years afterward. In Davie's case, he was believed to have been dead by the time his body hit the infield grass.

The funeral was held in Barclay. I'd made the decision to have Davie buried next to Anne in the town cemetery. I would join them someday, as there were four plots he and Anne had purchased right after they were married even though she was from Pemberton. I accepted the numerous suggestions that the calling and the funeral be held in the high school gymnasium because of the anticipated crowd. It was a wise decision.

The calling began at 2:00 p.m. Friday and was scheduled for six hours. That, too, was a good decision because a line still existed at 8:00 p.m. Davie's physically and emotionally drained parents, Peggy Sue, and I stayed until the last one expressed regret and wished us well.

I was proud of myself and commanded a strength within me I didn't know existed. I was the new Gibraltar of the family in these dark hours, supporting Davie's side of the family and mine, too. At the same time, I got great comfort from Lydia, Jillian, my mother, and my faith.

▬ ▬ ▬

When the funeral began at 1:00 Saturday, the open-lid, steel-burgundy casket sat along the free-throw line at the high school stage end of the gym floor, under the raised basketball backboard and goal. Floral arrangements and planters were stationed at both ends of the casket, too many to count. The largest—no one recalled ever seeing one so big—was an arrangement of flowers from the Phoenix. Davie had been dressed in a dark-blue suit with a red tie and white pocket handkerchief. A Barclay High School pin was in one lapel and his college's in the other. A folded burgundy Jacksonville Phoenix warm-up jacket lay to one side of his hands and a dark-blue LA Dodgers cap to the other.

White folding chairs sat on large sheets of drab-olive tarpaulin that covered the hardwood floor, and all but a few in the rear rows were filled. The lower stands on both sides of the floor were mostly full. Capacity for basketball games was 2,700, and someone said later the crowd was estimated at 1,500. A green covering similar to AstroTurf lay under the casket, floral arrangements, and a lectern stationed at the forward edge of it, approximately ten feet from the front row of padded chairs. The closed, tall, dark-blue, velvety stage drapery provided the background.

Three people sat in wheelchairs. Andy Ludlow and Ernie Hittle were in two, just to the right side of the front row. A grieving, weakened, dark-eyed Mary June was in the third, where a folding chair had been removed right in the middle of the front row, with a slump-shouldered, emotionally crushed Matt on one side of her and me on the other. My mother and daughters were to my right. Mary June's widowed mother was too ill to travel from Illinois. Matt's parents were deceased. Others in the reserved first and second rows included Peggy Sue, her husband, and their three children, Davie's widowed uncle John, cousin Marcy Lynn, her husband and two children, Aunt Sarah Mae Hutchison, Bruce Wilson and Gary McGlasson and their wives, Terry Koriath, Donnie Hazelett, Anne's parents, Benjamin Goldfarb, Fred Marshall, and Jerry Wilkes who represented the players. The Phoenix game with the Tigers that day was postponed. Mr. Wilkes carried guilt for not calling time before the last pitch, although doctors assured him it wouldn't have mattered.

Others toward the front in the crowd included the president and the board chair of the University of Evansville, the mayor of Evansville, Davie's high school coach Steve Anderson, the Evansville Dodgers' general manager and his wife, Davie's secretary BJ and other colleagues from the agency, the Latimore College president and every member of the board of trustees, Mildred Alexander (Fred's widow), and a contingent of Davie's closest childhood friends that included Randy, Dannie, and Dickie. Former Southern Illinois slugger Clyde Voss who'd hit the line drive that helped end Davie's career joined men who had been my husband's UE teammates. Sitting by himself on the top row near the bowl end of the stands, too embarrassed to be seen by the masses, was Davie's only best friend after Billy died, Bobby Hatcher, shabbily dressed, with unkempt hair, his thin body ravaged by too many years of abusing drugs, and looking far older than his fifty years.

By contrast, Davie's and my distinguished-looking Evansville church pastor Reverend Harold Vernon opened the service smiling pleasantly and speaking as he surveyed the crowd. "It's a great day to be alive. The sun is shining, spring is in the air, daffodils and forsythia are blooming, and the buds that fill the trees are ready to burst to life or have just produced baby leaves that will begin their journey to adulthood. It's a rebirth of our earth here in southwestern Indiana, a new life." The moderately deep voice of this tall, salt-and-pepper-haired, white-robed man resonated through the public address system. Light-gray speakers hung from the ceiling, and others were mounted on floor stands to the left and right of the front row. "And that's what we're here to celebrate today, the blessings we have from the life of David Harold Miller and the new life to which he has been called for eternity."

The minister's opening message continued briefly and was followed by scripture read by his fellow United Methodist man of the cloth, the pastor of Matt and Mary June's church in Barclay, the one where Davie grew up and accepted the calling of Christ when he was a teen.

There was only one song. I didn't want the service to be overly long or maudlin or somber. The song, sung at a microphone on a floor stand off to the right of the lectern by an outstanding UE senior soprano accompanied by a pianist, was, however, a slow one, preceded by Reverend Vernon's introduction. "Diane has chosen Davie's favorite hymn, 'How Great Thou Art,' one of the greatest ever written, and for one reason. She wants you to not only listen to the music but also concentrate on the words that are printed on the inside cover of the folded program you were given. Those words sum up some of Davie's strongest feelings about life and his love of nature. The writer recognized the wonderful power of God, the awesome beauty of nature and the world, and the praise our creator should receive for all of it. Every time you see this song in a hymnal or anywhere else, think of Davie."

As the auburn-haired student of average build sang, one could feel the power and emotion of the words.

Based on what Davie had shared with me, I sensed Peggy Sue probably had a slight grin, thinking it was exactly the type of slow song she and Davie hated with a passion when they were young and sitting with their parents in worship services, but in her mature years, she knew its words were the message Davie believed with all his heart.

"How *great* thou art," Pastor Vernon emphasized when he began the eulogy that summarized Davie's life—his passions, contributions to mankind, beliefs, love of family and close friends, and his legacy. "Whatever you remember about Davie Miller, remember that he loved life and through his strong faith in God, he tried his best to follow Christ's example. If you need an earthly role model, you couldn't choose any better than David Harold Miller."

There were only two other speakers. Fred Marshall had asked me for permission to say a few words.

Struggling to control the quiver in his voice, the Phoenix general manager stood, hands clasped behind him. He cleared his throat, swallowed, and began. "I'm here on behalf of the Jacksonville Phoenix—our players, staff, and ownership including the president and board chairman…" He motioned to the well-dressed man at the left end of the second row. "…Ben Goldfarb. Also with us is Davie's Phoenix catcher, Jerry Wilkes. It was our blessing and major league baseball's blessing to have met, known, and loved Davie Miller. Over the course of fifty-four days, we found out about his unique skills on the diamond but learned he was so much more as a human being. There was a competiveness, a fire to Davie but a compassionate, caring side as well, and that entire package is why he was so admired. When he arrived for our adult fantasy baseball camp at Sailors' Village on February 8, he was just another player looking to return to his childhood and teen days for a week of playing and learning to properly play baseball. But by the grace of God, we found out he was something else, something as unique as there ever has been in this game that is America's favorite pastime."

Not an extraneous sound was heard as Mr. Marshall permitted his eyes to rove tearstained faces in the stands and seats in front of him and his hands gripped the top sides of the lectern. "Our entire organization grieves with each of you. We *loved* Davie Miller." Then his voice broke. Surveying the audience while composing himself, he paused. "Davie was good for the game of baseball. It was a tragedy he didn't get an opportunity to play at the professional level when he was younger. It's obvious he was gifted. What he achieved when the media discovered him during spring training and the resultant public attention all the way through ..." His voice broke again. "... the first inning of Monday's game ..." He stopped, words caught in his throat. He removed a pressed white handkerchief from his back right suit trouser pocket and dabbed his eyes.

"In memory of him and in thankfulness to him, our organization will establish a Davie Miller scholarship program at the University of Evansville." UE's president was caught off guard at the news, but his facial expression showed he was obviously pleased. Andy Ludlow displayed a slight grin as well. "We haven't worked out any details, but we want the scholarship to honor baseball talent combined with evidence of compassion and community service." There was light applause, the first break in the thick emotion of the gymnasium. A baby cried, and its mother could be seen patting its back as she walked up the concrete steps of the stands. "Additionally, because Davie learned baseball here, we will work with town leaders and provide a very significant gift to help maintain the organized summer league program in Barclay." More applause, respectfully light.

"Our hearts go out to Diane and the children." He focused his eyes on us. "Our prayers for comfort, support, and, hopefully, understanding are with you, Diane, and Lydia and Jillian, as they are with Davie's wonderful parents and sister. We are thankful for knowing your husband, father, son, and brother and for all the joy he brought to untold thousands who learned it is never too late to realize a dream."

Mr. Marshall paused to shake hands with each of the six he'd named on the front row and then somberly took his seat between his boss and Wilkes on row two.

I was the other speaker. The fact I could muster the courage, the fortitude to stand in front of that crowd of grievers and supporters was apparently attributable to inner strength and prayers. I knew I couldn't do it alone.

Clutching a small, white, lace handkerchief in my left hand as I held the sides of the rostrum, I looked out over the stands and rows in front of me and then adjusted the flexible microphone holder built into the plain, wooden stand. "Don't cry for me and my children and Davie's parents and sister. Don't cry for the loss of Davie. Instead, be thankful, so very, very thankful, that you personally knew Davie or that he might have had some positive influence on you and your life. We were all blessed to know him or of him."

I paused to gather thoughts that I'd rehearsed in my mind through the night and morning after receiving so many comments at the calling. My eyes were moist, but I spoke with amazing clarity and confidence.

"Whatever you do, don't blame God that Davie is no longer with us. I heard so many well-meaning comments last night that it was a shame God took Davie to heaven far too early and how unfair it was to him and to his family and friends. He and I had the conversation many times over the all-too-brief seven and a half years we were married about whether God does indeed take some people and let others live, about why so many good people die earlier than they should, and why so many terribly bad people continue living. If God used such power, the world would be filled with wonderfully good people and we would all live harmoniously in peace.

"But both Davie and I believed God created us to live on our own on this earth and be productive in the most positive ways possible and to find ways to get along with one another. Some, unfortunately, do a horrible job of that. Most of us are blessed to live fairly long lives, some, luckily, quite long. But others die far, far too early. And that's the way life happens to be. We can live long or we can die early. It's important for each of us to remember that, that we have a limited time here and we don't know when we get out of bed in the morning if it's going to be our last day—whether a month from now, or a year or five years from now will be our last."

I paused again, a little longer this time, wanting to be very certain of my important next words. "Unfortunately, I've heard rumors that some people are blaming the Jacksonville Phoenix for allowing Davie to play, as though his playing had something to do with his death. For goodness sake, be thankful to the Phoenix for giving him an opportunity to make a dream come true. Davie has always been a person of faith and a positive attitude, but I have never, *never* seen him as happy as he was those last five days in Jacksonville.

"Think about this. Here was a young man twenty-nine years ago next month whose dream was shattered along with his eye socket. Here was a young man whose aspirations to play professional baseball were cut down in an instant. Then for him to have nearly three decades later an opportunity to live out that dream was one of the greatest gifts he could ever have had, perhaps *the* greatest gift. So, don't blame, but praise Mr. Goldfarb and Mr. Marshall for what they did.

"No routine physical would ever have discovered the aneurysm that eventually ended Davie's life. It was one of those horribly unfortunate things that can develop in the human body, just as we can suddenly be told we have cancer or suffer a heart attack. That's the way life is, and that's why we have to dedicate each day to being the best we can be."

Another long pause. "Finally, *please* take this thought with you, that you be determined to live your life as God wants you to live it. You can dedicate it to trying to be, as Reverend Vernon said, a role model like Davie while keeping him always in your thoughts. Was he perfect? Certainly not. He made mistakes like anyone else. But his intent always was to try to do what he believed God wanted of him. Likewise, the most important thing for you is that you dedicate yourself to good and noble service with a life that uses the talents and abilities God gave you so others can benefit and have a better life of their own. It's an obligation you have; we all have."

With that, I turned to Reverend Vernon, who responded with a warm embrace, and walked to my seat, my face radiating a look of peace and one I wanted the audience to remember.

Following the benediction, as was traditional in small Indiana towns, while the pianist softly played a series of upbeat religious songs, persons who wished to say good-bye to Davie walked slowly in a line that began at the far end of the gym floor and snaked its way past the open casket, some pausing but a moment to stare or utter prayerful words. Many made their way to me as I stood there, receiving their handshakes and wishes.

It took more than an hour for the procession to reach the end, and then, led by the hearse and Flanagan Family Funeral Home's polished black Cadillac containing my mother, my daughters, and me, the procession of cars made its way less than a mile to Barclay Community Cemetery.

The crowd wasn't large, no more than one hundred, and while a soft, warm April breeze floated across the small hillside where Davie was laid to rest, Reverend Vernon finished the brief graveside service with "... ashes to ashes and dust to dust. Amen." He turned to the gathering and said, "God bless each of you. Go in peace."

No one said a word as friends walked to their cars, leaving our immediate family to our own thoughts on the front row of folding chairs under the small harvest-green tent. Matt withheld his emotions except for tears that silently slid downward. Mary June sobbed as did my children. I held an arm tightly around Lydia and pulled her to me. My mother did her best to comfort Jillian. Lydia was now seventeen, and her sister fifteen. They'd experienced the deaths of older persons in their family, but this was far different, and I would have more talks with them later about understanding the meaning of what had happened to their stepfather who, to them, had been their only father.

With one exception, only the funeral home and family's parked cars remained when we arose from our chairs, placed yellow roses on top of the casket, and began walking from the grave site. I glanced up and saw Ben Goldfarb, Fred Marshall, and Jerry Wilkes moving slowly toward me through the unmowed grass that was greening after a winter of hibernation. I stepped aside and into the shade of a massive Bradford pear filled with small white blossoms.

"Diane," Mr. Goldfarb began, "we haven't had an opportunity to talk much privately since last Monday but I do hope you know how deeply saddened we are and how we grieve for you."

"Oh, I want all three of you to know, I do. I can't thank you enough, for Davie's opportunity, for how well you took care of all of us during the spring training visits, for all you've done to try to comfort us this week, and for the announcements you made at the service. Davie would be *so* proud of what has taken place." I glanced up past the overhanging blossomed limbs, with a look of peace. "I'm certain he is."

"We don't want to keep you from your family, but there are a couple of things we need to tell you," the chairman continued. "First, and I suppose I don't have to say this, it should be obvious, but there will be no expenses to bear in connection with anything that took place from the time Davie collapsed until this moment here at the cemetery. We'll see that everything is paid. The second is our ball club will provide you with a check for one and a half million dollars."

Mr. Marshall grabbed my right bicep when he detected I was about to sink. "Oh, my God! Oh, my God, you don't mean it?" I managed to gasp, my pent-up emotions on the verge of unraveling, and my hands covering my nose and mouth in disbelief.

"Yes, ma'am, we do. As we'd stipulated in the contract Davie signed, our club's insurance covered him for five hundred thousand life and all medical. Our organization will provide the rest. A life is worth far more than one and a half million dollars, we understand, but we hope you will accept our good-faith effort to assist you and your daughters as you begin your lives without Davie."

I was now sobbing, and Mr. Marshall embraced me, letting my tears dampen his tie. Seeing I was without a handkerchief, Jerry Wilkes produced his. Wiping tears, I managed to stand on my own. "This is unbelievable. It is far beyond what you said you'd do in the contract, and you certainly don't have to do it. I don't expect it."

Reaching out and lightly gripping my left forearm, Mr. Goldfarb responded, "I know, but we and our board wanted to do this because of what Davie meant to our club and to all of baseball."

I looked at one face and then the other, cast a faint smile, returned Mr. Wilkes's handkerchief, and extended my right arm. Shaking hands, I said, "God bless all of you, your club, the other players, and fans. All of you have been a blessing to Davie and to me."

Only the tweeting of birds and the rustling of the tall evergreen, pink-blossomed flowering crab, and the leafless branches of oak, tulip, and maple as the breeze grew stronger could be heard after the cars drove down the asphalt lane in the cemetery, leaving Davie in peace. My children and I were headed to an unknown life without him, but we would be dedicated to serving it with good purpose.

EPILOGUE

L ater that summer, just in time for their first-ever Eastern Division playoff games, following a season dedicated to their spring training hero from southwestern Indiana, as Phoenix fans arrived at Duval County Stadium, they were greeted by a new, life-size bronze statue on the concrete plaza outside the main gates. It was the perfect likeness of Davie in his forward motion, the tips of the middle three fingers of his right hand dug into the top of a baseball as he was about to release it toward home plate. Etched in white on each side of the three-foot-high black marble base on which it sat were the words:

The Knuckleballer
It's never too late to realize your dream.

An identical statue with inscription stood at the main entrance to Sailors' Village.

The back of each statue's uniform faced the sky: **MILLER 42**.

CPSIA information can be obtained at www.ICGtesting.com
Printed in the USA
LVOW042333230312

274562LV00002B/1/P